One's Posterity

One's Posterity

Where Love for Man, clashes with Love for Philosophy

Daniel Mistir

Mistir's Messages

Published 2022
Printed in the United States of America
ISBN: 978-0-578-39841-9

Cover Design by Bouhadda Abderrahmane
Interior Design by Daniel Mistir

For information, address:
Mistir's Messages
2400 Pole Line Rd, Apt. 92
Davis, CA 95618
mistirsmessages@gmail.com

Dedicated to those I call, family. For those who feel as if their voices have been muted, as if they are not heard and feel discarded, keep speaking, keep expressing yourself. I wish to hear it, to bring it to light, always caring for what you have to say.

CONTENTS

Preface

The events of this book take place in all three instances of time: past, present and future. It is important to understand the characters and settings are comprised of many events, conversations, and obstacles taken from the things I have faced in my life, things we all experience in life. These events were taken and mixed with an exaggerated component historians and strategists would say they expect to see in the near future.

While the bulk of the entertainment was intended for college-aged and middle-aged audiences, I wish for different generations of people to understand the characters and examine how the events shape their lives and relate to the common desire for more. Foundations of the structure of family need to be discussed to end curses passed down. The story was created with this question in mind: who deserves a family, who doesn't?

Posterity, meaning all future generations, is an interesting concept, a word used in different ways. How can one own a piece? This is the guiding question of the book.

REVIVAL

one:
Letters of the Past

The night before, his thoughts raced. Swirling around in moments of deep anguish, the room his stupors customarily took part in bore witness to reenactments of his demented ideas and shelved memories. A parable, a story he was once told in an older part of the world, lingered about in his head.

An old man, before the age of understanding, roamed the Earth in search of an individual capable of helping his daughter. He was consumed by a deep hatred of her condition, for she could only see blackness. Communicating this to her was to the detriment of his daughter. She was plagued by the misery of his beliefs. Healers tried and failed, repeatedly emptying all manners of mystique medicine and demands to deities. The man's wife attempted and failed herself, to show him what he believed to be a curse was indeed a unique ability. The man nearly went crazy, and in a time of desperation, asked his daughter what she felt. She told him the truth, she wanted to make him prideful again. Ashamed of his lack of self-control, his love poured out. He grabbed a shining rock, smashing his eyes till all he could see was blackness. He laughed and laughed in madness, finally able to see what others could only wish to see, the world through the eyes of their child.

The man fell into a deep sleep rethinking the allegorical story once told to him by a Pakistani friend. He did not realize a letter arrived at his home promptly at 8:10 A.M. The seasoned man grew accustomed to a retiree lifestyle and was not yet awake. The days were too similar for him to differentiate.

Three pages rested patiently at his doormat for hours. This day seemed to differ. His nights were acquainted with restless jostling and visitations from the departed. He dreamt of his forgotten days, the plans he once made, obstructed by the divine roadblocks of chance. Treks in the park were what he remembered the most when he would wake, but on this day, he was able to avoid the dreams. Instead of rising at noon, he was given a jolt from the back of his mind. He was reminded it was his day, his birthday. This one, being the sixty-eighth, started like those of the last decade. He arose to the celebratory yells of Suzie. She was overly ecstatic for his taste, souring his morning. He covered the humiliation of being commemorated by an automated home system by retreating to the bright beige silk sheets he laid in throughout the hours of the night.

After he felt cleansed from Suzie's singing, he decided to go about his business as he would any other day. He rose high enough from his bed to have his back pressed against the black faux leather headboard.

"Morning messages, Suzie?" asked the man.

"28 messages, sir," replied the AI.

The man was surprised to begin the day with so many notifications. He quickly understood why the day differed from the arduous others.

"Delete all the subscription-based birthday messages. How many still remain?"

"Five, sir."

"Delete advertisements. How many remain?" asked the man.

"Two, sir. Both are from schools. They are asking if you could guest lecture again, one in Berkeley, the other on the Los Angeles campus. They are asking for the first lecture to be about a week from today and the other, a few weeks…four weeks from now."

"Is the topic the same?" asked the man.

"Yes, they want you to discuss your brother."

The topic he dreaded most was the topic every university wanted to hear as he toured around the country.

He rose out of bed after he commanded Suzie to unscramble the obscured view of the windows. He reminisced on the times he would get berated by his father to close the blinds in the house before he slept. *If only he could see me now,* thought the man. Technology greatly advanced in the time since he was raised in the early 2000s. The money he received from the universities he spoke at allowed him to live in the chic home. The seclusion was synonymous to his introverted lifestyle. He knew no one would recognize his face, however, the small few who were highly attentive and educated on the politics of the 2030s and 2040s might cause a commotion if they knew where he resided, depending on their affiliations. This lonely landscape of a life protected him from intruders and protected others from his decisions.

He walked to the window and stared at the forestation outside. He wondered if this was the last piece of nature untouched in Sacramento. He focused on a pair of ravens interacting as Suzie gave him a report on the day's weather and required tasks.

"Suzie, turn on the shower and keep it lukewarm."

Following his rushed sightseeing, he once again made his way to his bed. He slept naked after the drunken night he found himself in after his pre-celebratory festivities. He ordered Suzie to begin playing the smooth blues he loved in the mornings. Instead of staying in all day, as he normally would on his birthday, he chose to instead be productive. He began the notable day by making his bed. The music was his motivation to make something of himself, as well as the fact this was, in all probability, the last birthday he would see. Unbeknownst to him, his attempt towards productivity was not in vain, for this was truly to be his last.

Whilst still bare, he did the stretches ordered by the doctors he frequently visited. After completing the stretches, the disorderly man found himself sweating an abnormal amount. The causes were alarming, and he tried to narrow down the root of the perspiration. The least alarming was his instruction to Suzie to keep the thermostat at a welcoming seventy-eight degrees to counter the freezing temperatures he experienced during his trip to the liquor store the night before. The room had become even warmer as the sunlight shone directly into the room, following the removal of the obscurity settings. The liquor from the previous night could have also played a factor, but he knew dehydration would not have made him sweat like this. He narrowed it down to the recurring liver issues his doctors constantly treated.

The doctors warned him of the effects of drinking while being treated and, for the most part, he ignored their advice. The night before, he desired to drink enough alcohol to sleep through the depressing birthday. There was nothing he could do about his loneliness without swallowing his mounting pride. The spritz of liquor in his nights helped pacify the ailments of his dreams. The drinks turned his mind black, freeing him from his mind's need to relive the past.

Before going into the bathroom, he took the pills Suzie dispensed in the electric contraption the pharmacy gave him. The master bathroom was incredibly spacious, especially for one person. The crisp white tiled floors were a nudge to his body every morning he stepped on them. He despised their rude awakening for they began the long days for him.

He brushed his teeth and quickly made his way into his shower as the rhythmic music reverberated through the home's speakers. The shower was always clean to his liking, a result of the automatic cleaning settings Suzie was assigned to. The man had no desire nor motivation to clean a home he shared with no one. He set the sliding door in the shower to obscure and washed the filth of his dazed night off, unaware of the devastating letter sitting at his doorstep.

When the shower concluded, he turned the dry setting on and stood still as the heated air blew from the tiles. Suzie updated him with more notifications for the day and reiterated the beautiful weather continuing through the rest of the month. She attempted to manipulate him into going on a walk since the doctors recommended daily exercise.

The man, wanting to make a change, believing he had come to the decision on his own, thought it to be a good idea for a walk. He left the bathroom and first returned to his bed, wanting to get off his feet, falling into the trap of reminiscing on some of his past birthdays. He remembered *her* in his earlier years, never forgetting to bring his favorite dessert out, marble cake. He remembered his twenty-first birthday he shared with the first woman to break his heart. He could not forget his fortieth either, as he and his brother were deadlocked with the nation's power players as they readied for political battle. His memories began to slowly fade into those of the last few years. His strenuous battles with helplessness and mortality were taking their toll.

His emotions were as dull as the setup of his room. There were no paintings or pictures hung in his home. His pill dispenser and antique arc lamp were the only decoration in the master bedroom. The man had been devoid of creativity for the last ten years. His only outstanding gift, which he recently stumbled upon again, was as an instructor and the realization of the power his voice had with the students in the universities. Since he had another week before his next lecture, he knew a mental release was in order to cleanse himself from the filth. A walk, he believed, was a great place to start.

He started by first putting on his green boxer briefs and black tapered sweatpants. He matched his black bottoms with the complementary gray pullover sweater with the faded labels of his alma mater. After quickly putting on his generic athletic black shoes, he rechecked the weather report. He did not trust the seventy-degree reading Suzie reported, so he grabbed his black beanie before he proceeded to leave the room.

He refused to leave the house without eating a meal. This was the rule he followed since his mother beat it into him in his youth. He made his way out of the master bedroom and into the hallway of the second floor of his home. The man walked past the guest room to get to the stairs every day. He learned to despise the additional room in the house. In the twenty-four years he resided there, decades had passed since he last entertained a guest, and there was not a day he did not loathe walking past the empty room. The room was a symbol of the betrayal and tragedy of his life, a reminder he was the last man standing. He quickly returned to close the door of the unwelcoming room, the room he conducted his drunken celebration in. He did not know how his body maneuvered back to his bed in the night. His own shame left him blind to the empty half-pint glass of whiskey lying on the floor of the unoccupied guest room. He made his way down the spiraling staircase and into the kitchen of the modernized two-story home.

"Suzie, turn the obscure setting off the windows."

"Yes, sir."

The wooden-tiled floors squeaked at his every step while he searched for his granola bars. Suzie was aware of his imminent arrival in the kitchen and began boiling water for his tea.

"Where are the granola bars?" asked the man.

"They are to the left of the refrigerator. They are on the top of the cabinet," replied Suzie.

The bars were placed very high up in the cabinet to make room for the most recent provisions Suzie ordered. He detested shopping because of all the options offered to ungrateful shoppers. However, to his dismay, the granola bars were not the flavor he expected them to be, a repercussion of automated shopping. He angrily cursed the growing frustration of the day's events thus far, annoyed by the complications and his deteriorating health.

"Shall I make you oatmeal, sir?" asked Suzie.

"No. I'll eat this."

He sat down at his wooden oval dining table. The wood was stained by his negligent behavior. He did not care for coasters, but the stains irritated him to a point of recurring disgust whenever he sat down to eat. Another point of annoyance were the two chairs placed at the table. So much time had passed since he had a guest visit his home. He reverted to focusing on his granola bar and his black ginger tea. His frustration continued to grow as his attention returned to the rapid staining process. The coasters sat with the unclean mats in the middle of the table, beyond his arm's length. He instead rolled up the napkin he brought with him from the kitchen and placed the folded replacement under the bright red mug. The improvisation would have to do as he ordered Suzie to update him on the day's news.

Suzie projected the abhorrent news onto the wall he was facing, after first scanning his eyes so she could place the screen in its premier location. The plain wall in front of him was the chosen location, for it always was the position he sat at for his morbid breakfasts. He began to sip his tea and eat the stale blueberry flavored bar as he looked up at the headlines. The news was as useless as his papier-mâché coaster.

Headlines: 31/03/2067
Daughter of Entente Party's Speaker of House dies at the mere age of
32.
Saudi Arabia places bid to host next soccer competition; says they'll
welcome all. Skeptics unsure.
Where a Master's Degree Isn't Needed...

He ignored the meaningless headlines. He did not care for anything politics related, especially the Entente Party. Tragedy being tragedy, he let an ounce of empathy sneak out for the Speaker of the House.

"Suzie, anything from sports?" asked the man.

The rugged man finished his breakfast and watched highlights from his favorite basketball team. He still held the passion for the sport he and his brother grew up watching. Even Suzie, glaring through the cameras, took notice of his smile when he watched the highlights of his team. He sat for a half-hour watching highlights for all the sports he held a vested interest in. Once he refueled and was prepared for his walk, he arose from his seat and instructed Suzie to turn off the news. He walked over to the kitchen and put his dishes in the dishwasher.

"Clean the dishes when I go for my walk, Suzie."

"Yes, sir."

"Clean the rest of the house as well. I fixed the vacuum the other day."

He brought out the robotic vacuum Suzie was linked up to. After the command, he could hear the toilets and the oven go into self-clean mode on her order.

"Yes, sir. The self-clean action has commenced."

"Notify me of any new messages during my walk. I will have my watch with me."

He pulled out his headphones and turned them on through his watch.

"Yes sir, I'll notify you if anything comes up. Any other orders?"

"Lock up the doors behind me, obscure the upstairs windows and blacken the downstairs windows. Notify me if anyone approaches."

"Yes sir."

She blackened the windows all throughout the downstairs level. The man did not think the order through, the kitchen was very far from the front door. His ignorance ruined his plan to stretch inside the house before his walk. He began to stumble along as he walked blindly to the front door. He looked for his worn-out white leather sofas and rosewood mini bar, but there was no way he could locate his furniture in the pitch-black abyss. He continued to push through and finally made his way to the door.

He did not see the letter when he walked out of the house. He stepped on and over the letter encased in the white envelope. The words sat on his amaranth red doormat. He stepped over the doormat for years with indifference. The day was no different. Writing letters and physical mail was an archaic form of sharing news especially following the rise of the green initiatives in the late 2030s. A man with his level of detachment could not imagine receiving a letter in his time. His impassivity left a symmetrical excrement-shaded boot stain in the bottom left corner of the envelope.

The walks were different from the morning routines he learned as a child. He began looking around the home three times to inspect the home for damage. The man's house was originally a cabin and was altered in the late 2040s right before he bought it. The newly painted home was much larger and elegant on the inside than on the outside. From the front of the house, it may look as if it was a small two-story cabin, but onlookers would be mistaken. The house's length was more considerable, especially after the original owners made a plethora of alterations to the home. The home, technologically, matched the times as well. He was given Suzie already downloaded into the home's mainframe. He painted the home, but the alterations would go unnoticed by most since he did not decorate or include many appliances in the home. The man had only a two-piece sofa set and a mini bar to go along with his bed. He was never one for decorating and the bland home shamed him every ticking day he strolled around.

Regardless, the man did still maintain the needs of the home. After he checked, he continued to walk along the recently cemented road leading out of the porch. There was not a house for another two and a half miles, so he walked freely.

He walked with a faster pace than he expected, weaving through the trees and fallen leaves. He quickly backtracked from his walk after seeing he approached the next home. He realized on his journey back he did not stretch enough, so he did so on the return. The grimacing looks on his face was evidence enough to any bystander the man either overextended or inflamed some muscle in his body. He decided to keep the pain in and wait till he was home. The feeling was always in the same place, right under his right pectoral muscle.

He did not realize the severity of the pain, however, until he finally reached his doorstep. He was stunned by the presence of the stained envelope. He was not able to be notified because Suzie's blind spot was near the mat, under the front of the door. She could see the fields and the forestation, but his laziness stalled him from repairing the doorbell camera. She might have mistaken a delivery drone for a nosy adolescent. It did not matter; he had an envelope. He had not seen one in over two decades. The anxiety the man was feeling went beyond the levels someone in his state of health should feel. The man's bronze hands were shaking as he composed himself and knelt to grab the letter. Shakingly, he spoke into his watch and waited as Suzie unscrambled the door's locks.

Once he made his way into his home, he immediately began to interrogate Suzie.

"Suzie, did you see a deliverer, or any unidentified device drop off a package?"

"No sir, there were not any devices that caught my attention. I had a reboot in my system between five and six this morning. You know that I am blind at that hour."

"Damn it! I forgot to schedule your reboot earlier."

The man was completely frightened. The only living individual he shared his address with was long departed. The universities would not have shared his address without his consent, and they never sent him a package. There, however, was no way he was going to let the envelope stay closed any longer.

The letter was addressed to him directly, to one of the campuses he frequently spoke at in Northern California. He did not recognize the handwriting on the outside of the envelope.

To: Markos Solomons

"Un-blacken the windows," said the man as he paced to the kitchen.

The knives were still being cleaned by Suzie.

"Suzie, these should all be done."

He waited impatiently for her to finish cleaning the knives. He did not want to accidentally cut any part of the content within the envelope.

"I apologize for the inconvenience sir. The knives are ready."

He quickly opened the unlocked dishwasher and searched for his knife. His impatience allowed him to get cut by one of the knives he sought. In one motion, he dampened a napkin and wiped off the blood on the knife as well as his finger.

He methodically sliced open the letter and pulled out the three pages of folded white paper. He deduced the school sent the letter to him, in an old envelope they had, since envelopes no longer were available. He was alarmed he recognized the handwriting of the letter. His knees weakened and crumbled as a cracker does in a mug filled with hot milk. Slowly, he got through the first of the three pages. His heart turned into a cinder block as it sank to the bottom of his stomach. He could not speak, but more importantly, his body froze. The muscles in his chest contracted with abrupt quickness. Each word was synonymous to a samurai's blade slicing his opponent on a path to a slow death. By the end, he attempted to compose himself.

His unlubricated fingers awakened and refolded the letter and he placed the contents into his drawer, to the right of the recently used dishwasher. The pain from his chest did not retreat, but he did not feel nor fear the pain. The words did enough of the damage and sent him to the heavens prematurely.

As he attempted to take one step forward, his body crumbled and fell, naturally, before wildly tightening. His body was seizing into what seemed to be a heart attack as he laid there alone as a newborn in a cradle, on the day of his sixty-eighth birthday.

two:
Faces

The man was experiencing the past and the present, simultaneously, as his body resisted any attempt he made to take back control. Markos was not only facing attacks on his body, but his mind was also being invaded.

He was experiencing something he never felt before. His body was drenched with sweat and his muscles tightened as that of a grip between lion's teeth. He could not move, and he was struggling to understand the concept of reality, blasted with past images of the faces he had once known and seen.

He recognized the laughing image of the young man he was once in the trenches with. He recognized his kinky, nappy hair and his ungroomed beard. Markos did not know the extent of the episode, because he was seeing flashes of a badge he could not misidentify. It read, *California Protected Responders,* the state's ambulance respondents. He was unaware Suzie, observing his condition, watched through her miniature cameras as her *person* remained unresponsive. She called the responders while Markos slipped into his fantasy. The bombardment of faces continued, reminding him of active ventures in his youthful years. The responders tried speaking to him, but he was completely unresponsive to their requests. They noticed a tear trickle down his left eye. One face shone in the darkness of his lids, the once angelic image of *her.*

The piercing eyes are what he remembered best. The volume of the dark black hair was what most people complimented her for, but the eyes told the truth of the lost convictions. Her personality was not one of temperance or restraint, but one of hidden discipline and respect, a product of the religious upbringing she passed up on. His eyes trickled with burning tears as his constant rampage of memories took him on a journey to the time of her departure, a near end to the repeated calamities he endured. This was his last memory before *it* went black, a result of the shot the responders gave him to relax his body.

A face appeared to the man; one he did not recognize when he woke. She was of a dark bronze complexion, only a shade darker than he was. Her black hair was laid on her back as she watched him with her round eyes. She had a small frame, but the straightened posture, with the piercings in her ears, allowed Solomons to infer she was older than a first glance could show. She looked at him, up and down, with curiosity. She analyzed, taking mental notes of his defining features. She held a bright green clipboard in front of her, watching him with judgment.

They sat on the top floor of the hospital where he received his check-ups. He hated the visits. The staff took precautions to treat him like he was a celebrity or dignitary, even putting him in an elegant, private hospital suite. He moved his eyes around the room. Once he realized where he was and gained full consciousness, questions piled into his head.

"Who are you?" abruptly asked Solomons.

"*Who are you?*" replied the girl with sincerity, pointing at him.

"You aren't a nurse, so who are you? Please tell me you are not with the media."

"The media? I'm a friendly neighbor," said the girl sarcastically.

Her face carried familiarity with him, but he was unaware where this feeling came from. They sat in silence due to her combativeness. His head shook at the obscurity. He scanned the room again, fighting the urge to leave. He knew and accepted the state of his body.

"Listen, security is close if need be."

He reached over to the table next to his bed, but his watch was too far for him to reach without the tubes connected to him being taken out. He felt the exertion take its toll. She moved faster than him. She took the watch, taking control of the room.

"Ah, ah, ah, old man, let's not get security involved. I don't even think you could if you wanted to. Don't worry though, you're safe. I'm on *your* team. "

The girl enjoyed the demonic reign she held over him. She was much mischievous to his liking, but he angrily admired the mystery. This was the most interaction he had outside of lecture halls. His smile masked the concern over his body's condition.

"Can you at least get the doctor and let him know I'm here?"

"You can notify the doctors on the tablet, and they'll come in here. We've been waiting hours for you to wake up."

We? thought Solomons. He did not waste time thinking about it. He found the Pad sitting against the railing on the hospital bed. He unlocked the tablet with his finger and scrolled through and clicked *"Call Doctor"*. It was now a waiting game.

"If you aren't going to tell me who you are, can you tell me how long they said I've been here?" asked Solomons.

"They said thirty-six hours. A baby *coma*," said the girl, with a devilish laugh.

That is not something to joke about, thought Markos, triggered by the word.

Regardless of his condition, he felt lucky. He was shocked to learn of the duration of his state, but he was grateful he did not miss his speaking engagement.

"Why are you here?" asked the man.

"Good question? I'm going to go see wha–,"

"No!" said the man abruptly.

The natural response did not feel right leaving his mouth, but it was necessary. It was a response for a man who had become overly acquainted with solitude. His vulnerable interjection made the girl aware of the delicate, frail nature of the person she sat with. She slowly sat back down in her cushioned chair and let out a small smile, a sign of peace.

"Okay, Markos Solomons, what would you like to discuss?"

Embarrassed, the man moved to joke with the girl.

"Let's start with your first name."

"What do I look like to you?" asked the girl.

"Maybe a 'Destiny' or a 'Marissa'?"

"Well, not at all. My first name is *Anna,*" said the girl with a Latin accent.

Information is crucial, thought Markos. *With a name, she's unaware I know who she is.*

"Ok, Anna. How did you know my name?"

She held up the clipboard and waved the papers in front of him. She let out a large smile.

"Markos Solomons, sixty-eight, and by the way, happy belated birthday. Born March 31, 1999, he is currently undergoing treatment for liver cancer. I'm sorry to hear that. He is five feet and eleven inches tall and weighs one hundred and seventy-two pounds, a little light on your feet ain't ya?" said Anna.

Her cruelty would normally torment and anger a man like Solomons, but the comedic attitude enabled him to laugh at her sarcasm. He knew facts she did not, and the slight control stalled his feeling of nakedness as she read his chart.

"It's been tough, but why don't you enlighten my day and share with me your last name?" asked Markos, creeping a smile out from his chapped lips.

"I don't know, you'll have to pay for that one. I'm liking this game of twenty-one questions. How about we go with *Solomons* for now," said Anna.

"Oh, so now we're family?" joked Markos.

"You should be so lucky," said Anna, under her breath.

Markos calmly laughed at her remark. The laugh surprised her, but she was interested in his mannerisms, he reminded her of his vibrant brother, from the videos she had seen.

"I think it's the other way around. Regardless, I heard you say 'we' earlier. Who is it you came with?"

"Me and my whole psychology team. They told our team that there was a case they couldn't crack so they asked for the best and they sent me," said the girl, following her self-appraisal with her hands running down her body, as if she displayed a diamond.

"You will join a long list of people who have tried," answered Markos. He turned away from her face, giving them a break between their small talk.

This was the truth he accepted about his social nature and his ability to maintain relationships. His initial cheery attitude soured, dwelling on his conclusion.

"Are you married or have a girlfriend?" inquired Anna.

"That isn't your business. Didn't your parents teach you to not ask those questions?"

"Psychology 101, you friend, are as open as a book can be. You look sad. I felt it when I walked into this room, while you slept."

The man did not like the assessment. He opened his mouth but recanted the verbal assault he was going to levy at her. He shifted his attention elsewhere, looking outside toward the city. The city's downtown skyscrapers were a few miles away and they were lighting up the city, hours after midnight. He wanted to be distracted from the truth Anna plied out of him within a few minutes of talking. He wanted to compose himself. After careful contemplation, he decided he was going to apologize for his belittling attitude and avoid this topic. As he turned, his soul left his body for a moment as the doctor walked in with a ghost.

"A... Alondra?" asked the man.

He was in complete shock. He did not mean to blurt the name out, but he was confused. He could not fathom her coming through the door, even with Anna serving as a warning.

"Anna, can you please go and ask where we could get snacks and drinks? See if they have vending machines," said the ghost.

She placed the bag she walked in with on the brown leather sofa by the window. She ignored his call to her.

"Hello, Mr. Solomons, we are glad that you are awake. You were very lucky. I have told you the risks of taking the pills and the effects that can happen with alcohol," said the doctor.

Markos wondered if the doctor was able to deduce the life he lived from the conversations they carried through their checkups. The doctor knew who walked through the door, yet he talked of alcohol, frustrating Markos. Doctors could have told him they cured him, and he would not flinch. His eyes followed the ghost as she looked through her bag on the sofa. She was listening to what the doctor said, but she was already briefed on the state of his health before they appeared together. His eyes refused to move away from her. He owed the doctor.

"Mr. Solomons, Mr. Solomons, can you hear me?"

"Yes, doctor. I can hear you," said Markos, still focused on her.

"Well, nothing has changed from your previous diagnosis. You've had a reaction due to the pills and alcohol mixing, which induced a state of paralysis. Your reaction was worsened from what seemed to be a panic attack as well," continued the doctor.

The revelation forced him to refocus on the doctor. He quickly jerked his head towards him in shock. He felt the recoil of his quick movement from the sharp pain in his neck, an indicator of his body's weak state. He did not believe he had a panic attack, he believed something divine was at play.

"A panic attack?" asked Markos.

"Yes, your condition worsened because of your stress levels. Your elevated blood pressure forced us to call your next of kin in case things were to take a turn for the worse. We found the only phone number we had available to us. It took us some time, but after we finally found it, your family said they would come," said the doctor.

He's lying, he had their number. He's making it easier on me.

The word, family, changed the mood of the room. It stung Markos and he felt his stomach turn. Even the ghost felt a chill because she turned her head towards the doctor as soon as she heard the word herself. The doctor was aware of the awkwardness of the situation and made the best decision possible in his position.

"I've updated your family on your condition and what the next steps are for you, Mr. Solomons. The nurses will check on you throughout the night and we'll discharge you in the morning. Utilize the Pad for any of your concerns."

Markos nodded his head to acknowledge the doctor. The doctor looked at the woman and immediately left the room after she gave her own nod of acknowledgement.

The room was silent in the aftermath of the doctor's exit. The woman found the photo trapped in her worn out backpack. She rested her bag on the leather cushions of the sofas and began to slowly approach the cushioned rolling stool Anna was sitting on. She refused to speak until she correctly positioned herself on the seat. She looked at Mr. Solomons and evaluated him, head to toe, as Anna previously did. This was her first time looking at Markos and immediately, she recognized the fragileness. She waited until he found her eyes. He was amazed at the sight of her. He was not able to get a good look while she rustled through the bag, but she was in front of him now.

"The doctor tells me you're in a very bad state and that you're making it worse."

"Ma'am, please do not torture me as your daughter did. Are, are you Alondra?" asked the man shakingly. He could not even say the right name.

He was worried and on the verge of tears as his past collided with his current existence. Quickly, life escalated for Markos. As it once did, tragedy brought confusion.

"No, they tell me your mind is sound, but I'm not Alondra. She died a few years ago, about six years ago in two months actually. I am Alondra's daughter. It's been a while," said the woman.

He was momentarily speechless to the news. He was hurt by his sister-in-law's death, but his disconnection from her kept his emotions at bay. The man was frozen as he marveled at the woman in front of him. Time passed since he last saw her, and she was a photocopy of Alondra. She moved like her, she dressed like her, and after the realization sunk in, she even talked with the slight Puerto Rican accent Alondra once spoke with. He remembered the ghost in front of him as a little girl who used to bring him and his brother tea when they prepared arguments for their opposition's strategies.

"I'm sorry, I wasn't aware of Alondra's death. Uh...I'm sorry you had to uh...come down here and see me, especially like this," lied Markos.

He was puzzled. Why did they come see him? The family was separated long before his condition ravaged his body.

"I'm sorry we came unannounced. We didn't know how we would find you. The doctors notified us that your condition could go either way and we didn't want your body to go to the state. We have been here for a few hours," said the woman.

"Please don't apologize to me. There's nothing you or your family must apologize to me for, *ever*. I'll be fine, thanks for coming. This is not your burden or the family's burden," said Markos, rustling to find a better position on the bed.

The man was very appreciative of Anna and her mother coming to see him. He was saddened by the death of his sister-in-law, but he was glad to find some type of closure with the soldier of a woman. He, however, was not looking for charity or forced compassion, especially in the position he found himself in. In nearly all instances of decision, pride clouded his choices. The moment would not be any different in another defining juncture in life.

"I know *our* family hasn't been perfect, but we *are* family. This was given to me right after my father died, lying on a bed, in peace. I was young then. My mother gave this to me when they collected his body in the morning. She said he asked her to promise him if anything happened, a few weeks before, to give this to me. I know you two weren't speaking then, but I didn't understand the meaning of this photo until much later," said the woman.

The photo regurgitated feelings deeply suppressed in Markos. He remembered the exact moment the photo was taken. They experienced betrayal and his brother announced their form of retribution for the traitor's superiors. After the speech, alerting others of their intentions, they took a photo and marked it as their pivoting moment as a group. The photo was folded, with remnants of details faded into the creases. The image alone had a profound effect on Markos. The statement on the back of the folded photo nearly moved him to tears:

"The House divided shall burn. The House divided shall erode,
As enemies surround the home with the barrels of their guns,
Pointed squarely at the House of God's Soldiers.
The security against the Godless trespassers
Is, and can only be, Family."

"Your father had a magical way with words. That was his gift and curse," said Markos.

"My mother took this back from me after the funeral and told me to not worry about it. She said it was yours and his responsibility to fix the relationship. After she passed, I found it in her wallet."

"She did the right thing."

The man was ashamed, consumed by disappointment while he clutched the photo. He was not looking for family, nor did he want them to reappear under false pretenses.

"Please, the doctor says you aren't taking care of yourself. He said the treatments were improving your health, but your stress and drinking is worsening your chances. You were given a reasonable chance of success—"

"No! No, no, no, please stop"

He took a moment to calm himself.

"The treatment is unnecessary. I have weeks, a few months at best. I don't know what you were told," said Markos, knowing she hoped to blend the line between reason and encouraging optimism.

"I'm asking, for my father's sake, for time to make certain things right."

"Listen, Olivia," said the man as he leaned forward and grabbed her arm.

"Your father has nothing to make right, he did many things in his life that have allowed me to breathe the air I am breathing today. He has nothing to make right and neither do you. Your father has done enough for not only me, but for a lot of people. You're free of any burden that you may think you must fulfill," said Markos.

He looked deep into her large eyes.

The man refused to be taken care of under any obligatory or misguided oaths. He shelved out lies in order to satisfy his stubbornness. He did not waiver for he would never shame his family into any type of aid for him. He knew the difficult truth of the circumstances regarding the family's relationship.

"Okay, I'm sorry. There is no way I can just let you go home alone after what transpired. I can only offer you a room and ask you to stay awhile?" asked Olivia.

"I appreciate the offer, but I think it's best if I go home."

"Well, I would talk to Dr. Galloway then."

Her tone shifted.

"Why would I do that?" replied Markos.

"Because of the incident, the doctor would recommend that you go into the state's care."

Olivia's veiled attempt at offering him a place to stay felt like a better option to Markos as he contemplated his future. They all lived in the same city, but her suburban life was the polar opposite of the isolation he existed in. With her assault, she extinguished his prideful barrier.

"Jesus," said the man sarcastically.

"There is no way I'd go into the state's care," continued Markos.

"If we don't come to some arrangement, they'll begin the transfer in the morning."

Oh, that doctor. Brilliant, believed Markos.

"Can we come to an agreement, and you tell them we're going to stay together?"

"I'm sorry, I can't do that in good conscience," said Olivia, a smile accompanying the witty response.

She had not seen her uncle in a very long time, but she dealt with overthinkers in her profession, self-conscious beasts enabling themselves with their attempts at fortitude.

"The apple never truly veers too far, you're much worse than your father. What choices do I have?"

Olivia shook her head, waiting for his response.

"If I stay with you for a while, granted I live long, and I show I'm good by myself, can I then return to my home?"

"I think we can do that," said Olivia.

His hands weakly appeared in front of her chest. She shook his meek hand, sealing the sudden transaction.

"I'll go with you, but you have to keep that little devil away from me," said Markos as he pressed down on the firm bed. He lifted himself, again, to match her rigid posture.

"Who? Anna? She didn't tell you who she was?" asked Olivia.

Markos turned away and shook his head, laughing. He knew, after she spoke her name, who he was with. He was smiling as if he was joking with his family the other day. For the first time in more than two and a half decades, the man looked forward to the mystery of the next second. He knew many questions would arise as the family reconnected. He was to mind his words, not only due to the delicate nature of the family name and its history, but also due to the promises made to stay away. He thought of all the risks as he watched closely at what his brother left the world. He watched as Anna came into the room, juggling snacks and soft drinks in her hands. He watched with awe at an opportunity to learn more about the two women who would carry on his family's name.

"Anna, I would like to introduce you to your great-uncle, Markos Solomons," said Olivia. She proudly watched Anna smile at him, shaking hands with the man of mystery.

The morning came faster than Markos would have liked. He spent the night contemplating past decisions and how they all lead to his present. Olivia left the old, crumpled photo with him for the night while she and Anna went home to sleep. The reunion was plagued with occasional awkward silences shadowing their good intentions for each other. He insisted they return home to rest after repeatedly thanking them for coming. He assured them he would be waiting where the doctors left him.

He wished he remembered to ask them to bring food in the morning when they arrived. He was tired of the second-rate hospital food, even in the luxury suite. He refused to eat anything throughout the night. His hunger and his insomnia did not affect him, though. He maintained his focus on the stand to his left.

He remembered the passionate address his brother made, serving as the precursor to the photo taken. The contentious debates and the weeks of tormented strategizing was hidden by the pleasing smiles of the two young men. The fervor of the night resurfaced. He remembered how they found themselves at the mercy of Alana's camera. He thought about the flurry of news stations and cameras running around them, digging for what they could find, as they embarked on their ill-fated journey together.

He was appreciative of the photo given to him, but as the hours passed through the night, the photo was a catalyst for the memories flooding in at an unholy pace. He remembered all the actions leading to the picture being captured. None could foresee the prophetic hell let loose by the announcements. He trembled at the consequences. Fear and doubt crept in during the remaining hours of his stay. He did not want to bring the family down this path again and open closed wounds, but he yearned for the second chance he never expected. He could not rush into the relationship, nor could he reveal too much with the family without leaving them open to risks. He believed it to be a kamikaze-like affair, where he was going down regardless. He reassured himself by focusing on the idea he would be dead before any of the past resurfaced.

Innocent and intrigued, Anna and Olivia, unbeknownst to Markos, were searching for a deeper connection to family as well. They themselves needed to strategize ways to avoid the repercussions of past family grievances. They tabled the discussion for the night, but once morning came, they could not avoid it.

"So, do you want to talk about this? You kind of sprung it up yesterday without…uh, really asking me?" asked Anna.

They awoke before their timid suburban community started to file to their workspaces. Olivia, after locking the door to the cul-de-sac encapsulated home, turned to her daughter and made her a victim of her powerful scowls. Olivia chose to answer the inconsiderate question once she settled into her electric midsize sanctuary.

"When do I ever need to ask you permission to bring someone into *my* home, especially someone who's family?" replied Olivia as she pressed a round inconspicuous button. The consequence of her action began smoothly turning the car's insides.

"He's interesting, at least for the few minutes I talked to him, but we don't know that much about him," said Anna.

She was not bothered by the thought of having her great-uncle live with her, but she wondered why her introverted mother would take a leap of faith in someone she did not know.

"Your grandfather never spoke ill of him. He always said there was bad blood that kept us away from him, but he never doubted or distrusted him. You know how much about us is online. Don't believe it all, that's what Mom always said," added Olivia. She tinkered with the attached tablet in the car, activating the defoggers.

Olivia was just as terrified about the family's past being reignited. As a group, they never discussed any of the news coverage the family received. They were forbidden to speak about certain topics in the home. Her reserved lifestyle was a product of the privacy her parents always demanded from the public and the people they worked with. Her parents made it their mission to never involve their kids in the work Ephraim was doing in the public eye. Their efforts could not stop all the questions and critique other children had of her parents, an outcome that pushed her towards a recluse lifestyle. Nevertheless, Olivia's mother and father taught her to never disrespect or leave the family when one was in need. Her decision to allow Markos to come and live with them was devoid of hesitation and welcomed with good intentions.

"I'm okay with it, I'm just asking if you thought about it. Did you talk to Darius about this?" said Anna.

"No, why would he care? He probably doesn't even remember Uncle Markos; he was young when Markos and Dad fell out. Why? Did you say something to him?" replied Olivia irritably.

"No, I haven't told him. Should I?"

"No, don't tell your uncle anything. He'll turn it all political. He treasured the ground your grandpa walked on. Sometimes...he cares too much about the name more than the people he shares it with," said Olivia, letting her voice trail off while taking control of the steering wheel.

Once the car began to reverse off the cracked driveway, the conversation ended. She wanted to take her mind away from the topic, choosing to drive the car herself instead of leaving the car on the automatic setting. The result of the quick exchange served to embed doubt in both of their heads. Olivia tried to focus on the terrain on the way to the hospital, while Anna tried to contemplate the coming changes in their life. She used the driver's side window as her canvas, drawing out her future on the smudged glass. The smooth and soulful rhythms attempted to calm their nerves as they glided along the empty highway. Tension rose while they slowly approached. They entered the suite to Markos struggling to put down the hospital's vanilla pudding.

"Hello, I didn't expect you guys early," said Markos forcefully.

"We didn't want the hospital charging you for an extra day. They told us to get here before 8," said Olivia.

"Ah, I see. Let me call the nurse in and get my clothes so we can leave," replied Markos.

He grabbed the tablet and pushed the "*Nurse Attendant*" button. Anna took a seat by the windows and looked out towards the city. She watched the calm cluster of trees sway in the direction of the soft spring wind. Olivia, wanting to look busy to avoid awkward encounters, chose to examine his chart to see if there were any changes to his condition from the night before. The eye-popping statistics pushed her to intrude on the subtle silence in the room.

"It says you haven't been eating. Are you okay?" asked Olivia.

"I'm good. This food is not the best," said Markos. He started to stretch his upper body.

Anna took her eyes off the fluorescent Sacramento morning sunshine and started chuckling. She turned to Markos.

"I can smell that nasty pudding over here," uttered Anna.

"They told me they won't discharge me without taking this down. The hospital is obligated to do so if they want to touch that state money," replied Markos, forcing another spoonful of pudding down his throat.

"Seems barbaric," said Anna.

"Why don't you help me out? Can you take this *barbaric* pudding and empty it out into the toilet before the nurse comes to the room and chastises me?" asked Markos.

Anna looked to her mother for approval, completely aware of the tough position she was put in by her great-uncle. Anna was not worried about getting in trouble, or the repercussions of breaking rules in a VIP suite, but she was worried about her mother. Olivia was completely uncomfortable with the concept of infringing upon any rules or indulging in deceit or trickery. Anna looked upon her mother for her next course of action.

"Hurry, hurry up before they walk in here," added Olivia.

Both Markos and Anna saw she was out of her comfort zone and watched awkwardly as she became flustered by the situation. Anna quickly walked a few paces forward in the wide empty space of the hospital room and grabbed the cup of pudding. She slid across the white tiled floors to motion towards the spacious private bathroom. She took his plastic spoon and emptied the clunky pudding into the tiny toilet. Disgusted, she threw the cup into the garbage can next to the toilet and walked out to find the nurse in the room with her smiling mother, practically unable to control her laughter, with Markos anxiously waiting to leave the hospital.

Anna misunderstood the reason for her mother's devilish laughter. Her lack of control over her deviant nature showed it's form for a different reason.

"Anna, can you please go down to the shop and buy Markos some new clothes. It seems the hospital chose to discard them after bringing him here," said Olivia, smirking uncontrollably.

"You guys are lucky I didn't care for the clothes I was wearing. Why would you guys throw it away?!"

"Markos!"

Olivia's laughter quickly subsided as her piercing gaze focused on his vulnerable eyes. Her act of discipline shamed him. He turned to the nurse.

"I apologize, Violet. This whole ordeal has taken a toll on my attitude. I didn't mean to yell at you."

Anna walked over to the cushioned stool by Markos. She could not refrain from the opportunity of undermining the elder statesman. As she slowly made her way past the lime green seat by his bed, she mouthed a derogative capable of collapsing any man's pride. She was smart in her approach, hidden from the view of her delirious mother and the nurse.

Markos noted the insult and chose to keep a mental note of the action. He was more concerned with the nurse contemplating her response to Markos. In 2067, he could find himself in a serious dilemma for harassing a registered nurse.

"No worries, Mr. Solomons. It's been a difficult time for you and your family. I'll see if we can get some extra scrubs for you."

Anna was grateful she did not have to travel nearly thirty floors down for his clothes.

"That'd be wonderful, Violet. Thank you."

The nurse quickly made herself scarce. She knew the trouble she could have got Markos in, but she was more worried about what the brother of her childhood hero thought of her after she discarded his sweat-riddled clothes.

"They're about to make me look like one of these nurses from those shows," uttered Markos, disgruntled.

"You know how much trouble you could've gotten all of us in. You know what that would do," murmured Olivia.

"Is your mother always this paranoid?" asked Markos.

She smiled and nodded to him.

"Call me that again and I'll respond in kind," said Markos, comically mimicking a serious tone.

"What?" asked the ignorant mother.

"Come on, lighten up," suggested Anna.

"If either of you curse, I promise I'll kick both of you out of my house."

Both Anna and Markos were silent, like children awaiting their parents in the principal's office. Markos did not care for the threat; he and the nurse shared similar discomfort. He was attempting to quickly immerse himself into his estranged family, socially, without due diligence. His realization that he did not know who these people were finally sunk in. His sigh of displeasure showed others of his remorse. He cautiously avoided speaking until the nurse returned with the leftover hospital garments.

"Thank you, Violet. I'm very appreciative of all the things you've done for me in the past few years. You were a glimmer of sun on the gloomy days I came in for treatment."

She extended her pale arms towards Markos, sharing the bland purple scrubs she found in storage. She fought back tears of joy after the reaffirmation of her confidence from his graceful statement. He, of course, decided this to be an opportune time to impress his new landlord, a cure for his recent remarks of negligence with his use of vulgarity. Anna found herself in a state of complete disgust by the gullible nature of her mother, while being impressed by the man's abnormal whit. She began to recognize the man in front of her as one who could either be a formidable opponent, or an unlikely ally.

Markos slowly arose from the firm bed. He started taking off his garments before a loud commotion arose within the room.

"Aye, woah, woah, woah. What are you doing!?"

"I'm changing. What?" asked Markos.

"*What?* Give me a heads up. Mom is he senile?"

He was ashamed to tell them he had not worried about covering his decency in some time. The words could not leave his mouth. The women turned around and decided to remain quiet as the man reacquainted himself with clothes. He quickly put the light scrubs on and headed to the restroom to wash his hands before they left.

"Now you want to go to the bathroom," said Anna. She arose and gathered her things.

"I have to get some of my things that I had on me when they took me. I'll be back and then we can leave."

"Sounds good, we'll wait here," said Olivia, sitting down at the end of the bed.

She stared, inquisitively, at the window, looking for answers for what future awaited her new family dynamic. She never liked to yell, let alone at family, but she was unprepared for the variation in culture with someone she was related to. She was unsure how to approach the situation. She had an opportunity, years ago, to do the right thing, but fate and her inability to come to terms with the ugly nature of family grudges stalled her from the window of chance. Olivia contemplated if she made the right decision years before and whether she was going down a rabbit hole, especially with all she was told about her uncle. Both her parents switched their tones from ignorance to endearment following a test of their mortality. Their forgiving nature at the end of both of their lives was a saddening moment for Olivia. She saw the regret in both of her parents' eyes and refused to follow in the same path. The shame stayed with her while the daily battles of life distracted the two women. Her parents spoke in riddles when it came to the hatred spewed between the family in the early 40s. As she sat with her uncle earlier, she felt joy along with a plethora of emotions resembling fear of what type of man she was allowing into her home. His political and social reputation was not what she feared, but the baffling philosophy her parents believed he had when they spoke of his quiet charisma. Her grandmother, in the few years she had with her, was never a revealing woman and went to the grave without saying much regarding the end of the unstable family. She never uttered anything detailing the controlling grasp the family had on American politics.

All Olivia could worry about was if they were safe, not only from the enigma they knew their uncle was, but the emotional toll old stories would bring back. She feared new information with potential to damage the perception of who her parents were. She thought of what type of man was coming home, was he scorned by the past or had the years allowed the man to find solace from the ripples in time? Who was at fault? She knew nothing and the mystery of it all intrigued her along with the ability to fulfill the promise she made to keep the family close.

Her time of contemplation quickly ran its course as they dashed out of the hospital. Markos was in a hurry because the medical director always wanted to discuss the state of his health and reassure him of the excellent treatment. Markos never appreciated any form of higher treatment or celebrity status. It defied the logic and tenets he and his brother were raised with and more importantly, this form of subtleness was the way they conducted business in the Party.

The group found themselves in front of the car as the shine from the reflection of the white tint blinded them. A minor scuffle about who would sit in the front of the car quickly occurred before they began on their way home.

Once he was in the car, Markos was at their behest.

"What's the plan for today?" asked Markos.

"Right now, I'm headed to the address you gave me last night. I assume it's your house," said Olivia. She stayed keyed in on the road in front of her. She still chose to drive manually.

"Yes, that's my house."

Markos was nervous about showing his home to anyone. His lonely lifestyle never obligated him to reinvent the AI in his home. He was afraid what state he would find the house in. He hoped Suzie cleaned all that she could.

"We'll head there to get the stuff you may need for work and a few weeks' worth of clothes, whatever you got. Then we'll head to a diner to get some food," said Olivia.

"That sounds great."

The drive to his home was very quiet because it was obvious how stiff Olivia and Markos were. Anna was more focused on the news she was ingesting on her tablet to even attempt to spark up a conversation with them. As they pushed out of the city, the stiffness worsened. Markos was weary of facing judgment on his living habits or the location of his home.

"This is beautiful," assessed Anna. Her head shifted outwards, towards the terrain from the backseat of the car.

They were just passing the elegant trees huddled over the long road into his home. Markos remembered the last time he went down the path. Grace started to appear in his demeanor as he subtly brushed his fingers on the clear window. He was very lucky to still be breathing. His time was running out, but it was like his brother said, *it is written.*

Anna's comment eased the queasiness in Markos's stomach.

"The trees remind me of a movie your grandfather loved."

"The movie with the disabled or autistic guy?" uttered Anna.

"Hmm, yes. How'd you know that?"

"All the movies you and grandpa have are with me. I watched all of them in my spare time. I got all your stuff. What are all the movies on again, Mom?"

"DVDs."

"They were archaic back then, too. I'm glad they went to a good cause. That's how we learned about *people*," said Markos.

His insightful comment was cut short. They pulled up to the stand alone home. They stared at the home with rigorous intrigue for they had never seen one positioned alone with no neighboring houses or businesses. Everything in the city, including in the suburbs, became compacted as the land in the state's capital was bought up at a rapid pace. They looked upon his home with shock and slight envy.

"I'd kill to live here. There isn't a thing out here," said Anna.

"Did you build this?" asked Olivia.

"No, I knew the previous owner. I've had some renovations done on the home over the years I've lived here."

"Who knew universities paid so well," said Anna. She tilted her head to see the trees surrounding the home.

The comment caught Markos off-guard as he stepped out of the parked car.

"How'd you know I worked with universities?"

"I read the news, no matter how far back page they are."

Markos wanted to be mad at her disparaging comment, but he smiled in disbelief of her wit. Her attentiveness and ability to disrupt reminded him of the past molders of his story.

"I'll wait in the car if that's okay. I have to make a call to work and let them know I won't be in today," said Olivia.

Markos turned back to check with her from the front door of his home, but she already dove into her watch, linking to the car to make a call. He felt more comfortable taking Anna inside because he knew she was going to judge regardless of what the home looked like.

"What does your mom do?" asked Markos as he typed in the code to get into his home.

"She, uh, is a clinical psychiatrist, behavior type things. She and a friend opened up their own small practice."

"Wow. What about you?"

"I graduated from school, but I'm at home trying to figure my situation out," said Anna.

"Ahh, so you're freeloading."

She quickly glanced back first and proceeded to give him a suggestive hand signal.

The house was unusually warm when both of them walked in to Suzie's welcome. Anna refused to acknowledge the housing system. Her generation rejected all forms of artificial intelligence interfering with daily functions. He complied with her request by shutting down Suzie. Markos felt like he was betraying the one friend who stayed true for a new, popular acquaintance. He concluded it was the right decision because he was getting too attached. Anna refused to judge him for it. She did ask if he had a fetish for Suzie, a fetish one of the characters in one of the movies in his collection had for an artificial system. He vehemently denied it. *She's just someone to talk to,* he said. He made a fatal mistake in divulging the fact as she ripped into him about a softer side.

Markos walked her all around the first floor of the two-story home. She did not care for the bland theme of the interior because she was so focused on how much freedom one must have away from all the noise and the people. He looked at her as she marveled at the privacy and loneliness of the home, the unfortunate characteristics enabling him to drink in sadness every night. It was when she made her way to the kitchen he remembered.

The man nearly forgot the devastating pieces of paper lying in his drawer, left of the sink.

"Hey, I don't want to keep your mother waiting, could you do me a favor and get my stuff from upstairs?" said Markos, his voice trailing away as he stumbled into the kitchen.

"What, how am I supposed to do that?" answered Anna, walking up behind him.

"All my clothes are still in the bags I travel in. Can you grab the two bags to the right of the closet door? They should be the red and dark gray duffle bags. I'll grab a toothbrush."

"You are weird…weird is good though," said Anna. She hurried away to his room.

He slowly made his way into his dimly lit kitchen. Days passed since Suzie had turned on the air conditioning, so the kitchen held a heavy stench of molded fruit. He grabbed a toothbrush from the drawer next to the letter and put it in his left pocket. The scrubs were crucial in fitting not only the toothbrush in the pockets, but the letter as well. The man looked upon his hand as he took the envelope from the drawer. Everything was the same as the time before, his bronze ashy hands were shaking as he grabbed the letter, and his stomach was once again beginning to turn. He quickly stuffed the letter into his pocket and remained still. He believed he was going to go into shock again, but he was able to deviate from the course this time. He waited and waited, still as a snake before attacking its prey. Solomons took it slow as he continued with his tasks. He began to empty out any perishable food into the garbage and save all the unhealthy snacks he could, knowing people of Olivia's age converted to veganism. He walked around with the weight of ten men, the letter weighing him down, along with the snacks. He patiently waited for Anna to appear, finally hearing her come down from her loud groans from the top of the steps.

"You need to buy me some dinner! These bags are heavy!!" yelled Anna.

"I apologize, I really didn't want to carry that stuff down the stairs," said Markos.

"It's okay, this'll do as payment," said Anna.

She held up an unopened one-liter bottle of cognac.

"What are you doing? Why'd you look through my cabinets?"

"I was trying to see the type of person you are. You had a few bottles up there, this looked the most elegant."

Even with the door closed, he feared Olivia's eyes. He turned, and after knowing he was safe, he spoke.

"Alright, put this stuff in the duffle bag. Don't tell your mother."

She stuffed the snacks he held in the bag, along with the bottle she took from his bathroom.

"That's the sound of it, you may be my favorite family member already Mr. Solomons," replied Anna while she placed her hand on his shoulders.

The touch was euphoric for Markos, unaware of the jumpstart she was to give in the few remaining moments of his life. He still hid his emotions as they figured one another out, but he let a smile escape his face. A small smirk crept from the birth of optimism, borne from a man scarred lifetimes over by distrust and nihilism.

three:
Visions

Sweating was the worst symptom. The moist stench he left worsened his embarrassment. He thought it better to be an insomniac, because he could understand and compartmentalize the treatments for his sleep troubles. This was much worse, and the physicality of the situation reverberated noise throughout the home. He was lucky the yelling subsided years ago. He repeatedly thanked the doctor in private for his advice to speak to a specialist for the screaming in the nights. Suzie's recordings were shocking, forcing him to come to terms with his psyche. Still, sleeping pills held him down for a few hours before his mind would spiral, again, out of control. He desperately craved the bottle Anna stashed in his bag four days prior.

That little devil, he thought. She took it out of the bag when they were getting situated. *If only she knew what the alcohol was for,* thought Markos. He refused to ask her for the bottle out of fear of compromising his moral standing with her. He woke from his demonic trance due to the pain from falling off the twin-sized bed Olivia provided. After searching for any semblance of time, Markos was pleased to learn he had slept for four hours. He knew, without a sliver of doubt, they could hear him scrambling in the middle of the night. He worried they were annoyed by the noises he would make when he struck the walls. There was no headboard in the small guest room, so his punches could be heard throughout the second floor of the house.

He never liked his brother's room growing up. Their parents quickly bought a house without showing the kids the rooms or allowing them to hash out specifics. Markos was older, so he was able to steal the room facing the driveway of the cul-de-sac. He was thankful his room was close to the stairs, giving him the ability to hear anyone sneak in and out. Now, he laid in the room decorated with cardboard boxes as Anna slept in his old sanctuary.

His old home reignited mixed emotions about the way he was raised. His mother's Ethiopian heritage and his father's American upbringing had a large influence on his views of the world. Everything he learned in this home triggered every infinitesimal reaction, to every obstacle he faced in life, for better or worse. He remembered his mother knocking on his door in her all-white traditional garments to obtain confirmation of his safe return from the nights he worked in high school. He remembered all the photos of historical figures and tourist posters put up in his room and how he dreamed one day of visiting every foreign nation under the sun. More importantly, he remembered his father's heavy hand in making sure his kids understood he demanded superior discipline from them. He remembered the dusty bookshelf he put in the living room by the front door. His mother abhorred the light brown, four-layered bookshelf. It's stocky and wooden features were an eyesore, but it was a reminder of what was necessary to become a citizen of the world, intelligence. Little did their father know his faulty policies would push his children to make education the forefront policy in their movement. He thought of it all as he lay stuck in the room his brother plotted the future in.

His nostalgic trips took time to dissipate. Notable pieces of the home were changed. Olivia painted the inside of the home a baby blue color, a color his father would have detested. As he imagined his father's disgust, he reveled in what his father's reaction would be if he walked in and saw what the home had become. The carpet was changed to hardwood floors and the cabinets were remodeled and painted white. Markos appreciated the changes because it represented the continuity Markos and Ephraim always wanted, not only with the family, but the people they encountered over the years. He was sad, however, to see that the garage shifted to a storage unit. There were groups of midsize brown boxes filled with all the lost remnants of the time passed. Markos spent some time in the garage when he lived in his home growing up. The two-car garage was once his gym, instead, reconfigured with boxes pushed towards the walls and extra kitchen equipment. He did not get a chance to talk to Olivia about the garage or the home, but he did not want to overstay nor intrude on his welcome. Olivia was busy scrambling around, trying to balance her work and feed an extra mouth in her home.

Most of his time was spent outside of the home. He walked around his old neighborhood, a practice he made a routine when he was growing up in the quiet, suburban neighborhood. The changes to the neighborhood were more disturbing and unsettling than the home's renovations.

Cameras were installed on all the light posts on the streets leading out of the cul-de-sac, along with a police car constantly patrolling every two hundred houses in the neighborhood. Markos was not a fan of the new policing and zoning laws in these older and secure neighborhoods, but he could not complain if the neighborhood was safe. He did not understand the use of promoting neighborhood patrol officers to police officers and equipping them with more fatal weapons to handle an already quiet and safe area.

Markos's walks were always carried out alone, however, Olivia stressed to her daughter about taking the necessary actions to help her uncle get acclimated. In the first few days, he was able to live with the independence he required. They had an eye on him, but slowly did they begin to encroach on his sovereignty. Markos understood they had good intentions, but he wished to be trusted with things such as his routine walks. For any familial relationship to be sparked, for him, it needed to be birthed out of desire instead of worry.

Olivia did not trust Markos in his current state of health. She had no reason to, and she did not attempt to hide her worries. She watched him closely every opportunity she had. The banging on the wall was not the only aspect drawing her nurturing tendencies closer to him. She assessed his calibrated movements and began to slowly understand, not only the physical toll of his sickness, but the detriment to his mental stability, in part due to the solitude. She was weary of his constant charade, reassuring her of his peak health, knowing deep down the pain he was in and the difficulties of understanding the finality of the impending death. They knew it, and she was right to worry about his mentality. She wanted him to feel comfortable in his new quarters before she would delve into the topic of what was to come for him. Nevertheless, things were to keep going on as is for the Solomons family.

Markos gazed deep into the alarm clock, waiting for the sun to meet him halfway. He was excited for his next guest lecture at the university. He already laid out and ironed his shirt as well as his customary navy blue, three-piece suit for the lecture. He decided to accompany his look with his black silk tie and black dress shoes with stiff laces. He wanted to look prepared. This would be the first time a member of his family would see him lecture.

The fear of Anna's judgment haunted him. Visions interrupted his night's rest. New faces he forgot reappeared in the worst way. The letter's weight never released itself from Markos's mind.

He insisted on driving to the event himself, or at least renting a car, but Olivia insisted on Anna taking him to Berkeley for the day. He resented the youthful tone Olivia was taking with him regarding Anna's assistance. Her subtle, demeaning tone mirrored the overall care he was receiving in the home. He did not like Anna being forced to hear him speak, but he resigned respectfully from any conflict with Olivia since the hospital. He was told by Olivia earlier in the night she wanted Anna to get close to her family. Anna did not make the effort with Olivia's brother. Olivia's mother did not spend enough time with her before her death. Topics surrounding the theme of family were tough for Markos to swallow, so he guiltily complied with her wishes. She reiterated Anna was in a tough situation in her life and that she was trying to figure out which path to take. He read through the lines of her soliloquy. Anna was unstable and she could be set off without some adult guidance. No one could tell him differently, the girl was special and intelligent, far smarter than anyone at her age of twenty in the day's social societal structure. The butterflies in his stomach were surging whilst Olivia spoke. A forgotten emotion compiled within, affection, brought about by Olivia's anxious request.

Olivia was the next to rise on the misty Sacramento morning. Spring recently turned the corner and was beginning its long stride into full fruition. The bees could be heard buzzing on the moist, vibrant flowers on both sides of the home. Markos was stretching when he heard the faint footsteps. Olivia carried a similar routine he and Ephraim had as kids. He chuckled at the fact the strict habits of his parents were still plaguing the Solomons' household. His brother detested the drill sergeant attitude of his father but was unaware of the importance of the strict discipline at the time. He heard her steps, in the same hall once obstructed by fatigued and innocent children. Her noticeable pause in front of Markos's door was accompanied with the slight brush of her head on the door. Markos wanted to smack the door as punishment for her attempt of eavesdropping, but acknowledging the good intentions, he chose another route.

"Good morning."

"Ah...good morning. I'm sorry if I disturbed you. I'm gonna go to the gym. Do you want me to bring any breakfast on the way back?" asked Olivia softly.

"No, I'll be okay."

"Okay, I'll be back for breakfast before I go to work."

"*Ishee, dehina huni,*" said Markos, in his mother's tongue.

Olivia hesitated and Markos could feel her smile through the door. He wanted to test what Olivia remembered about their family. Language was his mother's trade. She stressed the importance of knowing and understanding one's culture and being able to communicate in more than just the majority's speech. *Education is communication, communication is key to more education,* she would say. *If only the people knew where that came from*, thought Markos.

The importance of his witty remark was that he remembered his mother teaching Ephraim's children the language when they were on the road. He did not have time, with Olivia's busy schedule, to have a full conversation with her. Even though he was telling her to be safe, he was finally acknowledging he remembered her. Markos understood his kin's noticeable worry for him. He was going to pass on soon and the totality of his life was blanketed by morbid conditions. He simply wanted to remind her he was alright.

He rose and after waiting for Olivia to leave, he quietly left the home to go on his calming walk. The days he spoke at the university, he always would drink the night before in order to keep his sleep uninterrupted. He feared the consequence of deviating from his drunken routine. Surprisingly, he felt fresh. He had spunk in his attitude, and he was much more observant of his surroundings. The alcohol kept him impaired and emotionless during his lectures. Many students noticed his lack of emotion and took that as resentment of the party. It was true of his resentment for the *Entente Party,* for a different reason altogether, but his attitude was severely affected by the years and decades of isolated alcohol consumption. Artificial intelligence, he believed, was sufficient for a man who was a victim and a perceived cause of hurt and dissolution. He wondered why he was never booed or heckled, an adopted practice of students in lecture halls after the student strikes of the late 30s for professors who did not take their job seriously. He wondered if it was because his name was associated with the successful strikes. *Alana would laugh at the status she once warned us of,* thought Markos.

The times had changed, and he was granted another opportunity with his family. Both sides tried to keep tabs on the other in the past, but actors in between stalled efforts and eventually fizzled the family into mutual ignorance. The first few days of his return were silently awkward, but attempting to acknowledge the past with such remarks, he hoped, would ease the tension and bring him peace at the end of his life. The day would be an opportunity to open a path to connection with his family. He knew Ephraim would be smiling, watching them together.

He walked to the park he so often dreamt about, next to his family's cul-de-sac. Markos looked forward to reigniting his old practices of waking up and running a few laps around the wet soccer field. His father always watched him from the master bedroom window, at least until he left for work, to make sure he and his brother did their morning laps. He attempted to reintegrate a subtle jog into his slow pacing, but he inflamed his already upset insides and decided to go with the trusted walking. He looked over at the large elementary school across the field, opposite to the park's entrance by his home. He ignored his distasteful feelings towards his memories of the school and continued his laps. He anticipated the questions he would be asked at the lecture and the clever answers he was going to give, all in order to impress Anna. He began a very colorful conversation with himself in the park as he discussed a strategy for the day. His pacing increased as the tension of the conversation elevated. He knew the path to follow, but he feared its truth. He was afraid to be himself and share who he used to be. A day did not pass where he did not believe himself to be flawed.

Markos Solomons was once a member of the United States Air Force. Markos was an electrical engineering honors graduate of one of the leading universities in the world. He was a former Signals Intelligence Analyst in the Air Force turned political strategist of one of the most polarizing American political movements of not only the twentieth first century, but of the two-hundred-and-ninety-year history of the United States. He was a man who served the pleasure of others and helped move mountains for the people he loved, a relatively average man whose external outlook prepared his team to face the worst of his brother's enemies. He was a man who thrived in the shadows of powerful orators. Markos spent time as people's anchor until the ground beneath him gave way to the mounting weight. There was no one who carried his anchor in his tough times as he lost those who tried their best. Markos was a unique individual whose sanity and ability to comprehend tough situations brought him to that exact moment, as the last man standing. All of this was done despite his fear of people. He repeatedly felt the burning sensation of loss, as *they* all left him, one way or another. Others were much more important to the movement than he ever was, but who could speak to it?

Importance was not the key, for none could tell the story other than the man who was behind the scenes of it all. He remembered all those who came along with him: Ephraim, Alana, Jamie, Jonathan, Peter, Alondra, *Elsa.* Three were dead, three of them escaped the futile situation they created for themselves, only leaving Peter to profit from it all, as he always believed they could. None of them expected the oldest to live long nor would they believe the meekest to be the one passing the history of their movement to students. He tried locating Alana, but she warned him she would be leaving for good, never to return. Regardless, the story required retelling, for there was not a reason for him to outlive the others who morally, existed far better off than he could ever wish to be.

The others were vital to the movement's growth, however, the secrets shared between the core four were impenetrable and incredibly damaging to the party. Revelations, without a doubt, could shake up the structure and foundation of party leaders and power brokers. Unbeknownst to Markos originally, politicians kept close tabs on his guest lectures about the politics of the 2030s and 2040s grassroots efforts his brother made in conceptualizing the controlling party in the House of Representatives.

The rapid pace of the events back then mirrored the speed in which Markos was attempting to rekindle relations with the people who carried his name. He quickly darted back home after completing the ten required

laps his parents once forced him to do as a child. He came back to a livid
Anna who was unaware of his trek through the old neighborhood.

"Where did you go?!"

Markos froze at the door, unprepared for any interference on his
entry. He looked up to find Anna eyeing him down from a few steps
above the start of the staircase.

"I went to go walk Anna," said Markos, slowly shutting the light
brown door with the oval top.

"Listen, I almost had to call Mom. I couldn't find you for like an
hour. Your demented punches in the wall made me think you were out
there going crazy!" yelled Anna.

"I apologize for the antics last night. As for the walk, I always used to
do that as a kid, you don't have to worry about that."

"Uh, forget that no way. I saw your chart, and so did Mom. I've been
told not to leave your sight. You go outside, you wake me up, or you
wait here," demanded Anna.

Markos smiled and simply nodded at the young woman. He was
delighted because of the worry in her voice. He felt exposed, once again,
but he kept a dying man's attitude of positivity.

They went their separate ways and each prepared for the day the way
they normally would do so. Anna retreated upstairs to her room and
chose to come out when she figured out the outfit for the day's occasion.
Her vibrant presence could be felt anywhere in the home, no matter her
location. She stood around the average height of five feet six inches, but
she held the mentality of an elite athlete. She moved with confidence,
complemented with witty intelligence and unadulterated security. She
always kept her natural curls away from her sculpted cheekbones. They
were interrupted with miniature acne bumps, subtly blended with
distinctive bone structure. Her hair was always tied up, braided, or put in
a bun; a practice shared by the working women of the Solomons
household. She had the athletic build of a soccer player which was
attributed to her mother's vegan lifestyle. Her confident strides were
synonymous to her colorful and carefully chosen daily attire.

Her conservative decision to wear a black pantsuit and a clear white blouse surprised Markos. He looked upon her with admiration, because she reminded him of the great matriarch who held the family together as best she could. The white blouse allowed for her maple syrup skin to glisten in the artificial light coming from the middle of the upstairs hallway. He peered through his room, past the open door, as she emerged from the bathroom.

"What?" asked Anna, blushing embarrassedly.

"You remind me of your great-grandmother, in more ways than you know;" said Markos as he laid out his navy-blue slacks.

"Thank you, I think."

Her hair was put into a bun sitting above the top of her dome. Anna applied minimal makeup, enough to show others of her effort, sharing with others how effortless it was for her. She walked over to her mother's room to utilize her mother's large collection of perfume. After Anna nodded to show she concluded her preparation for the event, Markos entered the restroom and showered. He quickly put his navy-blue suit and black tie on and descended to the living room to find Olivia and Anna having breakfast.

"Anna says you went for a walk Markos?" asked Olivia.

"Yes, I used to do that as a kid when I lived here. I'm now being told I need her with me. I've been walking alone for the past few days," said Markos as he put his shoes on.

"It's for your own safety, we just want to keep an eye on you and make sure you stay safe. That's what this whole arrangement is about," replied Olivia, concerned about the comfort of her guest.

"Safety shouldn't be a worry of a dying man."

"Listen, if you're in tip top shape, they said you could tack on a few more months," added Anna.

"Something every dying man has been told by his doctor," commented Markos.

"So, safety and longevity shouldn't matter?"

"Again, not to a dying man," said Markos, doubling down.

Olivia placed herself next to him on the scarlet contemporary sofas and looked with curiosity as to why he was fighting them. Her warm cinnamon bagel triggered his hunger as he focused on her meal. *Jesus, she looks like her mother,* thought Markos.

Her sense of worry emanated from the thought of losing an opportunity at learning about the past. His earlier remark trapped her in recurring thought whilst at the gym. Her mind spun into an eternal loop of reignited feelings of the warmth and connection she missed from her parents and grandmother. She agreed, with herself at least, to bind Markos to some form of social contract to the family, the family of two who were still trying their best.

"We're all dying old man," added Anna.

"Anna, I'm trying to be serious," stressed Olivia.

"I am, too. Listen, I don't know what happened between you and Grandpa, but you need to get it in order. If you want to die alone, that can be arranged. This is a patient house, and you are definitely pushing it," calmly said Anna.

A switch clicked in Markos's mind before he reverted into a state of confusion. He was dazed and began to sluggishly forget where he stood. Vulnerability showed and he chose to do what he always did when he found himself in a similar spot.

"I think this arrangement has been great for a few days, but as I expected, we're just different people. I think it'd be best if I moved back, and we worked out some sort of visitation schedule so you two can tell the doctor I'm fine. I've never really been good at connecting with people, especially family. Regarding your grandfather, he was a spectacular man who brought the best out of me. I'm not going to burden his family with the same burden I put on him and my mother," said Markos, standing, focused on the eyes of the disappointed mother and daughter.

They both sat frozen and unsatisfied at his words. The mother and daughter were much more taken aback than expected. They too lived together, alone, for so long. Anna's grandparents held onto enough struggles in their lives, forcing them to be virtually inattentive to others. She was able to meet her grandmother before her demise, but she was never able to connect. Her mother's busy schedule stalled her from any deeper connections. Both, Anna and Olivia, detested the lack of effort being made by Olivia's distant brother, but they still reciprocated love after years of his negligence. He made more efforts running with the name than acknowledging those he shared the name with. Anna's collegiate years were the loneliest of times for her and her mother, but this was an opportunity possibly wasting away. After her graduation, the pressure of being Ephraim's granddaughter seemed to alleviate when she was told about the great-uncle they were going to visit at the hospital. Markos was not able to see the effect he could have on the family. With a subtle remark, he ignited a flame in Olivia and with his back and forth with Anna, he became the first to challenge her. Markos could not comprehend himself as a catalyst, because like him, they adapted to mask their emotions. And like him, they were riddled with pain by his request to depart.

"I can't do anything to stop you, wha...what would you like to do?" asked Olivia.

Anna lost any form of interest in the conversation. Patiently, she pushed in her kitchen stool and returned to her room with a raisin riddled cinnamon bagel in hand. Both Olivia and Markos's eyes were glued to Anna's movements as she retreated to her room. They waited for her to completely close the door to her room before they began to speak again.

"She wants to understand you. I told you, this is a vulnerable time for her. She's read why her family was important, but she has no idea what really happened because her loved ones never told her anything. She knows nothing, I mean, I know nothing. I lost Dad early, but losing Mom the way we did, was much harder on Anna."

"There's truly nothing I could do for you. Your parents were always wise to keep you guys away from not only me, but the things we took interest in. It's a lot. I speak for a source of income, and I lie most of the time. I think it's best if I go home and drive to the Bay Area alone."

Olivia took time to consider her next course of action. She could not allow herself to deviate from the orders the doctor gave her, especially so soon into Markos's stay.

"I can't let you in good conscience go to Berkeley alone."

"Look, I can do this on my own. Believe me, I'm not a kid," replied Markos sternly.

She maneuvered back to the kitchen to refill her cup with the rich Ethiopian coffee he always could identify. He waited for a response, yet she chose to continue to refill her drink from the steel dispenser. In the awkward stalemate, Markos decided to go into the dishwasher and grab the miniature green mug to pour the hot coffee into.

"I'll grant your request to go home, without contest. However, you have to do a few things for me. One, you can't go to Berkeley alone. You have to take my car, it's a whole lot safer than your car. Second, take Anna to the event today. She's pouting right now, but she really wants to go, this is just one of her moods. After all this, if you still want to leave, we can work something out," said Olivia.

She turned from the dispenser and reverted to the sofas.

"That works. That makes it easier for me. Does the girl drive well?" asked Markos.

"Yes."

"Okay, if you can convince her, I'm leaving in ten minutes. She can drive me."

"Alright."

The car ride was a silent disaster. Anxiety was never a friend to the family and Markos struggled building confidence for his lecture. He was to speak to the college students for roughly one hour and answer their repetitive questions for the duration of the time allotted. The campus changed the location after Markos refused to speak twice in the form of back-to-back lectures. The campus refused to pay him his flat fee twice and asked if he could take a higher percentage of the ticket sales. His refusal forced the university's hand for two major reasons. He spoke at many universities, and he usually spoke to them two to three times a year. However, he only spoke at this university once a year. They tried to negotiate against his flat fee, and he responded by refusing to lecture there for years. He returned the year before, but the campus could not fulfill the demand for tickets with seats. They settled the problem by renting out a neighboring facility able to hold a little above three thousand seats. The university decided it was best to overestimate and insult him with a small crowd, but to their surprise, he kept selling out the venue.

The Solomons name was very important in student communities across the United States. Smearing or attacking the name would cause a frenzy within student ranks. If he was not invited and treated with the utmost dignity, his influence would prove detrimental to the school. The students' naivete hid them from the fact Markos only came for the compensation. He sold out decades ago.

Nevertheless, his family was with him. He believed he would have to be at his best for his living family, if he could not do so for his dead loved ones. The silence in the car was unnerving. His brother was instrumental in teaching him ways to combat stage fright and nervous attacks in large crowds, but occasionally, when he would turn to his darker impulses, he would revert to his shy nature. They were nearly to the venue when they came upon devastating traffic, triggering Markos.

"I can't take this silence anymore."

"What do you want me to do about it?"

"Say something. You're around your actual family and don't have anything to say? All you've been doing since I've been with you both is judge. Then you chose anger when I said I wanted to leave," yelled Markos as he pointed his clubby fingers in her face.

"Get your fingers out of my face, I'm driving," replied Anna while pushing his hand away from her face.

He was surprised by her disrespectful courage: "Your father didn't teach you manners?"

"Yeah, right, you two were probably similar, drinking your lonely lives away?"

The topic of fathers was a taboo in the family. The experiences Ephraim and Markos were subject to were difficult to discuss and dissect, especially for Markos. He was the oldest and the one who communicated with his father, Daveed, the most. He noticed the same painstaking expressions in Anna that he had when anyone asked him of his father in his childhood. The ambience of the car turned dim. Markos leaned back against the noisy leather seats and held his fingers slightly below his chin. He clutched his scrappy beard with his index and middle finger. He looked out the window as he tried to remember the ordeal his father put his family through as a child. He hated the attention he received in the aftermath of his father's choices. Every child carries the trauma caused by their parents, but it is the trauma that disavows the idea of eternal love for an unsuspecting child that hurts most. His memories allowed him to understand what she was feeling, what she needed. He chose his next words carefully.

"Where's your father?" asked Markos to the focused driver, ending the timid silence.

"No clue, you have a better shot of answering that, *professor*."

Markos continued his line of questioning, out of curiosity.

"He's never come to see you? I honestly don't know how things are done nowadays."

"This isn't so different from your generation, *professor*."

Does this title bother her? thought Markos.

"What do you mean?" asked Markos.

Anna took a few deep breaths before she gave out personal information. Markos interpreted it as a mechanism against pain, when she was in fact contemplating trusting him with sensitive facts.

"Well, I hope you could keep a secret."

"We keep secrets from family?" sarcastically asked Markos.

She was taken aback by the ignorance of her guest. She squinted in anger at his attempt at humor. The timing of his jokes was off.

"Okay, truth teller, tell me the reason you fell out with Grandpa?" asked Anna cleverly.

Markos sat shaken. He took off the black brim reading glasses he wore while studying his notes. It was his turn to decide if he could trust a stranger. His contemplation and frustrated look attracted the attention of the focused driver, who looked over to check on the silenced passenger. She recognized pain and pitied the man for her own lack of self-control. As she scrambled to change the subject, she shared her truth.

"Well, anyways, my *father* knocked up my mom when she was in college when she was nineteen. He was her boyfriend for a few months, but he seemed more interested in making love to her last name, if you get what I mean," said Anna.

He then first took notice of the vein pulsating on her right temple. He recognized and admired the family's distinct, rigid physique passed down generations. *We're all the same.*

"The families talked, and since she was ineligible for an abortion, the family decided the grandparents would co-parent until the two finished all their schooling. Boys being boys, he psyched himself out and left the equation, and with that, his parents left too. It really hit the fan when that happened though. His family was concerned about the child support Mom was entitled to. They said they would shame my mom and call her a slut or say she seduced their *innocent* son. It was an attempt to try and smear our name. Grandma turned ballistic and tried to bully the family back," continued Anna.

Alondra, mmm, always force? He knew of her tactics.

"Okay, what happened next?" asked Markos. He was still, waiting for more. There were holes in the story he was once told.

"Grandma called in the big guns. She tracked down and found Alana. Sh—"

"Wait, how did she do that?" worryingly asked Markos.

"I don't know, but if you find her, I would like to meet her, please. That woman got his family to sign a non-disclosure agreement where the family put their car and house into the contract as collateral. They also had to pay Grandma until my mom graduated, even though we didn't need the money."

He despised the culture of NDA's and their prevalence, for he was also bound by an agreement, an agreement carrying implications for the family and the party's dominance.

"Alana doesn't like any form of belittling or extortion, you were lucky," added Markos.

"Yeah, and then Mom used that money to go to grad school near me and Grandma. The rest is history."

"So, your father never came to try and see you? Do you even know what he looks like?" asked the frustrated Markos.

"No, he's never come for me. I did see a picture, though. He's half-Puerto Rican, like Mom. I think that's why they were getting along so well."

They waited in silence as the traffic began to open up. He took time before continuing.

"And you can trust this story?"

"Uh...yeah. I don't see a reason to lie. And if they were going to lie, saying your father knocked up your mom for your name is a horrible thing to lie to your daughter and granddaughter about."

Markos sat in uncontrollable frustration. *Alondra was always too blunt. How much damage we have done, Ephraim? You always said we were doing this for the kids and the ones who would come much later than us. Was it worth it?* She saw as he patted an envelope in his jacket pocket. He took a moment to recalibrate himself.

"So, what do you think?"

"I'm mad this problem still plagues our people," uttered Markos.

Anna burst out laughing. She did not expect a spontaneous response from a man she felt was thinking too hard.

"Did your mother do good by you?"

"She's done what every single mother would, try. She's never missed a school debate, a graduation, a sporting event. We've always had money and a nice house. She sometimes tries too hard and forgets to connect, you know. I want to break all the rules and she wants to maintain order. I also think she's never recovered from the idiot who impregnated her. But she's my mother and I love her. Plus, we're close in age which is cool," said Anna, giving him a genuine assessment of her loving mother.

Damn, the mother is not only loving, but she's brilliant. She knew I wouldn't leave, thought Markos. There were too many moving parts running around in his head at the moment while he tried to process information thrown at him so quickly. The car finally picked up speed as they got closer to the venue.

"So, we're about to pull up to the convention center in about five minutes. Is that enough time for you to tell me what really happened with Grandpa?" asked Anna.

"It isn't, but I'll repay your show of honesty. When we get back, I think we'll have enough time to discuss some events of the past," said Markos, as he cracked a smile of confirmation towards Anna.

Their renewed jubilation and happiness carried into the first hour of his crowded lecture. The large convention center seated all the ticket holders in red polyester cushioned seats, fitting the late comers on the stairs between the rows. It was a fire hazard the venue despised, but Markos refused to speak until all were seated. Markos convinced his kin to meet and sit with him on the stage next to the large curtains. The curtains, matching the maroon red of the seats, served as a backdrop to the stage. The lights were connected along the outer walls and were covered by gray lampshades to illuminate the back of the room. They were dimmed while the patient man spoke to the crowd. The curiosity of the young students showed its form in their sheer silence as their eyes locked in with his every movement. Anna was surprised by how he utilized the crowd's emotions and interests, how he maneuvered his way through the details of the past. He gave the crowd the normal spiel his brother always said, *Education is communication, communication is key to more education* and *people were desperate to agree in a time of turmoil. We just gave them a push.* The moment that caught Anna by surprise was the thoroughness of the students during the question-and-answer portion of the lecture. Markos kept his introductory speech to an hour since he always answered every student's question, a practice heavily influenced by his brother's policy of transparency.

"Mr. Solomons, many of us weren't born when your brother's movement took full shape. We learned all we could in our classrooms, but I have a question we hope you can answer to settle a debate. How was he, and the rest of you of course, able to expedite a grassroots movement, to become a reckoning force in the political arena in one lifetime?" asked the well-dressed Caucasian student.

Markos politely scoffed at her attempt at an encompassing, posturing question.

"Before I answer, what is the consensus you all agree on or at least argue for?" replied Markos before shifting to the right corner of the stage.

The lights started to slightly rise in order to familiarize Markos with the students.

"We argue that it was the reach of his politics in the 'red' states that enabled you to do what you were able to do."

"Yes, we became quite formidable after crossing state lines, but there's a key point people forget when learning about my brother's movement. He was very coordinated and formed a rigid plan for this movement after it exploded. He also made sure he himself was an enigma socially. In the beginning, he wanted people focused on the party, not him. His ability to control his own narrative and conceal his motives until people needed to know was a powerful tool that made us formidable against folks who didn't respond well to what he preached."

Many hands rose after he talked about his brother's social practices. It was always a topic of conversation regarding his ability to hide his ulterior motives.

Helped when we were forced to negotiate, thought Markos.

"Who was Ephraim Solomons behind closed doors?" asked a soft-spoken blond woman, resembling Alana.

"Ephraim was a man of academic discipline. He was patient and *calculated*, an attribute we have forgotten about. His ability to understand problems propelled others towards his movement. He was no different from you, but what separated him from the rest of us at times, was the fact he focused on *one* problem in our society to fix, and that was disunity. My brother would always argue that it is our nature to want to agree with one another. He abhorred the division and antagonistic culture propelled by our entertainment mediums. He believed they would try their best to distract and polarize people. He really believed unity could sell more than hate. We didn't have to let each other know everything about ourselves, we merely had to respect one other," said Markos, wiping the sweat from his forehead with a towel in his back pocket.

He was now amongst the students who were in attendance, leaving the stage. He never liked stages, but preferred walking amongst the crowd when they asked questions. The intimacy was synonymous to the motivations for the family's actions.

Questions, both irrelevant and inconsiderate, about his past were asked. They wanted him to comment on Alana's rumored bisexuality and Peter's overall role in the conception of the movement. He gave them half-truths to satisfy their thirst for the dirt on the party. The House of Representatives also sent an individual to take notes on his lectures to reassure themselves he was not endangering the integrity of the party. Congress was unaware of the true motives of the representative and his awareness of an existing NDA. It did not matter anyhow, Markos always kept everything close to the vest. He understood the students were not here to learn about the truth of his brother's organization, they wanted to know the stories of yesterday and meet someone a part of a movement larger than himself. Markos remembered the student mindset and how they desire a purpose, to matter to others. *Especially during the superhero era, everyone wanted power over other humans,* thought Markos, answering another question about Alana's mystique.

The closer he got to the back of the room, the more challenging the questions got. They started asking about his current attachment to the party. Anna never lost track of Markos, she focused on signs of degrading health and more importantly, lies.

"Mr. Solomons, do you have any comment about the violence of the strikes of the early 40s, whether the student ones or the civilian boards?" asked a young Chinese student.

The young student was no older than 15, but made Markos pause. The room's energetic atmosphere turned tense as eyes shifted to Mr. Solomons. The correspondent of the House of Representatives tightened as he watched. Markos took a breath before answering.

"The violence...in all *our* ambition, we didn't see it coming. I believe in 2042 or 2043 it was, we were there. I can never forget it. I was glad to see both sides come to the table after years of protests. I wished it would've come sooner so people didn't have to get hurt."

"Why is it that you then left the party shortly after that, a year or two before your brother passed?" continued the teenager.

Markos looked at the child with admiration. *Finally, an attentive one. The truth won't come out, but you paid attention.*

"Differences. I was getting older, and the movement was growing into what it is today. The rest of us were leaving and the ones that stayed were looking past what we were and how we started. After Alana left, I lost my loving friend who kept me grounded. I think I was looking for a reason and I found it. My brother should have left for his health though, that's known."

Anna noticed it, and she made sure to make note of it for later. *A lie is always blanketed by truth or humor.*

"Thank you, Mr. Solomons."

Mr. Solomons nodded at the boy as one would to a worthy adversary following a match.

"Well, young lady, we have made it to what seems to be the last question. I lost count after forty-five, but I'll say it. Make it count."

The woman stood up like the others did. He noticed her hoodie was illustrated with his brother's famous picture taken near Lake Merritt. Oakland welcomed them for one of his most powerful speeches. The merchandise was Peter's idea and his clever marketing led to unforeseen capital for the family: politically, socially, and monetarily. The young African woman put her foggy glasses in her pocket. Sweat trickled down her face, but she stood up confident. She arose and locked eyes with the exhausted Mr. Solomons in the back of the warm convention center.

"Mr. Solomons, I'm glad to ask the last question. I have a series of them I believe only you could answer. First, um, do you think this party's current platform and policies have sold out to larger audiences and watered down your brother's original purpose?"

"I'll be honest with you; the party is its own entity. I don't much associate this party to my brother except by acknowledging his creation of the foundational principles. They do their own thing, and it would've been different if it was him who was here. But that's the truth about politics, it gobbles up idealists and turns them into company men," replied Markos, focused on the eyes of the woman.

Her braided hair reminded him of Angela in her youth. He wondered if she was her daughter, the resemblance and the similar speech was uncanny. He refocused as the woman continued.

"Well, why did Ephraim...uh excuse me, Mr. Solomons, choose to create a political party instead of keeping it a grassroots movement that was *so* popular with locals and students?"

Markos chuckled at her truthful informalities.

"Don't worry, Ephraim hated formalities, they distracted people from the truth he used to say. To answer your question, our hand was forced. I can simplify it to influence and betrayal."

"How'd you feel about the move?"

"I was against it."

"Even now?"

"Even now."

"Why didn't you stop your brother?"

"I am but a man, young lady. A man who joined the leader you have on your sweater out of love and pain. My advice were unvoiced thoughts I believed were to be outvoted."

"Which way did Alana vote?"

"She abstained, but it was known which way she swung."

"So, it's true, it was led by Mr. Clemmings," said the young woman as she clenched her fists in fulfillment.

Markos grabbed the conversation back from the clever girl.

"Be careful who you try to point your finger to. The judgments we made back then were as a team, and we voted, so the numbers spoke for themselves after the debates," said Markos. He tried at dominance, instead shaking with his retort. His play at control was too late.

Another one, thought Anna. Markos could feel the correspondent's anger.

"I apologize for the deduction. One last question, why don't you advise the party or participate in the actions of an entity that was built by your family?"

"Time, my dear. An old man cannot do what kids were once doing. It's in the hands of much smarter folks. While the party may have forgotten some of the tenets of my brother's movement, they are the best option and don't need the help of a man playing chess with death."

"*Jesus,*" whispered Anna.

Mr. Solomons quickly turned and focused on his retreat to the elevated stage. The silence of the group was piercing as Anna focused on Markos's walk back. The audience's eyes watched the man with amazement, amazement from a point of view of curiosity and reverence for a man who was part of a group that redefined the meaning of service.

There were no more questions to be answered or stories to be told. The end had come.

"I want to leave you with something," said the nervous man, who finally reached the stage. He wished he began his talk with this.

"Many of you were too young to remember. There are past remnants and messages that are important to discuss and reignite. You all have learned those things as children: do good daily, talk to others as you would like to be talked to, and love trumps hate. You've heard all this gooey stuff before," said Markos, giving the crowd time for a subtle chuckle.

"I'm not interested in acting like anyone's parent, believe me, you all can do whatever you want. But if you came here to learn, there are some important things I want to leave you with. As you can see, I've been engulfed with new vigor recently. My brother's granddaughter is here, and I've been lucky to reconnect with my family. This new rejuvenation reminded me of old lessons I was once taught. Walks in the park and morning stretches evolved into philosophical discussions and you kids face the consequences of those talks, so listen up.

"Rules, tenets, morals, they are nothing if you don't believe them and truly live by them. We have lists and calendars that we create, but do we follow them? Do we? How many times have you looked at your schedule and given up on your day after a singular event ruined it? One saying we forgot during my brother's time, an archaic one at that is, *actions speak louder than words,"* added Markos.

The group went silent and surrendered mental control to him. His attack, on them and their society, turned the most opinionated back into toddlers open to new information.

"You are students, and whether you understand it or not, you are the most powerful group of people. We always hoped to enlighten you. You saw the shifts of power in education after the holdouts. However, these causes are not simple requests or disagreements with parents. They are not the systems that represent your conservative moms and dads. You must care for the people, people who stand next to you. Care for your neighbors. My mother taught my brother something important. 'Pass along the good fortunes passed to you and repay them to two people. One by one, as they pass along the simple logic of kindness,' which is a forgotten art by the way, 'they will uplift your neighbor and the people you hope to pull from the struggle.'

"Certain practices you think are doing something good will give rise to the rules and regimes you fear. Don't become like the systems you wish to reform. Actions, shaped in acts of kindness, are important for unity. Acts of brutality will always be glorified, but arduous acts of kindness are immortal. Disagreements and competition are our nature. It's something we desire as we grow, but respect will separate us from animals. That's one part of my brother's logic that always surprised me. In times of hate, he never wavered or chose to match hate with his own piercing words. It is our nature to agree, but we must not be afraid to agree with people who seem so different. It will take discipline, but don't speak on it, become it, *do it.* Grow with the understanding that the indifferences put before you will be the water to the growing plants of your own movements and ideologies. Just leave the doors open to others who will slowly migrate to your disciplined ideology."

Wow, hmm, interesting, thought Anna.

The crowd arose with roaring applause. He reached his hand out and grabbed Anna's. Together, they waved to the crowd, aware his words would likely die there without the birthing of action by the short-minded students. He only wished to touch the mind of one.

four:
Entente

Anna's inquisitive urges were buzzing inside of her, awaiting to be released. As soon as they both finished shaking the hands of the different groups and organizations in attendance, they rushed to the car to beat the traffic they knew was accumulating. An hour into their drive back, Anna put her bun down and let her hair breath. She had a plethora of questions regarding the lecture. She wanted to wait until they were comfortably at home before they dove in.

They slowly approached the dormant neighborhood at its simmered six o'clock hour. The newly introduced neighborhood cameras were sanctioned by the elected city council and were manned throughout the day. The increased security served to disgust Anna and Markos, and both hoped to avoid any interactions with neighborhood security.

Security became a resounding issue after fears of protests and extremism grew after the party conceptualized. Heretics chose to attack members of the Entente Party following their splash into mainstream politics. Aberrant followers of the newly formed party met the violence with disorganized protests, protests that split the Solomons household. It not only splintered the household, but served as the rationale for newly rising political actors to begin utilizing the technology departments of corporate lobbyists in the name of security. Decades passed with humanity sitting stagnant, and security still lingering at the forefront of politics.

Feelings of happiness subsided as they passed each four-by-four-inch lens obstructing the peaceful path to Olivia's home. They strolled into the driveway with soured emotions, finding Olivia at peace in her bed when they arrived.

"Where's your mother," asked Markos loudly.

He loosened his tie and fell into the clutches of the sofa.

Anna slowly descended from the winding stairs on her tiptoes, signaling to Markos with her index finger over her lips.

"She's sleeping, keep your voice down," whispered Anna.

"Don't wake her. It's been a crazy day."

"She'll be excited to hear that you'll be staying."

Markos refused to reply to her cheering remark. His attitude towards showing weakness did not change over the decades. His affectionate capabilities departed with his mother and Elsa's death. Still, he was ecstatic to bring a smile to Olivia's face, but as the stoic stalwart of his brother's movement, he refused to show it.

"I'll be asleep by the time she wakes up. Let her know how well today went and mention to her that I'll be staying. I think we all deserve a small moment to relax. Please bring the bottle you rudely stole from me and *some* cups. *Don't tell your mother.*"

"Give me a minute," said Anna with a mischievous smile.

She quickly ascended the stairs again, unaware of the squeaky cracks being made with each step. Olivia's day was consumed by worry of Markos's threat and the hostile environment the house was evolving into. The household's atmosphere was not just shaped by Markos's arrival. The women were feeling the effects of the concern they shared for Anna's future. The displaced emotions were frustrating them. Anna's anger was evident in her reserved attitude during important discussions while Olivia pushed her struggles onto her work, focusing on things outside of the home. Anna was excited to put that behind her for a moment. She rushed to find the bottle hidden in the floor of her closet.

She avoided the future with the presence of the man who represented the lost past.

Her quick return to Markos with the alcohol and cups was stained by a frightful encounter, bringing fear to both.

"Are you guys, okay?" asked Olivia, leaning over a barrier wall on the second floor, near the stairs.

"We're good, Mom. We're just talking about Markos's lecture. Um, he also said he is going to stay with us."

"Is that so? That's great to hear," replied Olivia, her words sprinkled with a sly chuckle.

Markos recognized the awareness of a successful plan in Olivia's clever laugh. He was well prepared to hear a form of celebration of the woman's plan. She followed her chuckle with a quick remark they did not comprehend. She returned to her room and closed the door. Both Markos and Anna let out a small sigh of relief.

"She would've killed me if she saw this bottle," uttered Anna.

"Why? Didn't you graduate from college?" asked Markos as he poured a drink. He let it sink in, pouring a drink for family.

"Yeah, I graduated, but I'm still twenty. No hard liquor for me."

"How does that work?"

"I graduated school in three years?"

"Damn. It took me four and a half years to graduate college, five if you count the semester I didn't take classes. You started at seventeen, too?" wondered Markos, taking a sip of his drink.

"Yeah, I was put in an accelerated program at my school, Grandpa's alum. They let me have whatever I wanted out there."

"Yeah, it's a good school. They have some good people that work there. Interesting?"

"What?"

"You're telling me you never drank in college?"

Anna took a moment to answer. She wondered what the best course of action was.

"I didn't ever really get accustomed to alcohol or drugs. That was never my thing in high school or college," said Anna as she took another sip of her drink.

"Really?"

"Yeah?" said Anna nervously as she continued with her small sips of the rum.

He avoided eye contact with young Anna because he disapproved of being lied to. Lies proved to be fatal to his friendships and relationships, ruining nearly all his social experiences. The girl's persistence to ignore the questioning annoyed the man who attempted to break the ice.

"Do you not believe me?"

Markos ignored the irrelevant question Anna tried hiding her lies in. She did not have the ability to hold the lie against the seasoned man. She struggled to give her hands a purpose when the conversation was shrouded in silence. She fumbled under the control of Markos's attentive gaze. Markos felt inconsiderate in his torture of the young host, but he detested fiction.

"Alright, I'll give you a few easy reasons why I know you're lying. First, when you stole my drink, you asked no questions about the drink. The way you handled it with care showed me you understood the monetary value of the bottle. Secondly, most novice drinkers who've never drank before make uncontrollable, reflexive faces when they taste alcohol without a chaser. Plus, you've been taking baby sips every few instances, so even if you don't usually drink alcohol of this caliber, you absolutely do drink."

Anna sat with her hands on her knees. She was afraid of his high-level perception. It terrified her how he did not take long to make certain deductions about her drinking. She wanted to desperately get the heat off her shoulders. Her eyes made their way to Markos's hands as he lifted the plastic cup to his dry, parched lips.

"Years of experience of dealing with men and women who attempt to belittle you and do harm to your brother teaches you skills of perception and awareness," said Markos after touching his dry tongue to the roof of his mouth.

Anna had no choice but to divulge the truth.

"Alright, I'm sorry. I couldn't drink unless I was alone. Do you know how much pressure is on me while being at Grandpa's alma mater? I can't go out to parties and get drunk or high, I had to do that alone and in confidence. Do you think I wanted to be used like my mother was when she was nineteen? My whole father's movement would've been dissected and judged by my actions if I was drunk at some frat party. There's a whole political party that could be affected by my actions, so being out and about and drinking and smoking was out of the question. I had to do that stuff alone," softly answered Anna.

Markos let a few seconds pass as Anna recuperated her lost breath. She began to calm her nerves and the veins on her anger-riddled face began to fade at a similar calming pace.

"The truth is liberating, isn't it? You have to let it out, in every difficult dilemma. Drink up," added Markos, nonchalantly finishing his drink. He poured himself a second drink that was anything but modest.

Anna mirrored the actions of the sickly man. She looked him over and was astonished by his keen sense for truth. She tried her best to dissect him from his actions, but as a novice, she was not able to see things at his level. Still Anna noticed, first, that he was sicker than some could see on the surface. His face was riddled with the scars of dried tears, with loose skin hanging behind his scruffy beard. The dried hands and the energy required to move them were noticeable. He was not prepared to hide the signs of the overwhelming symptoms, the tradeoff to coming home. She recognized pain and dormant anger, but she could not find a chink in the armor to chip away at truth. Anna resorted to the simplest way to find it.

"Why don't you tell the truth? I caught a few lies today in your colorful lecture, specifically about Grandpa's involvement in the end." She paused for dramatic retort: "Why don't you let the truth liberate you?"

"There's a small percentage of the truths that lie in this world that wouldn't liberate but would cave you deeper into a prison. These truths should be hidden."

"They will die with you. That's not fair to those that live here with your name."

She thinks much like her mother.

"Some things never need to see the light of day," uttered Markos.

"And why is it you who has the final say about what must, *come to light?* Don't I deserve to know the truth about my own grandfather? You weren't here to pick up the pieces of this family's legacy," said Anna, pouring another drink into her cup.

Markos was uncomfortable in the tight spot he was placed in by Anna's insightful questions. His back slowly found the sofa as he laid back and scratched his goatee. He took small sips of his honey-flavored bourbon while he decided on his next course of action. She gazed upon his puzzled face with determination. Anna purposely pressured him into a corner, but she did not come from a place of hurt, more so out of curiosity. She wanted to know more, and her intelligent use of guilt forced Markos to examine what truths he could share.

He foresaw the colossal consequences of continuing. He looked at the girl and let his mind run. He ran the simulations and knew her arrogance was a mask for innocence, a piece of ignorant life he would take from her if he went further. Her eyes were his mother's. How could he see the reflection of his nurturer and deny her?

"What do you want to know?" asked Markos, resting his drink on the clear glass table.

Anna was stunned her guilt-glaring trap worked on Markos. Markos did not desire to hide much of the pain, joy, and loss of the past. His admiration for his estranged family was no different from the respect he shared for his mother and brother and those he was raised with, regardless of the little time shared between them.

"Everything."

"Narrow it down. Specific things can't be told. I have made and kept promises that I will never break."

"To whom?" wondered Anna.

"That too, is confidential."

"What can you tell me?"

"The answers to what you ask me."

Terribly brilliant, thought Anna. Markos realized from her abrupt show of joy he was hoodwinked by her show of sadness. His sarcastic and enigmatic tone was his defense mechanism to her wit. She took time to return to Markos with a prepared question.

"Why *Entente?"*

Markos smiled because of the simplicity of the question. He did not favor the times when he had to lie to people, especially family. He was glad he was not forced to come up with fables to explain the interesting conception of the name. He looked at her after pouring, once again, another piece of slow poison in his cup.

"*Entente* was one of the last names we discussed. When the decision was made to move forward as a political party, the discussion about nomenclature was very intense because we wanted to avoid certain ideologies. We carried so many people who were on both sides of the political spectrum, it was important we take precautions to stay away from words like freedom or labor in order to not sound too leftist. We did the same to avoid anything resembling tradition based or nationalistic in order to not cushion to conservatives. We got into heated battles over what to call the party. Finally, he went with *Entente.*"

"What does it mean?"

"Now, it means something like underground fighting or grassroots-like mobilization. The word was redefined by Ephraim after all he did. Back then, it meant an understanding or unofficial alliance. It was the *exact* definition of what Ephraim wanted to do. It was also the exact word we needed to describe the argument we were having over the name. But we really wanted people, basically neighbors in a community, to discard extremist viewpoints and stop the continuing divide that came from 'picking a side'. Extremism reached peak levels in the late 20s, and your brother did his best to curb the political machines feeding on the disunity."

Anna sat back on the sofas as she recalled how much she heard the name *Entente* and how often it was plastered in the news. She remembered from the classes she took, how the party-system was given a jolt by the entrance of the Ententes.

All this time, people have been misusing it, thought Anna.

"Why was it you guys to do it? What made all of you...special?" asked Anna.

Markos looked at his drink and remembered the grueling upbringing, his father and mother's strict guidelines. The discipline was needed, even his father's righteous heavy hand.

"I never have been and never was, the special one. The whole party was uplifted by the humble and righteous shoulders of a near perfect man. He was built different."

The superfluous half-truths made him pause.

"We came up in the exact same circumstances, one came out so very pessimistic about life, and one emerged believing the right message simply was lost in translation. I'd like to say we were smart, but he had the patience to act on his ideas. He calculated and anticipated nearly all the things he experienced in the beginning," said Markos.

He could not withhold his reflexes as smiles sieged his face. He recollected how detailed his brother's interactions with people were, even those who did not hide the disgust they had for him. Markos's smile opened Anna to a piece of his scarred heart.

"I heard many of the same things. But no one ever talks about him leaving the party. What really happened?"

"He didn't anticipate himself and his health," replied Markos, quickly and coldly.

"What is that supposed to mean?"

"Exactly what I said. There are things that happen to someone with so much sway and power. When it comes to good men, they know it can consume them, so they attempt to disperse the power and share it. Trusting others is always the difficult part, and when you lose trust in those around you, you're lost."

"You're really good at not answering any of my questions," uttered Anna, annoyed by his dancing.

"*Anna,* there's too much there for you to know. You don't know the facts, and the things, the choices that were made for this family. Hiding from cameras was the least of our worries. There's pain that lies deep in the truth that forces us all to be reclusive. *Leave it be,*" answered Markos. He attempted to end her quest for unedited truths.

"What are you so afraid of?"

Can she not see that her purity is treasured? He dug his face low into his hands for a moment, parallel to his resting knees.

Markos laughingly scoffed at Anna's childlike antagonization. His brother despised people's idea of the blissfulness of ignorant behavior. He wondered how quickly his brother would change his mind if he was there with them.

"Our mother used to say, 'Acts in darkness will be guided to the light. It will be guided to the light by God.' She was half-right. Sometimes, those acts escape the depths of His abyss with the help of fire. But they weren't being guided by God. He was keeping them there. It's the devil that releases them."

Markos slowly arose from his seat and walked to the first-floor bathroom, believing Anna dropped the subject altogether. After relieving himself, he returned to the seat which had taken the shape of his body. He picked up the fingerprint-ridden tablet. He was satisfied to find his return from the restroom basked in silence. He appreciated the brief fact that Anna somehow knew. He wanted her to understand the weight of the burden on the family.

"I'm not afraid," blurted out Anna.

"What?"

"You heard me. I'm not scared."

Markos turned the television off and quickly turned to the drunk girl. He was taken aback by her words. They were abrupt. He stared at her, confused by her stance.

"Listen, what don't you understand? Any secrets I share with you will have to die with you and they never can be unloaded to your mother. Once I go, which is pretty soon by the way, you'll have to carry all these burdens and secrets alone. I can't even share all of them and you still want half-truths, half-truths that are enough to blow your head open."

"You still care about knowing?" asked the frustrated man.

He was out of breath from how fast he quietly yelled at the girl. He somehow avoided waking her mother. He began feeling familiar pains in his stomach, serving as a warning to calm down and distance himself from the alcohol. His hand's reflexive shaking was enough for Anna to realize what happened. She snatched the bottle and retreated to the kitchen where she hid it in the drawer with her junk food. She returned with her answer.

"It's all a lie, old man. I have figured you out in these last few days. You have some noticeable markers when you are lying. Why torture yourself? I know you're anxious to unload all that stuff. Stop making it hard on yourself."

Markos thought about the time ahead. It was true he wanted to unload decades of facts, but portions needed to be redacted from the child or enemies could lurk out from the past. He knew he would steal her innocence, there was no way around the reality of his life. Depending on Anna's actions after hearing the truth, she could avoid the inevitable enemies. He wanted to protect her whilst protecting he and Ephraim's secrets. The onus of dissecting a way without leaving her in the dark was on him. Her ability to catch him in his effortless lies was a danger. Markos also recognized the risk of Anna inferring specific facts on her own.

"Promises have been made to protect certain secrets. This family has always been raised to understand the meaning and purity of one's word. I'll reveal what I can, without breaking certain promises I've sworn to take to the grave. Whatever revelations that come from us talking, must stay between us, till your death and mine. Understood?" asked Markos.

There was no fight in him anymore. Reminders of mortality were powerful in putting truth in perspective. The placement of his hand on his white, unbuttoned and now wrinkled dress shirt, near his stomach, caught Anna's attention as a deal was put forth.

"Understood."

"All stories desire a good beginning and so we'll start from the beginning, my beginning because everything being shared is from my point of view. You need to understand me before you can understand the choices I made. The opinions I carry on certain things that happened are my own, not Ephraim's. You must assess my actions from my position without making deductions based on your viewpoints, only based on what I experienced. Again, for a little while at least, we discuss things like these when your mother is out of sight. She has to ask to take part, we won't just involve her."

"All questions are allowed but I will tell you when I cannot answer certain things. I will grant you your request of knowing why I cannot speak on certain things, but what you must never do, and I beg you not to, is to infer things that have not been said or withheld. You do not deserve nor are you qualified to infer things for one reason and one reason only, you weren't there. Understood?" asked Markos again. *How could she?*

"Understood."

"Questions?"

Before they began, he wanted to make sure they asked what they wanted to know about one another.

"What's that letter in your pocket that you never seem to separate from?"

Markos did not realize anyone noticed the letter, but he remembered in the car, she caught a glimpse of it.

"This is one thing you must never touch. This line can never be broken. If you touch this letter, the trust between us dies. I know how curiosity is a drug to you and your generation. This is for me and me only. *It's the only way the dead still speak after they pass on*," said Markos.

"Understood."

Markos traced his bronze hands down his jacket to reassure himself the sanctity of the letter remained unbroken. It was not sealed but folded and placed in his left jacket pocket. His comfort in its stillness allowed him to return to the conversation at hand.

"I'll need a good night's sleep. Some type of prayer will need to be had before these things come to light. You said you weren't scared, but I surely am," said Markos, as he slowly stood up and stretched his arms, preparing to retreat to his room.

"You're not serious?"

"Listen, I pray on certain things, and this fits the description of things in need of prayer. You'll learn of this family's faith, too. What I can give you is that you carry intelligence that both Ephraim and I could never have obtained. You're a smart one, but you'll have to work for the things you want to hear and understand difficult choices that were made in tough positions. We'll discuss more when we walk tomorrow, bright and early."

Markos walked to the kitchen to dispense the evidence of their unhealthy drinking. He lifted a few of the distasteful objects in the compost can and placed the cups slightly beneath them. As he walked back past the couch to reach the stairs, Anna caught his attention. She was wondering what she was to learn, the fear of the unknown creeping into her mind. She looked out to the brick fence separating the park from her cul-de-sac.

Tomorrow, she thought.

"Hey, um, don't taint my knowledge of my family. What I mean is, don't try to lie to me. I picked up some things from school and Mom's work, but sooner or later I'm gonna get too comfortable with you and won't be able to know when you're lying. Please, don't lie, hide the truth if need be. I want to learn what it was like and what happened to our family," said Anna.

Her show of rare vulnerability finally enlightened Markos of the fragility of Anna's current state, the truth Olivia tried to warn him about. He thought her trek upstairs in the heat of an argument was the extent of it, but he understood there were levels to Anna.

He moved closer to her, avoiding her touch due to the unfamiliarity. He looked down towards her face and she matched his gaze with her hazel eyes. She looked up to her only connection to her ancestry.

"I won't lie."

"Just half-truths?" teased Anna.

"Just half-truths," reassured Markos.

Anna, unexpectedly put out her hand. Markos looked and shook the hand.

"An *entente?*"

"Yes…an *entente.*"

five:
Parasite

Walks around the park were as important to Markos as any one of his childhood practices. Forced morning runs around the park turned to comfortable pacing after his father's departure. His brother abhorred physical exercise and immediately reverted to his avid reading following the absence of his father's forceful hand. His brother later changed his stance on the practice, later returning to use the time as an opportunity to decompress with his brother. With something as simple as morning walks, they believed the senses could become recalibrated, and an individual realigned with one's purpose.

Anna was very much unprepared for the five A.M. stretching. Olivia's inability to control her laughter while watching her daughter struggle irritated Anna. She met Markos outside in front of their home. The house was in prime position for entering and exiting since it sat closest to the entrance of the cul-de-sac. They began stretching after waving away Olivia as she left for the gym. Anna's age became more apparent to Markos after seeing her come out of the house in her exercise attire. Her cotton, winter holiday themed socks stood out more than the double strapped slippers she wore. Her extremely revealing shorts were not a problem to Markos as much as the slippers and her oversized hoodie were.

"Jesus Christ," said Markos, watching her struggle to figure out what to do.

"Even he's sleeping right now."

"Have you never worked out?"

"Never had to. This is how one looks when you master a diet of coffee over meat."

Markos's laugh was accompanied by a friendly wave to follow him over to the street. There was no point in waiting for her to finish stretching because he knew her healthy bones could withstand long treks in the park. He paid attention to her dietary habits and knew she was not lying about her health.

"Alright, where should we start?" asked Anna. They began walking out of the boxed in, cul-de-sac.

"One's childhood always provides a good basis for an origin story," replied Markos.

"No way, forget that. I didn't just wake up at 5:15 for you to tell me about a boo-hoo childhood story. We all have experienced messed up childhoods. Start somewhere else."

Markos let out a large laugh, loud enough for cameras to move in on him and some neighbors to peer out of their windows. They continued towards the park and reached it within a minute. The park's close proximity from the home pushed the camera operators away as they recognized the man and the girl's destination. They needed to pass a few homes before they reached the next cul-de-sac where the opening of the park stood. They walked in silence for a few seconds while waiting for the cameras to return away from their line of sight. Their conversation restarted after they reached the shade covered entrance to the park. Leaves from the trees above the entrance of the park fell on their shoulders. The squirrels dispersed after hearing their loud footsteps.

"It's okay. You'll ask about our upbringing later," said Markos.

They began their laps on entry.

"Can you give me a quick abridged version?" asked Anna.

"I was raised by an African mother and a father whose family had roots in Chicago. As we grew up, we started to see things that seemed off with our upbringing and the way our father's relationship with the family was. Then, he left."

"That was quick and easy. Why'd he leave?"

"Prideful men can't show emotional pain when they lose the respect from the people who built them up," said the man, staring into the quiet streets of his old suburban neighborhood.

"You speak in more parables than a faulty prophet. Anyways, did he ever come forward after seeing Grandpa on TV?"

"No, he was too prideful for that. He was probably happy and believed it was him who created that. He never approached Ephraim though," said Markos.

He continued his emotionless stare, now focused on the school he was forced to attend.

They turned a corner in the park's cemented walkway. They were to travel in circles for the duration of their talk.

"Interesting, what were your parents like? This is my last question before we get to the juicy stuff, I'm just curious?"

"It was a combination every child deserves. My parents, at least for the first fourteen years of my life, worked together to discipline us and keep us aware of not only the present, but the past. They had met in college and came from two different types of families, families we were kept apart from. They were educated and forced that on us one way or another. We had bookshelves of old books and newspapers, but we also had a litany of films we were also forced to watch. We learned different languages our parents knew, and we were told to never waste our time for that was life's real currency. Even after our father and mother separated, the disciplinary force may have dissolved, but the work ethic never did. Their faith had trickled to us, or at least me, and the strict schedules never changed. It wasn't a normal upbringing with family getting together, going places and that sweet stuff. We had a few glimpses of fun in our times together, but the older we got, the more we realized our family was conducted in the basic form of the meaning. It wasn't like the families we watched on TV. Regardless, everything was done for us, and we never struggled. They were workers to the core, and never complained. That's what became of us, we became workers," echoed Markos.

"Interesting. Really interesting. Sounds tough and it kind of correlates with the things I find every once in a while, in the garage. We'll get to that later. Let's begin with the interesting stuff though," exclaimed Anna.

They completed one revolution around the park and were beginning lap two when they started with the desirables.

"Alright, my story will be told from my point of view and will be based on what I saw. Please…please, *remember that.*"

Anna quickly nodded in order to signal to him to proceed. She did not know what he meant, instead excited for what came next.

"Nothing is juicy about this story. You already know the tragic ending of all the people in the story, so please don't think this is some alternate ending. Plus, this stays with you. Any whiffs to your mother and I will not only stop, but I'll be leaving. There are some pieces that will ruin reputations and land some people in jail if you can't keep your happiness settled," reiterated Markos. He focused on Anna's curious eyes before going further.

"Empty threats…but whatever, yeah, I agree."

Markos rubbed his hands together to warm himself and provide comedic drama to his storytelling. Piece by piece, she unlocked token points to his personality, parts of him students did not see in his lectures. Storytelling was how he paid his bills in the last decade, but it would be the first time he would share certain truths he once kept away.

"For me, it starts with a young woman named Angela. I was a senior in college, and you know I went to school not too far from home, about 30 minutes depending on traffic."

"Near the farms, right?" asked Anna.

"Yeah, I didn't want to leave Mom alone. Ephraim had started his first year over in Los Angeles and he was already starting to do big things. He wasn't really known, outside of Sacramento and a few pockets in Los Angeles, but he was already planting the seeds. Anyways, I was a few months from graduating and I had no idea what I was going to do."

"Something we finally share."

"Yes, very similar. Basically, this woman, Angela, had been my girlfriend for the past two years. I was never close to anyone in college, but friends were made from pickup basketball and my jobs on campus. Then, this beautiful girl walked into the gym where I worked. My eyes couldn't look anywhere else. She came in a few more times and it seemed like whenever I worked, she was there."

Anna was not one to let a moment pass without making Markos feel uncomfortable: "Aww."

"She had me from the first glance," said Markos embarrassingly, smiling, gushing over the protected image of Angela.

"There was not much I could do. I had been with a number of women in college, simply because it wasn't hard to talk with women who had already decided they were going to have sex with you."

"Ew, what?"

"This story is far from kid friendly. You're gonna have to grow up. These stories are important to understand before we get to the meaty portions," said Markos.

"Alright, keep it superficial. I don't need gory details."

Markos snickered at her immaturity, smiling at the memories.

"Going back to my point, relationships, especially in my youth, were taught to be trivial. There were so many crazy stories I would hear in high school and college of psycho-crazed relationships and lovesick students. I never partook in anything that really lasted more than a few days, a week max. Me and my brother really only had one friend growing up, so you can say we stuck together most of the time, and even then, he was a much better socializer than I was."

"Basically, you are what women call *shy*?" said Anna.

"Interestingly enough, the shy approach got me closer to them."

"Alright, alright, continue the story."

He began after turning another corner, completing lap two. He avoided looking at the school every time it was in view.

"I just stared at this girl for weeks. She was beautiful and more importantly, she was intelligent. I did not want to make her uncomfortable, that is the worst thing anyone can do to another person, but she was beautiful. Anyways, a lot of the women that I had been with were other races, with a few Black women in the mix. I never thought anything ill towards interracial unions, but it always helped that she was Black. Anyways, the moment I started to forget about this girl, she ended up getting hired at my job."

It was Anna's turn to let out a booming laugh.

"And what did you do?"

"I didn't say anything to her. We worked a few shifts together, and I avoided talking to her. What led to us finally talking, was when she saw me at the campus cafe one day."

"What did she say?"

"Everything I wish I said. She was quick, smart, and very witty."

"She basically said she knew I was staring before and that I was interested. She knew an introvert when she saw one and she thought it to be wise to meet outside of work. I barely let a word out and she did most of the talking. She was very clever and articulate. Angela was always the big thing at school, and guys lined up for her. She had been a party girl and one of those women who had gotten caught in the spin cycle of football players, but she dodged that lifestyle once she was about to be dismissed from the university. Her attitude and demeanor changed once the idea of going home to Oakland empty-handed began to worry her. She was different than most people but was very similar to the people Ephraim and I were raised to be. I was never going to be enough for that woman and I knew it, but every man should try to find *it.*"

"It?" asked Anna.

"Love."

"Wow, how poetic. While I *love* this story, what does this have to do with anything?"

"You've heard people live two lives, one when they are mysteriously awakened, and one where they lived before the awakening. Many people claim money or finding purpose is the true awakening. It's the closest thing to an absolute lie there is. I don't believe a true man's character and actions could be judged and evaluated before they fall in love with someone. It's the only time a man will drop all of their pride because that's what it takes. You cannot judge me or my choices until you understand the moment I began changing, and shifting away from…*shyness*, as you call it."

"Hmm, okay. What happened to Angela?" asked Anna.

"What any individual would have guessed, she left me."

"Hey? Hey! What are you looking at?" asked the irritated woman.

The young man was thinking about the speakers at the event he and his girlfriend returned from. He wished he allotted more time for personal interactions with them, but he was only there at the invitation of the proactive woman. She became impatient with the supplemental time given to the students as they talked to the presenters and representatives. Markos took much of his time socializing with what she called *undesirables*. She nearly lost it when he shared his information with them. Her needs were already satisfied, but Markos's growing curiosity got the best of him, and in turn, made her miss the phone interview for her internship.

"Sorry, I was thinking about the midterm I took yesterday," lied the young man.

"Don't lie to me," pleaded the woman.

Markos sat quietly atop Angela's worn out, leather sofa. Markos tried to shift his focus from the poster-filled walls to the misty, stained windows. The dimly lit bedroom of his girlfriend's second story townhome was not as peaceful as it normally could be trusted to be. Their graduation date had been approaching and the conversations between them were becoming stale and negligent. The career fair they returned from soured the taste of the relationship. Angela was pushed to the point of beginning the discussion they were trying their best to curtail.

"Hello, are you just gonna look at the trees outside?"

"Angela, what's the problem?" softly inquired young Markos, omitting enthusiasm.

"Come on, Mark. Why are you acting like this? You know where the problem in this situation lies."

"I don't Angela, why don't you lay it out for me?"

Angela protested his sarcasm by silently removing herself from her room. She moved downstairs towards the kitchen, where she waited for Markos to continue their argument. She refused to let her anger get the best of her.

The discomfort felt by both was caused by more than the misleading argument. The career fair's demanding prerequisites asked that students appear in interview attire and bring their resumes if they wished to discuss anything with the representatives.

Markos forced himself into a bland gray suit and black tie he was given by his mother following his high school graduation. The suit, originally, came in much better condition and was quite expensive, but the location he stored the suit in ruined the quality and the material. He did not appreciate the tightness of the pants, squirming in his wrinkled clothes during the event. His lack of preparation embarrassed Angela, angering her in a time of seriousness.

Markos started to play along with Angela's difficult charade down the stairs. The creaking of the worn-out steps warned her of his arrival. He found her pouring a drink.

"Want a drink?" asked Angela. She wanted them to be on even ground.

Markos declined her subtle request with a slight shake of his head. He did not like drinking during the weekdays.

"Could we finish, whatever this is? I have work tonight at eight and I'm trying to leave on good terms before I come back."

"Be truthful, then. Why are you trying to deviate from the plan we talked about this last year and a half?" asked Angela.

Markos took a second before he answered her trivial question. *Nothing is set in stone. You planned and I nodded. I've enjoyed my time in the company of a good woman like you, but the cost of being a good man is too much in times of stress.*

"I'm sorry, I was interested in what they had to say. Plus… never mind," said Markos.

A nerve was struck, and Angela was on the verge of violently lashing out at Markos. Discussions were had regarding his passive aggressive behavior and his bottling of vital emotions. His reasons were to avoid detrimental arguments both could not control, but the causal relationship between his passive behavior and their arguments were intertwined with underlying issues.

"Are you serious?" asked Angela helplessly.

The gloomy graduation day was approaching, and the crossroads of their relationship followed. They both knew the instability of their connection and were fighting their own forms of a cold war, stuck in a lazy form of brinkmanship.

"Listen, Angela, there's not much I've promised you. We've talked for years on how everything is new to me. I've never made you any promises and my future with you is as questionable as my future outside of school," calmly assessed Markos.

Angela's sip of orange juice and rum quickly turned sour after his cold statement. She did not know how to respond, but her articulate acumen chose to stay reserved in the moment of danger. Her headstrong attitude was not going to let another man dictate what she was going to do in her life. What she could not fathom was Markos, a man she molded into one who could hold his own in a stable relationship, not falling in line with her in times of calamity. She remembered his blissful attitude when they discussed their futures but never, would he commit to something he could not see directly in front of him. Finality was difficult to grasp for Markos and he feared situations he could get stuck in. He rationalized his inability to hold relationships with women by telling them he was taught all the superficial things attached with a relationship at this age, and how they were distracting. The few women who passed his basic screening process were then told about his parents' struggles to stay together and how his father's treatment of the family ended his ability to form any semblance of a relationship. Angela was the first to get through the cloud coverage hiding her from the truth, Markos could not fathom any commitment leaving him in any metaphoric form of claustrophobia.

"So, what do you want to do?" asked Angela. Surrender was difficult to hide.

She grabbed her drink and sat on the wooden stools behind the kitchen counter. Unconsciously, she began to grab the napkins from the restaurant they went out to the night before and started folding them. Angela was far from ignorant. Her intellect awarded her multiple grants and scholarships paying half her tuition costs. To pay for the rest, she worked at the campus bookstore before she moved to the gym for more hours. Her honor roll status and oration skills garnered campus notoriety and put her in a position of power in multiple student organizations and student panels. As a president of one of two black sororities on campus, she was also very respected in social circles. Her transformation from an irresponsible extrovert to the connected scholar was one of the determining factors in Markos's decision to let her in. Her discipline was very similar to the discipline he was taught from a young age, and she was what he believed he would never see from a woman. The deterioration of their relationship recently was heartbreaking. They tried to avoid what they expected since the inception of their union.

Markos looked at her, one last time, before he pushed his chips in and hedged his bets with her. The beautiful reflection from the slowly reemerging sun and the crimson and cream colors of her sorority's flag put up behind her made her glisten in the light, on the day their relationship came to an end.

"There's not much to do. I can't go back to school. You know how much I've been happy, especially the last few months. I'd love to make you and my mom proud and become this person, this engineer with all the money and all this 'status'. I can't, I can't Angela. You know what'll happen if I go with you to Palo Alto, I'll drive you crazy and put myself in a deeper hole," stressed Markos.

She continued to play with the napkin. Her short curly hair was covering her eyes. Her hair was untied, the definition as profound as the enchanted beauty she commanded. Markos tried, each time, to eat up his words before saying his piece.

"I don't know what you want me to do. I've told you, if I get this internship with a firm out there, I won't be able to be around as much. I'd be in school at the same time. I want what's best for you, but it's time for me to be selfish," replied the woman.

Her napkin was now being shaped by her sharp nails. She attempted to fold the napkin into a shape Markos could not make out. Her eyes were glued to the napkin, speaking the words meant for him, towards the napkin.

"You don't think I want what's best for you? Angela, we both know I've never been good enough to maintain this or hold you down. This day was coming, and I thought it'd be you bringing this up to me, but I know what'll happen if we deviate from the path we both want to take."

"*What do you want to do*, Markos?" asked Angela again, sadly deducing in her head that she had asked him this twice in a few minutes, but never before.

"I don't know. I really haven't thought about it. I've always tried to move forward in the best situation possible, even since I was a kid. It was always, 'Work towards getting into a good middle school.' Then it was, 'Get the best grades to get into the best high school program.' Then it was college. There isn't anything to work towards because I don't know what's best."

"*What do you want to do though, Markos?*" asked Angela. She wanted him to do *it*.

"I honestly don't know Angela. Some of the presenters were talking to me about some things," said Markos.

Angela briefly stopped meddling with her napkin before she spoke.

"Come on Markos, the recruiters? They'll just use you and throw you away once you get done serving," said Angela as she switched her attention back to the napkin.

"I don't know, it sounds alright. It'd get me out of this, whatever situation I'm in right now. I know the stereotypes about the military, but what else is there to do?"

"I don't know, did you talk to your family?"

"My brother is busy, he's playing Jesus. You know how he is, studying till he solves the human problem. Mom will only put limitations on me to make sure I don't go too far. Whatever decision I make, I'll need to make it alone."

"Well, don't think anyone out here will show love. Veterans make less than people who pretend to be them with their fingers today," said Angela, wrapping up her masterpiece.

"I'm not doing it for love or recognition from people, there aren't people I want to impress anymore. I truly don't know, but I think they have something I can really learn from, and they gave me a pamphlet of jobs. This is what I want, I think. It's only four years, and at least these four years would be more purpose-filled than these last four. I want to get into teaching, and I don't know if I want to get a PhD and be a professor or be some form of high school teacher. I think they'll pay for that after I get out, *if* I go," said Markos softly.

His soft attitude was due to his uncertainty of the coming days and the advice he desperately wanted from Angela. She remained silent as she continued her folding. Her subtle creativity began to catch the attention of Markos. All the talk about the later days stalled as they focused on her skinny, delicate fingers folding the napkin. Both Markos and Angela's minds shifted to an empty chasm.

"I can't be here for all this soul searching. You know what I hope to do and how my life is in overdrive. You need to figure your life out because I can't be the one that suffers and compromises for your future," said Angela eloquently.

Her finished project was less flattering than the sensual nature of her folding and creative cutting. The simplicity of the design of her napkin-based sculpture angered Markos for the attention he gave it. Her stunning statement against their relationship carried no effect compared to his anger he fought to hold back from her version of origami. Markos shifted his body and turned his back, as subtle as he could, and looked around her worn down yellowed cabinets. She could say nothing more to entice his attention and he was speechless to the first woman he chose to open his heart to, the woman he believed would keep it open for all his days.

"It's on you," said Angela dramatically.

She walked off, leaving the folded piece on the table. The clean-cut and folded napkin was turned into an arrow, like the arrows on the bright yellow street signs a few feet outside her door. The arrow was squarely pointed at him, the young twenty-two-year-old, feeling the brushing feeling of anger and emptiness, similar to the feelings he felt the day he discovered his father left him. The feeling of having one's heartbreak was hard to miss for Markos, for a sudden pain in the stomach always arose from the inexplicable feeling. He looked at the arrow, its stillness made the neat edges and careful folding quite impressive in his opinion. His anger fumed at the idea of Angela taking more time to fold the napkin than to listen to what he wanted for his future. There was not more for him to do, but pick up the napkin, and in one last act of desperate frustration, carefully place it in the garbage as he walked out a man who knew love.

"Men's hearts aren't as cold and basic as women believe. Entering a relationship is easy, as easy as they show us in the movies. Leaving a relationship, that is what's often dramatized. There aren't phone calls and late-night texts to meet up when there are two responsible people who've been in a relationship. It's lonely and the next few months are quite routine. You live and move on. I don't understand how it is so easy for so many people. I question if some were really in love with their partners, because the act of ending a prolific relationship is too much," said the parabolic Markos.

The sixteen laps around the elliptic park went unnoticed by the unprepared walkers. The wisdom and storytelling of Markos charged both as they pushed forward for a bit longer. Anna's eyes enlarged at every revelation of his character. Opinions of his actions formed in her head. He embraced sharing the past with her, and he was encouraged by her ability to learn from elders, a lost art in the generation he spoke to at the universities. Many would instead come to compare their daily practices and social participation to his.

Anna shocked him, for he thought he could get away with rushing the stories he planned on sharing with her and moving to the topics he prepared. They spent a few hours in the park discussing the complications of keeping a relationship at that age, which directly correlated with problems Anna could potentially face on her own. He shared the awkwardness of graduating alone after planning a future with someone who taught him about holding a relationship. Markos shared opinions of getting families involved in unions such as his due to the questions arising when the relationship ends. He explained the tough times of having to share to their families all the issues in the relationship and the truths he had to hide about himself.

He ended his vivid story of his formation by recounting how he shook her hand after Black graduation. He believed he was lucky the social science majors would walk the stage on a different day than the engineers, but he did not anticipate Black graduation. He did not care for all the flash and optimism of graduations, so without the forceful nature of Angela, he would not have signed up for Black grad. He remembered seeing her with her family and he with his mother and brother. Both their families were aware of the break-up a month prior, and still, they forced a photo. They chose to shake hands and awkwardly snap a photo before they permanently parted.

"She made you take a photo?" asked Anna.

"My mother gets what she wants."

"I don't know if I could've done that."

"So, your mom, a single mother who raised and put you through school alone, wants you to take a photo with someone who's family also wants a photo. On one of the happiest days of her life, you comply," said Markos.

"I guess, did you guys say anything to each other?" asked Anna.

"Just 'congratulations' and 'good luck'. It was over and we knew, if we tried to work it out, we'd mess up each other's future."

Markos and Anna, as they approached lap twenty, chose to take a seat on the green, steel park tables. The path cut into another, leaving an option on the opposite side of the entrance to those who needed rest. Outside of the cemented path, they were surrounded by hills of grass, elevated before leveling out to the walkway, as well as trees providing minimal shade, placed more for the aesthetic. The picnic tables were coated with dust from the slight breeze moving through the park the night before. It made no difference due to the fatigue and sweating of Anna and Markos. The sun rose to a height the two story homes in their suburban neighborhood could no longer hide. Armies of children began funneling through the park, pushing forward towards the gate of the school, opened by the school policeman.

"Alright, so were you awoken?"

"Unfortunately, yes."

"Unfortunately? I thought you said every man lives two lives or something," said Anna.

She attempted to wipe the dust away.

"Yeah, pain is terrible to live with. You got to wake up with it, but you know how strong the feeling of wanting to go back to sleep keeps you exhausted."

"What'd you learn?" asked the young girl, looking up at Markos.

"Uh...about?"

"Love."

"In honesty, I learned it wasn't trivial as I had been taught to look at it. Regardless of the age, it could be fifteen or fifty, love is important. Love has to be respected at all ages, as dumb as it may seem. The same obsessive boy at thirteen is the same lovestruck man at thirty. They act the same, but for some reason, we make fun of the kid, because we're envious that the kid still gets to feels that way. Us older people have forgotten to keep loving after we've been accustomed to the ugliness," said Markos, interlocking his hands.

He was incredibly vulnerable, and he knew where the words brought him. At that moment, he was gushing out all the emotions and knowledge he withheld from the generations after him. His posture and demeanor were like a man who loved life, not of one scorned by time. His stationery form, which acted as a thinking position, was as revealing as his words. He interlocked his fingers and placed them under his chin as he looked up in the sky, remembering the good and the ugly of his past. The meshing motions of his hands as he spoke were to the delight and laughter of Anna as he told his stories and served as a source of ridicule for her. Her questions were short and concise, and she sat patiently hearing all his wisdom, allowing it to enter her memory bank and begin screening for any fiction. Her engaged participation was a response to his sharing.

"What else did you learn...about love?"

Anna, while smiling at the kids walking behind the seated Markos, smiled to ease her invasive question. He did not look at the kids, focused instead on her powerful eyes in the sun.

"Ah, many things I learned about love came years later for me. I can tell you one thing I remember experiencing about the process of learning love. I learned information is always key when trying to figure out which way to move. Learning something can also be very disappointing. Something we were taught as kids was ignorance isn't bliss, but curiosity surely kills," said Markos, his mood briefly darkening by the tensing of his arms.

Anna looked puzzled at the head spinner of a statement.

He knows how to mess up a happy mood, thought Anna.

"I'll explain. You never want to walk into a room with people you expect are gonna bring up a certain topic and attempt to act as if you know everything about the topic. For example, if you're going to walk into a room of people who run dog shelters, you need to be prepared to talk about dogs. Ignorance would be walking in and acting like you know everything about dogs. You can't discuss the politics of dogs without knowing about dogs, so you walk in, and you ask questions, and you drill them about all things dog. You attempt to learn everything you can from these people before you walk into another room of dog owners. You ask more and more questions and the ignorance on the topic fades. As you go deeper and deeper into the topic of dogs with these people, you learn everything about dogs, and you may even learn to love dogs. However, there's another side of this. You learn the dark side of the topic you are learning. You learn that these people must put down the animals they so love, in accordance with the regulations that are set upon them."

Anna quickly took a moment to think on his enthusiastic rant. He tried to catch his breath.

"How does any of this have to do with love?"

"Well, love is fantastic, illuminating, and for someone who's reserved as I am, it's liberating. I've only loved two women in my life, and I can say, they liberated me, but they nearly killed me. The side of love we don't discuss is the pain of the road to the end and in certain instances, the rushed endings."

Anna saw sorrow in the release of his interlocked fingers. He retreated his hands from under his chin to his lap. He glanced toward the sky once again, searching for his train of thought as he hoped to escape the memory of *her*.

"Who's the other woman you loved? I assumed Angela was the main woman in your life to affect you."

Markos was stunned by the question, as if he forgot he had mentioned the presence of another woman. His searching quickly subsided, and he looked directly into her eyes. Anna took notice of the dark brown bags under his eyes. She had not spotted them in the last few days they had spoken. His goatee, with the gray flakes, took the attention of his fingers as he pondered.

"We'll get to that another day."

Markos turned to watch the young children dash into the school. He remembered how he and his brother would race to the open gate in the mornings. He thought of the trouble they used to get into when they would accidently bump into the young mothers walking their children to class. He watched as the officer locked up the gate once the bell rang and classes began. Anna was combing through the news on her watch, attempting to kill some time for the unpleasant silence to pass.

She waited for Markos to break the seal but was disappointed as he continued to look at the children being guided to class.

"Hey! Hey, what are you looking at?"

"The kids. The circle of life is crazy. I used to be running around like those kids, but I know if I tried that, my hips would go, and my liver would burst."

Out of comfort, they laughed after the delicate quietness ended from the revival of his memories.

"Question, what was going on with your family when all this was happening? Specifically, what was Grandpa doing during this time?" asked Anna.

Her question brought him back from the sunken void he was in. Markos was very similar to the lady who sat in front of him. His emotions were riding on a rollercoaster since his reintroduction to his family and he shared Anna's characteristic instability. The family dynamics changed many things for him, but his instinctual response to people did not. Nothing could change him anymore. A few moments of good had an opportunity to provide people a glimpse of the man he once was. The once introverted and charismatic approach he took with people shattered following the devastating events of his life.

Anna pushed him to linger about with the fragments and pieces he remembered of his mother and Ephraim, and even his father. They were mixed with moments of shine and happiness. He appreciated the lessons he was taught by the powerful people he was surrounded by. However, his memories of *Elsa,* those memories and the pain with those times, still had not healed. The memories that led to her, those memories deteriorated his stability and were liable to force him down the path he followed the last twenty odd years.

"Your grandfather, he had already done so much, much more than anyone his age at that time was doing."

"What do you mean?"

"He was enrolled in this program in high school forcing kids to do community service. I believe it was something like twenty something hours every four months. Many kids BS'ed it and had their parents sign the form or they did something they always did like clean up their church. Your grandfather, uh, your grandfather, he was always gifted and different," said Markos as he brushed his face. He was caught thinking of Ephraim's early sincerity.

"He wanted to do something he could not only help out at, but something he could learn from. His honest approach landed him at the local veterans' center. He walked in there with his forms and asked around to see if there was any way he could make some form of impact. He asked to talk to the veterans that returned recently or the ones who spent most of their lives out there."

"Is that where the *Neighborhood Warrior Program* began?" asked the excited Anna, learning new information.

"Yes, good catch. People thought it was a political move to unite folks of liberal and conservative thinking, which was based on false pretenses and outdated information. He genuinely cared for veterans. He walked in there and he cleaned up around the center. He was referred to the VA hospitals where he would talk to career veterans and veterans who had lost limbs and pieces of their mainframe. It had a profound effect on him, and me as well because when I would come home, when he was in high school, we'd go together," said Markos.

Anna's face lit up like a child's at a carnival: "How come you guys never said that?"

"We did, he really did. People believe what they choose to believe and build their own stories or narratives when they deem you an opponent."

Anna was once a member of the program. The program grew tremendously under Ephraim's leadership and when he moved to college, eager students flocked towards him to become members. As his popularity grew, however, more came for Ephraim than they did for the veterans. Ephraim appreciated the attention of the people and the local media outlets, but a point came when the message behind his program was lost. His notoriety grew from the program's expansion to different college campuses and the heavy enrollment he obtained. Over time, what first began as an intimate relationship with veterans and the younger generation, turned into a resume stuffer. Nevertheless, for some, it was a brilliant and eye-opening experience with forgotten individuals. The program educated young teenagers, which served to provide Ephraim insight into a platform able to make true progress for people who needed it most. His initial actions proved his belief it was the innate nature for people to agree, propelling him forward.

"Huh, what pushed him to make it as big as it was?" asked Anna as she fiddled with a fallen leaf sitting still on the steel bench.

Markos looked at her fidgeting. He focused on her mannerisms trying to figure out who she most resembled. Her grandmother was a fidgeter, but she seemed to follow Ephraim's practicality. Ephraim's calculations were far beyond people's understanding. His ability to not only process, but distract, was as powerful a tool he had. Markos was keen enough to spot these mannerisms, but it was Ephraim who practiced these forms of preparation, with an innocent form of manipulation embedded. Anna was fidgeting, but her quick glance toward Markos revealed her deviant intentions.

Markos barely contained a hint of a smile as he thought of the similarities she shared with various members of the Solomons family. The sun was to Markos's back, so the slight luminescence detailed her features many of the women in his family had. Her skinny, but pointed nose was surely from Markos's mother, but the luscious, soft hair came from the other side of the family. Her hazel eyes were a trademark, but they were masked by dark bags, hiding the eagerness in them. She looked once again, attempting to see if her passive maneuvers worked.

"Who taught you that?" asked Markos, intentionally ignoring her question.

"Taught me what?" said the lying girl.

"Your fiddly maneuver. Who taught you that?"

"I don't know what you mean."

Markos brushed off her lie, but refused to answer questions until she chose to give in. She looked up at him and waited for him to speak. They both watched as the leaf she dropped floated to the ground. Both playing at the other's stubbornness, waited for someone to speak. Ephraim used these techniques when he wanted to know something without revealing his true motives. He had many more maneuvers that served different purposes, but the fidgeting was one he used on their parents the most. It signaled loss of attention and boredom, but underneath the show of simple idiocy, was coordination. Ephraim would use this to force a feeling of easiness and comfort in an adversary to extract information he would need.

"Where did you learn that?" desperately asked Markos again, as he lasered in on the girl.

Initially, her stubbornness stood fast, and she refused to acknowledge his request. Recognizing she met her equal, again, she conceded the truth.

"No one. Sitting by yourself and watching people allowed me to figure them out. People aren't difficult to understand if you just listen," said Anna as she avoided eye contact.

"That's how we were taught. Hm, be careful, there's a tradeoff."

"Early on, we made some friends, but once Dad left, we were alone, and we couldn't fix that. While Ephraim made new friends later on, I stayed alone, other than Alana of course," said Markos.

"When did you meet Alana?" asked the puzzled Anna.

"Really young," answered Markos.

"Wait, what? Nobody knows that. Why doesn't anybody know?" asked Anna.

"Alana is an incredibly private person, we all were. Jamie and Jonathan were the more outspoken ones, but they, like all of us, kept their personal lives out of the mix. Peter stuck with me, while Alana and Ephraim took each other's time up. We all avoided getting mixed up with others, for we knew we couldn't trust people. Your grandparents did a great job hiding your mother and the family away from all the mess going on. But, Alana, why do people think a white girl, who happened to be one of the best lawyers in the country, just happened to follow the movement of an outspoken black man?"

"I don't know...there are rumors."

"Like what?"

Anna paused before bringing up a piece of information she was dying to ask him since they met. She looked at the perplexed man. They shared curiosity, but she did not want to overstep or show an ounce of immaturity. She decided to hold the question.

"For another time."

"If it is so," said the man, slowly rising from the seat.

"We're done?" asked Anna.

"No, not by the closest margin. However, it is time to eat. These kids will be out here soon running around for P.E. and I'm hungry."

Anna grunted in frustration. She planned for much more to be revealed in her first session with the all-knowing man. There were many secrets and truths in his head, but at that moment, he had not yet told her a lie. Manipulation was a weapon he stole from his brother. She could no longer know whether he was telling the truth. She would need to be extremely sharp in her evaluation of Markos, but emotional desires clouded her mind. Throughout their whole session, he was laying out fillers and feelers, trying to identify the girl's mannerisms and tells. The whole morning, getting her to wake up early and conduct meaningless stretches, all served to throw her off her guard as he laid the foundations of the past. Markos was ecstatic she shared the Solomons' intelligence, but he needed to see where her mental state was at.

He looked upon the girl and put out a hand to the child as she meekly rose from the uncomfortable seating. The grueling workout did a number on Anna. She did not feel the strain when they were walking, only after she tried to move again.

There was a steady spark Markos felt, from the light brush of her cold fingers. It was the touch of his kin, and even though small interactions occurred in the previous days, this was one that brought him complacency and a sense of preparedness for death. The slow touch of the girl was enough, as they walked half a lap towards the entrance of the park, leading them back home.

He was uncomfortable with the deceptive nature of the stories, but there was reason for such caution. His previous worries of the seriousness and devastation of the truth multiplied after he started to mouth the words of the past. There was still much he did not reveal of his upbringing, nor did he discuss the brutal endings to his connection with the family.

His philosophy clashed with the necessity to reveal facts. Protection was a must, but the events needed to be relayed in a sequential order, for who would be next to speak for him? Who could understand the dilemma in the penned words sitting on the eight in a half by eleven pieces of paper in his left breast pocket?

six:
Mom n'Pop

"How about the fashion?" asked Anna as she took a sip of her strawberry lemonade.

"What about fashion?"

"Was it better, you know, was it cooler? I don't know, the outfits we saw you guys in, and the photos of actors and actresses are nice. Was fashion better then or now?" asked the stuffed girl.

They chose to sneak out in the night after Olivia went to bed. Their sly mission sent them to the small burger place near the school. Olivia was busy all week trying to catch up on the two days she took off work to tend to the family. She was running in and out and did not have the chance for face time with the two during their times of discussion. She found comfort in the growing relationship between them, and she hoped to free up time to do the same. Markos and Anna's conversations were endless. Nothing else was serious enough to distract them from each other. In the day, both spent their time watching the daily programs available on the television and streaming the current movies and shows they enjoyed. They showed each other the big-name films and programs from their respective eras. They enjoyed each other's company, and when the irresponsible binging bored them, they found themselves once again wrapped up in the stories he began sharing a few days earlier.

Anna tried pestering him into choosing to get the food delivered, but he insisted on driving there. He told her of how all food services came to rely on the delivery system and how the laziness of the people allowed the delivery system to stay in place. She was unaware of the once shared attraction of dressing and meeting to eat, for in the current times, the bars and a few select restaurants enjoyed indoor dining, a luxurious opportunity the bourgeoisie afforded.

They sat outside the house as they finished up their food. Their heads were both lifted to the sky, watching the clear night, the myriad of sparkling stars on display through the sunroof. Anna attempted to get a feel for popular culture during the period she began to call his prime.

"I don't know, we were starting to get away from solid colors and wear tighter pants. My time lived through the tight pants and baggy top look, but you all took it to another level with the tighter clothes. Today, you wear tight clothes all around. I couldn't do it; my skin would act up. Many of the professional attire has stayed the same, though. You definitely accessorize more than us. Before, accessories used to be seen as childish or inappropriate, but a lot more people wear, uh, necklaces and bracelets with their expensive suits, in interviews too. That's kind of new, I'd say," reminisced Markos, taking a large bite of his three-by-three burger.

"Do you like the clothes we wear now more than the stuff you would wear back then?" asked Anna.

"I'm the wrong person to ask. I kept the look of my folks, the old school approach we were raised with. It matched our personalities. Some of us like Alana and the twins were good about fashion. What I'd ask is you bring back the looser formal wear, I'd love that. Before I joined my brother, my formal wear was slim fit, not a tight fit. I really didn't care about my look. When I joined them, I had to be more self-conscious and trendier."

"Loose fit clothes would give me space to move and stuff, while allowing for a decent sense of creativity, I think. To be honest, what you all need to do is take those ultra-skinny pants out of your closets and burn them. They don't make sense for guys. I don't know why guys want to show their 'bulges' now. Back then, you didn't wear skinny pants like that," said Markos, his face souring from the taste of the sugary lemonade.

"No, the pants are cool. I like them, I don't really see the problems with it. This stems from your generation's inability to conform to others' opinions," added Anna.

"No, biologically and comfort-wise, they don't make sense. I don't know what it is with your generation. We were the most accommodating. It's you that really doesn't give any ground now, huh?" asked Markos.

Anna took a second to finish chewing on her juicy double veggie burger. *Times have changed,* affirmed Markos in his thoughts. Her mother's rigid dietary practices hid her away from the unhealthy spoils of life. She took her time and enjoyed the temporary pleasures of the meal, at least before she began her assault.

"No, y'all weren't accommodating. Y'all were 'liberal' but not enough to the point that you were accommodating. You carried that same thing folks used to use on us with that 'I got a black friend' stuff. You couldn't be labeled homophobic or transphobic or whatever the hell it is because you all never even gave them a chance to be your friends. You allowed them in your protests and speeches, but even Grandpa didn't give *them* a voice or ever spoke for their group. Grandpa is still heavily criticized for that in these classrooms. Accommodating is the last word I'd use to describe your contributions to people who went outside tradition," rebutted Anna.

Markos laughed at her tirade, and she was powerless to stop the little smirk she let out. His laugh was contagiously childish. Her rant, in his eyes, was unjustified.

"Go to Hell, I'm serious though."

Markos took his time with his tangy lemonade before he answered her.

"Listen, you are one hundred percent right. We didn't do our best in accordance with our *allies.* Don't get me wrong, they are our allies, and believe it or not, back then, they had all the social power. It's much more normalized now, but back then, being gay or trans wasn't always a favorable attribute in certain circles, especially in conservative hotspots. They've maneuvered themselves into a powerful position today due to their solidarity. Solidarity was what we wanted and the reason so many people failed in their grassroots initiatives. It's because people tried to tackle everything at once that movements failed to move in one accord for a duration of time. They were allies, an ally in terms of similar philosophies and goals, but we supported one another when reinforcements were needed. That might be a problem we all have, especially back then and even worse now. You can't strap on some gloves and fight everyone in the room. You gotta ease into what it is you want and fight for it. They were our allies, but yeah, you're right, we weren't too involved. But we had some members of their community in our inner circles."

"Who?"

Markos let out a sneaky chuckle and nearly choked on how he set up Anna. As he stopped, he thought of a moment he once felt this mentally...*liberated.*

"See, you are part of the problem."

"How?"

"Why does it matter? Your grandfather, he redefined the meaning of an American. People were surprised to see Black men and women, Asian men and women, create an American party. You weren't born to see how people were surprised and shocked. Their rising was an awakening to others, showing people Americans were not just white people. People were shocked to see Alana, a woman, speaking for a party led by a Black man. It challenged a lot of people's perception of Black folks or women being innately challenged, that they couldn't do something because there was a biological shortcoming with their gender or race. They kept telling them they were the first this or first that, insinuating they weren't supposed to do something. Sexuality is sexuality, race is race, and gender is gender."

"Imagine creating a force of a political party, and people thinking of you and the people like you as an anomaly. They created a party with people who were unequivocally free of the judgment the founders of the parties before them still face. They were not enslavers, sexist, or took part in any social phobias. Award them for their merit, don't separate someone, they are a part of history, not a sect of history. They are a part of this life of normality. Instead, respect what one does and acknowledge that you aren't entitled to know what they do at home."

"Alright," sarcastically replied Anna. Her anger stemmed from the endearing sentiments, and the hypocrisy others hid using similar opinions.

She never appreciated the professor-like attitude of the man, but she keenly heard the lessons he shared. The holier than thou attitude was a part of Markos from the moment his life turned to scorched earth. He was always the smarter man in the room, at least when his brother was not in attendance. Anna was the most recent challenge to his intelligence, but none stood a chance when it came to the intellect of his parents, the people who carefully taught and ingrained a moral compass in the brothers, with a fierce work ethic.

"I'm sorry. I'm trying to share all I have before I go," sincerely spoke Markos.

Anna nodded, acknowledging his efforts with a slow smirk. She was not acquainted with death, but she understood the impending doom of Markos. Like clockwork, he hid emotions well, but his fear of losing time with his family was growing.

"Let's head back to the house."

Anna opened the tablet connected to the car and opened a new tab, allowing them to toggle with the sunroof. She quickly swiped to close and immediately walked out of the car. As Anna swung around to the back of the car, their eyes locked onto the downstairs living room window. The miniscule patch of grass and the hunter green bushes of leaves did not separate them far enough from the window. The horror that struck them when they saw the light turn on forced them to freeze in their tracks. They looked with surprising disgust. They did not know which Olivia was waiting for them, the worried mother waiting for her daughter to come home, or a sleepy Olivia who did not notice the two left to get food.

"What should we do?" asked Markos.

"I don't know. Hopefully she just came down for a snack or something. If she's gonna stay there, we might be screwed."

Markos accidentally slammed the door when he turned back to the car. The car was parked in the driveway, a few paces away from the bushes separating the house from the patches of grass. Anna was already walking along the cemented road at the edge of the patch.

"What...the hell?" Her angry whisper shocked the already knowing Markos.

Markos opened his mouth and gritted his teeth, to serve as his apology.

"She definitely knows we're here now."

"Forget it, I'm older than both of you. Open the door," said Markos confidently, striding up two cement steps leading towards the door.

"'I'm a grown man', huh," imitated Anna. She followed him through the brown door.

The encircled light bulb sitting right above the front door's entrance was on but dimmed by Olivia. She sat on the glass dining room table with a direct line of sight to the oval top door. Her tired eyes did not portray any forms of anger or disappointment, but rather a look of familial relief every mother feels when their child comes home after a night out.

"Where'd you guys go?"

"Markos took me to the burger spot by my old high school. We thought you were asleep," replied Anna.

They walked over with the greasy bag of salty French fries and their sour strawberry lemonade hand in hand.

Markos did not speak a word as his confident posture waned out of fear of irritating Olivia. He waited and said nothing while Anna looked at him with a humorous smile. From cheek to cheek, she enjoyed his exposure. Markos refused to relinquish his unnecessary fear until Olivia reached in and searched around for loose fries. Olivia did not hide the satisfaction of deviating from her rigid diet.

"It's been a long week," added Olivia as she stuffed her mouth with French fries.

The mood immediately lightened up after her conformity to Anna and Markos's side. She ate up what was left of Anna's food as they discussed what the past few days were like. Olivia debriefed the two about the difficulties of running her own practice when she expected to be on her own schedule. She explained her current predicament at work and how deadlines were approaching amid all this change. Markos inferred her disrupted sleep schedule stemmed from the overwhelming stress. They discussed how she built up her practice after being passed up on promotions at her alma mater in the biopsychology department. Markos attentively watched as she laid out all the little parts motivating her to create her own practice. The whole discussion turned quite a bit emotional as she explained how she sacrificed much of her time with Anna during Anna's high school years. With the eyes of determination, she explained there was no choice but to finish what she started. Anna watched as her mother spoke to Markos loosely, regarding how they never struggled with money or food, but how they, like him, struggled with maintaining connections. Markos sat through it and in the end, she said what she wanted to say from the beginning. She thanked him for the effort of staying and interacting with them both. He admired the openness, a curse of the family she overtly worked past. Throughout her soliloquy, he recognized the despair of feeling alone and away from others. After she finished, Markos signaled to Anna and they both understood what it meant. Anna quickly rose and darted off to the kitchen in excitement.

"Wha...what is she doing?"

"Bring three cups," said Markos as he ignored Olivia's remarks. He bit into the last fries he grabbed from the bottom of the bag.

Anna quickly returned with three coffee mugs and the bourbon hidden in the kitchen.

"Wait, I can't drink tonight, I have to wake up in the morning. You all shouldn't be drinking either," said Olivia, pointing to them.

"Just a small sip Mom, you won't feel a thing."

"It won't hurt," added Markos.

Her approving nod was followed with a shy, devious laugh. She let out a laugh of frustration at the secrets already being withheld from her. He smiled at the thought of taking stress from her shoulders. Liberation was key to each of their self-required tasks.

They complained of pain in their familial bony cheeks from their bouts with laughter. The conversations livened as the Solomons family continued exchanging the current events of their lives. Markos shared how well his previous speaking arrangement went and how he planned on one last one in a week or so. He planned for a brief hiatus due to the uncertainty surrounding his health. Anna followed, with a permissive wink and nod from Markos, revealing his recent revelations about the family and the past. Both Olivia and Markos were visibly worried after her anxious reveal. Markos was worried of what Olivia would think of him, while Olivia gained another source of worry as to what may blind side her. Markos, noticing the crossroads they came to, quickly changed the subject to the current state of the world around them.

The transition served them well as they shifted topics and vibrantly spoke of the changing dynamics of the neighborhood, noting the increased security and patrol officers at the schools. For nearly twenty minutes they debated the decade old legislation requiring an officer for every few hundred students to be on duty in the schools. Anna's eagerness to attack the legislation was to the dismay of Olivia. Anna could not understand how an adult's worry for a child would outweigh the invasive law. They debated the logic behind the bill and its debates, once propelled in the media due to unholy amounts of violence in several schools years before.

They moved to more pertinent topics and discussed the men both mother and daughter engaged with over the years. Markos took the time to step back and hear the stories of the women's upbringings and stumbles. They spoke of men who spent their time trying to get a scoop on their family name. They spoke of others who asked for pictures for bragging purposes and those who always asked questions about Ephraim. He barely listened, instead worried Elsa being brought up by Anna, for he had only told her of a name but not of who she was to him. Anna angered Markos by bringing up certain things about Angela and the contributions she made towards his life. She spoke of his knowledge of love and all he shared on the topic. The awkward stares and unforced blushing of both the women made Markos very uncomfortable. Anna revealed all the information: Ephraim's high school accomplishments and Markos's brief career in the Air Force as a Signals Intelligence Analyst. Markos's anger rapidly subsided as Olivia's face brightened up at each fact being revealed. She asked a healthy number of questions to avoid disturbing him, showing forms of educational curiousness. He graciously answered her questions, while noting to himself, he needed to remind Anna of discretion.

The conversations flowed from school and love to various explorations and the state of children. Markos took part more in the conversation of children for he was always fascinated with their development. His teaching background was the topic of choice.

"Why didn't you teach here, instead of out there?" asked Olivia.

"I don't know, I was applying for master's programs, but after being stationed abroad for the Air Force, I wanted to see more of what was out there."

Anna spotted a tiny, unnoticeable movement in his shoulder he attempted to brush off as an itch. She felt as if he was lying.

"Why?" pushed back Anna.

Markos, noticing her look of analysis, answered her truthfully.

"I didn't want to come home because I didn't think anything was here for me," confessed Markos. He shifted his view from Olivia's hunched body to Anna's eyes.

Anna was cradling her mug with her brown hands. Her interlocked fingers held her drink between her crisscrossed legs, placed on the black on gray dining room chairs. Markos sat facing Anna, with Olivia to his right. Olivia, who sat with her head leaning on her right hand, rested her drink with her left on the table, unaware of the chess match beginning between Anna and Markos. Her fatigue made her oblivious to their silent affair. Olivia sat, in her silk white robe, watching as Markos began to spill the truth.

"Why do you say that?" asked Olivia, worried about his answer.

"My parents ruined a lot of what I thought my future was going to look like. Ephraim was already doing his thing, and he never let anyone bother his bubble. After Angela was out of the picture, I was as clueless as one could be at that age," answered Markos.

Markos sat with his eyes glued to his sugar filled drink and the liquor posturing beside it. His eyes slowly traced his chest towards his sweatpants, and he found his hunter green sweat suit stained by a drop of his lemonade. He ignored the small pink droplets and looked up to find the women waiting for him to continue.

"I didn't want to really do anything that I was taught to do. We were donned as kids as a way to prophesy what we were to do, at least career wise. I was always supposed to be the engineer, and my brother, the great lawyer. The whole thing wasn't meant for our good fortune, but for our prideful parents, specifically my father, to be proud they had two of something they can show off. It was alright for a while, but as you get older and start to realize some things, especially about the intentions of your parents, it casts a shadow on a lot of things you look forward to," said Markos, taking a second for the finishing gulp of his subtle poison.

"While I deviated from the given path, Ephraim completely surpassed their expectations and pushed it as far as he could. I didn't have a purpose or anything that I was passionate about. There was not much emotion with anything I did. I just went with it, and it was like that for a while. I was happy to be a part of my family and I was happy with the opportunities they afforded me. I always wanted to make my parents proud, and once they betrayed me, there was nothing I could do. Everything feels temporary after you feel betrayed by your parents. It's hard not to become a narcissist or a mood killer when you grew up waiting for someone to leave or something to go wrong," continued Markos.

The pessimistic tone of Markos acted as a jolt to Olivia. The liquor began to warm her blood. She was unsure how to react as a family member, but she understood this type of pain from her job. It was rather elementary for her, but she understood the delicate nature of the problem. She wanted to warn her daughter not to make any rude remarks at this time. She quickly looked over to her daughter to see her mesmerized by his truthful story, anxiously anticipating his next words. She also recognized her daughter's inability to handle something as simple as a mug of bourbon, even with a full stomach. Olivia brought her elbows forward and rested them on the glass table to politely signal she wanted to speak.

"Can you elaborate on the betrayal? I ask because I see a lot of people talk of betrayal, but sometimes betrayal stems from the *presence* of the parents. I just want to know a little more to understand," said Olivia softly.

Both Markos and Anna looked towards Olivia's direction with a smile of relief. The past few days they both secretly wished to spend more time with the matriarch of the house and discuss the past with her. Anna, especially, knew how much her mother felt out of the loop when it came to the family. Olivia was kept in the dark much of her life, but that practice worsened once her issues with Anna's birth came.

The two retreated to their comfort positions. Anna began pouring a drink for herself and was astonished to see Markos decline a drink. Anna's show of surprise served to frustrate Olivia, but she chose to ignore it for now. Olivia gracefully accepted another drink which would send her to a slumber as soon as she reached her room.

Markos started by tracing back his mother and father's origins. They met at Ephraim's alma mater in Los Angeles, where his mother studied as an international student. The school was notorious for the international populace roaming its grounds. It was when a brown skinned girl with a few pimples on her sculpted cheeks, who always carried a red scarf around her neck, was trekking around campus, that a fairly large man noticed her for the first time on his way to the library. The large, bearded man followed her to the library only to lose her there and wonder for days where she had gone.

Days passed before he found her on the same route she used to walk from the gym to the library. His mother, being the smarter of the two, began to walk faster the day he finally tried to reach her. Markos remembered as she recounted this story years after he left, sharing how he ran after her and yelled whatever he could to get her attention. It was when she decided to give up the charade that the two second-year students sparked a conversation for the first time.

"My mother always lamented that he was always sweet and soft-natured. I can tell you, she never convinced me of it until the end. He wasn't when we were kids, I can definitely tell you that much. He was a tyrant who loved his kids but was too prideful to show it. We waited for love, but all that showed was discipline, and it wasn't until much later that we remembered and realized how important that really was. Look at Ephraim, he serves as an example of the saying that all great people had difficult parents," chimed Markos.

They watched as he continued to describe his parents with his colorful language.

He described how his father distracted his mother enough to convince her school was not the number one priority in life. This is another one of the surprises Markos did not believe about his father. His mother was an international student who was studying abroad from Ethiopia. She had no friends and had no social life, outside of the Ethiopian church community in inner city Los Angeles. Her conservative lifestyle was uprooted by the approach of a confident Chicagoan who was ironically studying education. Her focus had always been on her environmental studies program and her religious lifestyle. When Markos's father came into her life, he showed her all the things she never knew were part of college, let alone in the States. His charisma and understanding of her life's dynamics made them a great pair for he made sure never to compromise her socially religious morals. Their relationship grew and it took her a year before she would even call him her boyfriend. The relationship, according to Markos's mother, reached a peak when they both reentered into the same university for graduate school. Markos outlined to Anna and Olivia how eager his father Daveed was in trying to show his mother the life they could live once they received their doctorates. She had already deviated from the course her family outlined for her. She continued because she felt an aching in her stomach every instance she thought of leaving him, a feeling she identified to be anxiety, a first for her.

The playful mood of the home took a downturn after Markos explained how his mother's family disowned her once she graduated and chose to stay in the States with his father. Markos hit a nerve in Olivia, who experienced similar sacrifices due to perceived love. His mother was a woman scorned, but a woman grateful for the love she found, for it could never be replicated, regardless of his father's intentions. Markos shared how his mother's family were raised in opulence and chose to cut her off. She was grateful her father funded her whole education, but his mother resented the lack of faith he had in his daughter's emotions.

"She told me, she never regretted the whole interaction with my father in the beginning because of what they were to accomplish with the birth of their kids. Regardless of what happened, she never approved of bad mouthing a parent. It stemmed from the commandment that speaks on honoring parents. I thought her philosophy was BS because she hid her pain from us. We never saw it. She was able to hide it because we weren't allowed to talk about our father. It was after we were about to leave high school and go to college, she began to talk about him. She always said we couldn't leave without knowing the truth about ourselves," added Markos.

Both the women humbly scoffed at his words. They believed themselves to be alright without the truth. They were comfortable in the belief the truth could not be as bad to be hidden away from women who had the strength to find their own way out of struggle and hardship. Markos laughed under the straight face he allowed them to see, but he understood, because he had the same swagger and anger before he learned about his father.

The conversation found itself at the downfall his parents experienced as their relationship grew into a new form in Sacramento. The city itself drowned Daveed's personality, for he appreciated a larger city lifestyle. The isolation suffocated him. Daveed was not yet one to complain. He loved the opportunity to build a life with a woman he loved. He did much more, making a sacrifice for her career, as she did by turning her family away.

"This was the first problem they faced in their relationship. It wasn't just the fact that they had moved, but Mom, she had gotten a position at the local university in the environmental policy department. She was conducting research while also teaching for the school. She was on track to become a tenured professor, while my father struggled with assimilating and finding the same favor around those circles. He started reading a lot more literature, the type of literature that radicalizes an individual before he truly understands a given subject. Mom said he began blaming some of his struggles on things that had less to do with him, and more to do with the subtle differences between him and the interviewers. He would later find a job at the JuCo that's next to the high school over here, but certain things fundamentally changed as Mom spent her time at the university, while my father spent years soul searching. My mother noticed a few things that made her fear my father. His graceful attitude shifted to desperate anguish. Before she could act on it, her stomach began to swell with a new member of her family, and shortly after, a ring followed."

"The marriage was forced?" asked Anna loudly.

Oh, how I miss being young, thought Olivia and Markos.

"Forced is a strong word. They were in an awkward position and the relationship could've gone either way. My brother and I, when we were very young, talked about such scenarios. Relationships, whether you believe it or not, have never been consummated out of love. People get married for status and economics instead of true love, especially now. The most popular and followed accounts on the Internet have to do with couples and how they conduct their relationship. People want to emulate deep, true love, not for themselves, but to show others. You wouldn't vote for a single president, would you?"

Anna smacked her lips as loud as she could.

"There are too many questions surrounding that whole predicament, and I ask myself why that would be? We wouldn't care if he or she had actual love in their marriage, just as long as they were married. It's a form of acceptance we've come to lean on, however, we don't realize the detrimental effect these unions have on children. It's because the ignorance these relationships are borne out of. This greatly affects the children when they are born. As you grow up, and as aware as our parents made us, you realize certain shortcomings in your parents' relationship. We begin to carry deep anger because of their partnership. This began as empathy, but that leaves once it's our turn to relive the cycle. Why do you think it takes fifty years to forget the stuff our parents did to us? When they finally die, we forgive and forget," said Markos as he looked at Anna, angered, knowing she's cursed to repeat the doom Olivia went through.

Her innocence, briefly mourned Markos.

He knew the family was cursed because none of them were like the families they were surrounded by. He grimaced, sharing how his mother and father doomed him from love.

His father and mother continued on, less happy than they were in the beginning. After Ephraim was born a few years later, the deprived nerves of his father began to show. He was stricter on the children, for he demanded his children be the best. He did not desire his children to be like others, distracted from the pursuits of life. His mother bought into the benefits of the strict regimen of the household because of the semblance to her upbringing. This gave his father life as well, distracting him from the strain of his own mental concerns. They lived under his forced readings and physical standards. Much of the aspects of their father's demands were from various teachings in books and films, through analysis of certain characters and leaders he appreciated. The problem, Markos noted, lied with the intentions of his father.

Markos showed the women the demented principles his father held on to earlier on in the first decade of their great-uncle's life. His father was not doing it to make them the best they could be, he wanted them to be the best for himself. Markos shared how his father disconnected from his Chicagoan roots and claimed he was Caribbean instead of a Black man from inner city Chicago. He refused to accept calls from his family back home for he thought they subscribed too much to the "ghetto" mindset. He remained stuck in his job and his outspoken comments in his classroom hindered any chance of mobility, blaming much of his sorrows on structural things without reflecting on himself. Markos took a breath, for he once deeply loved his father, for they snuck a conversation in before he passed, but the disgusted feeling he felt for his practices never left.

"See, you can look at my father and think his struggles were synonymous to Black people's struggles, but that'd be a mistake. Much of the kids fighting their own fight at the time were too focused on trying to provide awareness for unchecked things overlooked over the years. My father was leaning on them to get away from his own problems. He once told us he didn't know why he left Chicago but refused to turn back and acknowledge the people he was raised around. He chose to remain in a polished mindset, that he was holier than thou. This mindset drove him to drop all forms of his past and culture and tack on to a culture he knew nothing about, nor had a connection to. He claimed the Caribbean because he had a family friend from there that he always spoke to, at least according to my Mom. I believe only his uncle by marriage was Caribbean. He scared my mother, in the fact that he chose to look down on Black folks, and act as if his ideas would fix problems. One thing he could never understand was the unique culture of the way he was raised, as a Black man from an inner city, an archetype important to any culture you wish to adapt or create here in the United States. He started to spew stronger statements against self-love and self-realization, and it served as the last straw for me. As a twelve-year-old who already knew and studied the lives of *Malcolm X* and *Frederick Douglass,* I knew what this was. He was not like them, he was projecting," added Markos.

After his father began to take more control around the house, his mother became less engaged in discussing anything with him. The house became still and with Markos and Ephraim both passed the age of ten, they were in the age of realizations, according to Ephraim. They both were becoming more tiresome of his misguided discipline and noticed the comfort Daveed took with the parents at their school. Some of their classmates discussed how their father enjoyed subtly bragging about the discipline of his children. He loved sharing how his teachings went a long way with them both.

"This pissed the other kids off, especially Black kids. He was having these parents shut off game consoles and forcing their kids to read, which will never work cause the one thing he got right, ironically, was that knowledge can't be forced. Kids hated us because he convinced some parents to forgo sports and get away from that mindset. All our classmates hated us because their parents would listen while others feared their parents would be next, and it didn't help that we always won awards at the school for our coursework," said Markos as he let out a chuckle.

"It was sad to see that this was what our father enjoyed, the bragging. We won these debate awards and came home with stellar grades, but the only way to make him happy was if others were jealous. We loved our mother, but she was to blame, too, because she never protected us. She always said that was how she was raised, and that made me come to the conclusion, not everyone deserves to have kids, for the simple fact, people don't know what they want from their kids. Without knowing what you want from them, you can't properly love them," continued Markos in his consistent somberness.

The stories continued towards the slow realization his father was much more harmful to his psyche than Anna and Olivia were aware. The influence he carried with other parents put his children in a difficult place. Markos reminded the women Ephraim was quite annoyed with their father and outwardly stuck closer to their mother. Markos shared how he first came to learn of his brother's special knowledge of people. The calculated personality came from understanding people like their father, for they would experience many people like him later on. Regardless, Ephraim was the first of the two to lose respect for their father after he repeatedly invaded their space with the parents at the school. He believed Ephraim knew what was to come next.

"After Ephraim refused to do certain things our father asked, my father would ask my mother for help. She quickly refused; Ephraim was her baby. There was nothing he could do, and he became much more frustrated with us. I soon followed out of solidarity, but I was always afraid to test my parents' power. Soon after, my Dad lost it, emotionally I mean. He became too reserved because he understood he'd lost all forms of control and respect from his family. Ephraim refused to speak to him, he already knew what he was, an egomaniac. It was too subtle, at first, for us to see it as a psychological problem, but with how he raised us, we nearly were conditioned to be the same. He crumbled against the pressure of his family, scrambling to fix the issues he created. The funny thing is, it probably could've been all fixed with a simple apology and a delayed promise to be better in the future, but a prideful man could never be asked to do something like that to people he believes he is superior to. My Dad, as loving as he was originally, began to change after that, for he was only there to provide and not love. He would come home and eat, then he would spend his time walking around our neighborhood for he could no longer teach his kids once they came home from school. His teachings were important in making sure we were aware of such things like *Harriet Tubman's* journeys or *Mandela's* prison sentence, going as far as *Simon Bolivar's* upheavals and *Haile Selassie's* reign, but again, knowledge not stemming from a good place feels like poison at times. We never forgot what we learned, but we separated him from what we were taught, and as we did, he separated from us."

Markos explained that after a year or so, his walks began coinciding with the walks of certain mothers of children in their classroom. His charisma and idealism found a home with some of them. His passion was rejuvenated, especially around the single mothers who were looking for a man with all the controlling qualities he possessed. It did not take their colorful father long to pick one from the pile and relocate his life with one of them. The revelation took the women by surprise, and they did not hold their disgust back.

"Wow, that explains some things!" yelled Anna.

Her drinking did not help mediate her angered frustration for she deeply sighed after he spoke. He was grateful he chose not to drink because reminiscing on this topic usually sent him towards the bottle. Olivia was shaken by the thought of her family's trauma. She would never have thought the angelic grandmother she knew could have gone through such things.

"You weren't kidding about the betrayal," said Olivia as she took a few moments to watch her daughter steadily process. Anna's thorough drinking slowed her reaction time.

"Yes, absolutely," replied Markos jokingly.

"It was crazy seeing my mother trying to cope with all of it. He was trying to be someone else by forgetting who he actually was in the first place. He attempted to reinvent his whole life without acknowledging how important his true self was. He missed the point of many of his teachings and the literature he was trying to share with me and my brother. By the end, he was disappointed in us, but it wasn't until much later that I would learn he was more so disappointed in himself.

"Things, however, drastically shifted after he left. Everyone knew him, but they didn't know my mother or us for that fact. People created the narrative that my mother had chased away someone who had so much charisma and respect. They started making up stories of how difficult it must've been to live with someone like her.

"Everyone enjoyed his company, so they couldn't possibly understand how a man like that can do wrong. Kids would make fun of us because another single mother and student had moved away with our father. Our whole family was chastised and casted out because no one knew the truth. We stopped going to school events and avoided community linkups at the Center because we felt the stares. We were ashamed of how much sway our father really had. That was the betrayal, in the time we needed the most protection, my mother didn't care, and my father wasn't there for us. Life was pretty ugly, but as Ephraim would say, *it was written to be like it was.* For there was an outcast who didn't pass the judgment like others. A young White girl who saw me and my brother eating lunch alone on the bleachers, walked up to us one day and asked if our father was the one who had slept with her aunt. He had run away with her cousin, who also was her only friend. That little White girl was the first person to make us laugh in a while. It was Alana," said Markos, with a large smile plastered across his face.

Anna shifted her head, asking for confirmation with a shy smile.

"Yes, that was how we met Alana for the first time and how we forged such a strong bond. That woman would do anything for anyone named Solomons and I would gladly reciprocate that. She was a friend that neither he nor I saw coming."

Olivia found herself smacking her lips and cracked a smile of her own, thinking Alana was a friend they met in college. Many of the papers and articles were filled with things far from the truth about her. She scoffed at the idea of a friendship arising from such an horrific experience.

What demons these two may have had, thought Olivia.

Markos concluded the rest of the story, saying his mother became much more involved in their lives after she took time away from work. She invested in the social aspect of their lives, understanding she had to do to us what Daveed once did for her. This was the moment, he highlighted, the two became more religious for their father was not and begged her to allow the children to make the choice. Markos shared how the brothers desired comfort from her, factoring in their decision to attend church with her and learn her language. Their father always thought her language was useless due to the fact only one country spoke it. They learned of their mother's culture more extensively and adopted her ancient form of Christianity, a form of Christianity that predated Catholicism. They would encounter a culture shock when they would meet their grandfather for the first time, in a land they would only refer to as *The Homeland* after visiting for the first time. They were accepted once the lost daughter came home, following Daveed's departure, for a recovery trip lasting a summer break.

"That's where we were finally radicalized, for a lack of a better term. We didn't just discuss the meaning of family. We weren't just on a vacation. We went somewhere that we had been taught about but never experienced, our home. I want you to imagine, *Malcolm X,* going to Mecca. We realized, for the first time, there were billions of people on this planet," said Markos.

"We discussed the world. Ephraim was the one who changed the most from the experience. We would take boat rides and caravans through the animated jungles and bustling streets, and we would sit and discuss things with anyone we met. People's worlds are much more than we could ever understand. We were only thirteen and sixteen and we were talking to others like adults. We processed everything like we were older. It was interesting looking at people's perspectives on life and how some with less move quicker than those with more. It was also talking to people with as much conviction as Ethiopians. We were never colonized so we don't have a humble fiber in our bodies. We came back with a mended heart and with time away from distractions, we felt we too deserve some happiness. Ephraim carried this and gained a new purpose to live well and do well. It sounds corny, but it was like dipping your toe in Heaven's waters. All the anger changed into understanding because our discussions, for months, were about philosophy. No books can teach what you can get from talking to people from foreign lands, a point we overlook in the movies and books we read, for they inform us, but they don't allow us to experience it."

"My grandfather died a few years after we visited, but one day, he pulled us aside and talked to both of us privately when our mother went out with her siblings. This is the last thing, and then we can all go to bed," said Markos, glancing at how the little hand sat a few ticks past the two.

They even kept our old clock.

The women all turned to look at the large and quite rare mahogany analog clock placed in front of the dining room table. It sat above the closed coat closet. Neither of the women cared because they were in a trance, trying to imagine the vivid details Markos was sharing about the trip he took as a child.

"He pulled us aside and apologized for not manning up and coming to see us when we were born. He cried as he shared his great shame of his old mentality of stern leadership, a sad behavior he said we were already victims of. He trembled as he held our hands with his wrinkled and heavy paws, as he began to bless us, a custom elders do to the children they love back home. He softly placed his hands over our heads as he whispered his prayer under his breath. It was beautiful.

"He continued on and said we shall not worry about any financial problems in our lives, for as long as he lives, our family will be alright, and that after, he has prayed to God to set us up, through his preparation of certain things like a will of course. He was unaware our father's pride forced Dad to continue paying the bills on our home, in addition to a given amount for childcare he and Mom agreed upon after their peaceful divorce.

"Regardless, this man cried his eyes out asking young kids for forgiveness, a sight I never understood till much, much later. This was one of two times I saw Ephraim shed tears in my life, or at least after his toddler years. We graciously accepted his apology and he continued teaching us on how to avoid the pitfalls that he had experienced. He left me with something so powerful. He said that our strict discipline is good to a point, but we become too stern and rigid when we believe we have some type of economic or unnatural purpose in this life. He said this planet was here long before us and will be here long after us. He told us both, do the good that you can, but do not look for a purpose, just experience it. He said *experience* the world or you'll be left in the end apologizing for everything that you've done. Listen to the wisdom of others now, for when you get to my age, you wish you had.

"Ephraim ate those words up and he let them consume him. When we returned, it all clicked, and he knew what he wanted to do. He wanted to help people experience life as he did, see things as he did, live with love as we all should," concluded Markos.

Anna and Olivia were shell shocked as they sat back and digested. Markos evaluated the two's responses and questions as he graciously answered them. *Ephraim, I know it's through your permission and prayers, I'm here again,* believed Markos.

He carried the thought in his head through the night. He listened to the remarks of his family until Olivia rose and prepared to depart.

"Well, I really, really enjoyed this story time. I hope to be here for the next one. I have to be up in a few hours, so I have to head out, good night."

"Goodnight."

"Goodnight, Mom."

The two remained quiet as they watched Olivia ascend onto the steps. The hallway lights on the stairs flickered on. They waited and listened to the footsteps reverberate throughout the intimate home as she made her way to her room, and finally, closed the door to end her night. They even heard her crash into the bed, letting herself fall and go straight to sleep.

"I really enjoyed that story, thanks for telling the truth," said Anna. She also stood, beginning to clean the garbage left on the table. Markos began to help out by picking some of the stranded objects she could not carry towards the kitchen.

"Hmm, I told you, it's important to know the truth about the beginning to understand the choices made in the end," said Markos. He pushed the crumbs on the table to the floor.

"Yeah, I get it now. I see how you couldn't trust people after your Dad, and a little about Angela, but I don't know how much it could affect anything else," said Anna.

Anna was toggling with the self-clean settings on the rectangular tablet above the refrigerator. She leaned on the dishwasher while toggling with the vacuum settings to vacuum the home before her mother woke. She set a supplemental room alarm for her mother so she could wake on time as well. The bright white dishwasher unit and its black buttons were always sticky since the buttons were never cleaned. She set the auto clean setting to wash the dishes as they went to their beds. She made sure the house would be clean before her mother left for work.

"Are you going to answer my question?"

"What question?" replied Markos.

"Where else would knowing your issues play a role?"

"You didn't ask a question. But…it's important to know how me and Ephraim became close and how we met Alana. But more importantly you need to understand my parents before you understand me and *Elsa.*"

"I keep hearing you talking about Elsa, who is she?" asked Anna.

He paused before the words spewed out uncontrollably.

"The one person who understood me, the real me. She was the one person I should've formed a life with."

Those were the only words he was prepared for her to hear. She was much more, the source of love, leaving him to emptiness and reliant on anonymity and isolation after her untimely departure. She was the person who guided him back to Ephraim and made sure he understood what and who was important in his life. She tied it all together, what faith was about, and she taught him how life was supposed to be experienced, as his grandfather did.

"When am I going to get to learn about her?"

"She tied my upbringing and my brother's movement together for me. I believe it's a story for tomorrow. I apologize, I haven't spoken her name in over twenty-five years, so it'll take me some time to prepare to really discuss her. She was and is still very important to me," said Markos shakingly.

"What happened to her?"

Markos paused his cleaning for a quick second as he patted his pockets for the papers. The quick and subtle reach gained the attention of the young Anna as she remembered the lost letter. This was the second time she recalled his hesitance regarding the note and his Elsa.

"My dear, she died," said Markos.

They stopped speaking, instead wiping off the crumbs and smudges on the table. They ascended up the staircase together and faded into their rooms, both thinking of the woman he called Elsa.

UPHEAVAL

seven:
Elsa

The flight itself left the young man nervously clutching at the hardened plastic seat handles. Comfort eluded him since connecting to his second flight in Frankfurt due to the flimsy turbulence in his time in the sky. The uneasy airtime made his in-flight reading difficult. The reading was meant to alleviate his growing anxiety.

His life was to begin so far away from the distractions in the States. Choices made were beginning to show the repercussions attached. On the surface, the stress was turning his insides while he felt no hemodynamic response in his legs. Sticking with him in his descent into the new kingdom were the last few pages of the book, the book he kept close to him while he packed and left the comfort of his disheartened mother. As he descended into the new land he would continue his schooling, the last words on the beige paperback book rang in his head. The melted ice in his ginger ale shook as the landing gear made contact with the cracked roads of Rabat, in the Kingdom of Morocco. Words spun in his head, over and over.

His detailed understanding of the book was due to the familiarity he had with the author. The woman served in the Air Force with him and asked for his company throughout her writing process. He resented the ask, but he could never decline such a request from someone he shared years in service with. To make situations worse, he was useless at home while other members of his family found purpose in the avenues they took.

The book did not sell many copies, he could not even recall if even fifty were sold, but while tagging along on a book tour with the woman, conversations with purposeful veterans sparked questions within him. They embraced openness and attacked many of the stereotypes regarding the military and the future of armed forces personnel once they returned home. He met people with great experiences in their respective branch along with horrific stories of their own, outside of the military. Overall, the book's journey was his journey, as he tagged along and met gracious people who would encourage him to leave and go forward on his own.

While the encouragement was helpful, he was livid about the amount of effort he made to interact with hundreds, maybe even a thousand people, when barely a few copies were sold. He expected as much with the impact of the recent economic downturn. An optimist could easily blame this for the weak initial book sales. Still, when he finished the book, his unmitigated anger regarding the sales felt justified. The last page was powerful in its lasting message, sticking with him as he prepared to unbuckle his steel seat belt.

Markos knew he was not close to the woman enough to call her a serious friend. They shared occasional awkward nights out or breakfast together following their years in the service, but she was one of the only few people he could recall maintaining a friendship with in his time in the Air Force. Only in school and the armed forces could people from different places form unanticipated friendships and mesh antagonistic cultures together. But after his experience in school, he avoided getting close to many people. His relationships with the competitive men and women in college were in the past, the distant past, even Angela. All he cared for at that moment was his brother and the ambitious Alana, the two already beginning to cause friction in the western part of the States. His mother engulfed that realm as well, for she was the one he remembered the most when he left California, and the burning he felt in his cheeks as he saw the tears flow down her face. Outside this small circle, people did not support him after recognizing his adopted, distant social practices. Nonetheless, he found the book to be profound. She ended the book with such a quote, a long one at that, which would continue to ring in his head for decades to come.

"Danger arises when men of action meet men of words. The danger lies in the fact that the men of words, who are oblivious to the importance of knowing when and when not to act, are under pressure to act when they are put into contest with powerful men of action. Due to the unfamiliarity, the danger arises because the initial actions of such cowardly people are agents of destruction, a destruction that leads to the loss of life of all men. For the eternal goal of men of words, is to limit and destroy the men of actions. Who are the men you support?"

Markos believed the woman took the words too far with the question in the end of the interesting piece. The dangers of such men and the idea of it were not unique, for the risk of putting such men in contention would always create certain problems as it does in the streets and in the military. He invested attention into the eternal portion of her last page, trying hard to decode what she meant by the silencing of men of action, did she mean the military or another group? He attempted to perform some form of psychoanalysis of the woman as he read the book, but he understood her personal experiences could not be decoded, for it was just that, personal.

The words still stuck like the teachings of his grandfather, and he associated the abnormal clinging to the worry he carried for his family back home, especially his brother. He wondered if his brother's current traction with university students would be labeled as one of a man with words or a man who has been working in accordance with his actions. Ephraim was forced to complete another quarter of his public relations studies and he chose to forego his law studies. The programs and events he coordinated in school created a large presence on social media, a facet of media Ephraim despised since its inception. Despite his countenance, this was the way he amassed a large social movement against the current brinkmanship people experienced from their political allegiances. These extracurriculars took much of his time and limited the amount of attention he had for studies.

The thought of his brother at the moment he was landing in a new land disgusted him. The people around him, including Ephraim, embraced him to be more selfish. They encouraged him to find places where he could better himself. Ephraim's rapid entrance into the political sphere applied a small, yet noticeable pinch of pressure on Markos. His reserved lifestyle slowed progress in his life, as he kept no meaningful relationships, nor did he show any signs of growth as an adult. Years passed, and he still did not recover from the devastation of discontinuing the connection he shared with Angela. His life was consumed with separating from the discomfort people's flaunted emotions towards him would bring. One could blame the people around him, but the reality was he was in recovery from the departure of his father, the one person he loved the most.

He chose to take the time to instead learn more about the mysteries around him. He hoped his brother could outlast the men of words and become a man of action, for he believed *they* would come for him. He placed the thought in the proverbial back burner as he looked towards the thick glass window. A few mysteries appeared to him in his brief time in the Air Force. He made sure to make the most of the training and time he spent with the most funded sector of the government. He had decoded the mystery of certain languages like Arabic and Spanish, the two languages he always cared to learn. The two went along with the Amharic and French he was taught as a child. Markos paid particular attention to the small weapons training in basic and utilized supplemental training to gain as many accreditations as possible. Much of the leisure time Markos was given was spent alone, consumed by immense reading he certainly had not forgotten to continue.

When the man refuses to obtain new information, he becomes arrogant and ignorant, for he believes he's aware of it all. Always,

always be in school, some form of school. Reading will be your school when you aren't there, his father used to say.

Don't think of them, pushed Markos.

Markos did not yet depart from the dust-covered airplane, and already, he was filled with anguish, brooding with his thoughts about family.

His deformed duffle bags hanging above in the shaky compartments were squished by the name brand bags of the foreigners in the flight. Markos was quite indifferent about his belongings, since the toiletries and the shoes he brought were not important to him. He was prepared to lose or damage all his trivial belongings, for his camera and his laptop were always on his person. However, he conducted a silent prayer for the safe landing and recovery of the overpacked checked suitcase with all his clothes.

The descent came faster than expected. He quickly stretched his muscles while looking down the long aisle at a fluid line beginning to form down the plane. A smile crept out from the side of his mouth as he recognized the different nations people came from. They shared their arrival into Rabat with him. His mindset was still of a young graduate's, one of eagerness and passion for travel and the diffusion of ideas from the idealists and patriots of different nations. He wished to learn how to verbalize those desires. He learned from his mother's fervent love for her nation, the States did not have a monopoly on patriotism. His excitement was masked by the face of displeasure from the jetlag of the long flights.

The initial drive from Sacramento to San Francisco, due to the influx and efflux of international flights from the terminal, made it difficult to say his unpleasant goodbyes to the family. His mother soured the departure with her irrational tears and Ephraim's slim availability rushed the pleasantries. Ephraim spent time answering calls. After his mother's warmly moist cheeks met his during her kiss goodbye, it was Alana who gave him a genuine farewell.

"Enjoy it, I know what you're looking for. If this is the last time, you already know how much I love you. Stay safe. You know how much they love you, and you know what you mean to them. Other than your mom, it's tough for anyone with the Solomons name to show real emotion," argued Alana, giving a steady embrace lasting, for Markos, forever.

His brother rushed an aberrant wave and mouthed the words, *stay safe,* focusing on his outline of arguments to be presented to the district councilmen of the Sacramento City Council.

He was in Rabat, not just for himself and his peculiar path, but to be better for his family. His decisions to go to the Air Force upended much of the family's dynamics, while still being positively received by his mother and brother. The time away had given him peace, yet the sobering sabbatical found a plethora of disturbances once he returned. After he reached home, the comfort of the food and the easing hands of his mother tightened her clutches on his life. His path was not his and his purpose was inconclusive for he was twenty-six, with no profession, nor did he have a home of his own.

He looked down the patchy white and bland gray interior of the two-story airplane and homed in on the recognizable recent graduates, arrogant businessmen and women, and even some overzealous diplomats. The smell of Rabat was mixed with the aroma of uncertainty, immature eagerness, and the distinguished smell of green tea and the flavorful couscous. The oblong line of clustered peoples slowly proceeded to exit when a familiar sight showed itself. He saw a mother and father scuffle to grab their children to finally leave the long flight.

Couldn't be me, thought Markos.

The two Arabian parents were copies of the once married parents of Markos Solomons. The distasteful picture of Daveed and his mother, at dinner, yelling at one another formed while the father's physicality showed form in the violent retrieval of his bags.

He watched as the mother was berated by the father and her eldest son for slowing the line. She tried to get the three little ones she accompanied in order, but the confusion regarding the children's bags thwarted her efforts towards efficiency. Markos watched as the two unsympathetic men worried about the troubles of others, angrily hurrying the desperate mother. The strangers were foreign to the land, he could not hear the distinct Arabic spoken, but instead heard a certain accent giving away their southern French citizenry. Markos could easily make out their French, he recognized the love language rather quickly, a taste acquired as his favorite tongue. He attempted to help the frantic mother and quell the yells of the children by reaching over the compartment and handing the smallest child the last remaining bag. The small ocean blue and scarlet red backpack was the cause for all the unrest.

"*Merci beaucoup*," yelled the woman as she darted off with the children.

De rien, thought Markos. He followed the pig-tailed hair of the small golden child out the airplane and into the chaotic airport.

He reveled in the distinct sounds and smells of the rambunctious environment. Markos attempted to key into the different languages of the racing travelers and enjoyed the challenge of identifying their dialects. There were few events or unanticipated situations able to bring a smile to the nihilistic young man. The heavy air of the mint in tourists' gunpowder tea stained the airport with thick humidity as he walked through the customs checkpoint. Everything about the new nation brought a hesitant smile to his face, for the simple fact it was his to discover. The pig-tailed young girl woke him from his trance, pulling the pockets of his black chino pants.

"*Merci, Monsieur, et...au revoir,*" screamed the child. She immediately raced over to her mother and father whose eyes were set on the surprised Black man.

Markos shared an awkward wave with the family and with their wave in return, he was reminded of his lone journey.

Step 1, they told me to go and find my luggage!

The Moroccan customs workers graciously accepted Markos. His country of residence had lost grace with nations who shared the continent with Morocco due to the instability from a new generation of rash leaders. He half-expected them to rescind his visa, but they lit up when he chose there to study for an Electrical Engineering Masters. A few of the workers were so impressed by Markos's visit to their home, they helped him to a carousel and even retrieved his hefty black suitcase. They could sense the youthful passion in his voice and believed the boy came from a good family. Markos was confused by their helpfulness, but willingly accepted for his Darija was not the best, leaning more on his exceptional Arabic.

Step 2, I must find a taxi. They told me to find a taxi.

As soon as he left the tinted sliding doors, he felt it. The air, the humidity, and the bustling streets carried a profound effect for a Westerner used to fluidity in industrial settings. The air commanded a stench that may have disgusted folks from his region of residence, but to a man who grew accustomed to the holistic frankincense his mother burned in the home, the land showed character, a mystic and foreign quality unable to be captured digitally.

He emulated the hand movements of others around him. They too hoped to obtain a taxi driver's attention. The golden dust sitting on the beige cars transferred to the bags of the tourists funneling into the vehicles once the drivers came to a stop. Rampant Arabic words and rhythmic honking plagued the ears of all leaving the airport. The cars were moving faster than he expected. Markos did not know how the whole interaction was to be carried out. He found himself already buckled up in the back, middle seat of an exuberant driver's taxi, the man quickly fitting his four bags into the trunk of the car.

"As-salamu alaykum," said Markos once the driver ran back into the car.

"Wa alaykum assalam, my friend. Are you *American?*" asked the driver, emphatically rolling his r's.

"Yes," answered the nervous Markos.

"Ahh!!" replied the driver while clapping in jubilation.

"Yes, my friend!! Is this your first time in Morocco, brother?"

"Mhmm, first time."

The driver's excited smile lifted the young man's spirits. His smile exposed his golden-brown teeth, teeth stained by the warm tea he rested in his sticky cup holder. Markos sat on the teal cushioned seats in the back, waiting for his arrival at the university. The car was itself a tourist attraction, covered in the wear and tear of people staining the car with the marks and smells of their own nations. Markos's hands brushed the mahogany stains to the right of him, feeling the memories of the travelers before him in the rough seats.

He notified the driver of his desired destination. The driver's process of reintroducing the car onto the road was much more chaotic than Markos wished. The shuttles, tourist buses, and the transport vans all vied for the single lane out of the airport's arrival gate. The middle-aged driver noticed the young man's nerves betraying his face.

"Don't worry, my friend, the driving is crazy here. Don't trust any big cars, they mess up the traffic," cautioned the confident man as disorderly honking from vans reverberated through the single funnel out to the city.

"Jesus…," whispered Markos under his breath.

"Yesus won't save you here my friend, this is Muhammed's territory."

Markos's brisk laughter exposed his anxiety of the driver's techniques. There were no ten and two techniques taught, but there was a subtle comfort he felt in the man's confidence on the road, even under the duress of drivers' honks.

The driver looked back again, finding Markos's eagerness boil over to worry once the highway appeared.

"What is your name my friend?"

"Markos, *Markos* Solomons," said Markos, already rolling his r's, following the driver's cadence.

"Ahh, your sound is different from Americans I have met. Where are your parents from?"

"My father, he's American. My mother is Ethiopian. She's the one that raised me," replied Markos.

The driver's animation reached new levels once he saw they shared a home.

"Friend, you are Ethiopian? My African brother, where do you come from in the States?"

"Sacramento."

"The capital of California, correct?" asked the driver, to the surprise of Markos.

"Yes, have you been?"

"No, I've never been to *California.* My brother lives in Michigan, I try to go visit him every two years," replied the driver.

"Ah, which city?"

"My brother lives in Lansing, a little town called Okemos. He used to live in New Jersey, but he wanted somewhere quieter."

Markos looked for any sign of familial connection in his car: a photo, a necklace, anything he could find to continue the conversation. Nothing hung from the rearview mirror, nor did the driver carry any identification in the car for travelers. He found nothing of note. His ability to carry small talk was hindered by his shelved personality, but Markos wanted a better path, a path of connection in this journey.

"What is your name, *my friend,*" asked Markos, hinting at a hidden humor in his persona.

The driver let out a small chuckle under his breath, recognizing the attempts being made from the reserved gentleman.

"My name is Elmahdi, *but* my friends in America call me *Jerry.*"

Markos's laughter could not be contained, humorously fusing with the man's own chuckles.

"Why is it they call you Jerry?"

"Ahh, me and my son, we loved the rat, the Jerry. We always watched that program."

A marker, thought Markos as he wiggled his way through the colorful conversation.

As the car moved forward in the traffic, the unevenness of the bumpy road was hidden by the slow pace they surrendered to in the noisy rush hour. The conversation lightened. They discussed the politics of Morocco, since the supposed fifteen-minute car ride turned into an interesting forty minutes. Elmahdi began to educate him on the complexity of the new nation he was entering. Towards the end of the drive, the two men, understanding the fact they would never cross paths again, turned the conversation more personable.

"Why'd you pick my home to continue your schooling? It is only a master's degree, correct?" asked Elmahdi.

Markos took a second to answer. He told people reasons that resonated with their personality. Elmahdi, being the first of the people he met in Morocco, learned the truth.

"After I left for the Air Force, you look around, and while you gain brothers and sisters, you are alone. You decide your fate as you go, and I knew I had to decide what became of me. Being home later on, it was tough to build something that's yours. There are many pictures, and many crafted stories that tell people what to live by. Money, family. They tell you when you graduate that you will get a nice job and live comfortably. My grandfather taught me to experience the world, don't look for a purpose, it's already a disgusting world," concluded Markos.

"Well said, my friend. But why here?"

"*I've never been here.* It would have been easy to lean on my mother's family in her homeland, but what would I have learned? I got a good position in the program in Johannesburg and Nairobi, but the reason Rabat was different from those places was that they offered me a job as well. I told you, I am going to teach English or Mathematics here, but the other places offered me research positions in their engineering departments. Teaching, as quiet as I am, is a passion of mine. I'll be teaching kids and adults, but all the while, they'll be teaching me about myself."

The truth's weight bore on him for a good minute. The smile and clapping of Elmahdi could have brought tears to his eyes if he was not consumed by laughter. The teaching greatly separated the two other opportunities. The European schools he received admission requests from all asked him to teach in the private schools of diplomats and businessmen, the more secluded areas of the countries. The university in

Rabat gave him an opportunity to make money on the side by securing him a position, through a third-party organization, in teaching the people in the Moroccan communities. There was not much to stop the young man from accepting what he believed to be a dream job, especially in a place where choices were his to make.

"Well, brother, we are a few minutes away. Call who you must call so they can come and receive you," warned the driver.

"They know I'm coming. They told me to go to the main office when I show up. They told me I am to stay in an apartment with two graduate students."

"Ahh, good. They'll be important in teaching you about our customs. Language isn't enough here," continued Elmahdi.

"Don't worry about politics here. The people define the nation, never our politicians. It isn't fair to tie politics to the people. I cannot judge you for Ethiopia or America, and I hope you don't judge me for this Kingdom. You will meet different people with different, uh...motivation. Trust in our faith, for I see the cross on your neck. Again, language is not enough here. Listen and feel my brothers and sisters here, as I listened to your brothers and sisters in your country," added Elmahdi.

Markos, noting the stern statement, made sure to keep his words in mind, sensing the serious tone Elmahdi took with him. He fiddled with his thoughts in order to somehow change the topic from himself. He wanted to get the most out of the man before they would depart from each other, but he was interrupted by the man's inquisitive approach to the car ride.

"You will finish your Electrical Engineering here, correct?"

"Yes, I'll get my second masters here. I studied while in the Air Force and got one in Bioengineering. After this, I may go back home and make my mother happy and get a job next to her," replied Markos with uncertainty.

"Ahh, mother's boy, huh? Never disappoint your mother, especially when you only have one," joked Elmahdi.

"Was your son a mother's boy?" pivoted Markos.

Elmahdi's mood did not change, but his smile gradually faded, his voice cracking in his reply.

"My boy, he was attached to his father. His mother's jealousy was my comedy," said Elmahdi. His smile reappeared at the memories.

"Was?" asked Markos shakingly, fearful of the tragic response awaiting him.

"Ahh, my boy. My boy, he was eight. I went to help my brother move from his New Jersey home about four years ago. I received a phone call that my boy's soccer ball had gone over the fence. They told me that he didn't hear the speeding taxi's uh…honking when he went and looked for the ball."

Elmahdi swallowed his sadness, still at war with his emotions after recounting the story to Markos. He became one of few tourists who asked him about his son.

"My friend, a heart should never break, the way my heart broke that day. I was stuck, my flight didn't leave Michigan for another four days. I come back home to my wife, dead from a broken heart. I came home and buried my life that day. My brother sent me money to come back and live with him in America. I told him; this is my home. I took his money, and I bought a taxi, like the one that killed my boy," declared the headstrong Elmahdi.

Markos, still as he was, saw no better reaction than to smile from the back seat. He admired the discipline, wishing he had similar resolve. He waited in silence for a moment before choosing to speak.

"You are a remarkable man, Elmahdi," said Markos.

They approached the dormitories of the large university. Markos took note of the tamed greenery, he did not expect the university to be so like the pictures online. His palms moistened the closer they inched towards the front doors.

Along the way, Markos marveled at the effervescent energy of the constantly moving population of Rabat. He witnessed the elegant coastline and how the sand lit up and highlighted the restless Atlantic Ocean, as a picture frame differentiates the setting of an antique photo.

The buildings and homes sitting near the water fit together with the natural design of the kingdom's capital. The architectural format of the city was incredibly proportional and meshed with the roads. Markos's eyes fixated on the rising levels of the street and saw as the slanted roads corresponded with the elevated houses. The tame colors of beige, brown and white shaded the homes and buildings around the city. The busy beaches were within eyesight from the car the entire length of the drive, but there was not much time to revel in the beautiful landscape of the energetic city.

Markos was entranced by the man driving him to his awaited location. His eyes were glued on the man, his mannerisms and all. The tapping of the steering wheel and the restless toggling of his wedding ring with his thumb showed unhealed trauma. Elmahdi's story explained Markos's desire to leave home. Markos grew up anxiously reading bombastic news stories and watching the verisimilitude of the films and books he consumed. The world in which people experienced life differently from his sheltered upbringing forced him to acknowledge his privilege. He wanted to learn from others, but he was not as prepared or social as his brother. There were many unresolved issues Markos did not come to terms with, nor did he wish to identify them. What he would attempt to do, what he already realized in the first hour of his time in Morocco, was to listen to the people and hear their struggles, for there may lie solutions in their stories. Elmahdi's interjection regarding people, those sentiments were powerful to Markos. Nothing would play a larger role in Markos's future in Morocco, and his awaiting doom back in the States. The people, to him, were the key to the next stages in his transformation. In this point of his life, sympathy and hope took space in his heart.

Still, Markos was better off home, but how could he know? Sympathy and hope would scar into isolated contempt for time, from the trials and tribulations felt in the city of Rabat, soon to be added on by Ephraim in decades to come. A man can only attack the present with the experiences in his tool belt.

Elmahdi chose to keep his words to a minimum in the last few minutes, recognizing the awkward praise coming from the glare of his passenger. The arrival masked the soft sadness in both of them as they would forever depart. As they arrived at the large, glass structure of the main office, they were exposed to more of the enormous green and spacious university. Elmahdi parked the car and looked at the young Markos before he continued.

"I thank you Elmahdi, you have done more for me than you know. I wish you good fortune, and good business. May God grant us another moment in the future."

"May He do so, my friend," replied Elmahdi, slowly walking out of the car. He gently tapped the top of his ordinary taxi, reminded of his boy as he went to retrieve Markos's things.

"No, Mom, don't get those ones, they're nasty," cautioned the disgusted girl.

Olivia ignored her daughter's request, she knew she needed to stay healthy in a time of increased stress.

"Relax, this is for my diet, we can get you the one that you want, too," replied the annoyed Olivia.

Olivia continued to scroll through the living room tablet and chose, for the first time to Anna's recollection, to screen mirror the tablet on the seventy-inch television as she picked out groceries. Anna believed this decision to be influenced by their new houseguest. Anna realized her testy attitude needed to shift before her mother reversed her decision to make her normal duties a communal activity.

Markos, enjoying the playful banter, relinquished the frustration from being interrupted. Olivia chose to be more visible around the two following the completion of her backlogged work. She was beginning to make more of an effort to build a relationship with her peculiar uncle. Her efforts included making her presence known during the storytelling and embedding herself in the conversations. Olivia was the last piece to their puzzled family.

She enjoyed the stories, however, her attention was placed on many of the problems she faced, including how to tell Markos and Anna her brother requested the three of them come visit him in Los Angeles in a week. He was to arrive to visit his ex-wife and daughter, and after hearing of Markos's reemergence, looked to knock two birds with one stone. Much of the onus of keeping the Solomons family together fell on her and she felt the weight, but all the while, she maintained a level of informality important to the easing theme of family. She had requested that Markos begin calling her Liv, the name she was called since middle school and the name her friends preferred over calling her Olivia each time. Reluctantly, he agreed, knowing how ashamed Ephraim felt about people reducing one's name.

The name change reminded him of the silly name Elmahdi was given by his American friends, simply because he shared an affinity for cartoons. The reluctance, he wished, should have been enough for her to see the displeasure in his voice, but he chose to take the high road to avoid all forms of conflict.

"Get some mangos, both the fruit and the dried packets," added the persistent Anna.

Markos could do nothing but smile and enthusiastically nod his head for those were both childhood favorites. Olivia's smile softly took form, seeing the benefits of the communal efforts paying off in their participation.

"Alright, all this stuff's already at three seventy-five. We gotta be wise about what we want," cautioned Olivia.

"Huh? We didn't even get pancakes, the bourbon is getting low too, right?" jokingly replied Anna.

"She's not lying," chimed Markos quickly.

The mother was getting impatient. She knew another bourbon and the pancakes would take the space of the four hundred she allotted for groceries. Markos anticipated the fight to ensue.

"Get the bourbon and the fruit you had originally on the list. Also get her pancakes, because those were pretty good last time. Charge all of it to my card," confidently spoke Markos.

Both the women turned to see Markos unphased by a five-hundred-dollar purchase. All who shared the Solomons name remained modest in their economic means over the generations, even with the lucrative name they carried.

"I can't ask you to do that, this is my home," replied Olivia, knowingly aware she did not put up the fight she should have.

"This is *our* home. I don't know how long I'll be in your home, depending on how long this situation lasts. I have no expenses due to your hospitality. I don't mind, I'll pay," calmly concluded Markos as he retrieved his identification number from his watch.

Markos thought of the time he would lose his wallet in high school, all to return home to find the money to pay for his school lunch. The times of complete automation of shopping and purchasing would have served the timid man well. He could not quantify the time and pleasure he could have retained avoiding the long lines with his mother at the grocery stores. His mother's distaste for the automation following the pandemic was the opposite of his sentiments. Teaching her all the online perks showed him what he learned from their personal shopping experiences, *it was healthy to see people.* Now, his life resided in the watches that stuck to each person's wrist, and the tablets connected to every device in the home.

While Olivia continued scrolling, Markos felt his irritation turn into childish anxiety. He was sitting on hot coals the way he itched to relieve himself of the rest of the story. He very much wanted to describe the Eastern chic of the apartment he was placed in and those he stayed with. He wanted to tell Anna of Henok, the Ethiopian Muslim he roomed with as well as the atheist Pakistani, Malek, who carried on his shoulders the weight of the cynical world. There was so much to be discussed of his introduction to Morocco, and on that day, he wished to begin to describe the beauty of his Elsa, and how two unlikely paths collided.

The man was on a clock. He was to present to a group of academics in a little over a week. He needed to be more prepared for this group's questions, the questions people would be dying to ask in his last speaking engagement.

He understood the drinking, the stress, and the letter worsened his condition in the last month. Time was running low on supply. He felt diminished and weaker on his walks and found himself requesting more time in bed in the mornings. The crunching of time worsened his anxiety, as he wished to reveal all information to his family before he was to talk to the students with them in attendance. Markos felt ashamed about how fast his health deteriorated, but he found himself desiring more from his existence, a novel feeling. He wanted to prolong his life if he could, for them at least. Questions would not only come from the students, but Anna and her protector. The recent days were filled with stories of his youth and his brief time in the Air Force, but after Morocco, he would reveal what they most desired.

"Anything else you guys want?" asked Olivia. Markos impatiently nodded his head.

"No, I think that's it," replied Anna.

"We have alcohol in the cart. They're about to ask for a scan, you have your watch on?"

Anna rudely rolled up her sleeve and flaunted her bony arms in the direction of Markos to answer his question. Olivia walked over and scanned both hers and Anna's watches to confirm they were all above the legal drinking age of eighteen for soft liquor. Delivery could still be applicable if all were above the drinking age.

"Total came out to $536.41. Is that good with you?" asked Olivia.

Markos shook his head with quick approval.

"Big man with big bucks," added the quirky girl.

"I don't spend money on anything but food and liquor," somberly replied Markos.

Olivia quickly scanned his barcode and confirmed the purchase with a receipt. She took a deep breath, acknowledging the burden of budgeting lifted off her.

"Great, thanks again. The dairy products should come in today, along with the alcohol, but the rest of the groceries will be here tomorrow by 5:30, so make sure you guys are here all day," requested Olivia.

Markos and Anna looked at one another, signaling tomorrow was perfect either way. They planned on making it a movie day, especially since they found another one of the boxes with all his DVDs. To their amazement, everything was in the shape it was packed up in.

"One more thing?"

"What is it?" asked Anna, sensing her mother's reserved tone. Markos took notice as well.

"Well, I just wanted to ask you both if you were okay with going to see Darius in Los Angeles after Markos is done with his lecture?"

Silence basked the home, an unamused stalemate. Her dazed look implored them to speak.

"Ugh," uttered Anna as she turned to lay on her side.

"Does he know I'm here?"

"Yes, Darius is asking for you to come. He wants to see you and is asking if you would come to dinner with his ex-wife and daughter," replied Olivia.

"Ex?"

"Yes, ex! He's never home for his daughter, just like he was never there for Mom, except to judge!" yelled Anna.

"Why does he live far from his daughter?" asked the disappointed uncle.

"He's head of the pediatric department in one of the hospitals he completed his residency in. Mom welcomed his requests to go to an out-of-state program for medical school. She was proud of her doctor," calmly responded Olivia.

"Not as proud as he was to carry his last name," added Anna under her breath, just loud enough for Markos to infer the behavior of his nephew.

"A man shouldn't be far from his family," cautioned Markos, understanding the hypocrisy of his statement after it rolled off his tongue.

"Are you guys okay with going? I have to answer him, I don't even know if you remember him, Markos."

"I never forgot any of you. I'm good with going if Anna is."

Anna, while her read rested on her pillow, raised her thumb up.

"Will he be there for the lecture at your father's school?" wondered Markos.

"Yeah. I planned to go to dinner the day before if you both didn't go. I didn't know if you guys were going to agree to going. I'll tell him after the lecture then," said the ignited woman, happy her family would not leave her unaccompanied with her pious sibling.

"That's fine, I would love to see Darius again, regardless of who he's become. He used to be always stuck to your father's hip, trying to vie for his attention. We used to have him be put to sleep before we could leave the house for any events," reminisced Markos.

"You'll be meeting a different Darius," warned Anna.

Markos did not care for their warnings, no Solomons was more of a stain on the family than him. His actions formed his recluse behavior, consequently creating a cloud over those he was raised with. The only good thing left for him to do was share the truth. Her warning shifted his energy towards the memories of his departure.

He thought about the consequences of breaking his NDA. *I'm taking the innocence of Anna, she chose this, but what about the mother, Darius if the situation demands it?* He was there to see both the children grow, children unaware of a father's activities.

He imagined the lecture, his last one and he remembered how a once shy boy was repackaged by the confidence of a young Elsa, along with Malek and Henok. He wanted to continue the story.

Time...time, it's running low. They must know all of it. Nearly all at least, forget the NDA. How ugly it'd look to them if they came for a dead man's family. How dumb we were Ephraim, we should have made sure it kept only me and you under its grasp, thought Markos.

"So, are you guys ready to continue?" asked Markos.

He felt the relief any storyteller gains once he sees the turning of heads, the reignited vigor of listeners. He saw the tiresome Anna rise from her fetal position on the sofa, and the distracted Olivia turn towards him, still slightly preoccupied with her work emails on a Sunday evening. She looked up to signal her readiness.

"Then continue we shall," said Markos.

"No, no, no. How?" asked the frustrated Malek as he finished his plate of pasta.

"What do you mean, 'How'?" retorted the puzzled Markos.

"Out of all the countries playing right now, this is the damn country you decide to go for?"

Fused with passion, the young man glided to the kitchen to retrieve his second plate of food.

"Cheese?" quickly added Markos in the form of a whisper, passing the parmesan to his fellow Ethiopian.

"See, if you rooted for an African nation, we would be with you. Even if you went with the king colonizer, the US, we would understand. But how, I mean how, could you go for Brazil right now?" continued the man while in the kitchen.

The rare soccer tournament heightened the emotions of all in the miniature apartment, as it did for all the students in their industrial neighborhood. Yells of tenants all coordinated with the delay each television set had in their apartment, serving to increase the blood pressure of all observers. In 2026, soccer was no joke to either three of the roommates, for what broke the ice, after months and months of silence, were the soccer matches each shared an investment in. Their initial shy, uncomfortable meetings in the living room were conducted in silence, but with quiet observing and celebrating, conversations sparked and moved toward shared meals during the games. As the ice smoothly melted, the scope of their discussions widened, and turned into daily hangouts around the campus. The immature boyish discussions turned their friendship, quickly, into a cordial brotherhood. The constant and rapid formation of certain relationships was a recurring concept for Markos in Rabat.

"Listen, as Henok knows, there is nothing for us to root for in our parents' homeland. And as for Africa, of course I root for all of them. But, you know, winners are winners. You grow up rooting for winners, and Brazil are winners, my friend."

"What about USA?" asked Henok, loud enough for Malek to hear in the kitchen.

"Eh, I told you. Good country, not good at soccer though."

Malek's defined laugh could be heard not only in the apartment, but through the complex and into the beach, near the apartment.

They all recognized how lucky they were to get an apartment so close to the water. They were disappointed in the practice of making guests feel more comfortable than the people who resided in the nation. The university made sure to reserve and make payments on these apartments until all the international students, who committed to paying the full price for tuition and board, would feel the comfort and hospitality of Morocco. All three studious and attentive men, recognizing the advantage they were given, abhorred such consideration after leaving the blessed lives they lived already. The optimal standards served to satisfy their reservations with the incentives, but they understood it as only a recruiting tool. They were aware of the fact they were to go home and share their experiences to bring others who would follow. None would recommend Morocco after their stay.

"Ahh, well, they are close to winning it all. France will fall to Spain, but can they get through England?" asked Malek.

Henok looked at Malek with a puzzled gaze as Markos smacked the marble table with arrogant confidence in his team.

"Are you kidding? You think my team will be the one to fall to England. Can they withstand our attack?"

Henok took the time to revel in the opening given to bash Malek.

"You give him hell for Brazil, but how terrible is it you love England, the queen colonizer," assessed Henok, chuckling throughout his jab at Malek.

The remark was met with great laughter at the table. Their evenings turned from a brash silence and avoidance to vulgar discussions spanning from the deviant children they taught, to the gossip they eavesdropped into on campus.

Markos looked to find an empty silver plate in front of him, stained with the blood red pasta sauce Henok took his time to prepare that evening. He stumbled to get up from the comfort of a full stomach and cushioned leather chair. The screeching from the garnet wooden floors turned the faces of the men at the table sour.

"Whoa, my friend, how come you can never pick the chair up?" asked Malek.

"On a full stomach, how can one think properly?"

The smacking of lips was the only response to his witty retort.

Markos smiled whilst walking to the marbled kitchen counters, where the warm Italian spaghetti sauce they lauded Henok for, was resting. The spaghetti sat in the first of the three pots, similar to the two other pots hosting the sauce and the shredded beef. Malek's discovery of the healthy lifestyle of vegetarianism forced them to split their food into multiple pans.

"Do you want me to put the pans back on the stove? They are warming up the counters," said Markos, eagerly scooping up his seconds, forcing more food down than he had space.

"No, it's marble, it'll be fine. Just make sure to cover the food," answered Henok.

Henok took special care with all the food he prepared. He treasured the holistic sanctuary of the kitchen and refused to eat food he did not cook himself, outside of the extravagance of Moroccan restaurants. The other two bland men, reaping the benefits of the man's rigid Muslim diet, brokered a deal where he would cook their dinner if they provided him, weekly, with groceries he required for the dinners. He preferred these two masters' students over his old PhD cohorts who previously shared the apartment with him during his first three years in Morocco. He preferred an atheist Pakistani and an Orthodox Ethiopian over the two English women before. They did not respect his space. His relief came when he put in a transfer with the school and was placed with two new students, newcomers to the culture of Morocco he was accustomed to.

"Were you able to make it to Algebra with your students today, Markos?" asked Henok, taking a sip of his flat sparkling water.

"No, the kids were disruptive today in class. They were worked up with the film Malek showed them today," replied Markos.

Malek let out a small laugh, recognizing he had not thought his Friday lesson through.

"Listen, the kids were really funny this week. One kid even had the audacity to question my British schooling and what made me qualified to teach English. He asked how someone darker than him could teach English."

The gargled laughter nearly turned to choking for Markos as he returned to the dining room. He watered down Henok's fanciful pasta with the bottled cola they picked up from the market.

"What'd you show?" asked Henok.

"The old movie on space travel, the time stuff."

"Jesus, why'd you show that? That probably distorted all the English and Math they have been taught these last few months. It's a difficult movie to understand," replied Markos.

"For you, maybe. The kids were on top of it," countered Malek.

The daily discussion of their course load and their afternoon curriculum with the countryside children carried on like the other days.

The university's partnership with Morocco's relief organizations gave all their international students the option of teaching their native tongue to young children or adults. The students also had the option of obtaining higher pay teaching at the private institutions many prominent diplomats and businessmen sent their children. The three men emphatically denied the request and chose to focus on the children in the inner city and the farmlands, where certain resources were scarce. It seemed planned, divinely Henok and Markos would argue, the three men, with all their similarities, met as they did and meshed like they did.

"The game is going to start soon, let's move this to the couch," chimed Malek.

"No, check your watch. You are still thinking on British time, friend, after all these months. It won't start for another two hours," said Henok.

"Well, we should still go to the sofa," retorted Malek, in his brute East London accent.

It seemed so sudden how they left their dishes and resorted to the sofas in the adjoining room of their three-bedroom apartment. One could easily mistake the behemoth of an apartment with a large condominium, but the different doors connecting the adjacent rooms showed the architectural ingenuity, as well as the privacy each individual was awarded. The kitchen and dining room were separated by a sliding door, a door similar in build to any in the home. The front door opened to the dining room on the left, a large square room with simply a black wooden table and six black leather seats. A sliding door was positioned in front of the main door, connecting the dining room to the hallway leading to the living room and the three bedrooms. The kitchen was past the dining room, separated by another sliding door, paces away from the table and chairs, towards the left most wall from the entrance. Every door remained open in the house, avoiding the nuisance of opening a stuck sliding door, a recurring problem in the home.

The white walls throughout the apartment were covered with the result of Henok's infatuation with photography. Photos of he and Markos's homeland covered the apartment. A bowl of the fruit the three picked from the market not too far from their home sat on the black table, along with six distinct, mosaic designed place mats. Light brown wooden coasters, a photo of a hyena at dusk, as well as Henok's first picture of the Rabat Airport filled the empty space and blank walls in the apartment's dining room. Henok took the time to correctly place each object of decoration in the home. He desired symmetry and symbiosis. Every inch of decoration was his, leaving the two to impress guests with his creativity.

"Well, well, it seems your team is going to get killed today."

"Friendly wager then?" asked Markos.

"One week's groceries?"

"Eh, you think so little of me. Why not do two?" asked Malek.

"Two it is."

"Degenerates," added Henok as he seated himself on the black futon placed in front of the LED flatscreen in the common room.

The view of the oceanic border of the lively city differentiated their apartment from the others. All the apartments were crafted similarly, but their view was priceless. Henok's pictures and paintings were ignored whenever dusk fell upon the city. Nothing could take their attention away from the lit-up alleyways and homes leading to the soundly waves pushing against the Moroccan sand. They could choose to watch their neighbors in the adjoining building lift their wet laundry to the wires tied through their balconies, or turn their heads a little to either direction and watch cars speed through the city. If they were to step outside in the darkness, closing their eyelids, the waves bounced to the cadence of their heartbeat. In the mornings, following the call to prayer, as they ate to the sound of the waves, the sound of spoons whisking sugar into tea and the seagulls fighting for garbage left on the beach filled the air.

Soccer games limited their vision of the city. Competition was their gasoline, and all their topics were plagued by its presence. Meaningless small talk and corny conversations moved to more interesting topics, once again, towards the topic Malek loved to discuss, women.

"Henok, when are you going to forget about your girlfriend and dive into the dating life of Moroccan women?"

"'Forget my girlfriend', who raised you? There's no woman above my Leah. You always talk of women, but I have not seen *one* walk through those doors in the last six months you've been here?"

"Hey, sometimes it's hard to talk to these women. They want a sheikh, and not a student, especially an international relations student. They want my parents' money, not me. But when are we going to meet the ghost, we call Leah?"

"When you grow up and are a big kid," warned Henok.

"Don't make him mad, he has no limits," interjected Markos.

"Hold on, you shouldn't be in the conversation. How does a man not recover from a relationship he ended, when there is a woman looking for you every day in your class?"

"Which woman?"

"*Which woman?* Idiot," added Malek.

"If I cursed, I would say the same exact thing."

"She's evaluated you enough. There's no reason she should not be in your room every night," argued Malek.

Markos was not out of loop, contrary to their thinking. He made the inferences needed to understand the evaluator of their curriculums, who would enter their rooms on a biweekly schedule, was spending an unfair amount of her time in his classroom. Markos first feared his curriculum and shy personality was the cause for the subtle disturbance of her presence, but his students were scoring at the top of all the mathematics students in the program.

"You sound jealous, Malek."

"Brother, a South African woman like that is nothing to not cause a little issue over. She is beautiful, and she's being wasted on a man like you," attacked Malek, avoiding eye contact with his adversary.

Henok looked over at the two men who were beginning to turn their playful banter into a hostile encounter. Location was important in the ensuing conflict. The spacious living room was separated to give students space. An informal dining table, where Malek sat alone with the four chairs, was at the back of the room. Along the left, leading down to the television, the room was bordered by windows displaying the Kingdom of Morocco. To the right, a brown Persian rug held the weight of two black futons facing each other on the garnet hardwood floors. The two men, Henok and Markos, sat on each futon, looking at one another with a glass table filled with their schoolbooks and magazines separating them. A single loveseat, between them, completed the decorated room.

Markos, analyzing the arrogance and limitless insults in Malek's arsenal, backed off to keep the peace. Malek was too unpredictable, and the insults he let sit in his mind were much too personal for the proximity between them. He knew the soft-skinned blonde was interested in him, but he lacked both the confidence and the will to keep an intelligent woman interested in him, at least for a length of time before she could realize how soulless he was.

"I meant no disrespect. She's yours, my friend," replied Markos.

"No, no, no. It won't be that easy. Her and her roommate are Morgan's neighbors. I'll tell them to bring them tonight. Then, we'll settle all this misplaced testosterone and effort," asserted Henok.

"Uh, wait, wait, Henok. If anything, just the South African one, what's her name, again?"

"Amy," answered Markos.

"Okay, just Amy though. Her roommate, she's a wild one, I don't want her coming in here and running around in the apartment," warned Malek.

"I'm not a fan of the girl, but I think it's very unlikely Amy would come if we didn't invite both. I'm not sure it matters if both come. If it gets weird, they live downstairs from us, they can just leave," said Henok.

"I don't know. That woman has gotten comfortable with enough men in Rabat. I don't want my name associated with that woman," continued Malek.

"Shut up. Just ignore her," said Henok.

Markos looked at both the men, clueless to who the woman was they discussed. He was privy to warnings like this from men here in Rabat and the States. He placed these warnings in the back of his mind, ignoring them, for he observed men were fearful of women who resembled them and practiced male habits.

"Clean up the bathroom and the kitchen. I just sent a text and they agreed. They'll be here in the next twenty minutes," added Henok.

Markos and Malek, looking at one another with slight mistrust, uncomfortably understood the tough position their words and actions put them in. Malek had to prove he had the aura he built for himself regarding his boasted approachability with women. Markos, similarly, was forced to prove his shy attitude with people was not out of fear. He was irritated with the dilemma, for these two and Morgan were the only people he cozily conversed with in Rabat.

His brief encounter with Elmahdi was the extent to which he branched out and attempted openness. He found his words still minced and distorted in front of people he was not familiar with. The children took time to get used to, but their shyness towards the new instructor was overcome by their youthful exuberance, a shared experience between them and him. The young man remained excited about teaching and learning from the kids, never cheating them from a sound education. Once he found the familiarity he desperately needed to let the words flow smoother, he found success in creating a glowing learning environment. The glow was from the excitement of the young children, who recognized they opened the hidden radiance of a young man, limited by the smothered past of his childhood. Many contributed to his social commitment, but there was one more to see the radiance he sheltered within.

When they showed up, the four women were greeted by the three men, along with two others Henok invited from next door. The two men next door sustained a cordial and neighborly friendship with the three, whose screams during the matches echoed theirs. Henok cleverly appreciated he was out of the game, and matched the four women with the nervous men, who regardless of the discomfort, were in his eyes capable of carrying some conversation with the open women. The night went nothing like Henok believed would unfold, because from the beginning, he did not anticipate the aggressive approach of his two neighbors.

The diverse group of men and women were immediately thrusted into the drinking games of Henok's two Swedish neighbors. Henok was the surveyor. He refereed the games and watched the eyes and strategy of the men. From his perceptive eyes, he recognized the hunger of the two Swedes as they locked into their sights, Morgan, the fellow American on the trip, and her Indian roommate, Dhriti. A small and energetic laugh left his mouth of the cluelessness of the Swedes, not recognizing the hidden relationship between the roommates, a fact only the three men knew.

The bright orange ping pong balls and the western pop music shaking the apartment hid the ten-minute announcement of kickoff. The restless noise hid the continued darting of Henok's eyes and the nerves of Markos. Henok could recognize both his roommates, who were placed between Amy and her pecan-skinned roommate, were beginning to perspire at a faster rate than the players of the game. Their moist handprints were distinct on the black table, but the two were lucky only Henok could see what the others could not. Malek, in Henok's point of view, was holding his own, maintaining the comedic undertones of the conversations and providing a competitive edge to the festivities on their common room table. Markos was where his worry lay. Henok saw as his nerves were ringing in his stomach.

Amy positioned herself to share looks of interest and fire off her quirky statements in Markos's direction. The chaotic scene hid her nervousness well. Markos was not prepared to open up and talk with her beyond her visits to his room. Out of the rooms she evaluated, she saw the most growth in his classroom, the transformation from reservation to a glaring instructor igniting students when he walked into the room. He was the first to learn all the children's names and he understood how to teach the children. Her biweekly evaluations in the back of the room turned to daily checkups as her curiosity turned to lust for the hidden, yet attractive man.

At the moment, she was distracted by Malek's statements directed at her, which Markos was quite grateful for. He tried, but nothing reasonable was leaving his mouth. Consequently, he forced his lips shut. The alcohol was inadequate to quench his nervous thirst, but Markos chose to remain conservative after intaking an ungodly amount into his system. The nerves turned his anxiety to self-hate, for the soft words he thought of would not leave him. There was nothing he could do but let Malek let his refined Londonian accent entrance the woman. Lust was insufficient to keep a woman's interest in a man who remained mute. Even Henok, in the last few months, discussed Markos's actions with the women they encountered out in the town to make life easier on him. Henok tried everything with Markos, but nothing would get the man to open up to people. Henok tried to teach him confidence was all women understood in the first encounter. Through their conversations, he understood only Markos could remedy the problem when he was ready. Henok accepted he could not do anything for him, but he realized Markos was not unaware of the desires and ways of women. In his time of reserved retreat, he paid attention to successful approaches and the terminated disasters of men. All the time, he watched with no meaningful practice. This was how Markos understood there was much Malek was doing incorrectly, serving his amusement. However, lust clouded the lack of playful wit, and with his targeted attempts and Markos's inattentive eyes, his dutiful effort in the last hour was enough.

The first hour and a half went by quite quickly for the group. The liquor consumed was the right amount Markos trained his body with over the years in the Air Force. The rest of the group was not as prepared as the American, for their livers were accustomed to modest drinking.

As is customary in such gatherings, the large group became fizzled into different satellite groups. Morgan walked with her joyful roommate towards the futons with Henok, who was glued to the game. The soccer game was in the rearview for the others. Only Morgan and Henok placed their eyes on the irrelevant television since the guests arrived. Morgan's roommate attracted one of the Swedes to meet her on the couch as she toyed with the incapable man's heart and mind. The other Swede, belligerently drunk and occupying their toilet's surroundings with his vomit, was creating a mess for the three men. The confused Amy and her roommate were glued to the dining room table, now near the entrance where the men had eaten dinner.

Awkwardness occupied the air of the platonic inhabitants sitting at the black table. They had turned the music off and watched the game, letting their conversations and the game's announcers hold audible sway over the night. Amy's impatience grew immensely due to the liquor and her insatiable appetite to feel a man's touch that gloomy night. Everything was in Markos's favor, her desire for him and her loose cadence as the night came to an end. He not only recognized all the signs but sat in agony and shame at the ability to not capitalize on a woman he believed to be normally unattainable.

His distaste for the night worsened as Malek's childish remarks began to score him some easy points, and as the points accumulated, the last stroke of death was Malek's noisy journey to the room with the illuminated Amy. His lack of humble fibers showed in a smile from the side of his mouth as he walked the beautiful woman to his room, enjoying the sulking eyes of the guests following him. He took his time to wish everyone a very blissful good night.

"Lucky bastard," uttered the Swede on the futon, as he watched in displeased jealousy, finally beginning to understand his meaningless struggle with Dhriti.

Henok immediately looked at Markos and felt the pain of his embarrassment at the loss of such a good opportunity, not just for sex, but for a connection capable of jolting him to the material world, for the children, and he and Malek, were not enough. He was left with the woman, victim of Malek's distasteful words, a woman whose hidden beauty was missed by the group due to a reputation she was unaware of.

His head sank to the table, under his folded arms, unaware of the hidden gem in front of him. She was the first to comment on his mishap.

"Well, that didn't take long, did it?" sarcastically said the woman, the first words he heard from the guest.

He immediately recognized her tongue, the prepossessing accent. It was, again, his favorite in fact, with a touch of grace tied in with her melodic tone that he never overlooked.

"You're French?" replied Markos, unable to hide his curiosity, as his head rose too quickly to hide his interest.

"Not completely. Good ear, I was raised in France, but my father is Lebanese and my mother's French and Senegalese," continued the woman.

Markos's nod of understanding carried into a silence the woman had no use for. She was very beautiful, especially when he took a careful second look while her eyes wandered around the room. He was lucky she was hiding from the silence he caused. His eyes glued onto her, evaluating the structure of her toned body. He immediately recognized the body of an athlete, track and field by the shape and definition of her bones, evident in how her complexion lit up in certain linkages of bone and joint. She wore a sleeveless red blouse allowing him to observe the definition in her neck and arms. The tight baby blue jeans and low-top white athletic shoes confirmed his inferences. His eyes slightly shifted upwards to the smooth skin sitting under her cheekbones, hidden by her subtle makeup. Her loose, wet curls sparkled in the light, a canvas to her proportional and symmetrical features. The circular eyes were weighed down by the darkened bags, serving to humanize a godly configured woman. Her pointy nose was glimmering, and with a large smile, was able to bring joy to any man blessed to court her with just an easy glance. She limited her words around strangers which served to hide the beauty and the unmistakable mystique surrounding the cinnamon shaded woman. His analysis of her social mobility and confidence brought him to a conclusion the woman was leagues ahead of the ignorant participant of love he was. He continued to analyze her, noticing a slight carelessness when it came to her presence. Unbeknownst to him, she had carefully surveyed each member in the room the moment she arrived. Nothing he could say or do would surprise her, but she was aware of how embarrassed he was, knowing how Amy felt about the shy bachelor.

"How do you feel?" asked the woman hoping to reignite the conversation.

"Huh? I'm a little drunk if that's what you mean...what do you mean?" ignorantly asked Markos.

"You lost out on something today. It was fun watching a novice squeal under pressure," added the lady with a devilish smile.

"Novice? A lot of jokes from a woman who seems to be the complete opposite of prude," retorted Markos.

"Ahh, men creating stories about a woman to save their pride. And which men have you seen me with?"

She sighed at his attack. Her body moved to the side to block others from their conversation. Their bodies faced one another, as their eyes did when they spoke.

"Word gets around," said Markos, still having his tired hands folded across the table.

"Never to the actual person it seems, shows you the loyalty of the friends around you," replied the slightly disappointed woman. She tried to remain unphased.

"Well, inconsiderate friends seem like the theme for today."

"Ahh, don't worry. You're not the only one who hasn't felt the touch of another in Morocco," said the woman, surprising the man sitting to the right of her.

"Enjoy the company," said Markos, not believing a word she said, hoping it was the truth.

Markos watched as he tried to look for tells in her story, the way his brother showed him. Ephraim was fearful people would take advantage of his apprehensive appearance. He could find no lies, but something told him he was making a mistake with the woman. He did not care for warnings ringing off in his head, for in hindsight, pain may have been avoided, but the memories were invaluable. She did not shy away from his remarks either, showing resolve.

He walked back from the kitchen with two plastic, blank white cups and handed his counterpart one of them as he poured the cheap vodka Malek bought off one of the Englishmen in the building. The small talk was very brief before the meat of the conversation began. Their social radars were off as the search for the truth started.

"Why didn't you try something with Amy, she was waiting for this since you came here," inquired the headstrong woman.

Her hazel eyes darted around his body as she began to feel a semblance of lustful connection to the rigidness of the man. She could see more clearly his defined and stocky features from his walk to the head seat of the table.

"Sometimes I go silent with strangers, it needs to be pried out. I've never fared well with judgment. She didn't look prepared to do all of that," truthfully replied Markos.

He could see Henok sneaking looks from the living room. The common room table was the closest to the dining room, enabling him to sneak a look or two from his seat.

"You can't be afraid of judgment; it won't work out for you."

"I've been told, but sometimes the words refuse to come out, the calculations don't add up in my head," uttered Markos, downing a shot after colliding the cups with his drinking mate.

"Have you ever had a girlfriend?"

"I had one for a few years in America. It was good, but even then, we had some awkwardness for a while."

"How did she get it out of you?"

"What?" replied Markos.

"Words," joked the inquisitive girl, drunk from the drinking of the day's activities.

"Ahh, she would wait for me to say something and refused to speak until I did. It was annoying, but it forced me to speak."

"Alright, what would you like to say to me?" asked the woman.

Markos took a second before replying to the tricky question. His pride flew out the window. *Tell her she's beautiful. She's divine. She definitely isn't modest, but she sure is interesting. She really is the most beautiful woman I've seen here, a sneaky beautiful we men desire, but are too dumb to notice until she is swept away by an idiot.* Markos's head spun at the idea of breaking the minute-long silence she forced on him. She nearly gave up on his cause as her hands retreated towards the table. Her sway over him motivated Markos to speak, surprising even himself.

She had moved when he had returned from the kitchen moments earlier. As he sat down at the head of the table, his legs pointed to her seat, diagonally left of him. Her legs nearly touched his, also pointed directly at him as she faced him. As his silence forced her hands to retreat to the table, she moved her legs away from him, making her presence feel smaller while remaining in her seat.

"Would you believe me if I told you there weren't words that could describe how beautiful you are," said Markos, feeling the corny statement slip out of his mouth.

The woman's cheeks lifted as she blushed uncontrollably and let out a methodical and soothing laugh, peculiar enough to grab the attention of all four on the sofa.

"Not bad, not bad at all. You're truthful, at least."

"My turn. I think you are very interesting, Markos. I think you're cute, enough for me to ask if you'd like to go to dinner with me because I know it'd take years before you'd ask me. You're the first genuine man I've met in this country, who'd respect me before attempting to bed me," requested the young woman.

The room went quiet, only the waves and anomalous honks in the streets slithered through the apartment. Markos was psychologically empty, for his world was flipped by a single request of an endearing woman. It came from somewhere farther than left field, a request he believed was sent first class by the One above. His answer could not be misconstrued. The beginning was as quick as the end. Like one walking through a door unaware of what lay ahead, a simple nod and an infectious smile served as the first step in their union.

"Well, Markos, for some reason, I very much look forward to what comes next with a man like you. It may seem weird now, but you have dazzled me with all the warning signs you are giving," said the woman in her tasteful accent.

"I apologize for my surprise, you surprised me. Can I at least get a name to match the personality?" asked the spell-bound man.

"I'm glad you like my personality, already. My name is *Elsa, Elsa Saleh.*"

"Elsa…I look forward to taking you to dinner," said Markos.

They continued their conversations through the night, long after the party, alone, both intrigued by the mystery of the other. Some judged, some looked with jealousy at the smiles and daring conversations shared between the two as they filed out. Intellect was how they began their journey towards intimacy. They talked; they spoke of many things that clouded their self-pursuit towards perfection. They shared far more than what was appropriate for the first night, but a spark grew between them, the potential of it all serving as amusement. It was rushed, but for both, everything about their lives in Rabat was a sprint and they each took a leap of faith towards the other. The leap of faith was all it took for the foundation to be built between the two.

eight:
She's Mine, In the End

Frozen stillness held the stagnant cries in place. The screams in the saddened atmosphere were for the recently lost souls. Time worked against the requests of their loved ones. Sitting beside the slightly opened door, dazed by the confusion of the last few days, was a man wondering why his deity was so cruel to him. Everything pointed towards the man continuing in solemn loneliness, but agony filled his system after finally obtaining a taste of the forbidden fruit for it to be ruinously whisked away. Joy ended with blood-stained fingers, blood laying still on his hands, stained from the catastrophic event three days prior.

He sat for three days and two nights, distanced from food and essential nutrients, looking through the glass door of the mediocre hospital room. The balking demeanor of the doctors and their hesitant orders meant nothing to the man who looked after his treasure. His beaming love was reduced to a gloomy, motionless figure. His life was in her hands, and she was deteriorating, cell by cell, organ by organ, losing all forms of mobility by the moment. The clutching of his cross served as a meaningless dichotomy, for his anger towards Him was rabid. If his tongue had not retreated to his liver, he would curse God. His faith was tested farther than he could go, a point where every man was told it could never.

Markos recognized his legs were going to give out, for only water accompanied him through the tearful nights alone in the hospital. He did not yet respond to the doctors, nor to the few friends who remained close to him. He slowly knelt, with his sweat-ridden back rubbing against the off-white walls, towards the ceramic floors where he finally rested his backside in frustration.

I can't close my eyes; I may miss her waking up...or her last moments. I'll see it all happen again and again in my sleep. Don't sleep! She's it...she's it. There's nothing but her, she's it.

She's it! She's it, roared his thoughts.

Markos's eyes began to betray him. They were leaning into oblivion. The three days of dried tears and baggage laying between his eyes and his moist nose began to pull its weight.

Thunderous cries were heard from the other rooms of what Rabat called an intensive care unit. This worsened the creeping anxiety he sat with in the waiting room. There was not a shred of power he had to change the situation. Few made the effort to explain her condition to him. He worsened the state of all the overthinking family members of patients waiting for their loved ones. The four others waiting for news were beginning to feel for him, forgetting their family members at moments when they watched him drown in his own anguish.

He never heard the phrase "touch and go" in Arabic so much in his life. One nurse snuck into the waiting room, for all feared the intimidating frustration young Markos sat with. She was the only one to acknowledge Elsa's chances were incredibly slim, let alone returning unscathed. The lightning rod of a statement came the second morning, where the nurse shared, she would be losing her mobility, legs and all, if she survived. Nothing she came with would leave the same. She explained overhearing a doctor saying an imam would have to come within the next few days to say the customary rites. They were overworked and had no time to address the frustration of those sitting in the waiting rooms, especially for someone as unstable as Markos. She asked him to prepare, since Elsa had less than a fighting chance to make it in the next few days. The bold nurse had no bedside manner to accompany the somber news she shared. In retrospect, he admired her confidence, but flaming emotions clouded his clarity in the moment.

Moist discharge fell from his darkened nose, fogging the reading glasses he continued to wear since *it* happened. He stained the discolored off-white walls with the blood, unknowingly leaning on the structure to hold his weak body up through the endless nights. He stood facing the automatic sliding doors, separating the parakeet green walls of the intensive care unit hallway from the tense waiting room. The flickering ghostlike lights in the dim waiting room did not take his attention away from the doors. He shook every time the doors directly to his right opened, letting the doctors in to change shifts. The sliding doors no more than fifteen feet in front of the back wall he leaned on, the one holding his attention, was where the nurse appearing with the news of Elsa would come through.

Hope and hell arrived nearly at the same time. His body violently shook at their entrance, visibly letting out clamorous sounds of horror. From within, the power of the unforced sounds weakened Markos as they entered. Markos could not bring the words out when the three showed up, all holding their own worries for the woman suffering in the poorly lit emergency room. Ephraim's grizzly hug nearly collapsed the overstressed Markos, acknowledging his older brother would be joining his beloved if he did not take better care of himself in the time of defining strife. Words jumbled together at the thought of portraying the weight of his feelings.

"I... I tri... there was nothi...," struggled Markos, accepting the tightened hug of his brother as tears trickled down their soft faces.

His brother knew she was never to come home, let alone with Markos. Ephraim understood the moment his flight took off from Los Angeles, with the loss of her life, his brother could be next. He, and only he, had to be the one to retrieve him. Ephraim's tears burned as they fell to his chin. He could not shake the shivering feeling of disappointment for his brother Markos, a man who was sufficiently forging his own path in Rabat the last two years.

"Sit here, I talked with the nurse when we walked in, and they said you won't make it either if you don't get rest. We'll handle it and discuss the next steps. Eat this, and please rest," softly assured Ephraim while handing his brother a granola bar.

Markos looked past his brother, noticing the parents of his dear Elsa, shaken and terrified with thoughts of losing their troublemaker of a child, their only offspring. He recognized the stocky Lebanese man, a man of great stature, offset by a friendly face. The Lebanese man tempered his emotions, holding his wife's tearful face close to the left side of his dark peacoat. Markos did not recognize the mysterious mother, the catalyst of Elsa's psychological ailments, the mother who refused to hold any conversations with her rebel. The unmanageable tears streaming down her face flooded her estranged husband's chest as he did what he could to console her shame and regret. The man walked over to Markos, who had moved to the opposite wall connected to the sliding door of the hallway, awaiting with sheer terror. He sat by Markos, massaging his own gray-black facial hair before he spoke. With ease and assurance in his manner and tone, Elsa's father put his hands on the bloodied fingers of his daughter's lover.

"Sleep, she is discussing her case for the both of you with Allah. She even is making a case for her father who always refused to walk into a mosque. There was nothing you could've done more. Rest and await His judgment," said the patient man.

The empathetic assurance was surely planned between the conniving Ephraim and the fearful father. Nothing could help his situation, but tragedy was to shortly arrive, and a rested Markos surely fit the bill over a shaky individual ready to snap.

The granola bars dormant taste was far too much for Markos. The dullness served as a reminder of his poor diet in his stay in the hospital. Even though the bar was bland, like an addict in need of more, his stomach grumbled and shook in frustration from the lack of a sufficient amount of food. The bar served its purpose in allowing him to quietly drift off, right before the afternoon sunshine snuck between the dusty hunter green shutters of the three-floor hospital. The dull bar did the job of putting him under, sheathing him from the long-awaited news. Her mother and father's cries at the instructions and details, stated by the truthful nurse, shook him awake. He trembled after understanding the catalyst of the cries and screams of the Nubian woman and the Lebanese businessman.

Was it over, it couldn't be? Hope faded so quickly.

His head sank to the ground as his soul left his body, whole and alone. He laid sulking, as a sack of meat, while his essence left to caress the love of his life, the woman who had opened him and cracked the mystery of Markos Solomons. She linked all his mysteries together. Ephraim gave his brother a reminder of his soul's place of residence.

"Hey, hey!" said Ephraim, snapping his fingers in front of him to get his attention.

"I'll take care of it, it's complicated here, but I'm here for you. Go home, and we'll take care of it. There's nothing left for you here, or in Morocco. Mom is waiting for you back home. Pack the apartment up. We need to leave soon, we go home tomorrow," said Ephraim, consulting him as he dangled with the last of his breath.

"May, may...can I see her?" asked the frozen Markos. His eyes focused on the black spots of the ceramic tiles below his feet. He did not move; his body did not shake. His eyes remained glued to the ground. He was leaning on the wall, his bottom plastered on the tiles. He spoke with mellowed confidence. Markos's head laid on his brother's sport coat, the soft cushion holding his body weight as he attempted to rise. The hands held the blood of his hope, one on the shoulder of his brother, the other, clung to the wall separating her flesh from his.

"No, it'll worsen this, this feeling, your feelings. Get up, she wouldn't want this for you. Please, go home, please," pleaded Ephraim, tightening his grip on the hand on his shoulder while doing his best to pull him up.

"Were you the one, the one she told her father of?" interjected the Nubian woman.

The woman walked over to the grief-stricken man. Distracted, they did not hear her pace over to them from the wall by the other door. The eyes of the few in the room drizzled with tears for him, while others feared what would come from her mouth.

"Ye...yes."

"Go home. You don't need to see this, she was my responsibility and I left her, and you protected her. The burden of this is ours," assured the mother.

Everything: the dashing doctors, the symphonic sounds of the machines, moved so fast in the hospital. Words were flying around, and Markos remained still, psychologically wobbled in the heat of tragedy. The aroma of sadness was powerful, a deplorable atmosphere for the malleable Markos. The others were aware of the risks, knowing what she was to him. The discussions between the three served as a precursor to their entrance to the room, planned and calculated, calculated by the caring Ephraim. His considerations were instrumental in getting Markos out of the hospital safely, for he was at the edge of death, death from the stabbing pain of heartbreak. Once dumbfounded by the death of Elmahdi's wife, he finally became cognizant of the force of the heart.

"I'll take him home, but I would like to see my daughter first if that is possible."

Elsa's father and Markos walked a few feet into the hallway, past the door, to see what remained. They were paces away from the glass window displaying Elsa. The voices of the disappointed doctors could be heard before the two obtained a full picture.

Markos stumbled, falling at the broken sanctity of her body. She laid lifeless, ripped and prodded, forcing the man to crumble, falling from a lack of sleep he avoided in the days of horror.

"How was the dinner though?" asked Anna.

"Yeah, what was that first encounter alone like?" inquired Olivia.

Markos looked at them, his uninformed kin. He wondered if they would ask for more of the story if they knew the tragic way things ended. He sat and smiled, remembering Elsa's warning, her one stern request if they were not to live an eternity conjoined.

"The first dinner...it was, it was interesting. I wasn't sure how a dinner would go, knowing how I would tighten up. But she expected it to happen, she was prepared for it all. I came cluelessly to her doorstep, and from then on, she was in control," said Markos.

His giggles warmed the spirit of the mildly lit apartment. The layout surprised Markos each time he came downstairs to eat with the family. The space remained the same, his mother's interior design defeating time. While the couches differed, as well as the hue of the walls of the home, the two-piece sofa set was framed the same, one faced the television and the kitchen along the back wall, while the other was placed parallel to the window, closest of the two to the door. Olivia placed one large glass table above an expensive rug on her newly hardwood floors, the only change from the once dirtied carpet. Another table served as an armrest for both couches if necessary, sitting between the two, connecting the set. A few paces passed the lounge area, the circular, glass dining table directly sat under the chandelier. The inexpensive adjustable light, holding one large ovular light, with five surrounding miniature lights, still outlasted most of the family. Connected to the ceiling, the light hung uncleaned, collecting dust over time. The sliding door, a little further from the table, ended the modest living room. The kitchen was directly connected to the communal space, to the right of the table, allowing anyone downstairs to speak to another. An intimate area, in a time, was once obstructed by his father's bookshelf near the front door. He was grateful for its relocation to the cluttered garage.

The stories were becoming a welcoming practice, a form of therapeutic recreation for the family. The three lived in blissful peace together, comfortable with each other's presence. Taking a few weeks, they continued with their uneventful routines without worrying about the misplaced questions they once had about one another. Markos tirelessly prepared for his last speech in his free time. With the help of the unoccupied Anna, they shared the announcement through a new social media account she opened for her muse. He in turn, began helping her apply for graduate programs and provided her with an ace in the hole as a reference. He was not diffident, whisking his name around for family.

Olivia's life slowed down to the pace she was accustomed to, and she enjoyed the growing relationship of the two. She took the time to build a similar relationship with the both of them, and so, the recurring leisure time together began to be a festive event. She knew this to be a defining moment for her daughter, a time where each minute with Markos would alter her existence.

The lights were dim, a dim red Anna preferred when the stories began to be told. *How Mom would have disliked the automatic lights, the switching of colors and all,* thought Markos.

Markos worked in the common room, his music simmering into the ears of his hosts. The soft rhythm and blues would play throughout the day as he worked, under the sound waves of his faint voice as he read through his written words. He lowered the music to play in the background during his stories as well, heightening his memory of the times with the music he once enjoyed with loved ones. Drinks would be drunk, laughs would be shared, and for his guests, memories would be made. Under the guise of his worsening health, they treasured the falling sands of time.

"I knocked on the door, and she immediately yelled from inside for me to come in. I heard another loud yell from the back of the apartment. I rushed her with my presence since I showed up fifteen minutes early," said Markos with a childish smile on his face.

Anna and Olivia felt the warmth of the love he had for Elsa. Their smiles and laughs echoed his. The vivacious details could not be emulated by a man of mystery who never felt emotions for another. They could trust a man more if he lived and loved. They were beginning to tap into a lost portion of his scarred soul.

"I walked in, and she said I should come towards the back of the apartment," said Markos, recounting the details.

"I went to the back of the apartment, and she had on these beautiful black pants or jeans, I couldn't tell, but they were tight on the hips and loose on her ankles. I looked up, and she had on just a white bra, and a heart-shaped gold necklace. I was stunned and didn't know what to do," said Markos, softly chuckling at his unfailing memory.

Anna's arms leaned forward on the glass table. She, with her mother, pondered about the same question.

"What did you do?" asked Anna.

"I tried to look away, but she told me to look at her, and help her pick a blouse. She asked me why I would be afraid of the body I hoped to become familiar with. When I tell you she knew exactly what she was doing with me, I'm not joking. I helped her pick the blouse and we went on with the night."

Olivia's dinky smile for her uncle's story of love had a hint of envy hidden within. Anna's laugh shook the table, allowing Olivia to fly under the radar.

"What was it like? It was your first time out without Henok and the rest of them, right?" wondered Olivia.

The intelligence, Markos found, of both Anna and Olivia, showed in the picky questions they posed in the opportune times. Markos noted the similarities of the women with the rest of the family, specifically his mother and Ephraim.

"It was awkward, I felt unsure, but I never felt unsafe. She knew every response I would have to every situation. She watched me. She studied each movement and reflex I had to each problem. She watched my eyes change up in the craziness of the streets. For the most part, I stayed indoors other than my time at the campus.

"If we were cut off by a taxi, bumped into in the market, or yelled at for breaking some custom, she saw how I would handle a situation. She assessed and analyzed me. I thought she was trying to figure out if I was worth her time, but that wasn't it. We had talked so much that first night, so if she didn't like me, there was no point to us meeting up. She cared to know me, so in a way, I felt much more comfortable with Elsa than I did with Henok and Malek. They were forced to know who I was."

The women watched him explain the inception of the unlikely pair. Familiarity sparked their interest. Untimely stories of love were rampant, but intimate recounts of a story so close to home were rare for anyone. A family tarnished by power, they lived apart from emotion.

Hours went into explaining the expedited relationship. A little over eighteen months was all he received from the verbal commitment of an eternity. While recounting her beauty, memories of the minutiae drifted from his grasp. As the details faded, subconsciously, he brushed his pockets, searching for the pieces of paper he used to jog his memory. He refused to open it again. The letter's only purpose was to be passed to his kin. Only task left for him to do was share his life, for all that mattered was *his* truth.

He explained how he built a relationship on a deeper foundation of empathy. The empathy and patience Elsa had for him as he adapted, went hand in hand with his slow approach to understanding a colorful individual as extroverted as her. He learned, from their similar upbringing, she would constantly talk to others to avoid the silence she was raised around. He repaid her attentive attitude towards him with his own keen awareness of her and her unique mannerisms.

Many of the connections Markos made were convenient like his roommates. He was unable to go deeper with those he befriended at times, believing they were all a means to an end. As much as he fought the feeling in the past, he knew his relationship with Angela would always end. All his friendships were the same. He knew his demeanor was a burden on their social life. He loved Angela and Henok, but they were not like him. They could not understand him, only a few could because a handful took the time to. Elsa put her all into Markos, and he could never understand why. Learning of her mother, he understood where the resilience came from.

Yet, the intrigued women ignored the underlying themes of his thoughts. They imagined a flurry of traffic and the tangy smell of the foreign land many of his memories resided in. They listened as he recounted holding her hand, following her through the backroads only a few knew, learning more about the place he once lived.

Elsa knew everyone, and everyone knew her. He conceded he was extremely jealous of how many men were so in tune with her, calling her by name, waving to her from afar with no fear of her lover. He understood where the misconception of her as a harlot came from. He even told the women how he addressed the nuisance, and how she quickly brushed it off with simplicity.

"I'm yours, for as long as you treat me as you do now, I'm yours," confirmed Elsa.

That was that, thought Markos, remembering the walk they took past the golden lights, illuminating the windows of all the family-owned shops in the streets of Rabat.

"She was different from most of the girls from Europe. She wasn't stuck up, but she was fearless and brave. Her courage allowed her to try new things in the face of whatever social adversity was present. She always dealt with some form of gossip because she was so energetic and talkative. She didn't care for anyone's opinions of her, though. She didn't care about any of it. She didn't care for the modest woman, she was *the* woman, the one they wanted to be."

"She would force me to try new food and new fasts. I tried to have her follow my religious fasts, like the ones your father and I used to follow, but she refused because she wasn't much of a religious person. She believed but she didn't practice because she lacked conviction in causes. It was some weird stuff, she would say, and I would just go with it. What was interesting though, was that you wouldn't expect someone like that to be as respectful as she was," continued Markos, taking important sips of water ahead of his checkup the following day.

"She would make all of us in the apartment, Malek and I, and anyone that would come to my place, observe Henok's religious practices out of respect for Henok. She respected all our faiths and practices and placed a deep meaning of it in our lives, even as a nonbeliever. She believed in the divine, but not a denomination. Elsa was the social butterfly who's landing spots would turn to gold after she left. She was unique in her own right, as any woman you share your heart with should be. Interestingly enough, she restored my once stagnant faith in God, and she rebuilt my perspective of people. I followed her with my eyes everywhere she went because my heart laid next to her soul, and it was crushed when she left me," recounted Markos.

Knowing her journey ended in death, curiosity loomed in the minds of Anna and Olivia. The girls were wary of asking about her demise, but the story would only continue for a day. Elsa's story was not vital to what the women really wanted to hear, but as Markos stressed, context clues were needed to understand certain decisions. The night would detail the sudden disasters making Markos who he was, but first a light was to be shone on the woman who cracked the puzzle. Neither of them were selfish. As much intrigue as there was in Markos's unique stories, they wanted to know of their direct lineage. They wanted to know about Ephraim, all his exploits and journeys. They wanted the gossip, the dirt, and all the facts in between regarding his movement. They were anxious as he got closer and closer, and they clutched at the brief tidbits shared about him. Markos could see from the corner of his eye; they were thirsting over any information about Alondra and Ephraim when he described his early experiences in Sacramento and Rabat. Nevertheless, the sympathetic women leaned closer to learn and inquire of his shortened journey with Elsa.

"What was she like?" asked Anna.

"Witty, very witty. She was intelligent and the closest thing to free-spirited as anyone was. She had her daily demons following her, but she never allowed those to spoil others' days. Elsa didn't allow people's premonitions of her to touch her attitude. She would make friends with anyone she met, as soon as she was able to conversate with them. She was socially superior, and she had a great understanding of human cues," answered Markos.

His mind's mixture of truth and slight revision of Elsa, and the words he shared, took a toll on his body. He took a minute to wipe the sweat off his forehead. Slowly, he placed his glasses on the table as he grabbed a napkin from the steel holder at the center of the table. First, he breathed on the glasses, clearing them of the fog from the perspiration. Then, he wiped the sweat off his balding head, the frontal lobe clearly wet with the weight of the moisture. He detested the balding pattern of his hair, beginning with the front of his head, leaving him with the larger forehead he feared as a child. The sweat suits he wore around the house did the aesthetic job they were tailored for, hiding the increasing dampness of his clothes. He broke the audible seal of shyness, but he was always nervous when he spoke to people, a habit he never outgrew.

He resumed describing how her vivid personality became contagious to anyone that spoke to her. Elsa was not enough for one man, but she constantly adapted in order to make a relationship work, a similar feat Markos attempted. Markos walked them through the memorable dates and the day trips she encouraged Amy, Henok, and Malek to tag along on. Her vibrant approach to each individual made it difficult to decline her requests. One with innocence in their voice could manipulate people's moral compasses. Her prowess was never limited to people she knew. The people at the markets and stores all recognized her. They were given satisfaction from her brief biweekly visits. Markos marveled at how beloved she was, constantly wondering if there was a woman he was less deserving of.

He recalled a trip to Casablanca, after nearly six months together. When Henok was to graduate, she convinced him to forgo studying for his last remaining final exam and take a trip with them. He not only went on the trip, but she was also able to persuade the disciplined PhD student to drive them all down.

Markos grew weary thinking of the ways she would leave him during the initial months of their relationship. Markos made the women aware of this embarrassing fact. They were not shocked, already aware of his timorous manner. They attempted to relive and imagine the sorrowful nights he described when she would leave him to return to her bed, early in the relationship. He shared how he tussled in the night at the bone chilling thoughts of being left high and dry by a woman he believed to be superior to him. He was not prepared to express this amount of the truth, for there was much he was forced to hide from the women. He blurted the facts of his psyche out as a reflex, trying to best explain the great disparities between he and Elsa. He hoped to use this point to better engage the women and build empathy he would need later. Much of the difficult decisions still needed to be revealed.

"When did it stop, these fears?" asked Olivia, concerned for the twenty-seven-year-old Markos, seeing the drenched man in front of her. She saw him like he was, years ago in bed struggling with self-doubt, drowning in his thoughts and bodily fluids.

"When we first acknowledged we loved each other," answered Markos quickly.

"How long did that take?"

"It took about five or six months...before she let me sleep well again," said Markos.

Anna sprung forward to quickly make her presence known. She had a question to ask.

"Who said it first?"

"Said what?"

"*I love you,*" awkwardly replied Anna in a soft whisper.

Markos pondered the intentions of the question. The words had its own effect on him. From the stories he had told, he believed the question to be trivial. He continued to think in order to save face. He agonized over how weak he looked, sharing a flurry of information regarding his emotions. Anna quickly recognized the showmanship and correctly interpreted the silence.

"Never mind, stop thinking about it. We know who it was."

Markos nodded in assurance, deciding to finish off the recollections of Elsa with the story of how she reminded him she would always be his.

"Hey, who thought driving in this idiot's car was the smart thing to do?" asked Malek as he squeezed into the middle seat, between Amy and Elsa.

The car smelled of the repeated spilled splashes of tea during their morning drives to the university. The cramped car would have to bear the weight of the four students celebrating the completion of their cherished mentor's PhD studies. The remaining final had no bearing on his academic record, since the disciplined Henok completed his reports and presentations for his rigorous courses prior to the exam. A measly university writing requirement forced him to take a late exam. He had done so well he could turn in his exam blank and remain unphased for graduation. Elsa's notorious tactics were still utilized to break his rigid study habits. A celebration was in order. He was the one who took care of them during his time in Rabat. His departure meant a piece of their life would leave with him.

"You aren't close to two meters tall, why would you sit up front?" asked Henok, smiling and finding Markos's stoic face in the front seat, unchanged by the joke.

Markos had not spoken a word, even as Henok cut his hair before the trip. He looked into the mirror, sulking, a masochistic moment for the evolving Markos.

The women fulfilled the assurance Henok desired for his joke with their gargled giggles, serving to anger Malek. They were nearing the famed city, the victim of recurring trips during break times and stressful encounters with the university's curriculum.

"Elsa, where to, first?" asked Henok as they entered the borders of the city.

"Corniche."

Henok nodded in approval, excited for the last trip to the city. His jubilation was shortened by the impatient tourists obstructing their path to the destination. The overflowing traffic emerged once they were within eye view of the beach's parking.

"I promise, I won't miss driving in Morocco," said Henok.

They included a last trip to the Central Market, but the bulk of their time in Casablanca would be enjoyed at the beach with the activities Elsa prepared for. Their youthful impatience quickly subsided once they reached the breezy shores of the beach. The weather permitted loose, comfortable wear, but for a Californian, the weather did not permit entrance into the active waves.

Markos, since the car left Rabat, remained quiet as they unloaded the packed car. Henok's departure raised questions for his future with Elsa. He waited weeks to ask the difficult ones, and after finding the courage, she ignored his moment of maturity. She deflected and hid her fear of committing to answers to his submissive questions. He was angered at the fear he lived with the past few months, the fear she would leave him for someone more deserving of her attention. In his time of bravery, she scoffed at the questions. Shortly after, he began experiencing an emotion unfamiliar to him in his brief time with Elsa, anger.

She attempted to use ignorance as a weapon in the car, trying to spark up group conversations and involve him in playful banter, but he refused to heed any ground. The car ride had its awkward moments, even the unfocused eyes of Malek recognized the tension, but Henok's positivity concealed the unappreciated mood of the couple. Amy and Malek's tricky situation played a role in easing the ride as well. Their cordial relationship was built on lust instead of true emotion. Nevertheless, Malek refused to end his pursuit of an arrangement like the one Markos and Elsa had. His hidden desires were constantly ridiculed, but Amy's tunneled vision allowed for the joke of a union to carry on farther than expected.

"Alright, get the food and drinks out, Malek. You and Markos bring them to the same spot we went to last time. I'll bring the soccer ball and the chairs, and the girls, if you could please bring the blankets and towels," added Henok.

The walk from the parking lot was a good distance away, keeping the noise of the traffic away from their afternoon festivities. He could see the ships in the background of his friends, floating on the water, motioning towards the port. He desired to partake in the scene. He attempted to fight what his mind decided to be a silent protest against his love.

Markos found himself sitting next to the vibrant speaker, in charge of the rhythms of the day. He sat on his towel, watching his friends enjoy while he remained a captive of his own crafted future. He dug his hands deep into the lukewarm sand in frustration. The air was soothingly neutral, carefully carrying the sounds of the birds and laughter of those on the beach, along with the music ringing from his speaker. He could see his friends enjoying the abrupt game of soccer beginning to form with their towels and hats as the posts of the goals.

He believed she was going to leave him. He believed himself to be holding her captive, unable to let her roam loose. He was keeping her as a caterpillar, when the time for metamorphosis had come. Others would bend over backwards for her, but he felt the silence was the only ultimatum he could sufficiently give her to make her understand what she meant to him.

He rationalized his lack of enthusiastic inclusion with a stomachache, a lie that hurt Henok's peaceful heart. Henok could do nothing but watch the one he cared for most, struggle with his own self-destructiveness, remembering Markos's tussling nights. The walls were too hollow for him to ignore his friend's shaking. Markos was pleased when they all sat for a break after the first hour and a half on the punishing sand. He felt joy, balancing the sand between his toes, watching the others curl near him as the sun reached its highest point for the day. A smile cracked as he inserted himself in the conversation, still avoiding Elsa, a cursed practice he inherited from his parents. She was aware of the tactic's origins and chose to avoid him when he would revert to those souring practices of ignorance. The posturing of the couple was ignored. The others enjoyed the time and would not let the issues become theirs.

Elsa believed her lover would be filled with regret if he did not enjoy the group's last day at the beach. She quickly glanced over at him and saw his forced smiles and decided action was needed. After the prepared meals were ingested, with the conversations reaching a stalemate, her swift hand signals and eye contact sent a silent yet resounding message to the others to disperse. Amy quickly grabbed Malek and challenged him to go into the water and he gladly agreed.

"This man will drown without me, I must go and help him," Henok quickly added as he left the sand-soaked towels he sat on.

The doubt Markos was battling crept in between his toes, his fingers, and his socks, all where the sand was pestering him. He could feel the pressure of the mental struggles. They both sat in silence for a few minutes. He was able to watch her as she faked a few smiles towards their friends running into the water. She felt his judgmental eyes on her. He reveled in her beauty, highlighted by the searing heat and sand sitting on her body. She chose a modest outfit of a white crop top and black athletic shorts. She had planned on not entering the water. In case she faltered, she chose to wear a baby blue bikini under her clothing, the color sneaking through her moisturized garments. After the heat of his eyes pushed her to the limits, she chose to remove the white tee, revealing the perky breasts and the sharp rounding of her hips she maintained through her rugged workouts in the university's gymnasium.

He succumbed to her vast beauty, how her luscious hair sat on her browned shoulders, a few strands escaping to her breasts. He tried to conceptualize how a woman like her dropped to his lap, how he could even choose anger as an emotion to feel towards her. His anger slowly turned into self-hatred as chilling quietness covered them. The city went silent to them, shuddering at the choice ignorance of their problems. Her abrupt questions would change the mood of the trip as she chose the ideal time to act.

"I talked to your mother yesterday, did you check on your brother?" asked Elsa, her eyes sticking to their joyful friends.

Markos, embarrassed at the curveball thrown at him, answered as best he could.

"I haven't. I heard he was touring through California, speaking at universities. He's starting to compile the list of demands the students were asking for," answered Markos.

"Not about what he's doing. She told me he has also found a woman, a Puerto Rican girl," said Elsa, surprising her love.

"I didn't know about that. We don't talk about those types of things when we talk. We barely talk anyhow. They are both asleep most of the time when I can call home."

"Well, you should call home, your mom misses your voice. Your brother is gaining more attention than she expected. She's hoping it'd be you that keeps him grounded. I just wanted to relay the message," softly asserted Elsa.

Markos was irritated at the direction of the conversation when there were much more important matters to discuss. He knew his brother was making his mother proud with the empowering voice he inherited from their father, using it for good, but he did not care for that, his time was his own. He needed Elsa to understand, he needed her to answer him.

"Your conversations with my mother are your conversations. Keep them to yourself, I know what my brother is doing, I talk enough with my family. Call your mother," said Markos.

He had gone too far with Elsa.

Her mother was a soft spot, a point of contact he always knew must be avoided. Her mother did not see eye to eye with her because of their trailblazing similarities. A French woman born into a Senegalese family who would become a practicing private lawyer in Nice, understood a certain amount of resilience and discipline is required in a lifestyle where luxury and gluttony were highlighted. When she married a Lebanese immigrant, the unexpected union was not accepted by her own family. Regardless of her mother's enduring attitude, she discouraged the same behavior in her only daughter. Her mother demanded complete obedience and when her daughter did not comply and chose to leave her side for Morocco, to build a path of her own, no calls registered from Nice to Rabat. Her father, under constant fear of her overbearing mother, called his golden child in secret.

The mother was taboo.

Elsa sat in incubated silence, registering Markos was truly under psychological fire to bring her mother up. She ignored his remark meant to stand as a slight. She forced him to endure an unsure silence while waiting for her opportunity.

Markos sat in instant regret.

He chose to eat whatever would come. He followed her path and focused on his friends a few paces ahead of them in the water. He saw Malek attempt to dunk the unsuspecting Amy in the water just to be slammed in by Henok. The two lovers sat centimeters away from each other. The mental miles separating the two was deeper than the current spiritual divide between the pair. Smaller arguments and constant confusion lead the love affair to stand at an impasse, unaware which way it could go since both concluded the first half of their master's program.

"Do you...do you think you betray God?" asked Elsa, still focused on the plots of the three hypnotized by the cooled waters.

Markos stiffened, completely aware of the mental warfare to ensue. The unsurety in which he waited for her words scared him into slowly rising from his seated position. He dug his feet into the sand and pushed himself up in order to avoid the misdirection of the question. Markos refused to begin a conversation he could not control, a conversation he feared would push for the end of their brief union.

"No, please, *s'il vous plait,* come sit next to me?" asked Elsa.

As he sat down, she spoke again: *"Kayf haal-ik?"*

Her angelic voice, in the accent he loved, weakened any resistance he had to her words. His retreat to her side left him completely in the sand, away from the area the towels rested.

Markos's eyes were prisoners of the moment, caught idolizing the woman to his right. The sun sat parallel to his love, glistening her skin and all the sharp curves of her body's outline. He found her eyes, and sat under her spell, unaware of where he would go. Deafening silence hijacked his ears, intaking the words she projected into the holy air between them.

"Please, have patience with me. It is as difficult for me, as it is to you," added Elsa.

Markos uncomfortably sat on the heated sand, confused at what she was trying to get at. Nothing lived beyond the truth of his feelings. Their months together meant nothing in the face of his truth. The relationship with Angela taught him about the importance of saying his peace.

"I love God, I have missteps, but I don't knowingly betray Him," spoke Markos, continuing with her game.

She fiddled with her hands, feeling the sun slowly shift towards her back, the heat of the conversation's momentum brewing.

"We all betray God. The ones he's blessed most are the ones who betray him the worst."

She paused before continuing further, taking her attention to the grains of sand before her.

"He's blessed some with the power of expression, the power of oration. Some have the power to manipulate others. Their words have powers even they don't understand, because it comes from Him, you don't think they, like us, can betray people?"

"I don't think orators can betray people. People betray themselves by giving men and women they think can fix their problems with words, power. There are enough warnings about trusting people, even people of the 'cloth'. Ignorance isn't betrayal."

"Says who?" asked Elsa.

"Me…" answered Markos.

Elsa, continuing with the persistence the questions required, pondered her retort to his reply.

"History says otherwise. You have seen the God you pray to give the greatest of men and women the power to speak to others, and most of the time they create enemies and cloud people's judgment. You don't think they can betray God?"

"We all ignore God at times. I'm taught not to fornicate, but I do. I'm told not to live with envy or jealousy, but I watch you talk with men, and I can't help myself. I watch others talk to you with no effort and I feel a way. We all ignore God and His rules at times, you can't blame just orators for their message, you have to look at those who listen and act on it. *Ignorance is not betrayal*," continued Markos, letting the reeking worries and stress out from within his soul.

"You don't believe that the great speakers of our time, politicians and all, are not guilty of some form of deception? Are their words not deceiving and full of guilt, like the thoughts you convince yourself of regarding me?" asked Elsa, patting her stomach to comfort the bubbling discomfort persisting from fear. More pain than she expected lingered in her stomach.

The heat, the sand, the voices of their friends: the environment was betraying them.

"They are no more guilty than those of us who love, cry, and hope each day. We lie to each other to perpetuate a fake courtship with one another. Your questions mean nothing because the examples are in the scriptures and the internet. Our thoughts are full of ignorance, but we blame people for what we can't control, for what we can't fathom. We must remain faithful, but above that, truthful," answered Markos.

Soon after he let his statement out, he understood what the ambiguous discussion was created for. The basis of their relationship was being tested. The trust was missing.

"Do you trust me and my words?" asked Elsa.

Markos looked to his hands for the answer. The brief hesitation was enough to worry both of their future.

"I love you, more than I have ever loved. I pray for forgiveness because I am taught to never love anything borne from this world, but I love you and I cherish you. To trust…hmm, I trust you and it doesn't lessen or increase due to the love I have for you. *However,* I do not trust that you will stay with me. I await the day you are to leave me," spoke Markos confidently.

Elsa, stunned by the statement, released the hold she had on her folded knees. She laid back, flat on the towel, thinking about the power of his love, the fact he had no belief in her loyalty to him. Her stomach worsened as the butterflies began to aggravate her mingling insides.

"I… I love you, though," said Elsa under her breath.

"Has it been enough for either of us to feel comfortable?" asked Markos, softening the motivation of his anger.

He mirrored her action and chose to lie next to her. Both their heads connected in the sand. The meaningless action served to calm the other with the touch they had forgotten the feel of. The sanctitude of the touch, their treasured bond, nearly became a distant memory to the other.

"What do you look for from me?" asked Markos.

"I don't know. I'm not sure I care for anything more of what you can give me. You're here, more than anyone else has been, even for the few months we've been together. I love you and I wish I can show you how much I love you while satisfying the fear I have of commitment. There's no man I want to share my life with other than you, I wish you could understand that. There are things in my life that have stunted my ability to show commitment to you, but I will try. I am yours, for as long as you want me. I don't want my words to betray God, that's the fear I have of sharing them with you and answering your questions. I don't want to fail you," said Elsa.

Markos sat unmoving, ecstatic about the promises, simultaneously feeling the statement betray her desires. His words would do the same, deceiving his perceptions of truth.

The echo of her words meshed with the cadence of the sloshing waves. The smiles and laughs of all on the beach lifted his energy. He waited in silence for her statements to sit with him. He laid there, happy she could not see the opening of his teeth, the slow warmth of his heart diffusing to the rest of his body. Elsa knew how to work around his insecurities with her words. Happy tears trickled down her eyes, a feedback of emotion Markos felt on the left side of his neglected hair. The tears were shared by the man who lied connected to her, like an arrow, pointing to the city from God's point of view.

Markos turned his body towards her, waiting for Elsa to match his movement.

"I promise you an eternity," softly said Markos.

He softly kissed her cheek, rushing her body with excitement. In the moment, they thought of the obstacles they overcame. As a bear would pounce on a prey, he wrapped her whole body with his, happy the rollercoaster of a conversation concluded in his favor, while still feeling as though a temporary solution was found. The adjournment was met with laughing admiration and excitement for the cursed eternity they promised each other. As he wrapped her body with his, she moved to sit above him, looking down at him while her body rested on his. Filled with elation, she covered him from the sun behind her. In unfamiliar spontaneity, she looked down on him. To remain unmoving, he dug his hands deep into the sand. No words could encapsulate his heart's desire. He attempted to steal what he could of the earth, taking a moment of time he believed he deserved as she smiled. Both forgetting the initial inquiry of the conversation, would go on to betray God, as they kissed one another.

"The rest of the day went as we all had hoped. We stayed for a few more hours into the evening than we had expected, playing soccer, volleyball, and all the things we hoped to do. We built a nice little fire on the beach and sent off Henok the right way," said Markos, watching tears dry on the faces of the two women.

He explained how they angered Henok by buying him a cake with his Western name, *Henry,* plastered over the cake. The enthusiasm he spoke with rejuvenated the emotions of the room, transforming their cheerful crying to hesitant laughs. He was saddened by how quickly their happiness would shift to hate, hatred of the unmitigated circumstances of life.

"All happiness comes to an end, though."

Anna showed her interest in the end of Markos's youthful stories by holding his hand as he walked through the mental journey of sorrow again. The touch was necessary, more for her than him. She felt his rough hands, callused by the dried, endless tears he let out in the nights alone in Suzie's presence. He thought of the guest room, the host to his drunken adventures when she first touched his palms.

She watched as his other hand began to fidget with the armrest of the sofa, waiting for Olivia to return with more of the soft tissues. Her crying helped disguise her trip to the kitchen for a snack. She was affected by the changing dynamics of his relationship with Elsa, and the envy of a love similar to theirs.

Anna's arm left Markos once her mother returned. He, unnoticeable to an inattentive eye, slightly shook at the loss of the touch of family. He would have to go on alone.

"We graduated together, we even lived together in our final year of school. Amy and Elsa had taken Henok's room, but she stayed in the room with me. As our relationship grew stronger and stronger, our families became more familiar with one other. Her father met my mother, and they sometimes spoke over the phone. It seemed like everything was going well, but it always was weird when we talked about anything after Morocco. We avoided it, knowing we'd go anywhere with each other, but the problem was where.

"After graduation, we chose to stay a month or so after, to not rush the move. It was supposed to give us time to choose where to go. We promised to spend time with each other's family to see where we best fit. Everything seemed to be going well, but it changed quickly. We were rushing to prepare for the move out. We had a long list of things to not only get rid of, but things to shop for."

"About three weeks before we were planning on leaving, I got a stomach flu and was unable to take Elsa shopping around the city. There were some things she wanted to bring back home to all her family and cousins. She had pledged to be a better daughter to her mother and father, and a better person to the rest of her family. She rubbed that off on me, so we were going to shop around for some collector type things to bring back to our families. We planned to help each other shop. After I got sick, she helped me out and did the shopping for Ephraim, Mom, and even Alana."

He paused, slowing before continuing. A somber laugh left his mouth before going on.

"It was like yesterday; I will always remember this day. I can see it every night I go to sleep," said Markos.

His body momentarily shivered at the preparation needed to recount the end. He avoided eye contact of both women, using the tragedy to mask the truths missing from the recollection.

"As she returned, Amy, God rest her soul, made the error of trying to drive home during the rush hour. She had returned to the apartment safely and as Malek and I walked out to help them with their bags, the traffic covered our vision of the street where they were parking. It's as difficult to park during rush hour as it is to drive. Regardless, Amy attempted to parallel park on the street. She was unaware of the coming blow from an impatient taxi driver, berating the pickup truck behind him for cutting him off on the street. He pressed on the gas in a show of force against the pickup truck. He passed up a few cars. He didn't know about the space the other courteous drivers were giving Amy to park. The unexpected space they had given them was taken over by the driver. He collided with them, instantly killing himself and Amy."

He needed a break to continue.

"Death was cruel to Elsa, sadly, taking its time with her. It whisked her away from me, providing me with the agony of a graphic image of what destruction looks like."

Anna and Olivia sat stunned and shaken by the revelations of their houseguest. His desolation and isolation were explained. They were in the company of a confessed lover, a man who faced more spiritual woes in his first twenty-eight years of life than most would encounter in two lifetimes. The sorrow of the gloomy man forced him to remove the revealing letter sitting in his pockets, day by day, shifting from outfit to outfit, accompanying him through his days.

"This letter, after all these years, was the only thing left for me, from my love. This was left for me, on my front doorstep, the day I had my accident. A few days later, the faces of two beautiful women claiming to be my family appeared. I am grateful for all I have experienced and the people I've lost and loved. There are things that test your faith, but at the end of the day, faith keeps you standing," lied Markos.

Tears accompanied the poetic ending to his formulated beginning. For the women, they believed triumph would follow. While he loved the women and spoke with invigoration, he made sure to lie by omission. Omission and emotion were useful when lying to those he loved.

"Faith? You still had faith after all that, finding love and getting that taken from you?" asked Anna.

"Anna!" yelled Olivia.

"No, it's okay. You are right in the fact that I wished to curse God in all the words and languages I knew. But sorrows were the only thing in my heart, not hate. Your grandfather took me under his wing and made sure I didn't succumb to my sorrows and watch it scab into hate."

Anna and Olivia's questions showered Markos after he shared his testaments of the past. There was not much more he could share with them, for he not only made promises to Ephraim, but he was separated from the tragedy after it occurred. There was a discussion, a hidden parlay, between Elsa's mother and father, and Ephraim. All he could remember was a handshake between her father and his brother. He was unsure of all that surrounded the peculiar embrace, but he knew of a few phone calls shared between the two following the tragedy. Ephraim's secrets could fill a lawyer's bookshelf, but he was opposed to sharing, even on his deathbed. He knew remnants of the deal struck, but he chose to remain oblivious of the facts. There was shame in his weak state following the crash. He broke promises to his love, and even when she left him, he did not have the boldness to face the necessary arrangements.

"The last few months in Africa were filled with so many issues prior to the crash. There were protests in Rabat towards the end of our studies. The people protested the corruption in Morocco and the gap in wages paid to schools and other important components of the community. Malek, surprisingly, found a passion in fighting for his students and had become somewhat of a voice in the university regarding these protests. Malek's pessimism was challenged by the innocent eyes of his students, whose parents faced the weight of certain wage gaps and corrupt officials. For his efforts, he was arrested, and it was me who had to go get him out. He was beaten to an inch of his life, completely naked when he came out of the cell, only covered in a blue towel. It was darkened by the stains of his blood. They handed me his bloodied clothes and told me, 'Fight what you know, idiot.' I was so full of shame I had not helped my friend. The shame didn't do anything for me or for him. The British embassy wanted nothing to do with him. After they refused to help him, the police continued to bully him and torment him, flattening his tires, bashing his windows, and giving him tickets. He couldn't even finish his studies. It brought me great shame that I couldn't do anything for him, a source of shame I promised I would never let happen to anyone I loved again," said Markos.

His sweaty hands balled up into a fist remembering the incident. He remembered how he started in Morocco with no friends seeking a righteous path, just to be left with sorrows and just as alone as he started. He wished he could have protested with Malek, another moment where courage was needed. *I asked for the experiences the world had to offer, and I got it all.*

"Was there nothing you took from Morocco, no happy memories?" asked Olivia.

"For months, I remembered the shame of my inaction and the loss of my love. There was not much good that came with my stay in Africa. There were many good memories locked away, etched in the back of my brain. I remembered a trip I took with Elsa during our second winter break to Ethiopia. It was as revealing a trip I can remember," said Markos.

The trip was the pinnacle, the high point, of his eventful correspondence with Elsa. He remembered the glaring concerns clouding his mind on the shaky flight. The twelve-hour layover did nothing to rest his fears. Ephraim and his mother were meeting him in their family home, a trip he believed as Ephraim would say, was written. A family wedding forced them to converge onto the city, coinciding with a trip Elsa desired. She berated him about visiting his family home, for he had already seen France through his work trips around Europe on the Air Force's dime. This trip worked his mind into anticipating the different storylines of what could go wrong. Henok reassured him he would be the one picking him up from the Addis Ababa airport, giving him time to gameplan his approach with the family.

He told his family he and Elsa required their own room. He was afraid of the judgmental eyes, living centuries behind what the current culture accepted. A French girl, not a Senegalese and Lebanese girl, would be what his family would key in on, a European. A country that was not colonized did not forget the attempts made, and the fact they were disrespected still left a repulsive taste in their mouth.

On arrival, pleasant surprises repeatedly presented themselves to him. He was not expecting to meet the treasure Henok periodically reminded his roommates was waiting for him. The young woman, clothed in her religious coverings, was as sharing and innocent as her partner. They talked, during the first hour of the drive home, of their own wedding happening in a year, an event Elsa and Markos promised to be in attendance for. Markos insisted they remain with them in the large, gated compound for the duration of his stay, not only for the enjoyable dialogue, but to avoid the three-hour round trips from their home to his.

Markos noted how Henok leaned on his fiancé for direction, a universal concept in any culture or religion. She reluctantly agreed once she laid her eyes on the palatial estate.

Markos saw the newly painted golden gates on arrival. Following the three honks from Henok's truck, the gates opened to another world. The dead vegetation outside the compound hid the surprise of what lay on the inside. The secluded home was over two miles away from any other victim of civilization, strategically stranded from others in hopes of a show of opulence. He thought of the home as one of his grandfather's early mistakes he once described to him.

Guarded by the family's security, the men lying on the other side waved them in, automatic weapons strapped to their backs. They smiled as they closed the gate behind him. The quarter mile drive from the gate to the multi-housed compound, Markos believed, was the essence of all Ethiopia had to offer. He saw in the night, from the bright radiance of the automobile's lights, with the fluorescent garden lights, the rainbow of flowers on each side of the road. They were lined up against the borders of the solid golden barriers, keeping the straying hyenas away from the property. The trimmed grass from the edges of the cemented road to the flowers placed near the barriers was no more than twenty feet, showing uniformity and symmetry in the design. The house was freshly painted, the shade of the black ginger tea he fell in love with in his first visit.

Surprise filled the place his fears of judgment and impartiality once took. Markos recounted how the trip showed the truth about the love of his family. Open arms were the least of the hospitality. He was the oldest of the long-lost daughter, the prize. The child that caused worry amongst the family was now the one bringing hope, a chance of further ownership of a piece of posterity. The opening of the gates initiated rhythmic clapping from the anxious family sitting a distance away. They bombarded them before they could reach the home. The guards' smiles misplaced his attention. He was tickled by the lack of anticipation, for he hated surprises, but none brought a smile to his face like the people hiding near the dark copper fences. Once they opened the car, he believed the cultural song and dance in the heat of the night could be heard kilometers away. The infectious happiness would have had others join in. He recognized his mother's elation from her exuberant singing, and he felt the helpful hand of his brother on his shoulder as he walked out of the car. Impossible to miss the only white woman in the dead of the African night, he admired the commitment Alana made to the family through her unsuccessful attempts at catching the tune.

There was no language barrier, no cultural barrier, no love lost. The family welcomed her as the savior of the boy. Elsa's excitement grew from the pulsating encouragement of Markos's mother. Their ghostly phone calls carried their illusory relationship on a thread, but their embrace once they met brought him nearly to tears, an image captured by his dynamic hazel eyes. Ephraim and Alana's enthusiasm in meeting his cohorts from Morocco carried into the morning, as they all escaped the lingering sleep their bodies required. The first night, the night of the introductory small talk turned into a story filled occasion, full of laughs and recollections of what each was currently entangled with. They barely retreated to their rooms in the morning as the sun rose, but he remembered as he returned, how his views on mortality had been challenged.

He expected an absence of love and a conservative form of judgment. The words Elsa shared with his mother, the biweekly checkups her son found uncomfortable, built character in her eyes. The welcome they gratefully received, the love he never expected from the childish uncles and aunts awaiting them, forced his cheeks to feel the brunt weight of his persistent smiles. It was *her*, the catalyst of it all.

He remembered, before they ended their first night in Ethiopia, looking at the woman he would love for the remainder of his perishable, celestial life and doubling down on his promise.

His deep gaze into her eyes as he entered the darkened room was meant for more than words. Markos looked at her with a consistent and fixed purpose, admiring the whites of her eyes, looking deep and seeing the disturbed past and glowing future. The stare given back by Elsa, in turn, caused all the accepted euphoria to ascend within their veins. He realized the truth in all the laughs shared in the night. In their lonely moment together, as one, he believed his words of promise would be words of action. In a stolen moment, as their eyes glued to one another while they guided each other to the firm mattress, he spoke to her.

"An eternity, that's what you will have from me, an eternity."

Pieces of the trip lingered in his mind: the boat ride into the mysterious island near the family home, drifting through the safari and stumbling onto a waterfall, and the treks through the city landscapes, all playing a role in rounding out the trip. He remembered Elsa's father agreeing to take time off to meet the man his daughter effortlessly gushed over. He enjoyed a free vacation, a stay in the large palace of a home, food served by those properly maintaining the needs of the well-off family. He remembered how he had forgotten the family wedding bringing all of them together to begin with. He recounted the minor field trip they were obligated to make for a tailored suit, both for he and Ephraim. Two peas in a pod, they were the only two to forget to bring the proper attire for the wedding. Much laid deep in the thoughts of the busy men.

The smiles of Anna and Olivia impeded the streaming waterworks.

"It was a memory that needed to be remembered. Thinking about her in a hospital room, lifeless, wasn't healthy. Months went by, accompanied with the alcohol that would go on to destroy my liver and kidneys, before I could remember the good and not the bad. At first, I remembered the sweat filled nights, not the promises, not the emphatic energy she had on our trip home. Losing her was enough to kill me, but I remembered that she was in here," concluded Markos, softly signaling towards his sweat covered head with his shaking finger.

The beating his body took to recount the chopped story removed an abnormal amount of liquid from his body. He did not expect the abnormal perspiration, nor the excitement of describing the godly memories of Elsa. The glimmer of the balmy lightbulb shining directly above flushed him of the brief desire in the memories. The clock, from a quick glimpse, passed the threshold of required rest. The once inquisitive and admiring eyes of the women turned to crimson, a side effect of the lost tears of the women, for Elsa and for their uncle.

The rest will be shared with them in the letter after I am gone.

Preparing for the much-needed sleep, their thoughts would be filled with a plethora of questions about his past. Going into another day, it would be filled with preparation for his last speaking engagement. The women were still to pack and prepare for the trip. There was still a question they had for Markos.

"Knowing what awaited, would you have lived and loved like you did?" asked Olivia.

She feared asking the question, but she desired an answer.

"Without hesitation," said Markos looking to the ceiling, mesmerized by the image of the first embrace shared between his mother and the overjoyed Elsa. The image would not leave.

"She linked me with life, she changed my existence. It was hard before her, and she helped me live. I survived day by day before her, avoiding touch, avoiding contact with people. The small stuff, saying 'hello' or 'good morning' to random people in the street or store, rubbed off on me. I learned to live, *experiencing* the atmosphere around me," concluded Markos.

Satisfied with the response, Anna spontaneously tapped his arm to give him reassurance. He was a man desperately in need of a touch of love. Her innocence stopped his tears, impervious to his emotions. To Olivia and Anna, strength was what was needed to survive what he went through and still share the past. The recollection was the first time they did not have Ephraim's legacy lingering in the back of their mind. Markos did not care to overthink the unfair practice of hiding key moments from the women, specifically Ephraim's involvement in certain situations.

Nevertheless, Olivia quickly joined in the embrace, putting an arm to his shoulder. The women heard his backstory, the man who endured. Markos treasured the unification before the veracity of his tales could be challenged. He let go of himself and was brave enough to meet their touch with one of his own. He brought his hand to theirs, connecting the missing link to the family. The embrace, an uneasy task, was well accepted. As a touch of love, it sat as a touch of thanks, an appreciation for hearing him, the first people to do so. He embraced them for his brother, for the sacrifices made allowing him to stand tall in this moment when others could not.

nine:
Repercussions

The shadow, a leering outline of a man deep into the trees, was all he could make out. He resented the decision to throw away his minacious weapons, unaware of who was approaching.

There was no one left.

He already had buried his mother and his brother, and he knew his sister-in-law would never return to see him. His morning began with the routine moping, focused on memories of love and his means of living. Choosing to have his black tea outside on the autumn morning, he hoped it to be as quiet as any other lost day.

Cursing himself for his lack of preparation, he held no premonition of whether it was a friend or foe coming to his home. He refused to run back inside, showing his hand and allowing the individual to see fear in their target.

The mysterious figure chose to walk in the middle of the road, eyeing the landscape of trees and fields encompassing his path. The leaves felt the disturbance of his stride, falling behind him as he inched closer. The environment's hemostasis was swayed adrift by the man. The birds, the scavenging squirrels and the existing creatures around, were only prepared for the rhythmic steps of Markos. They hid as the ghost came closer. The alertness in his walk eased Markos, believing at first a celestial being of some sort encroached. He was still unsure of who was near his enclosed space, the home deep in nature, away from the untrustworthy masses he hoped to avoid.

Years and years with no visitors. The mailmen don't come this late, and they never come in this far.

Markos looked upon the man as he made his slow strides towards his recently renovated home. The home was turned into a winter cabin-like structure, the architectural setup changed to match the peaceful seclusion of the area. This figure's attempt to disturb his solitude brought an uneasy fear. Markos was reaching retirement age, yet, despite his ailments, his mind was still sharp. He remembered the last time he spoke to someone outside of his university engagements. Devastation, along with hope, once had arrived at his doorstep, only to fade from memory with each endless day. With no neighbors, conversations were kept limited and impersonal outside of occasional discussions with his doctors. Rumors of the mail switching to an automated drone system threatened to take away his only form of daily human contact.

Markos invested all his visual prowess on the man walking towards him. His eyes were now glued on the trespasser and without his glasses, he could not make him out. His once sniper-like eyes succumbed to age. The man was now about half a mile out. Markos decidedly utilized the minute context clues to obtain an educated guess of who he was.

From the slow strides, Markos understood he was dealing with a man of age. The stocky fit of the man's attire showed Markos how much time the man had spent in flesh form. The solid dark colors of the clothing solidified his inferred ideas of the man's seniority. Markos believed the man to be much older than he originally began to think, for the gray in the man's facial hair began to show more as he got closer.

The angel of death, thought Markos.

The black dot, once creeping from nearly a mile away, was much closer. The face carried familiarity as it lingered closer and closer, striding straight from the original point of his journey. Markos focused his head in on his black tea, wondering if an angel was coming for him. He wondered if he, the man who deserved the least time of all those who rose with him, would finally see his end. Closer and closer, stride by stride, Markos's anxiety worsened. Years would go by before he welcomed death, losing all fear of those who would come for him.

A quarter of a mile.

Five hundred feet.

The angel's facial structures were covered by grayed out facial hair, a black knitted beanie, and thick lenses sitting in front of his aged eyes. The black overcoat was now much more apparent than originally perceived. Cluttered by lint, the grayish strands became clearer, matching the tight hairs on his chin. The angel was possessed by the demonic horrors of time and age. His charcoal slacks ended where his ankles rested, showing the creeping black socks lying in the dark suede shoes.

The man now slithered a hundred feet away, showing his yellowed teeth at first recognition of Markos. No angel was near, surely a lost article of time as the farsighted Markos caught the man's face. He was still unsure of his identity. There was fluff surrounding the man's aura, the formalwear and the facial hair, along with the subtle blur due to his distance.

The man passed the trail of trees, dodging the warning system of fallen leaves for trespassers. The farmlands were a sight to behold to the intruder, but he had one mission in mind. Another thirty feet or so, after passing the road of leaves, he would be at the grass field where the house lay. He saw Markos's car parked nearest to the road, on the left side of the house. The endless untamed terrain behind the home left the area unadulterated and private. The man would require such privacy before he spoke to Markos. He watched Markos sip his tea from the freshly painted white porch, hoping Markos caught his smile upon clear sight of him.

The man was nearly there.

Markos could sense the familiarity through an internal hunch. The warm tea should not have burned him as it did, it should not have awakened the senses as it did. An alert was sent through his body with every nearing step. He fought the feeling, acknowledging the impossibility of the man standing in front of him. As the man approached the first of the three steps lifting guests into Markos's abode, he took his beanie off, disclosing more of his identifiable structures. Markos sat frozen, clutching his beige mug of tea in his left hand. He sat confused of the intentions and the motivations of the individual to afflict him with his presence, now, of all times.

He refused his mind's request of muscular movement, any movement. Anger, love, and shame, all these emotions besieged his boiling blood pumping through his thickening veins. The blood within begged for some show of physical action. Still, as the wind chill suspended them on his front porch that Californian fall morning, he refused to move.

His father, basking in the happiness of seeing the boy he left decades before, pulled a white, porch chair beside his son, moving closer towards him. Markos, dazed, suddenly arose from his warmed seat and laid his tea on the wooden side table between them. As he stood up, ready to end the life of the man who shattered his existence a lifetime ago, he placed his hands in the large pockets of his sweatpants and retreated inside. He needed time before deciding to act. He did not want to live with any added regret in his endless sentence in solitary.

This daunting memory, a recollection he rarely revisited, reappeared that day of all days.

Judgment Day, he remembered.

There were many unmemorable moments between the defining days of his life, the ones that left him blank. In that fall morning with the visitor, every aspect was unexpected, a day in which he answered for his mishaps and failures.

The unfortunate encounter was alike to the looming disaster of the current day upon him. The day startled him with unscheduled visits. Anna's excitement and use of social media gave his last speaking engagement a large social following. He was not prepared for the ignorant reposts to spread the message so quickly, yet he was grateful his words had importance to Anna's generation of students.

The shortsighted announcement brought a representative of the Speaker of the House to his door before his undesired checkup with the doctors. The engagement with the young intern was quite brief, a reminder of the obscure confidentiality agreement he relinquished his voice to, years ago, at the request of his power-hungry brother.

The agreement defined their relationship.

The rushed encounter outside of the home on he and Olivia's way out caused the scrupulous woman to overthink the visit, only catching a brief view of the insignia on the tinted motorcade. Markos was incredulous at how lucky he was. Anna was out with a friend from college for the day, showing her friend around the uneventful tourist locations in Sacramento. Her pursuit for the truth would have been relentless and he promised Ephraim he would never discuss the agreement with anyone. Markos refused to recount all the facts, especially points in the past where his brother's image could be tarnished. Impatient with the lack of hospitality the Speaker had, ignoring the importance of calling first, he brushed off the intern with a swift declaration. The lies would remain the truth, and facts would remain shelved.

The prompt confrontation was not enough for Olivia. Markos could hear her ponder the racing thoughts in her head, unaware of what the issue could possibly be. The enigmatic question, which first entered her head when they were introduced, cyclically began to reappear. She thought about the question more after the motorcade took off.

Who was he? thought Olivia.

Very quickly, her guard went up. She became as fierce as one must be, protection was still needed for her young one. She required an answer, but she knew she was in no way entitled to one. Markos was very careful to avoid conflict with either of the women, yet, feeling the pressure to answer for this visitor, he betrayed the silence he was protected by. The man did not care about self-incrimination.

"I would appreciate it if we could keep the visitor between us," uttered Markos in fear.

She was in no mood for the dance around the facts. Her curiosity was not important, the protection of her daughter came first.

"Who was that?"

Markos hesitated. He weighed telling her the true purpose of the visit in order to hide it from the tenacious one. He vaguely remembered Anna suggesting her mother always told her the truth. A risk had to be taken.

"The man works for the Speaker," answered Markos.

Olivia thought of the magnitude of the word. *Speaker... speaker of what, the House? The insignia is enough to believe it, but why?*

The morning drive to the doctor's office turned stale for a few minutes. She refused to continue the line of questioning until she herself could identify who it was, he referred to.

Markos thought of the demon. Thinking of the demon, on this day of all days, he knew the long-awaited death was near. He knew the demon, whether it was his or one he created for himself, made the necessary preparations for his demise. Judgment day was again near, and his mysterious death date was cause for concern. He wondered if he would be able to finish the tales of his journey with Ephraim, and if he could use his death as a reason to bring the facts to light. He thought of his body fading as he let go of the truth, hiding him from the impending doom of his words. He pondered whether death transcended promises made to the living.

Prepare for me, my angels, for my demons have cursed me, surrounding me with the lies and serpents of the garden, thought Markos, remembering the words Ephraim once told him after he lost Elsa. He smiled into the misty passenger window, accepting, even welcoming death.

The smirk awakened a new line of questioning for Olivia. She would infer, understanding the importance of the man sitting in the passenger seat.

"Are you in trouble?"

"No, but I'd like the visit to stay between me and you. I am unsure of how the girl would act," calmly replied Markos.

"*Anna* is a grown woman. I think she's mature enough. Are *we* in trouble?" wondered Olivia, shaking at the thought of the man bringing trouble to them.

"No, and yes, she is grown. The girl is smarter than any of the people I've ever encountered. There's no telling how special she is, but the short time I've been with you all also has shown me how unpredictable she is. If I divulged the reason for the intrusion, any form of resistance would be met with punishment. In this time, intellect isn't needed, patience is," concluded Markos.

Olivia, frightened, demanded the truth with the look she gave Markos. The look was one Alondra mastered in her dismissal of Markos, a look ushering mixed feelings from the man.

Markos took a deep breath, using the in-between time to draft an acceptable half-truth.

"Years ago, when I had my falling out with your father, there were some things that needed to remain hidden. There were some meetings behind closed doors, promises made to certain individuals, and people we contacted to coordinate protests. Stuff like that all had to remain hidden. As you guys know, after Elsa died, my grief was treated by being given a new purpose of working for your father. I saw all the action from behind the scenes, and after I fell out with him and the people that worked with him, I agreed to sign a confidentiality agreement. It protected both me and Ephraim, from the law, and each other. I was reminded today of not only my failing health, but of the agreement I made years ago. I was reminded that a man who believed he had nothing to lose had things to lose."

She could not comprehend the mystery of the threat. She focused on the confidentiality agreement, a promise to keep secrets hidden. She focused on the fragment which Markos said the agreement protected them from each other. Olivia processed the information at a rapid pace, accepting his willingness to hide the worry from the family, for he was unphased. She did not understand his preparation for death, the weight of the mental warnings of the day.

"You're right. We can keep this between us," said Olivia, sarcastically smiling at how serious the situation was, showing false resolve in the face of the looming threats.

His undisturbed outlook on the problem calmed her. The rest of the ride was characterized by the blues of the music in her car. They each had their thoughts to accompany the ride, he with his figureless demons, and she with the confidentiality agreement. The stoic response from both emotionless creatures carried on through their trek to the top floor of the hospital.

Markos's mind went black as he finally took a seat on the cushioned bed, once again, the *V.I.P* room. The nurse held full control of his body, reporting on her tablet all the pertinent facts of the peripheral condition of her patient. Where she asked him to stand, he stood. When she asked him to cough, he coughed. A slave to the room's requirements, his mind remained black, refusing to think as the nurse drew his blood and conducted the imaging exams. Olivia's thoughts were as formless and bland as his. They were entranced by the day of demons.

They sat alone, feeling the fizzling heat emitted from the LED bulb above them. Neither spoke, nor did they acknowledge the long waiting time for the results. The pair did not notice the group of doctors and nurses outside his door, wondering if they could get some scoop of his last speaking engagement. They had questions, various questions spanning from rumors about the main members to the philosophical consequences of their words. He was among friends and foes in the hospital and the prying eyes were all around him. He and Olivia, shielded by their current worries, were blinded to the awe of their spectators.

Markos, finding Olivia in a similar state, put the silence to bed. She was not thinking of the full picture.

"I ask one more thing from you. Whatever we're told, good or bad, we keep it to ourselves. The girl doesn't need to know," requested Markos, aware of the signals his body was sending.

Olivia sensed the confidence in his voice. She nodded in agreement at the request.

Minutes passed until he could make out his doctor in the distance, walking towards him with the doomed results.

How similar, he thought.

The doctor approached, with the demeanor of sadness, unable to smile or walk with any encouraging endearment. Markos knew the news before he reached the room. He watched as he scowled at the prying eyes outside the room, sending onlookers away with an embarrassed wave. The doctor remained his only confidant over the years. The news he was bringing felt like betrayal to a friend. The doctor was the catalyst of it all, forcing Markos's hand, calling the family he encouraged him for years to talk to. Being his caretaker over the decades of isolation Markos faced in purgatory, the doctor showed him the living were not done with him.

This final act, for the doctor, was an act of cruelty.

The words used to share the news were a formality. Olivia's tears were professional and were more for Anna than Markos. The news came quickly, shared with meaningless options able to barely prolong his time with his family. The doctor attempted to do anything he could for his patient, the guest of honor who never requested anything from the hospital. Markos, in an act of humanity, shared a few shining moments of his past with the doctor with Olivia. She smiled at his attempts at considerate tolerance. In their last moments together, the images of the visits remained on a loop in their head. Following two decades of visits, the doctor, in a brief show of admiration and respect, shook the hand of his patient.

Markos was muted by the thought of his demon's plans coming into effect. Markos believed he heard a thank you, but only shared a morbid display of affection back to the doctor, appreciative of the connection he rekindled. The doctor soon left and allowed for his patient to prepare for the next steps with what remained of family.

The story must continue, it must be told, affirmed Markos.

"Nothing changes, we live like we have," said Markos calmly. He gathered his things.

"I've been with you for what, a little under a month. I'd trade my last fifteen years for another, but if all I have is a handful of moments, nothing changes. Like every relationship I've had with people, things have moved quickly, and at least I won't be here to see the downfall. I don't need sympathy, I need an open mind, from both of you," said Markos, still following his doctor through the glass doors with his gaze.

Again, the tearful Olivia nodded in agreement, forgetting the business with the Speaker.

Judgment day had come and ended its control over the events of his life. Markos expected the results from the moment the recollection reappeared to him. His stories needed to continue, but the simplified truths he told them were not enough. The confidentiality agreements handicapped many of his intentions, but they were miniscule to the promises he made to Ephraim that bound him. Nevertheless, the promises meant nothing in the face of the repercussions of an isolated life, a faulty existence. He pondered for hours and hours, in a day of isolation, the safeguards of his truths. They would die with him, an unfair dilemma he had to face head on, if he wanted to properly leave his family.

In fairness, what would they gain? The safeguards are necessary, but who are we protecting, history? Elsa gave me her truth in the end, I must share mine, concluded Markos.

The safeguards were made of flesh and bone, nothing meaningful to the women. His demons had finally located him. There was no way to defeat death, but Elsa taught him the importance of eluding the eternal collectors. In a day left to himself, Anna off to her friends, Olivia returning to work after the check-up, he held onto Elsa's letter. He thought of what truth meant to him, what it would mean to his family, to the women.

They're owed, believed Markos.

ten:
Death Is Quicker

"My entrance into Ephraim's movement starts with a photo. I remember a photo being taken in the park, over there, the spot we would take our walks on," said Markos.

Markos began the night with stern warnings of rekindling the conflict of his time. Over and over, he informed them they had to respect his infrequent requests for privacy. The day was full of trips to the local stores, preparing and completing the checklists motivated by their trip to Los Angeles. Their Sunday morning was diluted by the pollution of fraught shoppers, one after the other trying to catch the best of the repeated sales and deals. The summer heat was ruthless in its emanation of heat rays. It did no good to the man who received the devastating news of his terminal sickness the day before. He had put in the maximum effort, but he saw as his body began to crumble, more or so due to the news, instead of the actual condition outlined by the doctor. He felt rushed to finish the checklist he required of himself, but after taking rest in the food court of a large department store, he began to hammer out his tasks, facing the coming death with a pen and pad on the mustard-stained table. The editing of his speech took a backseat to the importance of the paper and pen in front of him. He was able to chisel away at the consequential matters at hand, writing the fatal sentences in front of the marching shoppers. He looked around, wondering if any could see the distressing words on his paper. He cursed himself whilst ripping the yellow paper from the pad, wrapping a token from his wallet in the paper, as he looked helplessly at the mustard stains from the table, smearing on the ripped page.

Regardless of the stain, he smiled at his courage.

Markos followed this by removing the letter his love wrote him. The letter was wrinkled, and the ripped envelope was plagued by creases. He removed her letter, still folded, and shakingly forced his hand to write the number "1" on it. The hesitation appeared out of the fear he felt defacing her words, as simple as his marking was. Markos then placed his letter behind it, and again forced himself to write the number "2" on it. The envelope encased the truths of two dead lovers, a romantic note he would leave to the inquisitive Anna. It would serve as a quirky note to his kin, an act of love giving purpose to a dying man. He nearly was caught by the two women, as they paid for their purposeless materials. He quickly placed the envelope and paper back into his pocket and forged a smile to show an improvement in his fatigued state.

Two of the three remaining tasks were complete.

He already made sure to contact his lawyer, years in advance, to leave everything to whoever carried the name of Solomons. He made sure to recently change the beneficiary to Anna and leave Olivia the option of changing certain things, unknowing of Darius's motives after their warnings to him.

All that remained was telling them of him and Ephraim. The rest of the day was consumed by their naps, the consequence of the steps taken around the different department stores, hunting for the optimal prices. They all retreated to their rooms, preparing for the informal nightly meetings. All fell easily into their sleep, but Olivia faced the effects of being burdened by her own questions. She wondered what thoughts sieged the mind of the dying Markos, unaware of the alleviating sleep he was enjoying. Olivia scoured through her mental records, peeling back from the near month of memories with the man. She still did not know what she required, what she truly desired from the man who shared a roof with her as a child. He reemerged in her life decades later, still a man plagued by secrecy. Desperately did she want to tell Anna of his condition, but soon her thoughts shut the heavy eyelids, along with the comfort of her freshly lubricated skin rubbing against the soft sheets following her shower.

Hours went by before the shuffling of the dining chairs and the opening of kitchen cabinets woke her from her troubled sleep. The home found peace in its own unambiguous solitude, lost in the mirage of houses sitting in all directions of the home. There were never visitors to the Solomons' estate, and there were no intruders or mundane prying eyes involved in the business of the family anymore. Any noise made in the home would ring through the empty hallways, as it had for over half a century. The home stood tall, through the years, and served as the holistic sanctuary to accusations flying towards the family from those unaware of proven facts.

Hearing the hints from the home indicating it was time to meet, she put a sweater on over her athletic shorts and made use of the clean socks sitting on the chair behind her desk. The room was quite blank, a staple of the decorative style of the family. Photos on miniature frames were placed near her tablet. The photos, displaced around her debonair black desk, were of her father, her mother, a family photo with her and Darius, and her Anna. Near those, a small photo of her grandmother, a woman she did not completely remember nor understand as a youth, sat connected to the frame holding her father's photo. The desk was the only object standing out from the antique feeling of the sixty-year-old room.

She had a large television on a black stand, as well as a mini fridge connected to the bottom right of the stand. No posters, photos, or tapestries were placed on the clear white walls. The dim lighting from the outdoor streetlights were enough to expose the chipping paint on the walls of the room. The uneven white surrounded her with the same lonely feeling Markos was once a victim of.

When she first woke, she found time to look at the enclosing space. Olivia sulked in the restless response to the nap. Her body rose perpendicular to the bed. It took her time to rise and put on the necessary garments. Her straightened back was stiff while her eyes scanned the walls and windows. She wondered if she would suffer the same fate as the man. She feared Anna leaving her. Anna's journey was just beginning, but hers would end if she left.

The dreadful thought was much to consider as problems stacked for the unprepared Olivia, but she had to continue forward.

"What'd I miss," asked the mother, rolling down her large gray sweater past her knees as she descended down the stairs with a cheerful smile.

"He's just going on, saying something about sleeping dogs, he can tell you while I get some cereal," replied Anna.

An auspicious look was shared between the two at the old saying being recognized. Markos went on explaining the importance of respecting the boundaries of a sensitive topic. He pointed out the two were well within their rights to judge and defend Ephraim. He simply asked for privacy and empathy.

"The photo was the thing I remembered during the first event I got invited to. I had just returned and was getting settled back into our home," said Markos, looking around the house.

The diseased walls were uneven downstairs as well but were hidden with conscious decorating. More effort was placed in hanging religious quotations in the form of paintings and framed photographs to hide uneven discolorations. The placed pieces of nature, artwork based on the images of the wildlife in the land of their lineage, hung throughout the communal space. Some were ones left in the past, unaltered by the descendants of the family.

"I found welcoming arms here when I came back, but I was asked to meet the family in the park after I arrived from the airport. I found a note placed for me in my room, along with a bunch of little girl's toys and some baby bottles," said Markos, smiling as he pointed to Anna's mother.

A blushing Olivia let another shy smile creep out of her lips.

"I was confused by what was happening, but I remember leaving my stuff. I dropped it and walked, in a button up and a tie, prepared to surprise my family. They had their own plans for me."

"Where were you?" asked Anna, running to the kitchen to place her dishes in the sink, before missing anything more.

"Rehab," boldly answered Markos.

The lack of hesitation in his reply surprised the women, accepting how open he was. His bold approach was successful in hiding the partial truth in plain sight.

"I expected open hands, but they were distracted. There was too much going on."

Markos felt the extent of his weight loss in the walk to the park. His feet weakened in every step he took, and his loose bones felt flimsy against the slight breeze, resisting his every step. He could hear laughter, the immature yells of adolescents surrounding the grassy fields of the park.

When he finally turned the corner into the neighboring cul-de-sac, he could see the cause of the commotion. The small opening between the wooden barriers to the park shared the view of the festivities. Ephraim's popularity were words to him. He heard the whispers and noticed the lengthy phone calls, but to see, it shocked Markos how Ephraim's manifested visions came to be.

The tents circled the outer rim of the soccer field, taking half the space of the park. The kids ran both, in front and behind Markos, as he cut through one of the stations to search for his family, now placing himself in the middle of the open area informally cordoned off by the tents. His light feet felt the weight of his steps, stepping deeper into the marshy grass, soaking the bottom of his beige cargo pants with every indecisive direction he took to find Ephraim.

"Markos! Markos!"

His violent turn caught the eye of a few of the people enjoying the festivities. Markos kept turning, nervously feeling the pressure of the gazes focused on him. Continuing his walk, he noticed the diverse group of people manning their stations; face painting, book sellers, dunk tanks, all in the name of fundraising. He put an end to the chase for the voice, deciding to dampen his rising uneasiness.

The endless laughter of the children could be assumed to be a happy thought. To Markos, it was a piercing reminder of Elsa, the woman he feared was calling him in his head. Two years and ten months was not enough time to heal. The treatment he received did not help. Alcohol was not his first impulse; however, limits were complex for him once he began. The act of repulsion was yet to be worked out by his preoccupied counselors before he left prematurely.

"Markos, Markos!" yelled the woman again.

I hear it, but I can't see it.

The trickling sweat foaming his spectacles escaped his forehead as he turned.

Jesus, I came home too early.

The tap on the left side of his shoulder alleviated his stress. He did not care who it was. As it had always been, the blonde guardian angel was there waiting.

The embrace was heavenly for Markos, fighting the tears he shed alone, fighting the urge of sifting through his sorrows with a bottle. The sweat on their backs from the inconsistent spring heat of Northern California ruined their needed embrace. Alana's cap nearly fell off as Markos tightened his grip around her back. Leaving his coat behind, his arms were exposed after he rolled up his sleeves. He felt her perspiration through her tee. After he released his grip, he looked her up and down, noticing a slight weight loss, highlighted by the fact she tucked her baggy shirt into her denim shorts. His smile was characterized by how impressed he was by the improvement of her wardrobe. She was once a young teenager, covered in pesky spots, who wore overalls in high school. She emerged with a new sense of spunk and confidence.

She was big time now.

"I told them to have someone wait for you, but Ephraim couldn't be late to something he promoted," asserted Alana.

"It's fine. I'm just happy to be home."

Alana did not know whether he was lying, but pain carried his soulless words. It robbed the joy in the air placed by the children's voices. The words levied the attitude of an unchanging face, refusing to form into anything revealing how he was suffering.

I'm fine, they must believe I'm fine. I'm fine.

"Come on, they're taking pictures," said Alana, grabbing his hand and guiding him towards the last tents. She pushed towards the north side of the park, near the school the three once dreaded.

Tent by tent, he realized how happy each person was. He saw in their smiles what Ephraim's goal was. He felt motivated by the people's thoughtless euphoria, tinkering with the memories in his mind if there was a chance to find similar satisfaction in this life.

The abrupt end to his walk ended the line of thinking.

His mother's tears after she caught a glimpse of her son nearly cracked his apathetic surface. He was able to make out her face in the distance before they crept closer. He deduced her mind was elsewhere as she awaited her chance to take a photo. The topic of which she was focused on was now in her hands.

"*Indate nuh?*" asked his mother, attempting to evaluate her son with a detailed look.

"I'm good, Mom, don't worry," said Markos. He slightly bent over to lean his tired weight on his mother's shoulder.

It was then his eyes found his brother, along with his wife and young daughter, taking photos with sponsors of the event.

His brother looked as if he severely aged since their last meeting, showing a hint of gray in his bushy beard. The bags resting beneath his restless eyes darkened, a different shade from his chocolate complexion. The casual golf shirt he wore was a miscalculation on his part. The years he spent expressing resentment towards physical exercise were beginning to take a toll on his weight, just enough for only family to notice.

Ephraim's eyes focused on the expensive camera placed on the tripod. They posed for the two newspapers belonging to the local universities. His brother's eyes, along with the smile, changed from the years of their adolescence. Markos could not identify what he saw in his face.

The time it took to position the impatient posing adults uncovered the urgency in Ephraim's manner. His shoulders were always in a defense position. Ephraim's fatigued eyes darted in all positions in the seconds between the insignificant small talk Ephraim held with the photographers. He did not get distracted with the eager people amongst the crowd.

Deficient of sleep, his brother's body was frail. *Was there a threat to worry about?* They snapped Markos from his thoughts with a request to join the second photo of the family.

The immediate click of the camera startled him. His mother felt his jolt and was reminded of her son's gentleness. She tightened her grip on her boy and he followed her action with a look of embarrassment, borne out of the feeling of comfort and safety.

"Markos, how are you?" softly asked his brother as he turned from the view of the lens.

Markos, again, was startled by how his brother made him out in the commotion, without making eye contact to alert him.

Markos was able to give a meek wave to Ephraim. He waved to his wife with a nervous smile, but only a dutiful nod was returned.

She never liked me, she will never like me, thought Markos.

"I'm good. How are you? Hello, Alondra," murmured Markos.

"Hello," said Alondra, holding up her baby girl in her arms.

The silence was tension in their midst. The five adults each avoided the eyes of the others. Markos remained unchanged in his posture while

Ephraim continued to wave at the people walking past the family, still in the fight or flight stance.

"Why don't we meet the others by the food vendors?" suggested Ephraim, moving about unbothered.

Still in the clutches of his mother, they strode through the crowd, dodging the football being passed around from corner to corner. None of them cared for a conversation with Markos, only his mother asked questions about his time away. To her surprise, the truth was shared with her, and he noticed as he slipped her more information, the others slithering closer, trying their best to overhear.

"Ah, I know you smell that," added Ephraim.

The charred smell of the honey spiced barbeque, with marinated and sauteed onions, watered Markos's mouth as he approached the food truck parked adjacent to the field. Leaving the grass, their ascent onto the sidewalk put them directly in front of the truck selling every form of meat.

Markos began to despise the people in the hallowed ground he once strolled around. The symmetrical lines in the grass, formed by landscapers the city sent, were destroyed. In his mind, the grass was sacred, his guiding tunnel of vision. He looked to the grass from the cemented walkway: for guidance, for advice, for peace. The event desecrated what was his, his home.

Ephraim's head spurred around looking for his friends.

"What do you want?" asked Alana.

Markos quickly scanned the menu. He divided his attention between the menu and his brother's quest for his friends.

"I'll take a hot dog and a BBQ...uh, a BBQ tri-tip plate with a side of onion rings," uttered Markos.

"When it's not on your dime, huh?" said Alana, moving to his mother's order before paying.

The first smile he allowed himself to enjoy informed him he was home. The empty stomach from the lack of food on the connecting flights was to the detriment of his mental state. Alana would not give him the option of remaining an outsider. His mother was equally as important in curing his recent recurring afflictions. The thought of ever returning home eluded him over the time he remained away.

His mother was defenseless against Alondra's arguments to remove the tragedy-stricken Markos from the home. Ephraim avoided causing further dissension within the family by politely providing Markos with the knowledge of the dilemma he was creating. The smell of distilled liquor as he returned home in the mystique hours of the night was the least of the problems. His insecurities were beyond the reach of any of his family. Markos needed to realize the bottles around the home and the late trips out were endangering the family's equilibrium. He worsened the hectic environment Olivia had to be raised in. Markos's time away put everything in perspective, providing him with the closure required under the adverse circumstances.

"Here."

"Thanks," said Markos, grabbing the red basket from Alana.

"I'm gonna go get some condiments," said his mother.

She stood in the street, on the opposite side of the truck. They retreated to the grass to wait for her. His mother drenched her food with barbecue sauce, a habit she loved when she did not fast. The seconds of privacy were crucial to Alana.

"How was it?" asked Alana.

"Which part? Being alone or staying sober?" replied Markos.

Alana did not want to anger him, but she wanted to learn more, she wanted to know if it worked.

"Did it help?"

"Sort of," said Markos.

"Sort of?"

"I picked up a bad habit of smoking cigarettes. I've only had three glasses of wine since rehab," said Markos, avoiding her glare.

She looked at him in silence, waiting for him to turn to catch her face. He refused.

"You're cutting it close, huh? You better not start it all up, again," warned Alana.

Markos could take their judgment, but he feared Alondra's anger. Since first hearing of her on his trip with Elsa to Ethiopia, he was excited to meet her. The first impression of him as a hopeless drunk was enough for her to deduce what type of man he was, regardless of the trauma. Still, Markos refused to stand up to her for he never lost respect for her. The head on her broad shoulders were strong, she was unbending, but was lenient enough to listen to the emotions of others. She made the effort early on when he returned, but she had more than herself to think about. He showed the couple no decency, not respecting her as his brother's fiancé when he returned from Morocco with his grief. He did not return from his hiatus from the family when they were to be married either. He did not even give them the pleasure of returning on Olivia's first birthday.

Years later, she chose forgiveness, but stubbornly, labored the shaky past over him.

"I plan on staying sober. I will get my own place in a few months. I don't want to cram into any of your lives."

"Talk to your brother first before making a decision like that," said Alana.

They both shifted towards his mother as she returned.

She said it like she knew something, what now?

Markos's irritation peaked when the family made plans for him. Leaving after he had enough of rehab was his idea, an initiative thought for him, by him. The brief time he spent with them was suffocating. Reclaiming his right to be home was difficult after returning to find his family unbothered by his years away in Rabat. Markos wanted to be selfish. He himself knew the attention he required in a difficult time in his life. Dealing with Elsa alone in Sacramento taught Markos how important it was to branch out. He continued his search for the independence he sought, avoiding the family in times of growth. The betrayal from his father and the inattentive ear of his beguiled brother warned him to avoid his hometown altogether, yet he was drawn to the city.

"Here he is," said Alana.

He could not get over the bushy bear Ephraim turned into. *This must help him in terms of photos and campaigns,* wondered Markos.

Alana was careful in her tap of Ephraim's shoulder, alerting him of their approach. As he turned, Alondra moved back, leaving extra space between her and Markos, evading any contact with him. The couple was not alone, standing with two familiar faces. The names escaped Markos, but he had seen them somewhere.

"Markos, I'm glad we found you. I want to introduce you to some friends you may have seen around," said Ephraim, a hint of advertising in his tone.

"These two, Jamie and Jonathan, were the ones who were important in making this all come together. They were right alongside Alana and I, since our college days," continued Ephraim.

"Nice to meet you," said both of them, awkwardly waving their hands in the air.

Markos, leaning in, chose to shake their hands. The looks he received from the twins displayed a sense of knowledgeable caution.

They're afraid of me.

He saw them in the local news reports he periodically scanned in his time away from the family. The four of them had grown in notoriety over the years. The beginning of Ephraim's importance in student movements was evident in his last year of high school, being a champion of revitalizing the meaning of community service. He was instrumental, especially for the misguided youth who searched for a purposeful cause to give their time to. Growing from his popularity, he was chosen to speak at youth conferences, still being limited to Sacramento and slowly spreading his name around social circles in Northern California. He reinvigorated the passion in the youth at the monotonous conferences, and as his commanding etiquette began to spread, his presence on social media platforms began to disseminate his piercing words. The efficacy of his decision to begin his collegiate studies in Los Angeles was crucial to his meteoric popularity amongst people. Alana's path would align with his. She began her pre-law studies there with him, sharing a passion to correct the deteriorating humanity around them.

Ephraim continued what he started in Sacramento, growing his volunteer servicing program for the returning veterans. He found support, since his ideas coincided with the city's plan to curb the growth of the homeless population. The stalled aid from the city weakened his faith in the established efforts in veteran affairs. Their efforts did not match the urgency of the good people he met in the ruinous streets of the city.

From there, he put his time in focusing on the strategic advantage of controlling local governments, studying the budgetary decisions being made and the importance of donors. Noticing the alarming rate of ignorance in people's understanding of local politics, he would make it a point to passionately inquire others to pay more attention in their local city councils. He outlined these points in his talks at small conferences, speaking to no more than forty-five people at a time.

It is written.

The twenties were a tough time for the country, dividing the nation, alienating and dismantling the relations one built with those living in the same community. Political and social affiliations, as well as religious preferences, dominated the influencing airwaves. Empathy showed weakness. Those placed in power believed sympathy was a career killer, showing their constituents this was a time to be as unyielding as ever. People believed they were at philosophical war. People were forced to be on edge, reviewing every piece of information they had access to. Ephraim's words, calculated and precise, effectively attacked power structures blinding people. He refused to name officials or decidedly point to others to cast blame. His words found a home in the worried ears of his counterparts at the universities, catching a glimpse of him on their one-sided feeds. He began to receive invitations to come speak to numerous clubs and unions on different campuses: The Politics of

Tomorrow, Black Student Union, Today's Democrats, Tomorrow's Republicans, Green Catalysts, International Student Unions. Amplified on a campus with an elite alumnus, his mother and father's former cohorts, Ephraim would find himself speaking at larger regional conferences throughout California. He marveled students with his patient composure and galvanized them with his brutal evaluations of both local politicians, and their constituents.

He was at a loss of words, when two American-born Korean students, awaiting their turn to ask a question, arose and asked if the use of words in a time of division and xenophobia were moot. They warned words were a double-edged sword without action. His reply was simple.

"Help me, I'm a person who is happens to be like you, a student."

The two, now looking at Markos, were the vigor of the four. The outspoken pair would link with Ephraim to list out the ten crucial points of attack for the group. The three met and outlined a ten-point list of their desired goals, a first for people of their age. Previously, movements were clouded by the lack of an end, a goal to aspire to. Youth movements in the early twenties opened themselves to opposition because no goals were listed. Movements were at the mercy of the opposition's narratives. With the list publicized, it began to trend, nationwide. Only the list itself began to trend, but in California, the three crafters were glorified. The newfound fame was used to conduct important roundtables with university chairs and donors, discussing the importance of funding numerous programs, fundamental in retaining students and preparing them for the world. Their voices could not be drowned out by the local politicians. Ephraim gained the necessary capital to begin asking for what he desired, disrupting the routine of deafening inquiring voices.

Soon after, Alana began to give her time to Ephraim, promising to continue her studies and split her time with him. The four assembled, and since then, they made use of their time by leading protests, guest lectures, sit-ins, and more importantly, graduating.

"If you guys don't mind, I'd like to show my brother around and talk with him?"

The group all nodded, all, except for Alondra. She turned to hide her face, ashamed efforts were being made in the betterment of a man who did not desire help. Markos, weakened at the disdain of his sister-in-law, soured at the hate he infused in her. She took Olivia in her arms and walked to his mother as they motioned towards the rest of the carnival.

Ephraim led Markos to the first station perpendicular to the food trucks, positioned on the corner of the grass, where the end of the grass met the paved sidewalks.

"Hello, Mr. Solomons!" yelled the two Mexican women, selling their savory pastries.

"Hello, hello. Those pastries you sold to my wife were great, I'll be sure to come back."

Markos tried his best to force a smile to the women. He could overhear the women discussing the slight resemblance of the two.

"They think we look alike," said Markos.

"I forgot you know Spanish. You remembered your teachings. I wish you could teach me when Alondra gets mad at me," jokingly remarked Ephraim, easing the light tension.

"No, you don't, the things she used to say about me are crazy. I used to overhear her on the phone through the walls."

Ephraim could not use his prowess and premeditated approach at times with Markos. Markos was older and studied human interaction by observing his childhood friendship with Alana and his brother Ephraim. The two certainly prepared him for the people in the world, and with the reinforcement of his teaching with Elsa, he surely would never be misled again.

Still heat accompanied them on their midday trek around the cemented path of the park, a memory of their youthful runs returning. Both refused to speak, dreading the yells of their father from first, his bedroom window, then the benches, barking at them to move faster. Necessity worsened the turning in their stomach. His teachings were vital for the two to enjoy the superior comprehension of others. They traded a higher understanding for emotional cognition.

"How was your time away?"

"Necessary."

"That's it?"

"Yeah."

"You missed a lot of things here. My wedding, Olivia's birthday, Mom removing a tumor from her breast, a lot of stuff, Markos. Necessary isn't enough? You only called Mom, and even she was afraid of telling you of her condition," said Ephraim, in his trademark monotone voice, hinting at a loss of composure with a forced show of passion.

Markos rejected his mind's request to stop. His brother sprang information he never could expect. If he had lost his mother, living would be difficult. He and his brother had a strong relationship, but his connection was tentative on how much effort Ephraim put in his life. With the recent growth of his name, and the new life he would create with Alondra, time was a commodity he could not allocate to his brother Markos.

"I'm sorry. I don't feel anything here, I couldn't come back the same way I left."

As least as possible, thought Markos.

Ephraim's voice lowered as they circled back to the half of the park with the tented vendors.

"You gotta do something. You've already lived an anomaly of a life, we both have. There are still things for you, here," said Ephraim, waving at the family while they interacted with vendors.

"I don't know. Mom's here and you'll be on the road soon. I was talking with Alana about moving away. I'm thinking of moving close to an apartment or a small house near where I went to school. It's secluded and it's what I need. I got all the money I saved up from the Air Force and working in Rabat. I've scraped a few coins from my time away, too," said Markos.

Ephraim took time to hear and analyze the meaning of his words. He thought about his remarks and waited for them to continue past the people. He remained focused, head held high, looking forward, waving past vendors who electrified as he acknowledged them.

"I hear you, Markos, but I have an opportunity for you. I want you to follow me on the road. The others have been made aware of the request and have agreed on it," said Ephraim.

He's lying, even Alana knows the risk of me blowing this up. Their rising, I can bring them down as fast as they've risen.

"What? In what capacity?" asked Markos.

"Any capacity you'd like. You need purpose, you can't be alone straight out of rehab. I sold it as a security gig, you were in the Air Force anyways. What do you think? It'd look good talking to some of the veterans, too."

Calculated, and still, he's using emotions as a variable, even in the name of good.

Markos let the request simmer. He sighed, letting a deep exhale slowly escape. His brother did not change. He was still the big man: round face, modest belly, a large statue of empathy. He gave things a quick thought before letting his mind focus on the eternal goal of helping others. Markos trembled at becoming a miniscule topic to his brother.

"It wouldn't work out, I'm unstable. The issue here also lies in the fact that as you rise, you'll actually need security, I read the articles. Your popular list also blew up because it ruffled some feathers. I was a Signals Analyst, I shuffled papers and left."

"Stop it, don't lie to me. When you were touring for that book, I talked to a few of your friends. I'm aware of your first year and a half in the Air Force, you were a Targeting Analyst. I heard you were pretty good at it, and then you asked to transfer because you wanted to have time to get into learning languages," said Ephraim.

"You're just like Dad, you wanted to learn all they had to offer," said Ephraim, continuing his analysis of him.

Markos shuffled around his pockets. He clenched his fist at his preparation for the pitch.

"What if I refuse, I don't care much for this fight. You're the righteous one, I have no dog in this. It'll get messier and as you amass popularity, you gain strong opposition."

"A fight, what fight are you referring to? If you read the papers, you'd know we're not like posturing freedom fighters who use their limited characters to spread their messages. You gotta see that people, everyone, are getting worse. We're truncating the facts that we were given. Yesterday, the Catholic Church removed a book from the Bible due to its incredulous interpretability and today, nations are passing laws limiting voting rights. From this headline you can see that the world is getting worse, but what you didn't hear about is the new laws that are getting passed enforcing new 'luxury taxes' in places like California, New York, and Texas. The standard of living is decreasing as the rich get richer, and bolder and bolder. We let this pass and they will handicap a demographic you belong to, as well as the same poor demographic fighting *us*.

"Don't belittle me or my purpose. These laws have been getting passed since the economy collapsed a few years ago. I know you didn't feel anything while you were in the Air Force or Rabat. 2026 was a tough year for all those working, and it worsened the already deep disparities between people. I'm trying to find a new sense of humanity and give it back to people. My opposition calls it blind sympathy. We clean the needles off the streets, we sit-in and argue for lowered tuition rates, we ask public schools to be supplied with the same programs as charter and private schools. We speak out at conferences and engage with students. We engage with young adults through guest lectures. We ask people to help us paint the neglected neighborhoods city's refuse to help. We listen to the homeless population. We help veterans like you reclaim a renewed sense of purpose after they've been discarded. Why wouldn't you want to help us do that?"

I envy his optimism. If he experienced people like I did, if he saw what I saw, he'd know. I've experienced them now, Ephraim. I've seen where it all goes.

They stopped as he concluded his prepared speech. They remained away from the people, covered by the risen hill of grass of the uneven field. The miniature hill split the park, hiding them from the gazes of prying eyes while others enjoyed the festivities at its peak hour.

"I provide nothing to this, and I can't see the purpose or reason for all of it. I can refuse and move out. I love you, but why can't I go out alone?"

Ephraim turned to Markos. He snapped. Soft rage took over.

"Look at me. Look at me. You left a knife out in the house next to your empty bottle of bourbon. Forgiveness, that's what you owe me and that should be your purpose. What if Olivia would have found that and not me? How about Alondra, I haven't even told her. After all I've done for you, you need to come with me so I can watch you. I am lying to my wife, Markos. You can't be alone. I know you have the ability to hurt yourself. The family cannot take that right now. You're now included in my number of worries and need to stick close to me," released Ephraim, portraying his emotion in a whisper. He beat his heavy hands on his chest as he spoke.

I do not have the courage to hurt myself, thought Markos.

Markos knew if he refused, he could not return home again. He desired solitude, but he wanted the option to do as he pleased. They continued towards the people. His brother was alluding to some form of suicide, but he could never go that far, his self-righteous promises kept him from it. Ephraim applied pressure on him using his own tenets to force Markos into a corner.

"I'll go with you, but if I'm there, I'm in the room for everything. I won't be segregated from anything. I'll remain dead silent, but I'll be respected. I'm your elder, remember that. You asked to not be belittled, I ask the same."

It was an immune response from Markos, a response he blurted in frustration. The statement would be instrumental in protecting Ephraim more than himself.

Markos cornered Ephraim. Ephraim was helpless, yet he enjoyed the dilemma. He put his hand out, and Markos gladly shook the hand, unaware of what it would entail.

"It was tough from that day."

Markos maneuvered towards the kitchen, pouring himself chilled cranberry juice. The cooled refreshment shared alarming similarities to his cold sweat wetting his relaxing nightwear. The strain recounting the tales of his time with Ephraim, embalmed with surface level lies, continued its toll. Markos loved the women, the inspiring attitude to learn was a desire he wished he held onto over the years. Returning to the circular table near the opened French door, Markos placed his drink down.

The current generation of the Solomons were oblivious of the extent of his bouts with alcohol addiction. He tiptoed around the topic and left small hints allowing the two to make deductions. Olivia remained in the know, however, recalling her time eavesdropping on certain conversations about her mysterious uncle. The stories did not click those memories back, but she did remember the cigarettes he smoked over the years. The pungent requests from her mother to avoid the stench of his substandard habits bothered her. It was the only habit, however, Markos was able to quit.

"What did they have you do?" asked Olivia.

"It was very difficult because I didn't have much to contribute originally. He learned I worked as a Targeting Analyst and believed I had the prerequisites to be their security. I would gameplan with the university's security and hire and coordinate with third parties for security at events. I just remained on my P's and Q's during private speaking engagements. I used to fog my glasses with the stress of staying on edge. It forced me to completely abandon drinking, for a while at least," jokingly added Markos.

"I learned a lot. The most important part for me was watching Ephraim. He served as my savior and my guide, but as he grew, he changed...something distinct in the eyes. I requested to be in those meetings to watch him. I wanted to be his spiritual guide. I was still his older brother. I learned more about people's motivations and how they change watching those four," continued Markos.

Olivia and Anna set their eyes on the movements of their uncle. Markos knew the reason. He recognized the look he once had when his father left, the face of an awakening.

The end of innocence does not occur when feeling the touch of another. The end of innocence, as Ephraim said, was when you look to those above you, the ones who raised you, and realize that they are far from infallible.

Markos slowed at the thought of betrayal. The story removed pieces of the image they created for Ephraim.

"He was a good man, your father, your grandfather. In my eyes, he began as my protector, the closest thing I had to a father figure, as weird as it may sound. The demands of the people he helped stressed him out. The heart has to work double time to keep it good, to keep it pure. A man reaches a point where he boils over."

Markos looked at the most important individual in the room, the future bearer of the Solomons' sins. As time dwindled, Anna listened to the stories and referred to the role of the wallflower. She noticed the rushed storytelling, unaware of the growing presence of his demons. Like the motivated students at his lectures, she held her questions to the end. She noted all the defining points said about her grandfather. As she became more invested in his words, her ability to analyze him waned. Anna was accustomed to her great-uncle's stories and presence. She was unable to break him down as she once did. She was only able to make out a sense of reserved speech.

Olivia took a moment to stroll along the vanilla tiled floors in the kitchen. She patiently warmed and poured the black ginger tea Markos requested. The tea Henok made in the apartment, a familiar taste of

Rabat, would ease the stress of his fitness. The tea became a favorite of Olivia, an unadulterated taste of maturity shared only between the two. Anna used the supplementary time to explain to everyone how her new job hunt was going. The vigorous excitement of the job interviews approaching put a smile on the face of both Markos and Olivia, remembering the times shared in the amusement of uncertainty.

He smiled, knowing through the unpredictability of the future, they would both be alright, as he overheard happiness shared in the conversation between mother and daughter.

He moved to the sofas and watched as the mother emerged from the kitchen with the tea and a smile, adoring her daughter's resilience. The two, one situated with the unhealthy company of potato chips and the other with the mug of tea, found a spot on both sides of Markos. He shared the sofa with Olivia, while Anna sat on the complementary two-seater. They dimmed the light directly above the table in the lounge area. The house was still, unchanged for a moment by the happiness and guilt consuming the members of the cryptic family.

"How's the speech going?" asked Olivia.

"Good, I should be good to go before we leave in a few days. At this point, I have the introduction and important points written out. I have to edit, and I'll be ready," said Markos.

"I have to first give you both everything before I share my life with others. I know there will be a lot of questions and a larger audience. I'm walking again to build up the stamina for the day. Father time shows no mercy. I'm glad I have a few days to prepare."

"What are you going to say?" asked Anna. Without modesty, she chewed and spoke.

"I feel like I've answered questions and discussed the things that happened in my time with Ephraim. I haven't done him justice though, because I haven't talked to people about his motivations and why he did it. I need to talk more about what he thought of people's habits. He was unique because he was able to divert people from their allegiances to form something new. He wanted to share that comfortable compliance was an enemy, a counterpart to progress. Something new was needed for hope," answered Markos, picking at the bottom of his beard.

Anna was interested, but the story of the brothers was critical, it meant more to her.

"Okay, I already...*we* already know it's beginning. I'm wondering about the middle, the unexplained things that split you two up. We deserve an explanation as to why we weren't close over the years, why we lived alone when you were thirty minutes away," vocalized Anna.

Markos remained relaxed as he thought of his reply. The righteous request alarmed him of the information the women craved.

"Okay, you already know why we split up. The protests, we disagreed on how those were handled. We were forgiven by the public, but we did not forgive each other," shared Markos.

"Well, things happen. We deserve to know the full story. We aren't here to learn about just Grandpa's time, we can look that up. You know what we want to hear," doubled down Anna.

Olivia shared her sentiments in silent approval. She nodded her head, ashamed of the attack on Markos, yet, standing in full agreement with her daughter.

"You don't care about him passing legislation and stuff like that?" asked Markos, confused. He smirked at the request.

"We know these things," arrogantly replied Anna.

"I don't mind, the dispute between us started in the very beginning with arguments over small things. I remember the first difficult task I was given after a speaking engagement here in Sacramento...I really don't mind talking about this, I feel like I've already deviated from my story. Our issues bled into some important decisions. If you're aware of what he's accomplished, and you've thought this through, I can begin with our *rift*," said Markos.

"I have," quickly replied Anna.

Markos ignored her insolence, waiting for silence. He favored this over a full recounting. They would learn more about the family with this path of discussion.

"May I continue?"

"You may."

"We've discussed the importance of knowing your friends and your enemies. There are important reasons for understanding your leaders and what they mean to your communities. We saw how it felt blindly following in the beginning of the twenties. The message I'm sharing with you is the same I give to students. I've attempted to calm their attacking tendencies, and to you, no different. I ask you, give leaders the time and attention required. They won't come to you as before.

"Some may look at me up here, a man who may follow the stereotype and support liberal politics. You haven't clapped as much as the students, but it means you are listening," said Ephraim, smiling at the minute laughs shared throughout the audience.

"Yes, I support typical liberal stances, but never have I closed my mind. I ask students to give leaders time for the same reason I ask you. Hold them to the same account you would hold your parents to. Be patient and watch as they change and get comfortable in their positions, locally, statewide, and nationwide. Their words, instead of uniting, discards people and steps on the toes of the people that put them in office. The ones you support, and ones I have supported, betray us by criticizing our neighbors and pitting us against the ones we should be locking hands with. The danger lies with the power we give them, for we need to remember, like us they have a job and desire promotion. They will do what's necessary, say what's necessary. I avoid the argument of politics. We need to understand we have different religions, denominations, even different motivations, that force us to view issues differently. I respect yours, and by inviting me here, I assume you respect mine. The amount of good people joining politics has decreased, for it is now men and women with agendas of their own going into politics," continued Ephraim, stopping before he chose to say what he meant to say.

"Nowadays, our next generation of leaders, even if they were to come into politics, would have to choose between two outdated juggernauts that have a hold on the politics of America," said Ephraim, feeling the shifts in the seats.

The speaking tour concluded in the Solomons' hometown. Markos, placed at the back of the church's dining hall, calmly sat listening to the crafted words of his brother's team. The last statement, words of debate, were to have considerable capital in the coming years. The remark was highly debated throughout the tour, while Alana, the lawyer, understood what those words could represent if the movement continued to grow.

The team was visible but remained elusive. They only gave personal access to media teams and journalists of universities they spoke to. Markos favored the team's form of media coverage, disavowing narratives given by other facets of media. They angered the others, referring them to the students or their bulleted list.

The speeches were routine, conducted the way Ephraim chose. Alana stayed as hidden from the stage as Markos did, unimpressed by the masses of people congregating to hear their words. Alana, however, was the team's spokeswoman when interviews or questions were asked by the representatives of the universities' media teams. One of the twins began every lecture and speech with the volunteer initiative they were introducing, along with a progress report on the ones in action, ending with an update on the goals of their famed list. The twins remained the voice of action, the desired voice Ephraim required to round out his group.

To achieve the outlined goals, the group shifted their efforts from volunteering in the community centers and after school youth programs, to advocating more in the local political arena. The popularity of the group skyrocketed due to their inconspicuous media coverage and viral sound bites. Their scheduled appearances at city hall and the shift in rhetoric towards politics made their endorsements and requests important in West Coast politics. The group would find various prospective politicians seated in their audience, some boldly participating in the question-and-answer portion of the rallies. However, they refused to be aligned with any individual due to the incapability of others to separate a face with movements. Any endorsements or unions would come from the whole team.

"Our endorsements of various politicians come down to their politics and their ethics. We'll endorse their ideas, never the individual, since the individual is susceptible to the benefits, monetary and otherwise, of the profession. I can't stress this enough, if you continue to follow us, we are party less, we have no investment nor do we receive money for our endorsements. We aren't donors or lobbyists; we hope to help educate and learn from others to share the idea of *one*. We are neighbors. It sounds mystical or romantic because we've been taught to believe this type of unity is unattainable or unbeneficial to the status of the community. It's like our religion. We listen to the teachings, and we hear it, day in and day out, love each other, love your neighbor, *love your enemies*. It's interesting literature, but you forget to apply it because you never realize it actually applies to you. It reminds me of my father."

"My brother is here, there in the back serving as our security, he can attest to this," continued Ephraim, pointing at his brother behind the seven rows of white foldable chairs.

"Our father would ask us, whenever we stayed up on the weekends and breaks, don't forget to lock the door, the door that opened to the garage. My brother, whenever we'd stay up to watch movies, he would be the first to always shut his eyes and I knew it. I'd keep saying it, out loud and in my head, *don't forget to lock the door, don't forget to lock the door*. Every time I'd go to the kitchen for an unhealthy late-night snack, I'd look at the door, every bathroom break, *don't forget to lock the door*. It's crazy, I'd wake my brother up to go up the stairs to call it a night, and still, I'd repeat it. I'd go all the way up to bed until I surrendered to my sleep, remembering to lock the door. I'd go to sleep remembering, but still, not locking it. I promise to apply the knowledge

I've learned from my failures, and I ask you to do the same. Hold your politicians to the same standards you hold yourselves to, your children, your spouses. We're here to reapply the standards we should've always had for each other. We should improve day by day, together, opening up possibilities of growth and the ability to teach others."

Such words, but like Ephraim, will they forget to act?

The questions piled in. They were the typical inquiries he received. They asked for his motivations, some requesting him to show proof of separation from the rest who picked up a cause in the last decade. Some echoed the voices of his critics, asking how he could achieve the required goals. Others fired inappropriate questions about his allegiances and how he saw America, being as he was raised by an Ethiopian mother. Patiently, he received each question with grace, understanding the biased feelings of all who came to see him. He was full of hope. He was appreciative they sat respectfully to hear his words.

Markos sat back, eyeing the rows of Evangelists, hearing the words and ethical requests they threw in Ephraim's direction. His mother requested they speak there, recalling a conversation with a coworker. Her coworker's church heard some of his words and wanted to see him personally. He never backed down from an influenced audience, adding a location pro bono, his last stop before returning home.

The dining hall seated seventy in the exclusive space. A small stage was placed near the kitchen, the seats facing the kitchen. Behind the speaker sat two doors, the door to the kitchen and one in the right corner, to a lot outside. Markos watched the doors, but secured the secondary exit behind all the seats, choosing to remain hidden in the back of the extravagant hall. He sat near another entrance to a hallway, near the back wall. The religious decorations: the fiery angels placing their feet at the indistinct demons, the Baby lit under the luminescence of the stars, and the sacred Mother, remained plastered on baby blue walls. The dining tables were placed at the edges, to the walls of the rectangular room, which choked the audience inwards. The space between left room for the team's and church's cameras. The church recorded for the rest of the congregation while the team, like athletes, required film to better prepare for other engagements.

Markos slithered about in the back, watching those with the look of disgust. A small few chose to go against the church's united front, unafraid of the conflict. The majority appeared to hear the optimistic words. They found a different tune from politicians and pundits who fed audiences parasitical words of fear. Nevertheless, race was still a divisive topic as they continued into 2032. Including the consecrated paintings, the team represented the only diversity in the room. Some looked upon them with disdain, representations of changing social dynamics of the country by radical newcomers. The adapting nation had yet to come to terms with the consequences of the social migration and integration of immigrants. The generation of leaders before them were hesitant to speak up, somewhat reserved in the noise they made during integration, simply because they held the power. The new generation that followed refused to remain silent as their power dissipated. The hateful noise rose to its peak in the late end of the previous decade. It rose as the economy worsened, and in that room, and similar rooms, the disparities and the barbs traded were not forgotten. Markos continued to linger and evade the hateful eyes while directing his attention to the safety of the four.

"I appreciate your time and your questions. I'll leave you with this, morality is increasingly important. The money doesn't win, morality does, whether it's in philosophical or political debate. The divisive news we hear daily, fights to be the source of your opinions and utilizes morality in their arguments. Sad stories of the important characters of movements are used to gain morality points and strengthen your opinions.

"Morality is forged and tested in the face of adversity. Thou shalt not kill, however, when facing the murderer of your family, one's morality is thrown out the window. For a more personal example, morality is tested when one challenges your opinions, and you can easily dismiss and hate them. When our Christian values are tested, we forget we must love those we disagree with. We also must remember not all follow the same faith. Our morality must stay intact and the ethical code we live by must remain solid in the face of competition. By keeping a cool head, an open mind, we keep the morality of our purpose we hope to teach others. We are also available to remain students if we can remain patient, for the moral adversity will show you the path you will follow...thank you."

His abrupt end was met with mild applause. He shifted the minds of a few, but merely gained the personal respect of most of the audience. It was enough in his quest to grow his political capital.

The four lingered through the crowd, enjoying the refreshments while holding small talk with the churchgoers. Markos chose to stay separated, watching the eyes of each of the four, anticipating their movement through the crowd. He respected the efforts of those who stayed engaged once the speaking concluded. Some chose to show their respectful sentiments, shake their hands, and politely leave. Others were open to a humble disagreement, comic debates that softened the blow of their scathing arguments. Markos assessed the room, saw no threat amongst the group, and enjoyed a refreshment himself. He awaited their departure, wanting to get home to his mother's cooking after briefly returning the morning of from their speaking tour.

The four made their way to the back to meet Markos.

"What did you think?" asked Alana.

"It's time to go home," answered Markos.

The comment, to his chagrin, angered the twins. Markos avoided them since the awkward introduction. Words were never shared between the three, and they saw his presence as unnecessary. They did not believe there was a perceived threat to their cause.

"You did well, Ephraim. You were very relatable," said Jamie, ignoring Markos.

Ephraim smiled at her words, still looking at his unamused brother. Markos was initially impressed with their cause. His joy was nullified by the crowds he saw come out, and his new profession. It was a mask. Inside, he remained profoundly proud. Like his father, however, he only showed his displeasure.

"Well, why don't we go get our stuff from the room and get out of here then," suggested Ephraim, clapping his hands together.

They were accompanied by his mother's coworker through the hallway to the backroom.

"I think it'd be smart if we start putting our time into town hall meetings," said Jonathan. They continued past the church's walls. The baby blue walls turned to stained beige as they got deeper in.

"I agree, it seems politics is the road our words end up at. It's still important we spend our time with the kids, they keep our momentum pure," replied Ephraim.

They ceased to speak as they got closer and closer to the room. Their feet, outside of their guide, moved to the same cadence.

A dichotomy to their mission of purity, they saw it. The horror in the woman's face mirrored theirs. Markos's face was still, wondering if other threats lingered about, preparing for a sort of ambush of reporters or young hecklers. Ephraim shared his worries, forced motionless by the sight of the debacle. All of them refused to move. They watched Markos move about and act. He paced through the hallway checking for stragglers. The woman, reddened by the hideous embarrassment, feared the repercussions.

Markos found slight comfort from the hall being empty. He grabbed the tied woolen noose and pulled it down. Half of the noose was behind the closed door of the backroom, while the goal of the charade was put in front, for everyone to see before entering. Without ample lighting, artificial or natural, the windowless hallway hid the noose from onlookers peering from afar. Only when they reached the door could they see the rope.

Markos slowly opened the door, distressed by the feeling he was going to be caught off-guard. He blamed his complacency on the presence of university campus security teams present during their routine events at schools. He shared in the woman's embarrassment. Slowly, he pushed the door open. He stood in a defensive stance and prepared for any threat on the other side.

Nothing stood out of place. They slowly filed in and checked their belongings as Markos held onto the symbolic rope. He laid the rope on the dusty table where the churchgoers conducted Bible study. The way he loosely discarded the shameful artifact on the table showed his frustration. He motioned to the corner of the room to await their instructions.

"Nothing's missing," said Alana.

Alana walked over to the frantic woman and tried her best to calm her. Markos and Ephraim's mother was her coworker, someone she would have to repeatedly apologize to for the position she put her children in. She was embarrassed for the church, for the mirage of criticism that would befall them, all due to her request to have Ephraim come and speak.

Ephraim walked over to the woman.

"Please, calm down, it wasn't meant for you. I'd like to know who you think did this. Do you have any idea who?" asked Ephraim.

Her face drastically shifted at the poise in his voice. She knew.

"There's no way to be one hundred percent sure, but I believe I know," said the woman. She took a seat on a stool Alana brought over from the table.

"Please bring whoever it is here, call them over."

"Sure, but he's a kid. I don't know what he would do in this situation. I'll call his parents to bring him over."

Jonathan helped her out. She walked a few steps through the door with Jonathan. After he returned, they shut it, allowing her some privacy before the animated phone call. They grouped closer to each other to discuss options, under the cover of her own voice.

"What do you want to do, Ephraim?" asked Alana.

He tried to shelve his emotions, to quantify it into a variable to manipulate the situation.

"We have to turn in the kid, point blank," said Jamie.

"I agree," concurred Jonathan, backing his sister.

Ephraim looked to his legal counsel, awaiting to hear options.

"You could turn in the boy; even gain some sympathy from the students we've spoken to. The boy would face heavy scrutiny. He'd be ruined with a record of a Hate Crime, possibly even serve some small time in jail depending on the judge."

"Serves the kid right, he should be crucified, it would be poetic," assessed Jamie.

She moved her dark black hair away from her face, an intrusion caused by her enthusiastic whispers. She was not going to back down. Some form of punishment was due. Markos was amazed by how much the others were offended by the suggestive act.

Patience, cooler heads, isn't that what you all preach?

They remained quiet while their minds raced. The room was plain, the walls recently repainted clear white. The setup of the room was purposely crafted in order to be colored by the emotions of those reading through the scriptures. No ounce of good laid in the room, instead, darkness and anger filled all who were present. The backpacks and handbags were placed on the small rectangular table where the rope lay, paces away from the door with chairs pushed to the brim of the walls. A wooden cross was hung on the door, an abrupt attempt to show the only path to salvation at the only entrance and exit into the room.

Markos lasered in on Ephraim. He was thinking of the ramifications of involving law enforcement. He was aware of the coverage this would receive, especially when at home.

"What would happen to the boy if he was taken by the police?" asked Ephraim, breaking the tense silence.

"I just told you, Ephraim. He'll be taken by the police. If he's over eighteen, the boy will see jail time under the H.C. Bill. He can see four to six if he confesses here, I'm an officer of the court. I can report him, but you'd also need a different lawyer," said Alana.

"What are we waiting for? We report the boy, we have the witnesses and I'm sure the woman will be happy to shame the boy as an outcast," continued Jamie.

"Eph... Ephraim," intruded Markos.

Nobody bothered to acknowledge his voice. They continued to argue. He walked closer to Ephraim, tapping his shoulder behind him. Ephraim's gaze jetted to catch the view of the man tapping him, still distressed by the presence of the noose.

"Yes, what is it?"

He inched closer to his brother to whisper, afraid of the opinions of the twins.

"No secrets!"

Markos backed up. He was surprised his brother did not recognize his fear.

"You don't want to alienate the people you just spoke to. As awkward as it was, you were able to gain their respect. They can sway and alter the path of your movement. If you involve the police, bring them here, their church...these people won't want to have anything to do with you. We don't need a spectacle, something private can be worked out."

Alana looked away and smiled. He stole the words out of her mouth. She avoided the point to avoid showing insensitivity.

"I agree," affirmed Alana.

Ephraim looked at the twins. "Thoughts?"

They refused to speak. They were frustrated by Markos's analysis. He was right.

"As long as the kid is severely punished," said Jonathan. He waved off his sister's anger to her dismay.

"Death is quicker," concluded Jamie.

They all subtly dispersed, avoiding each other's anger. This was their first test. They saw and heard angered opposition, but to see a noose, they were jerked out of sync.

Nobody took notice of the large room. One bulb hung above the table, connected to the low hanging ceiling. The fresh paint mustered an unpleasant hue as the light shined directly on the rope, underscoring the noose and the tasteless intentions. They were cornered in by the square set up of the room. There was one way in, with one glass window overlooking the rocky lot. The group felt the heat from the bright bulb, increasing the abnormal sweat caused by the paralytic adrenaline. They kept silent as they waited for the boy to show. Everyone wondered who would speak, how they would assess and carry out punishment on the boy and his family.

The message must still remain respectful, thought Markos, *they aren't people who can act on emotion. Punishment has to be calculated, too.*

Markos walked over to Ephraim. His position by the door was tactical. He wanted to avoid any surprise from behind the doors.

"I can talk for you, if need be. The twins are angry, and Alana can't help but talk like a lawyer, they'll see through that. You're out of it, I can do it," said Markos.

Ephraim remained calm and refused to relocate. He did not reply to his brother, instead admiring Markos's confidence as Markos pressed his body against the door. The door was the most important location in the room.

"We'll see. I'm blind right now. I have no idea what's taking so long. I'm still wondering if we've been set up. Right now, everyone should grab their stuff and prepare to leave," said Ephraim, loud enough for all to hear.

He wants to leave. What is he worried about?

They began to grab their handbags and backpacks. Fear struck as they started to walk out.

"The door's locked," whispered Markos.

"Say again?" uttered Alana.

"The door's locked," replied Markos. His voice barely carried to the rest of them.

The twins immediately reverted to the motivations of their nerves. Ephraim remained dazed by the situation he put himself in. Alana and Markos, poised to act, sought a rational explanation.

"Don't panic," said Markos, taking over.

"Do...not...panic. This is a private room, there's nothing here. This room isn't meant to keep people out, it's meant to keep them in. There are reasons it could be locked," continued Markos.

The others succumbed to their worst premonitions, becoming slaves to the room. The light screech of the bulb stressed the twins as Alana's tapping of the table intensified. Ephraim stood stunned by the surprises of the day. He was ashamed he was too trustworthy, too open. Markos detested the looks he received. He believed the security title would rarely be tested, a position in name only. Markos truncated his fears. He locked into their exit strategy.

Window is a last resort, but I don't expect anything to be planned. We're just too nervous.

He delicately knocked on the door. The rushed steps from the other side hardened his inner core. He tightened his lightning grip on the knob. Markos refused to succumb to any threat.

The person behind the door did not hide their anxiety. They struggled with the knob for a few seconds, and only after Markos let go, did the door open.

It was his mother's friend. *It'll just be an acquaintance after this.*

"Why was the door locked?" hammered Jamie, rushing in front of the woman's face.

The brothers were too focused on the three people emerging from the far door, by the stage. Both remained puzzled for there was no child among them. The long hallway to the common area was hollow, pointing towards the door. The adjacent wall cut their vision of the family as they made their way to the seats by the stage.

"I apologize, it's locked from the other side. It requires a key on your side so people don't come through the window for our food and supplies. I was trying to convince them to come back. I'm sorry, I'm so sorry... please, a lot is going on right now," said the woman.

"It's fine, Mariam. Are the people by the stage who we need to talk to?" asked Ephraim.

"Huh...oh yes. Have you decided on a course of action?"

"Thank you, Mariam. That is all we need, please wait outside," said Ephraim.

He was relieved because he was now in an arena of people, a place he believed to be his home court. The earlier ambush neutralized his abilities. There were no people to manipulate, no deals to be brokered. These three, mysterious as they were, now shifted under his control and he was aware of his renewed dominance. Markos feared what punishment he would choose to carry out on the suspect, but he wanted the others to watch.

He waited to grab his things. A patient thought was crucial in a moment where the movement could explode onto the political scene. They waited for Mariam to leave them before they continued.

"Ephraim, please, be careful. You have momentum, the students are with you. The veterans are with you. Your support is important for elected officials. If you send this kid to prison, you'll split your support and stall your progress," added Markos.

"Quiet, let him think. The choice is far from ours. That's no kid," rebutted Jamie.

Alana turned to scorn the woman with the sourest of looks. Jonathan grabbed his sister's hands and gently eased her fire. Jamie smacked her lips at his reprieve.

"Ephraim, we didn't start this to get into politics or become lobbyists. We're here for action. We want action," said Jonathan.

The disfigured circle they stood in was as fluid as their decisions. They had no idea how to punish the culprit, but action was required. Ephraim ignored their insignificant arguments and eyed his brother. With a nod from Markos, they began walking over. The others were slow to follow, but there was no confusion amongst the ranks, they knew who led them.

The brothers walked the pack through the hallway, not allowing a glimpse of meekness to creep out. Ephraim appreciated his brother's force, watching as he played the situation and maneuvered himself in front of the chairs the family sat at. He left room for Ephraim to enter, but his position allowed for a controlled view of all their hands. He wanted to protect everyone from the aggravated emotions in the room.

Markos was a few feet in front of them all, eyeing them as he rested on the wall. He laid his back on the baby blue background of a fluorescent painting, the glowing angel stomping on the vile, fiery demon. He looked at the confused mother and father, dressed in business casual attire, holding the pamphlets the twins handed out to the congregation before they spoke. Ephraim saw a puzzled innocence in the constricted movement of the fidgeting mother, yet the shame of the father's eyes reported the moment. He briefly looked at the two, purposely avoiding even recognizing the boy's presence: "Before we begin, we all know he's guilty, but we have a few requests," said Ephraim.

He slowly pulled a foldable chair in front of the two parents. His legs sat squarely in front of them, between the openness of their legs. His chest and the backrest of the chair were pressed together. He loosely rested his tired hands on the top of the chair.

"Please, the boy...he's smart, but influenced by others," frantically pleaded the mother.

Markos looked at the father and the familiarity of the man gradually introduced itself. He remembered the man's disapproval in the crowd. Still, he politely watched his brother speak. Markos saw the man feel disrespected by the presence of strangers in his church, at the behest of people he held no friendly accord with. His opinions were his, and they refused to fizzle down or adapt. His silence in the hall was as dangerous as the lack of discipline he heeded on his son. Markos knew the man was to blame for the day's situation, and his realization came as a comfort, for if he identified the man's flaws, Ephraim was ready to act on it.

"Ma'am, I truly have no sympathy for your cries, nor do I care for the shame I'd bring upon your family. From your husband's reserved sound and his disinterest during the speaking, I know where these types of actions arise. The boy is as innocent and as much of a victim of this as my brother or I am," coldly explained Ephraim. Markos saw as the boy looked up to defend his family. He was given a scolding by his mother. The action forced him to return to his neutral position.

The father's eyes popped open as the veins on the sides of his temple tightened. The man served no physical threat to the brothers. His age showed in the dry wrinkles of his wrist as his arms remained folded in his lap. The posture was one of distinction, a man who served in a prominent position at a respectable profession. His teeth were embarrassingly whitened, like the dye in the crystal gray of his hair. The bright red polo shirt and the loose khaki slacks would confuse many to his opulence, but the shoes were the giveaway. The cream patent leather shoes matched the look of the lawyer, for they were around so many. His clean-shaven face and the straight posture warned them of his rigidity. He still refused to speak, a precaution his wife surely chose as the route to follow.

His son mirrored his ghostly image.

"My lawyer wisely has informed me of the punishments for breaking The Hate Crime Bill. We have taken the rope and will dispose of it. Luckily, my brother has also chosen to refrain from getting the police involved and making this a shaky situation," continued Ephraim.

Ephraim took a pause as he saw the scarlet blood sink and dissipate from the father's face. His shock was justified, but he knew something was still in store for his son. He was embarrassed by the gasps of his oblivious wife. The boy looked up and felt a weight shift off his shoulder. He thought he escaped the danger.

Ephraim looked to his brother. Markos was focused on the anger and stiffness of the twins who stood by the exit with the bags. He felt their hatred for the family. They stood for the oppression the twins identified as the burdensome plague ailing so many people. He felt the sharp pain of the memory of Elsa, mentally chuckling at how the situation proved him wrong. Their disgust betrayed their beliefs, many of the orations they made regarding peace and the deflection of hatred. He looked at the proof of the betrayal Elsa asked him about on the sandy beach.

"What is it you want?" asked the father, barely moving his lips. His body was still.

"Well, that depends," said Ephraim.

He scratched at the few gray strands recently populating the smooth dark skin on his face. He moved the chair towards the boy, forgetting the two parents. The boy's head steadily rose. He saw from the squinting blue eyes how angry the boy was. He was angry at the embarrassment of being caught like an uneasy child in an administrator's office. The boy had no remorse, for he looked at Ephraim with arrogance. Ephraim had almost a decade over the boy, but in the boy's eyes, they were equals. The brothers saw in the boy's posture how much correction he needed.

Did Dad see this in us as kids?

The boy's wrinkled plaid shirt and tight black jeans stuck to his body as fluids released from his pores. Ephraim refused to be distracted and did not flinch as he kept eye contact. Markos felt uneasy about the risk of spontaneity arising from a staring contest of pride. The two would be like the moment, at a psychological impasse, for decades to come, as Markos shared the facts of the past. He shared the beginning, where the curly black-haired boy made his mark on the brothers.

"What's your name?"

The boy was beaten. Ephraim knew the boy was not in control, of his attitude or of his own actions. He was tricked into shifting his eyes from the bushy man, half a foot in front of him, to his mother and father as they nervously awaited his sentence. He looked for permission to divulge the information and received an approval from his mother.

"Pe...Peter."

"Are you in school, college?"

"Yeah, here in Sacramento, living at home."

"State or city?" asked Ephraim.

"State."

"Huh, okay. Peter, how old are you?"

"Nineteen."

"So much for being a kid?" said Ephraim as he looked at the focused Markos. "So, prison instead of juvie?"

"I guess," answered the boy with a hint of irritation.

"You are a feisty kid. You have gumption, but you're misguided. Do you want to go to jail?"

"No, not at all."

"Then why the noose on the door?" continued Ephraim.

Jesus, he's manipulating the kid. Yes, Ephraim, the parents are to blame. You're letting our woes with Dad confuse you. You are just punishing his parents. Please wrap this up.

"Hello?"

"Answer him!" demanded the father.

"Please sir, I'm having a conversation with your son. I have finished with you both," wittily replied Ephraim.

"Ephraim, finish this up, we need to get going," added Markos. He startled the family as all three looked at him.

They were at the mercy of Ephraim's patience. He was calm. He had decided before he began, the boy's parents were to blame for the crime. To him, Peter was a boy who had no control over the situation. The father's shame stemmed from the fact the boy was caught, not of the action itself. That's how Ephraim saw it. His perception of the events was the only that mattered in the moment.

"Continue, Peter," calmly ordered Ephraim.

"I'm...I'm not a fan of yours," said the boy.

The twins looked away in disdain from Peter. Jamie refused to watch any more of the sluggish interrogation. Her contempt was justified, and they all knew it.

"Can I wait by the car, I might say something?" asked Jamie.

"Yes, feel free, any of you. I'm nearly done," said Ephraim, locked into the eyes of Peter.

Jamie immediately rushed out with the bags. Jonathan remained for a few moments but decided it wiser to stay with his sister. He did not want to show dissension with blood.

"Okay, we're getting somewhere, what don't you like?"

Peter took his time as he thought of the question. The old curtains in the church were useless to the rays of sunshine creeping into the hall.

The light exposed the dust in the air between them. The warm air heightened the heat of the contentious room. The boy brushed his hair through with his hands. He kept thinking as the waiting seconds worsened the feverish anxiety of the parents. They desperately wanted to be rid of the situation, looking Ephraim up and down, praying in their heads for it all to conclude.

"I'm not a fan of the list," yelled Peter in his lightbulb moment.

"Which point?" rebutted Ephraim. He did not want to give him time to think.

"I'm really not a fan of the one about prison reform or changes to how certain things are done with the prison system. It's good as is," concluded Peter.

"*It's...good...as...is.* Interesting, did that warrant a noose?"

None of them spoke. Silence felt as if it fell on the whole neighborhood, not even cars could be heard outside.

"Okay you won't answer. Are you a racist?" asked Ephraim.

Peter's father smacked his lips as he cracked a sarcastic smile. The word lost its meaning in the twenties. It was overtly thrown around; an accusation one side saw as a tool to silence.

"I warn you sir, keep your remarks to yourself. I'm talking to the boy," warned Ephraim.

The man's wife calmly put her palm on her husband's hand to help his uneasiness. Markos saw how much the man reminded him of his father, crumbling at the thought of losing control. A loud sound removed the effect of Ephraim's show of power. The breeze of the cooling system as it turned on and smacked the curtains into the window served to break the ice in the room.

"Did it warrant a noose?"

Again, silence. Markos silently scoffed.

"You don't like the prison point, I heard you, I understand. Did it warrant a noose?"

"Yes!" hammered Peter.

"Peter!!" yelled his father.

Ephraim swiftly answered the father's disruption: "Sir, if you need to remove yourself, do so. If anything comes from you again, authorities will be alerted, and the next time you see us, that woman will be wrapping her closing arguments in court as your son is hauled away," said Ephraim. He pointed to Alana near the door without turning. His eyes never deviated from Peter.

The father froze at his helplessness. He looked up for strength.

"Okay, that's that. It warranted a noose. Are you a racist?"

"No, this is Sacramento, I was raised around all types of people," said Peter. He believed this freed him from suspicion.

"Okay, Peter, do you believe the noose is racist?"

"No, it's intended purpose was to scare you into stopping. I wanted you to never walk into a place like this. I wanted you to think twice before ever discussing your points again."

Ephraim could hear the father in his voice. Peter was acquainted with an infectious youthful passion for politics. Ephraim saw it in the people supporting him as well. They either went deeper into the beliefs of their parents, or outright rebelled against them, still following the path of politics. Politics became the guiding topic of conversation.

"Well, do you think you should be punished? I believe we both know you don't really understand the gravity of what you did, nor do I believe you actually know what I talk about. I believe the sound bites you see or the things on the news that trigger your parents caused this anger. But I'm here to tell you, I didn't want to come here. I know how much opposition awaited me. I don't really care what you or your parents believe in. I'm here because a community member, my mother's coworker, who you turned into a frantic woman, asked us to come. Out of respect, I briefly discussed my list and what we plan to do in the coming years. You brought that noose because you were scared and thought you could be a hero to you and yours. Look, look at your parents. You embarrassed them, well, your father may be a little proud after this all blows over. Either way, do you believe you should be punished?"

Peter slowly nodded his head. He was out of it, beguiled by the statement, thinking it over how he was quickly analyzed. The naked feeling he felt worsened the verbal assault he received.

"My fate is in your hands," said Peter, lowering his head.

Ephraim finally removed his invasive eyes from Peter and arose from his seat. He returned the chair back to the correct position. He looked at Markos, then to his watchful lawyer near the door. She stood motionless. She, like the rest, waited for the end.

"Alright, Peter. I don't know what type of person you are, but you aren't an idiot. You are just very…very, very ignorant. It may come from Mom and Dad, it could be from what you learned, I don't know," said Ephraim, insulting the family.

"I do know a way to rectify this situation. I could alert the authorities; you could go to prison, and I can hope for you to feel the effects of our efforts in four to six years. I believe we could get it done in that time. Then, I'm sure you'd feel differently about us.

"But, like other folks who falter, with time, there are other ways to rectify hateful actions. I look around, and I think of how many opportunities I have given my brother in this life. I look at how many times Alana over there had patience with the Solomons family. There are ways to reform without bars. I'll open a door for you, but if you don't accept it, prison it is."

Ephraim shifted his confidence towards the parents now.

"Alright Mom and Dad, I'm done. He was immature to put a noose in your place of worship, and it goes to show how far your parenting has gone with him. It's easy, the second option is, the boy becomes my…*underling*, an intern that works directly in the field with us. He would accompany us, when he's not in school, as an unpaid associate. He'd be filling out forms and such during the school year. He's ours, he is our errand boy. He'll also do important things like volunteering at the community center and going on trips to City Hall with us. He'll do any of the tasks we ask of him. He'd serve for four to six years, probably six to properly recondition him. He'll be my advocate. The way I see it, you condemned him, so you decide."

There was no choice to be discussed. The entire debate was concluded in a mere minute. Ephraim wanted to punish the irregular disciplining of the parents, accomplishing the goal by strong-arming them. He humiliated them in the process. Peter was practically given to him, for Ephraim knew the father would not sacrifice the name. Peter's father would sacrifice his son's idealism in order to stop his family name from being tarnished. The situation was finalized between the two lawyers in writing, using legal loopholes to get a simple non-disclosure agreement signed. Markos was surprised by how clever, yet distracted, his brother was. He previously saw the backroom deals being struck, but this was a direct manipulation of an opponent. He underestimated Ephraim's prowess, seeing how he turned the problem fortuitous. Markos saw, for the first time, a glimpse of a natural response, to their father's absence.

He feared what repercussions would come with the decision.

"The boy will serve under your wing. I have no use for him, except for small things like moving stuff and driving us. He'll have to be close to one of us for him to gain respect for us. He's our science project, we have to reform him in the next few years. As much as he had evil intentions, he was dealt bad conditions by those two. Teach him about security, whatever you have to do to get into his head," ordered Ephraim, days after the incident.

Markos thought about his new assignment as the twins argued their opposing views over the coming weeks. The twins saw the boy's invitation as a form of betrayal by Ephraim, a slight the twins would hearken back to. They believed the addition of an individual with his perceived intentions perverted their cause. The yells shared on the car ride home was the first instance of displeasure the group had with one another. The even argument, the twins against Ephraim and Alana, echoed through the car as Markos focused on the drive across town to their home.

The revelations of Peter's assimilation into the group were a shock to Anna and Olivia, their mouths agape at Peter's preliminary entrance on the scene. His efforts with the group were known to be transformative, legitimizing the longevity of the group with the future being secured. Peter opened the group to other demographics. Ephraim's calculations paid off in the long term in relation to the proposed plan of the group. However, the relationship and trust between the team did not heal as Markos became closer with the boy. Nevertheless, awe and shock were seen in the eyes of the few who knew where young Peter originated from.

Their shock was nothing compared to the surprise of the ramifications Markos would face if others knew he himself broke a part of his Non-Disclosure Agreement. He enjoyed, however, the liberation of a brief truth in a mirage of lies.

That night, one of the man's last remaining nights, the sleep was as peaceful as it was in his early years in the warm clutches of Elsa.

eleven:
Politics, The End All Be All

"1. Dedicate our services to educating others and ourselves in the importance of the existence of another, the importance of a dependable and knowledgeable neighbor."

- Entente Party's List of Goals, inherited from the social movement of founder, Ephraim Solomons.

His rise is covered. His failures demand attention.

Markos desired solitude the next morning. He walked around in what was a smoke-filled park. Summer wildfires were pushing smoke onto California's capital city. It took a great toll on the air quality of the masked sunny day. A thick layer of grayish haze surrounded the fiery circular spectacle, alone in the sky. Markos saw as the mist of the sprinklers rose from the ground and heightened the visage of the mystical landscape.

His trek around the park was dull, steadily feeling how his impending death was taking shape. His coughs were progressively worsening as they strung on longer with each initial burst. The shortening of his breath suffocated him in times of recollection. His disrupted airflow showed him the true limitations of mortality.

Markos found himself completing little over a lap before acquainting his backside with the unmoving metal benches. He looked on, then up, begging God for more time. He demanded strength to conclude his story.

What could be accomplished with the action of clutching a cross, he hoped for. Any source of aid would go a long way. Markos wondered how the condition worsened so rapidly. Whenever love crept into his hardened heart, death lingered, and he feared what was in store.

It's written, but why like this, like this for me?

He shrugged at the frustration and the lack of control he feared his father was victim to. He held back tears out of necessity. Nothing would come from them.

Two days remained before they would depart to his nephew's home, the day his speech would be heard and live streamed for the first time. Anna's wit demanded he allow the streaming in order to charge them extra for the additional audience.

The speech had been written and edited. He was fearful of its ramifications. He thought of how he would leave the family. He hoped to give them closure on the hidden darkness of the angel propelled by the media. Markos believed Ephraim to be far more than the angelic figure kids depicted him to be. He convinced himself the allure of his brother was, in part, created by the tough decisions and sacrifices he maintained were necessary to the safety of those around him. Markos thought of his brother as selfish at times, hesitant in disclosing facts when others needed to be privy to his thoughts. Ephraim's monopoly on secrets needed to be exposed. At a point, to Markos, the man felt himself to be more important than his listed goals, a movement many dedicated so much to.

Markos still shared great admiration for the soldier of the people, a champion, but the truth was glaring to those close to him. His enemies grew as his popularity did. He opened himself to the paranoia most feel from repeated bombardment from opposition. As those who built the foundation began to leave him, Markos saw his brother slowly wither away and deteriorate, sacrificing the tenets he first campaigned with.

Olivia and Anna did not desire to defend anyone. Accuracy of events is what they demanded. Their maturity was missing in times of Solomons' peril, in a period where disputes may have been resolved by their superior competence. They were appreciative, young and inquisitive, ready to hear the difficult journey the brothers pushed through. The two remained at home the morning of, spending the day packing and patiently waiting for Markos to return.

"Do you remember anything, like stuff that happened here at home?" asked Anna.

"Bits and pieces."

Olivia removed her hands from the backpack she placed her toiletries into. The two were sitting in front of each other, utilizing the rug on the hardwood floor like a blanket at a picnic. Their neatly folded garments and remaining toiletries were scattered around them as they sat together and handed each other the different objects on their packing checklist.

"I do remember Dad being on the road often, coming home and leaving as fast as he came. Mom would sometimes read to us about the stuff he was doing. We read about things like him endorsing someone or having an important meeting with some people."

Anna sat disappointed in the lacking memories of her mother. She wanted to see if she could gain an upper hand before Markos returned: "Do you remember him and Markos, what was their relationship like before...?" She paused before continuing. "I don't even know what happened, but what was it like?"

Olivia stopped her movements altogether. She considered the question and configured through remnants of broken memories.

"In the house, Markos stayed in his room. He was a reader. Another thing, he was always on the phone. I never knew who it was, but he always, *always* avoided people in the house when he was on the phone. He would share some small words with Grandma, but he was isolated here. Him and Dad shared some time together on their walks in the morning. That was their time to speak freely with each other. I'd tag along, bringing a ball or...uh, like a frisbee, whatever. I'd play out there and sometimes they'd play with me if they had nothing to talk over. Sometimes, Alana would meet them there, or the whole house would come while they walked around. Their conversations were interesting, the science of people, the way people react, stuff like that. They were interesting, but both were extremely reserved on their own. It didn't surprise me they fell out."

Anna hoped she would have had the strength to change the outcome of their relationship if she was there in the time of conflict. With their discussions, Markos led her towards the end of the spiraling journey of growing questions about Ephraim and the Solomons name. Markos was very important to them, in little under a month, providing them with satisfactory responses to intricacies they demanded answers for. His information served as the stimulation for Anna motioning towards him when he walked in, spontaneously hugging him with her might. The noticeable symptoms stalling the continuity of the stories gave her indication of a problem to his health. She found her mother's delicate, periodic warnings to give him space motivated by an agenda. She sensed the discomfort of the unfavorable news shared by the doctors. They would not be permitted to discuss all she hoped for in the time given. Anna used the prolonged time of the union to emphasize, he was no longer alone, nor would he be in the end. The embrace was well received, served with embarrassment and a look to Olivia.

She cheerfully shrugged at the inability to fool her intelligent pupil. As Olivia blushed, Markos softly placed his arms around the girl, remembering the first time he saw her in the photos Alondra shared with him.

"'We wither away once those who can carry the name come of age and become worthy of holding our truths.' It's something Ephraim told me when Mom died. When it's time, it's time," spoke Markos, ending their embrace. He looked, again, at the two as Anna returned to the spot rug.

"Worry occurs for the dead when things remain unsaid. I will say what needs to be said. But first, a shower is needed," said Markos. He dropped his spectacles on the table near them.

He ascended up the stairs and situated himself in the restroom, shakingly removing his sweat-filled garments. Markos glanced at his face in the mirror. He let the shameful tears roam down his puffed cheeks. Never would he think the young girl, once a baby in white angelic clothes in a photo captured at her christening, would embrace him in his lifetime. He was grateful for Alondra's mercy. She understood the dilemma of the family, but still she decided to share photos of Anna with him. She shared similarities with his mother who followed a similar policy of forgiveness.

The showerhead cleansed his ignited feelings of nostalgia. He remembered the efforts made by Alana to include him, as well as the small patience Alondra afforded him out of compassion. They owed him nothing. Markos thought of how his mother was pitted against her daughter-in-law because of his selfishness, how Ephraim bore the cross of all his sins. His last sin, a fatal one, weakened Ephraim's resolve with him. The heated water quenched the chill of past vicissitudes, thinking of where it all went sideways for the family.

When, he thought.

It was Ephraim. I was selfish in my wants and needs, my desired isolation. He chose to grab more and more when it was just a little the people wanted. He pushed it, he pushed me. Ephraim had time with the family. I wasn't selfish, not compared to you. You chose to get into it, you chose politics.

"He chose the route to expand," announced Markos, residing on the carpet near them, his back to the leather sofas. He watched the two of them file through the chaos of bags and clothes.

"Mmm, after you all came together, how fast did it all come to be?" asked Olivia.

Her attention was split with finding an antique doll she purchased for Darius's daughter.

"It wasn't fast at all. As quick as my life moved in Morocco, life dramatically slowed once I began to work with Ephraim. Over the next three years, as I got closer to Peter, we traveled and traveled. We met with academics and local social leaders. We held dinners, repainted old community shops and restaurants, held group clean-up events, and we fixed up community centers. As a group, we were always permitted to do anything by the city. Our events were always the safest. It was funny, Ephraim was well respected by those from city hall to those who roamed the streets in inner cities. He would always meet with people, respecting all their time and influence. He asked everyone what they wanted to see and what people like him should speak about. In turn, they attended his speeches and rallies, ensuring his safety with me. He was truly smart about the way he networked," said Markos. He paused to sneak in a sip of his iced water. His bowl of cinnamon oatmeal laid by his side. He sat patiently waiting for the bowl to cool for consumption.

"We started to travel to other states, typically liberal states like Oregon and Washington. Ephraim avoided leaning one way, but it was evident that reform was what he wanted. He was methodical about how though. His courtship with the universities, the only ones who he gave interviews to, allowed for his message to be challenged by those who at least respected his views. He controlled the narrative and allowed people like moderate conservatives and veterans who wouldn't typically side with a reformer, welcome him. He became very popular on the West Coast. He ended up endorsing candidates during local elections and mayoral elections in Oakland...Seattle, Tacoma, Eugene, and the rest of the big cities in the West."

He paused to conduct a temperature check of his oatmeal. He nearly burnt his hand when he felt the sides of the orange ceramic bowl. The noise the spoon made clinking the sides of the bowl alerted the two to his food. He took another sip of cooled water after almost dropping the bowl, only to suffer from violent coughs at the entrance of iced water into his system, again.

"I apologize for that, the coughs got worse in the night."

A worried look was shared between the girls before he continued.

"Anyways, he was smart about who he endorsed. It never leaned towards one party, he only endorsed those that took their time to hold meaningful, private conversations with him. He sometimes would even endorse multiple candidates in a race if they were to his liking. He would cash in favors as well, as any man would. He would ask for approval for certain projects in local centers, as well as aid in uplifting the local landscape and aesthetic of inner cities. He focused on showing other people their neighborhood didn't have to be what it was. His power resided in his oral skills. He could bring people out after long days to help him volunteer. He never needed the money or aid, for his power lay with people's actions. That's where his movement was different, how he had normal, everyday people coming to help out. It was very important to show people that money wasn't necessarily required. The twins were important in teaching him the large-scale effect of volunteering. The twins carried the voice of change with their initiatives and the projects they brought forth to the group. Peter's hard work legitimized the broadened thinking of his movement with the presence of a white male, young in age with a conservative background."

Anna smiled at the cleverness of Ephraim, how he turned a sick situation into a plus.

"How was young Peter, anyways? How was his *transformation?*" asked Anna.

"He was always scared, but we knew he was wronged. The boy would've been an immortal enemy of all Black people if we'd sent him to prison. After six months or so, he felt fulfilled by his work. He saw the happy faces he was surrounded by at the rallies. He stayed by my side and gave me a purpose beyond security."

He paused, thinking of the young man's innocence, pondering if it ever existed.

"In those times, the sun would rise, and I would not wake thinking of Elsa. We remained close in those early days, before his presence became of importance to Ephraim. I remember him telling me how popular he was on campus because of his affiliation with us. There wasn't a day the idiot didn't apologize for what he did. He taught me of hate, how ignorant, and how dangerous it could be when you fight it back with anger," answered Markos.

Olivia's eyes perked up as he concluded his thoughts on Peter. Her eyebrows rose as she questioned the morality of their actions.

"He wasn't punished though?"

"He wasn't. He was embarrassed, but what was better, he was freed from his old thinking. He was disowned by his family after he graduated college and chose to remain with us. The boy was okay with me and Ephraim, a successful science project."

"If people knew…?" uttered Olivia under her breath. The resentment worried Markos.

"They never will. Let dead dogs lie, awakening them has consequences, *for all of us.*"

Her shoulders rose as a sign of a forgetful retreat. She did not like it, but she was not clueless, secrets like those remained locked away for the benefit of others. A fact with this power gave Markos wiggle room to bend the truth, providing credibility for his half-truths without raising eyebrows.

"When did they have the explosive moment happen? I still can't see how it all blew up to be that big?" inquired Anna.

"*Our* conflict arises in the blow up. We began to appear in certain places we didn't expect…Austin, Phoenix, and Reno from what I can remember. Ephraim's words bled into the neighboring areas of those cities. He amassed a notable following in right leaning states. They appreciated our moderate stances and the stagnant patience we had with politicians. When hate is spewed between people, everyone welcomes a reformer they can appreciate. The volunteer programs exemplified action and mobilization, and Ephraim stressed that it's human to want to fight laziness to help others. He gave them something tangible to do.

"I want to say, sometime in the mid to late thirties, maybe 2034, midterm elections were testy. The tension of the twenties and early thirties began to wither away. People always want change, but they desire something more. They wanted honorable people in office. What you need to understand is that many of the candidates we endorsed, were now moving up. They entered into senatorial and representative races and from there, our stock skyrocketed. We were brought in, by both parties, since our movement was so popular on the West Coast.

"Shortly after, our support became worth a lot more. We were needed in different types of elections and found ourselves deep into national legislative races in Nevada, Texas and Washington. I'm trying to tell you. People really appreciated the time we took with candidates and how patient we were with our decisions. Everyone was tired of the divisive options they were given; they saw us break political lines, beyond the promises other politicians made.

"We were asked to begin drafting our own legislation for policies that could bring about the change people wanted. Candidates and politicians saw this as an opportunity to be seized. Our bills began to be introduced on the floors of all levels of government: local, state and federal. By 2038, the elections were a lock to win if the candidates received our tap on the shoulder. We felt powerful, a feeling of success, but we sacrificed our time with the community to help these politicians."

We, we, we, I didn't do anything. I was just there.

"The issue arose a year later, by the twins of course. They made good, strong points that politicians were reneging on all their promises of passing our legislation. The group waited six years to see some change, but there were no efforts, regardless of what audience we had. Some elected officials would briefly introduce legislation based on the ten points, but nothing came from their unpassionate effort. Ephraim began to openly defy the politicians they once endorsed. He stirred the pot amongst voters and officials. We sort of confused the people who had grown with us over the years. Students and fresh graduates, who were with us in the beginning, were now nearly a decade removed from school. They still trusted us though. We amassed a large industrial as well as corporate following, and the teachings were trickling down from university students to high school students as well. Thousands became hundreds of thousands. Out of nowhere, our decisions swayed opinions of millions. The underground became mainstream.

"Many politicians were forced to cave and reintroduce the legislation, but again, their efforts were for the cameras. Nothing passed the committee level. We sat at an impasse."

I need to eat this oatmeal before it goes cold.

"Excuse me, I am pretty hungry."

He grabbed the bowl, stalling the rushed history lesson. High school classrooms instructed children in the government and economics classes about Ephraim's rise. This was common practice for years since the Ententes took hold of the House. The techniques compartmentalized by the founders of the Entente Party were popular due to its mobilization capabilities and the patience Ephraim took in laying the pavement for his optimistic policies. Politicians started to implement similar tactics in their own campaign trails, approaching problems in their community with a more hands-on approach. The volunteer programs became incorporated into the budgets of many states, while becoming fully subsidized by others who saw the benefit of a motivated citizenry. Markos bashed states each time he took the podium for taking initiative instead of the people, crushing the innocent intentions of volunteering. They watered down the passion. *Deterioration comes with complacency Ephraim, something you pointed out but did not prevent.*

Markos arose to place his dishes in the automated dishwasher. He grabbed a blueberry flavored granola bar from the counter after putting his dishes away. The sugar engulfed his tongue with flavor. He watered the straggling chunks positioned in the cracks of his teeth with warmed almond milk, mixed into his caffeinated black tea. His detour into the kitchen concluded with him wallowing down the snack. He returned with his beverage to the seat where his chilled water still sat.

The exertion of his muscles stole his supply of oxygen and forced a rampant cough out of his mouth. Luckily, he escaped its terror seconds after.

"What's left to pack?"

"All this stuff you see behind Mom and some old pictures for Darius's daughter. Forget that, though, we'll take care of it, continue the story."

Markos ignored her request and countered with one of his own. "What pictures?"

"Some old stuff, we're gonna put it in an envelope. We're clueless about a lot of things, but Darius's daughter carries the name of her father and is as separated from it as we were. We just wanted to send her some things," said Olivia.

His disappointment triggered an empathetic response.

"Don't let that child be raised like that, hidden from this side of the family. There are a lot of unsaid things, I get it. She is as important as any of us, don't have her resent our family due to her father's shortcomings. The mother will need to have the resolve Alondra and my mother had to not bad mouth our name. It sounds like Darius followed my father's path."

Olivia motioned her head towards the inner workings of a miniature duffle bag. She was ashamed of her brother, for the pressure he put on her while avoiding his family, using his name to instead open doors for himself.

"Yeah, he's terrible."

"Anna!!" shouted Olivia. Markos laughed at her assessment.

"Still, you must correct your family, take the burden for his mistakes and when he falls short of certain duties, it's up to you to take care of it. The pictures are evidence of your understanding of the responsibility," declared Markos.

The women nodded their heads to humbly accept his comment, eyeing each other.

"Continue though," ordered Anna.

He smiled, taking the finishing sip of his tea.

"Ahh...well, like I was saying...an impasse. Rumblings and rumors were the name of the game. We share secrets with another close friend believing it will stay with us, neglecting the fact that we might not be the closest friends of our close friends. Well, Ephraim began having conversations with the team about breaking off from the politicians they had aligned with."

"I remember that. I was pretty young, but I remember reading about that," chimed in Olivia.

The two were lost. She did not previously speak about the past.

"What? He was my dad. It was everywhere," innocently rebutted Olivia. Smiles were put on their faces at her blushing response.

"Good, as we assumed," replied Markos.

"The debate was heated, heavy on the fact that they had fought each other to get into politics. The twins resembled the fierce socialists from the 1960s who fought against various establishments. They didn't care for politicians but were guaranteed by Ephraim they wouldn't go too deep if they started endorsing some. After initially witnessing the debates and backroom conversations, watching the way the game was played, the twins folded their reservations and saw a higher probability of change with their alignment with certain officials. They did not wish for it to go beyond that, just endorsements. Their acceptance was radical, but they had limits. Originally, when we discussed breaking away, Peter, years into the movement, shocked us and sided with Ephraim. While Alana abstained, the twins voted against it. I never voted on any of their addendums or legislation drafts, I only offered my opinion at times. As time continued on, from that point, their votes stopped being unanimous," said Markos.

"There was more on the line than just breaking away from politicians," alerted Markos.

He sipped water with a need for replenishment. He was liable to surrender to his coughs.

"*A political nation with three crutches is slowed and rendered unreliable,*" said Markos.

"I'm paraphrasing, but that quote came from one of the books our father made us read as a kid. It's a great book, but I remember thinking of this when Ephraim and Peter concocted the idea of breaking away from politicians and forming our own party. Conversations quickly soured and turned absolute. They marauded each other with ultimatums and threats. The twins were no match for the carnivorous attitude of those two. Peter, I later found out, leaked the debate under an anonymous tip, and created a frenzy."

The women turned their attention towards him and his uncorroborated story. The truth was in those words, however.

"What? Leaked it?" asked Anna. Markos nodded to confirm.

Olivia already knew the more important question; a fact Markos was going to gloss over if they did not ask: "Did Dad give the okay?"

Markos brushed his knees with both of his hands to hide the slight sadness of shaming their calculated patriarch: "Yes, Peter later revealed that to me when I left."

The women stopped packing, unsure of their peculiar feelings.

Anna snapped out of it first, asking, "What happened after?"

"They all regrouped, but without truth, threats are dangerous. He, of course, protected Ephraim, but me and Alana had our suspicions. Alana deflected when she spoke to the public, but warnings were given from the politicians who saw our rise as a legitimate threat to their reign. They were alarmed at how much social media was buzzing at our discussion to break away and create something new. We found resounding support with our friends in Texas, Nevada, and New Mexico. The liberal states were always going to ride with us, good or bad. Too much time was spent there, and they knew us. Threats are dangerous in a game of perception.

"We discussed certain things and in a time of solidarity, we chose to stall any talks and table any vote on breaking away. The damage was already done, though. You have to know, they were celebrities, especially in the United States. Their videos were receiving thousands of replies and reposts, amassing followings in various states, breaking past just here in the West Coast. We remained in the West, but our policies and the list were discussed among so many others, professors and students. They were equivalent to rockstars, especially Ephraim, the mastermind, and Alana, the loyal soldier and spokesperson. Once the news broke, the opinionated media outlets were repeatedly debating the ramifications of a third political party, especially when you have one as structured and as supported as Ephraim's movement. Years were already put in for the conception of something new.

"The news buildup was too much for leaders in Washington to ignore. They were against us breaking away. They worried themselves with scenarios they created in their own heads. Those men and women were conniving leaders who chose to blindside others rather than work out a deal with people they didn't understand. Both parties wanted to sit down with us, but they were fearful we would align with the other if we became at odds with one. Both instead chose to *let dead dogs lie.* It's funny how they scared each other into inaction, but soon, their supporters wanted a large sit down, a parlay of sorts because as I told you, going into the 40s now, people's demands required action. People wanted to know what Ephraim's thoughts were. This was a dangerous power to give to any man," said Markos.

"What did you all decide?" asked Anna.

"Out of fear we may change our minds at any time, we were asked to meet a delegation of two members from both parties. They wanted to speak to just Alana and Ephraim. They demanded we leave our dogs at home. They didn't want idealists in the room, only 'the visionaries.' That's how the group interpreted the invitation to Washington. They complied, but petitioned to allow me, their ridiculous form of security to also tag along. When I tell you the conversation between the group was vicious, I mean it. We were broken by the ordeal."

Markos delayed his insertion into the heated battle. He chose to abstain from the words and accusations slung between the allies. Markos slowly stretched his arms behind the glass dining table on the dirtied carpet. Avoiding the minefield of gazes, Markos headed to the kitchen, walking on pins and needles. He wished to defend his brother, even as he stood in the wrong.

"We're not getting anywhere; we have to come to a decision today. We've held out long enough," spoke Alana. She sat frustrated at the table, her sweaty palms brushing through her tied blond hair, placing her reading glasses on her forehead.

Peter sat near Alana under the chandelier. The five miniature lights circled the enlarged yellow light aligned directly above a hunter green, rose-covered vase. Peter's facial hair took over the once childish, smooth face seeking an adversary in the Solomons family. He scratched his slick backed hair, a neat transformation from his rugged curls. The discipline he adopted from his new family, the Solomons, shaped his look, head to toe.

The twins comfortably sat on the clear white couches with Jonathan's feet resting on the plain coffee table. The muted flat screen illuminated the room with news headlines bolded on the bottom of the screen. All the words focused on the meeting scheduled for three days from then. Jamie fumed at the coverage. She was weakened by the power she allowed to be taken from her, by Ephraim and the influences around him. Peter bested her, and now Washington was next. Her plastic bracelets collided with her new computer watch as she tied her hair into a ponytail.

Jamie wondered if the contest would turn physical, for they were at the apex of the dispute. Jonathan and Jamie admonished Peter for the leaking of the information, again, choosing to not let the issue subside. They were victims of their tunnel vision. They could not see how Ephraim served as the catalyst of the leak. Love for a man they did not understand clouded their rationale, but she did not care for the other. She could take the small Peter. To her, he would always remain a boy whose words meant more than his actions. She spent time as a volleyball player, sensibly coordinated and blessed with the physical capital, making her a petrifying figure. Her height was no more than seventy inches, but her broad shoulders and daunting expressions struck fear in opponents. There were reasons for her name to be missing in the invitation to Washington.

She blamed Peter for the weakened bond between them. He gave credibility to assailants who called them frauds looking for temporary popularity. She despised Peter and waited for justification to pounce on her prey. She found it, but the true challenge lied with the tensions between Jonathan and Ephraim. Ephraim was out of shape, diseased by the diet and stress of one distracted by other tasks. He was larger, but the growing gray in his beard was a facade, he could still handle himself. Jonathan was tall, resembling a professional basketball player. The two were quite similar in height, but Jonathan's bodily regiment was supreme. He was neatly chiseled, clean-shaved, carrying himself with the utmost respect of his body and posture. He, too, was fed up. He, however, remained the cooler one of the group, astounding Markos. His composure led Markos to worry if the twins were correct in this instance. Emotions clouded their mind, ignoring Markos in the dispute, a potential ally capable of stifling Ephraim.

"We don't need to do anything; I don't know why we won't allow this topic to remain tabled. We shouldn't allow people, let alone those in Washington, the ones we accused of stalling the progress we jumpstarted, to dictate our actions," interjected Jamie.

Markos returned from the kitchen, stepping out for refreshments. He saw how angry Ephraim was by Jamie's repetition. He continued with his arguments.

"I don't know what you want, Jamie. I told you, us three are going to represent your wishes. We're just asking for a new vote. If a deal isn't struck, we need to be able to act and announce as soon as we touch down back here."

"Why can't we wait, I don't see it the way you do?" asked Jonathan. His hands were placed in the air in doubt.

"Because…we speak at Lake Merritt a few days after we return. That's where the announcement would take place, if we chose to split and create our own thing," noted Ephraim.

Markos moved over to the table. He sat opposite Alana, next to Ephraim's ally. He looked at the face many women appealed to; the one Ephraim needed to convince. He needed her support.

"If a deal isn't struck, why must we choose to turn into a party? I've said it, we'll sell out. Money will shift our vision and you can be sure that our list will be nothing more than words. Vote or not, you know where I stand," added Jamie.

"Let's vote then," said Peter under his breath.

"Shut up! You don't dictate anything here," yelled Jamie.

All eyes rested on the sweating Jamie and her uncontrolled temper. Silence carried the brooding thoughts of each marauder. They wondered where the others' allegiances lied, scared of ultimatums capable of splitting their progressing union.

"During the last election, 41% of people who voted believed that the two-party system was waning. People were asked why they thought that. They said the two parties were too old and that they were worsening their tactics to distinguish and disunify the other side. The people suffered through a pandemic of distrust and accusations, as well as an economic downturn. We have millions who follow us. We are well respected. Do you understand how old these parties are? Regardless of what we think, they have done some things in the centuries they've been around. Forget ourselves, even our names and legacies, this political party can stand tall for centuries to come if we think in terms of decades instead of months and years. That's what separates people from the governments and corporations. We can do something for people, with all this momentum, we can do it in this lifetime and the next. Our name will die out, the party could carry on with the path *we* set it on. Why are you against this Jamie?" asked Ephraim.

"Don't forget where these parties ended up. Look where they are now. The money, Ephraim, we have been able to do it all without the money. Discipline, the word of the century according to you, will it really be the word to describe us? There'll be donors who want a piece of the pie we're selling, attached requests that come with the cash. You're playing a dangerous game, again, *you* know where I stand," concluded Jamie as she pointed at Ephraim.

The mist of her perspired shirt made its way to the carpet. The passion with which she spoke froze the thought processes of the others. They sat, four hours into their dinner and the debate that followed, stalled in how to finish. Jamie, to her credit, sat unchanged and unaffected by the arguments of those who never saw money corrupt a loved one. Her and Jonathan, victims of a mother addicted to the buttering sound of slots and the euphoric shift of chips, knew the effects of loans. They understood where taking chances with other people's money could take you, working themselves through school after their mother ate a bullet to pay her debts.

"Money could also propel our voice," continued Peter.

This time, his point was met with wit, instead of hatred.

"More cake at the table will lead to more peeping mouths to feed. I don't know...I'm done."

Jonathan carefully moved the heels of his feet from the table. He softly placed them on the darkened beige carpet below and clasped his hands in front of his lips. He balled them up into a fist and soothingly blew into his hands.

"I'm okay with voting right now. I want to be clear what we're voting about though," said Jonathan. He could no longer hold out, choosing instead to table the conversation and move on the ultimatum he and his sister offered to the group months before. He would act on it if they were given no choice, for they made a promise to remain as pure as possible.

"Alana, will you?" requested Ephraim, sighing in relief.

"We just want to be able to threaten and seriously act on the idea of creating our own political party if need be. We don't want to threaten them if we can't act on it. The announcement would come in Oakland during our address after the roundtable discussion with leaders hoping to return Black families into the city, after the BBQ their hosting. Our goal is to work something out and obtain a much more vital role in Washington. Anything further?" forced out Alana.

Ephraim shook his head. Markos remained puzzled the others did not understand what he and Alana knew, unless they could agree, the twins would leave. *Did you already know, Ephraim?*

"Before we vote, I'd like to say something," interrupted Peter.

"We'll remain stagnant. Everything you started and allowed me to join will end. They'll see us as a failure if we don't adapt. People look to us to help them understand what politicians are doing. They look to us for who to vote for. We could be doing more for them," finished Peter.

"What is he getting out of this, Ephraim? What'd you promise the kid? Are you going to bury the photos you took of him with the noose?" asked Jamie, going below the belt.

"Jamie, are you ready to vote?" asked Ephraim. He did not want to reopen the closed wounds of the knife fight of an argument. He outright ignored her.

"I'm. A. No."

"Peter?"

"Yes!"

"I'm a yes. Alana? Jonathan?"

"I abstain," said Alana.

Jonathan searched for wisdom in the seconds between votes. He felt the direction of the wind and understood its trajectory. He considered himself loyal and battle-tested for difficult decisions such as these. The twins provided action to Ephraim's words, but Jonathan would never stay if it meant handicapping Ephraim's intentions. His decision came out of respect.

"I... abstain," answered Jonathan.

Peter cracked a smile, knowing where the results would stand with his abstention. Jamie stepped out of the house, calmly through the front door following his vote. Alana felt devastated for Jamie, a betrayal of blood. No return was in store for the twins. Markos was sickened at how fast the group crumbled after nearly a decade slowly pushing through each of their agendas.

Betrayal Elsa, how did you see it? One by one, whether they feel it heroic or necessary, it is and always will be, betrayal.

"Markos?" asked Ephraim out of respect.

Nothing. Markos turned to his brother, empty. He was ashamed of Ephraim's ambition.

"We'll continue on. I know where you stand."

Jonathan rose and firmly shook each of their hands. It was the end. He promised he and Jamie would support their speech at Lake Merritt following their decision. Alana looked in his eyes when he shook their hands, stout and respectful. After a prideful loss, he would make sure to leave a lasting impression of coordinated chivalry. Peter and Ephraim were entertained with the endless possibilities, only Ephraim kept his composure though, enough to walk out his two partners to their car and wave them away. This was an avoidable crisis, materializing a sour feeling for Markos regarding his brother, a feeling that grew from that point. He wanted to address it, but after Ephraim's return from a gloating farewell, Markos walked out with Alana. He left as the family descended down the stairs. He walked her a few blocks past the park to her home, discussing the vote.

"I saw your eyes after Jonathan got up, you wanted to vote with Jamie?" inquired Alana.

"I can't go against my brother, he's done a lot for me. I don't want to betray him, but I might've just done so. He's in the wrong."

"He could do good with a larger range of resources and support."

"His eyes have changed, *permanently*. He's no longer the loving bear that people can come hug on the street. The people see it, some mistake it for him being big time. It's not him being big time, he's untrusting. He approached the twins as enemies, and he drowned out their voices. Jamie warned him of his discipline in staying pure and he didn't see it. I love Peter, but he's traded ignorance for a hunger for power, and that's where his and Ephraim's relationship will grow. I can't risk him turning on me, I won't say anything," announced Markos.

A weight relinquished itself from his chest. Alana saw it fall.

"I fear he'll one day see me as an obsolete figure that he can discard, I see how he turns when girls yell when I come out and speak. I'm worried, but he's always been a step ahead, an overseer of sorts," presumed Alana. They neared the doorstep, paces away from her driveway.

"I think it's time to see Ephraim as a chess piece instead of the master making the moves. It'll worsen if politicians begin taking a vested interest in him. Each person requires differentiation, that's what everything is about: business, statistics, physics. We study trends and plots, and he's trying to differentiate himself and form something. The twins showed him you can't focus too much on the formation without actually getting something done. He's in trouble."

They left each other fearing Ephraim becoming a pawn in the game Washington played. A few mornings later, a crowded passenger plane was surprised by a visit from the brothers and the famed lawyer. The turbulent flight was a direct, Sacramento to Washington, six hours of worry and task delegating. Research was given to Markos, talking points to Alana, and potential rebuttal points of the opposition and their rebukes to Ephraim. The small breaks in between their work were consumed by the hopeful people sitting in the plane, requesting pictures and soundbites on certain topics. There was not one in the plane unaware of their trip.

Friends and foes lay amongst the crowd in the plane. The early flight subjugated passengers to comforting sleep whilst the plane glided through the Midwest. Markos eased into his task after seeing most of the people's eyes fall into a slumber. The three tried to keep their heads down. Goals were within reach, and with decades invested, this was their time to collect. Ephraim and Alana, especially, were full of admiration and pride for what they had completed. This was not their perfect scenario where they were with the full team, but the three comrades always maintained it would be them, together in the end.

Taxpayer dollars were at work to pick them up from the airport and drive over to their complimentary stay at a nearby hotel. Opulence and pleasure were not a theme of their road trips. Each speaking ordeal paid for the next. The group's split of the money was their only income. They all lived with family, a lovable talking point of their supporters. To appear in a four-star hotel, with full amenities and prepaid service, they became privy to the brokering of power and the appearance of wealth. Once they arrived, Markos scanned through the hotel, walking throughout the numerous floors and establishing a form of contact with the hotel's security. The hotel security brushed him off after noticing his ignorance of the guests staying in the hotel. They knew who Ephraim was, he was a typical guest to them. Foreign dignitaries and performers were among the guests the hotel housed. The manager politely ordered him to his room after showing him the crazed protocols and the excess of cameras and personnel on each floor.

"The security is airtight," shared Markos, returning to the room.

"Good, let's keep all of our discussions limited to this room. This is their turf; you never know who's listening. Alana's gonna take this bed, and we'll bunk on the other one, Markos," said Ephraim.

Markos nodded at his commands. As soon as they were out of the clothes they flew in, they got to work. The comfort in each other's presence reminded them of their youth. The boys had no issue changing in front of Alana, and her with them. Prying eyes could not be helped due to carnal desires, but Alana and Markos were too mature to think twice about such a thing. The three had not been alone in some time. They ate together, taking in the unhealthy room service without any manners, quickly devouring the meals. Hours and hours went by as they finished their tasks and discussed the various talking points. Markos helped where he could, seeing the potential ramifications of rash decisions being made in their meeting. He played the different scenarios, again and again, in his head. He thought of what his prayers that night would entail.

Fatigue betrayed the eyes of the middle-aged giants, even as anxiety grew for their meeting. They had worked tirelessly since landing, but time felt different in the nation's capital. They had six hours before their 10 A.M. meeting in the hotel conference room. The green and red mural of the city on the brown fabric walls began to become less distinctive as the city's lights dimmed. Lamplights in the room flickered due to the overuse. They no longer could look at the material in their hands without fading into some form of sleep. Heads bobbed uncontrollably until all three retreated to lying down, Alana and Ephraim on their respective beds while Markos took his doughy pillow and placed it against the desk chair between them. He lay down on the ground, reviewing his work before he gave it to them to check, worried of his mistakes. Alana and Ephraim could feel the sweat of his forehead hitting the ground. They were all worried, yet they each closed their eyes for a few minutes before they consolidated their notes following hours of discussions.

The power naps were disturbed by a trickling noise coming from the roof of the hotel.

"I didn't believe the forecast when it said it was going to rain," said Ephraim. He faced the window, being the one closest to it, talking away from the other two.

"Jesus…it's going to be ninety degrees today. I'm glad the meeting's here, it's going to be humid," replied Alana, choosing to keep her eyes shut.

The trickling noise rose to a formidable swooshing sound. The rain picked up in no less than two minutes, easing the stressful tension within the room. The television's headlines, as well as a lamp set on the desk between them, remained as the only sources of light. The rest of the lamplights had given out to the fraught stillness of the room.

"So much for four stars," joked Markos, looking at the dead bulbs on the wall lamplights.

They were all able to let out a laugh at the forced darkness. The laughs awkwardly died down as the spacious room chose silence. Markos wondered when they were going to rise to prepare the notes.

Markos grabbed the tablet connected to the room. The new device became normalized in hotels and suburban neighborhoods. They controlled the electronics in the room. Avoiding the plethora of remotes in a home, the tablet served to control any lights or television sets. He used it to embed music in the air, hoping for any relief from their rigid fears, as music once did for him in rehab. He lessened the radiance of the large light above him and closed his eyes. For a second, he was able to see moments of time he was afforded hope: Elsa at the beach, walks in the park. The recollections were purely joyful. Markos wanted to share the ecstasy with them.

It felt like an angel's vocals expanded through the room. Markos looked up at the heavyweights, feeling the pressure they put on themselves from the shift of their bodies on the beds above him.

"Great choice," heard Markos, unaware of who spoke.

A playlist was curated from the music he queued up for the room, so they rested as the rain drizzled down. Brilliant displays of lightning and the rumbling of the ground curated a blissful sense of peace. They surrendered to the moment, resting longer than they hoped. The room was in disarray with no plan to arise. No alarms were set, and no notes were put together. The bags laid open, clothes hanging out of them near another wooden desk by the door. The serene sounds of trumpets and the soothing keys of pianos slithered into their ears, momentarily distracting them from what came next.

"Are y'all awake?" asked Markos.

"I was never asleep."

"Neither was I."

Markos did not expect to hear a quick reply from them.

"Are we...Are y'all doing the right thing?" again asked Markos.

A quick reply did not come this time. Markos could hear them shift and breathe heavily. Ephraim cleared his throat.

"I honestly don't know, I'm not sure," interrupted Alana.

Markos could hear Ephraim pause and tighten at her response. Ephraim shifted to get into the position he desired before he spoke. He turned towards them, on his side, with his elbow pressed perpendicular to the headboard, holding his head up.

"When I first started volunteering...uh with the veterans, I wanted to be useful, I didn't really want a lot. I just wanted to do something, something worth my time. Talking to them was what pushed me to be here. I spent time with combat veterans, and if they physically came back whole, they never came back all there. Regardless, something was interesting to me. I always asked them why, why they fought, because we only love them in name. Once they come back, we don't really care, and we ask them to get used to life here. Anyways, a lot of them said they do it out of respect for their home, respect for the people here."

He paused before continuing, again, clearing his throat.

"Most of them are religious. They believe they've earned respect from God, sacrificing a lot to fight. They believed they kept their words as Christians to protect and act. Some went crazy at the disrespect they received here, while others gave up and wondered if it was worth it. They talked to me about sleep, how they could hear the wailing mothers of comrades at funerals. It didn't help when they woke, because they could only think about the amount of mothers they sent to sleep wailing as well. I say this to give you something to think about, the similarities with other folks about that point of respect and your word."

"What point?" curiously asked Alana, confused where he was going. She nearly gave in to the twins' way of thinking hours before, losing pieces of her sense of strong purpose.

"Many of the people who hit the inner streets, hustling or part of gangs would tell me the same thing of the oaths they took. I agree it wasn't as righteous as the soldiers, but they said it gave them purpose while also earning them respect and a name that may possibly live on. The people on the streets also believed themselves to be soldiers of their neighborhood, protecting their own. This movement...this thing we've created, it's been done in history. Socialist movements, civil rights movements, even the hippie movement, it's all been done, but they've all subsided and died down, breaking into different sects. We've put in years and years, and we'll have to put even more time. Out of respect for our community and in an effort to keep our word, if we can consolidate our ideas into these parties or even create something of our own, we can give others a renewed purpose and keep our word, our promise. Things will surely change and be shaken up, but we can create something after we're done, something for...our descendants," said Ephraim. He rose to sit with his legs hanging over the side of the bed, back straightened.

"People are still with us, but they don't know what to do. This is us fulfilling a large portion of our oath to them. We could easily fade because of the firepower of these politicians. They recognize us as a threat, but they don't know how to act without angering their voters. We owe it to all the people we've talked to, the people that we've *listened* to, the businesses we've helped get off the ground and the kids we have tutored and mentored. We can lessen people's stress about the government and alleviate the political worry so many have about this country. They've given me purpose because for once, I can see something in the horizon beyond us, beyond our time. I finally understood and saw what the soldiers saw, what the hustlers envisioned, a position beyond me. I believe we can plant the seeds here, but we must be on the same page," argued Ephraim.

Seconds passed before he took the tablet from the desk and raised the level of the light. He maneuvered over Markos and motioned to the desk near the bathroom to continue his work.

Alana and Markos were moved by Ephraim's vision, still worried of the consequences of his vivid, yet narrowed hopes. They saw purpose, with something beautiful beyond. They, too, continued their work, continuing for two more hours before they napped. An hour of sleep is all they afforded themselves before they prepared for the meeting.

The misty heat fogged the windows, hiding the exhausted occupants of the room from onlookers. They were awake two hours before they were needed in the conference room downstairs. The lobby's wakeup call was not needed, Alana and Ephraim were already up. Markos was sluggish to wake, feeling the shifting presence of Elsa in his sleep, as he did through all his difficult nights. He dreamt of the park near his home, Elsa strolling through with him, carrying her eye-opening discussions while they watched the family play with the little ones. The small kick from Ephraim on the back of his foot woke him from his misrepresented hopes. The feeling saddened Markos while he hobbled towards the bathroom, experiencing the side effects of such a dream. A flickering feeling loitered about, like the effects of a distorted memory.

"Shower up, Markos. We're about to shower after reading this stuff. We need to get dressed and gather our things before we go eat, unless you want to have breakfast up here?" asked Ephraim.

"No, I think it'd be good to be around people, we've been alone up here too long. We need a taste of sanity before we go in there," replied Markos.

He closed the door before he warmed the shower and opened the bag with his toothpaste and toothbrush. Markos was in the bathroom no more than ten minutes, finishing up and returning with nothing but his towel wrapped around his waist.

"Good, you're done. I'll go next unless you want Alana?" suggested Ephraim.

"Go ahead," said Alana. Her head remained sunk into the papers.

Ephraim grabbed his suit before entering the bathroom, choosing to spend his time mentally preparing in the shower and in front of the mirror. He wanted to completely be ready before he would emerge from the restroom.

Markos remained half-naked in the room while he looked for his clothes. The discipline the Air Force reinforced in the rigorous dieting and exercise taught by his father, exemplified itself in the shape of his cut muscles. The ripping definition in his chest and abdomen were a hidden asset of his, for he forever remained a timid man, especially before his diagnosis. His relapse into alcohol would be the catalyst for the end of his shy modesty and bodily regimen.

Nevertheless, his body shined as his glands perspired after the heated shower, glistening as he applied his shea butter lotion. He first placed his spectacles on his face. His tiresome eyes refused to put in the effort the morning of the meeting. He slid the glasses into the ungroomed hair on the sides of his head, aligning with the proportional peak of his untamed, nappy mini afro. He used a small washcloth to rub the mist from his skin off before applying more lotion and deodorant.

"Nothing new will come from looking that hard, Alana."

"The man who stood quietly in rooms sure has a lot of advice these days," replied Alana.

He could do nothing but smile, pulling out the clothes in the closet, still only in his towel.

"Your efforts would be better served helping me pick an outfit."

He offered her a lifeline. She put her notes in order, filing them in the folder next to an array of papers. She placed them in Ephraim's arm bag before turning her attention away.

She walked over to the closet commenting on his improper fashion sense: "I hope you brought something presentable."

Markos investigated the contents of the closet, confused on how coordinated they were to appear at the meeting.

"I think I brought some good things. I don't really know which shirt and shoes to wear."

"Okay, I'm here, let's see what we got," said Alana.

She threw the suits he brought on the bed she slept on. His lack of decision making was the reason for the extra fees they paid to check baggage in. Alana knew what she was going to wear, but the brothers chose to bring more clothes than necessary for their two-day trip. She unzipped the protective packaging for the suits, seeing the navy blue and gray suits he brought with him.

"What color shirts?" asked Alana, studying the two suits.

Markos looked in the opposite direction, to the three shirts hanging in the closet.

"I got one that's red, one black, and one white."

"Hmm. Red won't work with either. Wear either a white shirt and a black tie or a black shirt and a black tie," commanded Alana.

He turned around to look her in the eye.

"Why only black tie, I have others?" softly added Markos.

"None of us will be wearing anything with bright blue or red on it, we won't be showing that we're leaning one way. These people are already fearful that we will side with one of them."

"Well, I didn't get that memo," said Markos, grabbing the black shirt from the closet.

She softly grabbed his arm to stop him from pulling the wrinkled black shirt from the rack. She looked up at him as she instructed him: "Let's not go with that one. Let's...let's go with the one normal people would wear, the white."

The lack of sleep was a large factor, for he could not move his stare from her restless eyes behind her small black frames. Neither of them would act on insatiable desires, baseless of emotion, but the shared look was profound. Words stalled from their mouths. Markos was in the desired attire for what their bodies fancied. Alana's blond hair was loosely hanging, her baggy pajama pants resting partly on the toes of Markos. Sounds of the city's traffic matched the cadence of the sounds of their breathing, her air meeting his chest while his were felt slightly above her forehead. The sound of the water hitting the tub held the background noise of the moment together. Her cropped shirt was a small barrier for Markos, but almost half a century of boundaries sat between the centimeters of space between them. With all the power they amassed, connections and emotions were long muted and cast aside to achieve what they needed.

"I... I think hmm, uh...white is the better shirt. I'm gonna go see what's taking him so long," said Alana.

Markos looked at his suits as she walked away. Moments like those were shared between the two in a few instances, but they were not genuine. In times of heartbreak and stress, their bodies asked for something their friendship would not repair itself from. This, of all the moments, a brief thirty seconds, was the closest they came to capitulating to their flesh. He looked at his gray suit, the one acquired in his visit to Ethiopia with Elsa. He was weakened by the betrayal he nearly committed if he would have succumbed to his desire. His eyes glued to the suit after Alana moved away from him. Elsa was attached to all the material objects of his life.

Alana, herself, was near her limit. She was occupied with her own thoughts and promises. She had begun to think beyond the movement. Since Ephraim's paranoia worsened, she thought of her own life. She turned the corner as Markos began to change, shaking off the lust from her body. It was comedic for her, thinking about sleeping with Markos. She knew there was never anything there, but the stresses of the moment were boiling over for each of them.

It was Ephraim, calmly thinking over the moment he was about to have, personally and for his family. He left the shower and slipped into a suit. The expensive suit was a gift his wife gave him. She requested he only wear it on the days he would be defined as a man. They smiled at the all-black attire: the shirt, the tie, and the suede loafers he wore. He came out of the room, showered and shaved, groomed from head to toe. Of all of them, he was most excited.

"We still have an hour and a half. We're good on time, I want to get there about fifteen minutes early," encouraged Ephraim.

Alana came out of the restroom much more elegant as either of them expected. Her black pantsuit and bright white blouse left peers a peek of her clear skinned chest. She accompanied her look with her black heels. The fiery red on the outsoles defied her own request of neutrality.

Breakfast was dull. They did not have an appetite, at least not Ephraim and Alana. They tried a cinnamon bagel with cream cheese, only being able to down cups of coffee and a few bites of the toasty bagels. Markos on the other hand went into the meeting on a full stomach, enjoying the complimentary continental breakfast. He comfortably ate the scrambled eggs, the oily buttermilk pancakes, and the rounds of turkey bacon the hotel staff kept refilling. He found joy in the black tea they kept warm in the thermoses.

The group looked around, humbly stunned no one tried at conversing with them. They wondered of the support they had in the East, but to have no one talk with them was shocking. Breakfast remained a slow nuisance to their nerves and anxiety. Before long, they made their way to the conference room, punctual, thinking the feeling was to be reciprocated. They hurried Markos, nearly staining his sentimental navy blue suit as he left the table with his tea.

They waited for the representatives by the door of the room, sitting for thirty minutes as they motioned, back and forth, near a long hallway by the lobby. The hallway was devoid of doors on one side, only a shaded mix of white and red paint on the walls for forty feet. The only doors were for the two conference rooms, on the same side, separated by a good distance from each other. Only a vending machine laid in between the two rooms. To one end, an emergency exit was visible and on the other, a pathway to the lobby's elevator. Markos sat on the ground while the others stood searching through their phones for any relevant headlines.

"Is the room even open?" asked Markos.

"It's locked. This is the right room; I asked the front desk when you were getting your tea. I just think they're trying to get a rise out of us, make us feel uncomfortable," assured Ephraim.

He's worried.

"Well, it's unprofessional. They are fifteen minutes late. We have to wait," said Alana.

"Or we could just tell them we'll make our own party and be done with it," joked Ephraim.

His joke triggered the army. A stampede of staffers emerged from the lobby pathway, numbering at least twenty-five, walking in some sort of sync. Markos tried to catch a detailed glimpse of the overworked collection of political science majors. He made out an abundance of white men and a few women. He saw one black woman in the crowd, quickly striding past them, as they were ordered to. He could not see any faces, but the nameless soldiers strode on until they were out of sight. The representatives walked directly behind them, along with their security detail. The gesture was meant to intimidate the three, but only Markos was stunned.

Jesus, thought Markos as he stood up from the ground.

The staffers filed to the second conference room, deeper down the hallway. They walked by fast without acknowledging them. The collective four representatives of the two parties emerged and slowed as they approached the three, putting their hands out. The security personnel were the only few who saw beyond Alana and Ephraim, shaking Markos's hand and sharing pleasantries. Of the security detail, four of them remained outside while two went in with them. The four covered the exits in the hallway. Markos saw the preparation in their protocols, embarrassed by the full belly and fatigue slowing his reaction time. He remained, for all purposes of the meeting, behind Alana and Ephraim as a fly on the wall.

The room was well prepared for the meeting. It was quite large, a room better suited for a conference or a seminar. Instead, a long dining table was set up in the middle of the room, equidistant from all four corners. The table's edges were parallel to all the walls. A circular light, giving off a clear white color, was directly above the long table while four lights were lit in each of the corners of the room. The small, bright yellow bulbs were like the flickering lamps in the rooms. The smaller lights were all connected to the walls. Extra chairs were stacked and equally distributed to the corners, under the lamps. The off-white walls were a few shades darker than those in the hallway, giving off a tan brownish reflection with the light. The room was meant to be darkened. A large white projector screen was fully unrolled against the wall adjacent to the next room. The projector was connected to the ceiling in front of the large light, between it and the wall farthest from the entrance holding the projector screen.

The long table, covered in a white cloth, was able to seat the representatives in the manner in which they delegated. Two representatives, one dressed in a black suit and blue tie, and another male in a similar outfit with a pin of his party on the left collar of his coat, sat on the left side of the table, closest to the door. Their seats, a navy-blue cushioned chair with an arched top, were put closer together. The other two, a woman in an exquisitely made scarlet red dress, and an elder gentleman in a red tie and black suit, sat on the same side, yet a bit farther from the other representatives. These two, again, were seated near each other, but the two groups were placed equally separated from the middle. The two outsiders were sitting on the other side, together, directly in the middle. Their backs were to the entrance.

Markos wondered who decided the clever seating arrangement. He mimicked the security detail's protocol of pulling the chair out for each of his *clients*. He followed their lead and retreated to the wall behind the two. He faced the Secret Service agent, leaning on the wall, positioning herself behind the chairs between the representatives facing Ephraim from across the table. The other agent went to guard the only door into the room, left of Markos.

We're here. I've seen these four before, the quiet members of the legislative branch. I see why they didn't want the twins. This is business. This would've made Elsa laugh, how important they all must each think they are. Maybe they were, but all men die.

Small talk carried on in a low tone of voice. Markos did not hear their words, but friendly jokes were shared. He cursed the agent opposite of him. She stood too far, and he could not get closer unless she did. It would break his newly adopted protocol. He stood over five paces away.

He waited for an opportunity to get closer and was awarded when the refreshments were brought in by the hotel staff. Pitchers of water and finger foods, buttered bread and the typical spread, were brought in for their meeting. He used the opportunity to get closer and Ephraim was the first to notice it.

"Want some water before we begin, Markos?" asked Ephraim, wanting his brother to experience the moment with him.

Markos shared an emotionless nod, edging closer to grab the water to the chagrin of the security agents, who themselves were parched. He did not return to the same position, now only a few paces behind his brother and Alana.

Markos took an opportunity to evaluate the guests during their time of refreshments. He saw from the blue side, two young males, patient and methodical. He saw a young black male from a well-off family, completely bought into his party's politics due to the position he was afforded. The pin was enough for Markos to see how deep he was in, and how he saw them as a threat. He was a bald man, easily under forty, a climber of the political ladder and someone who could use a win from this for his party. He was not a senator, a member of the House, but the man's stagnant facial movements showed he eyed a career beyond senatorial leadership. The other man, a white man, slightly older seemed to be one of more liberal stances. Markos saw that the lengthy man was barely able to fit his clothes, knowing he was uncomfortable in a suit. He had a friendly face, his large spectacles hiding inquisitive eyes of a man with a unique approach to politics. Markos wondered if he stumbled into this, being a yes man that delivered. A feeling of innocence emanated from him. *A powerful weapon to have,* thought Markos.

The other side, a conservative look of politics, was confident. They were interested in what could come from the meeting, yet they saw the newcomers as children. The two, the seasoned gentleman and the middle-aged woman, were true politicians, eyeing their competition and attempting to see how they could spin these discussions into a benefit for their party. Markos was easily able to break down the mold of the man, for he was a man of military background. The straightened posture and the groomed facial hair, as well as his poise, was enough. He could tell the man served in the Army. He knew the man was a senator, a formidable opponent, but one who broke the rules, limiting his ability to work. He paid for it in his lack of upward mobility. He was insubordinate to those he did not respect. *He's a weapon,* thought Markos, *they point him in a direction and he's there.* The woman, to Markos, was the keenest of the group. She was a negotiator, one who valued the words said in a room. She did not smile or joke with the others, only shaking hands when they walked in. Of the four, she was the only one who debated as if she had five opponents instead of one. She found Markos's probing eyes and she recognized he saw her as the fiercest. He first believed they sent in a woman for Alana, but this was out of merit.

Markos did not care for politicians, only reading about politics to stay informed for his brother. He saw fraudulent martyrs come and go, worsening from his childhood.

The debates began soon after the refreshments were removed from the table, leaving only the iced water between them.

They need names. I didn't hear their names, recalled Markos.

They asked a question first: "What is it you all want?" asked the man with the spectacles.

The friendly one first.

Markos watched as Ephraim outlined betrayal and the reversal of old promises made by the people, they themselves, got elected. The word 'betrayal' opened the other sides' arguments as they continued to argue over the relevance of Ephraim's movement to Washington.

"Our parties owe you virtually nothing, it's the game of politics," said the man with the pin in the middle of the debate.

"The reversal of promises is the name of the game," uttered the old man in agreement.

Alana was a fierce opponent to the rough game of politics. She shared how several of their initiatives were adopted from the team's programs. She did not like their excuses. She outlined to them the states, East or West, appreciated the ten-point plan and the volunteering opportunities. She explained their influence in places they saw as battleground areas.

"We are more formidable than you seem to let on, they wouldn't have sent their attack dogs if we weren't a force," continued Alana.

Ephraim was surprisingly shy through the negotiations. The initial talking points were a slug fest where insults were hurled, and pride was the prize sought. Nothing regarding people was discussed, simply the limits of their reach. The first hour went by without a meaningful word being shared, with Ephraim only speaking up a few times.

"We certainly can't hide the fact that what you've done is profound. What can our parties do for your movement, something to maintain the order in which we've kept where we all benefit?" asked the man with the pin.

A dangerous question, you opened yourself up to him.

"Joseph, who do you represent at these talks? 'We all benefit'? I'm not here to benefit the parties you all are representing. People on the streets, your constituents, are tired of your two parties, *because you* are representing your parties, the politicians and the actual establishment of the party, instead of the people. Pose your question differently," advised Ephraim.

Ephraim was annoyed at an irresponsible question from a man he believed knew better, knowing they came from the same people.

The talks soured after Ephraim's interjecting attack on Joseph. Joseph retreated to his water and refused to speak as a napkin was needed to rub off the sweat from his forehead. There was no frustration visible, it was anger. Ephraim pushed the envelope with their party specifically.

"I appreciate your programs, your initiatives. I would love to discuss that in private more, but I seriously question whether you believe you can break away into your own party? We've heard the whispers, is that what you please?" asked the senator.

He's baiting, tread lightly, mentally ordered Markos.

"Senator Campbell, we want to find a resolution here with you. We know the success rate of a party, a third-party parading independence. The trajectory of your parties has negatively trended downwards since the twenties, after all the hate that was spewed in the eyes of recession and fear. We've done our part to rejuvenate your youthful members and educate the voters in certain regions, but it's what you can offer here that can make a difference, we don't need you as much as you require our services," asserted Alana.

Good, really great. They know after these two hours; concession statements have to be given. We don't need them, they need us.

"I wouldn't necessarily say we need you. Over the years, you've confused your voters. We'd just have to leave you all alone and point out your errors, for errors will come with doing things like this without experience. People change with the wind, we've been around for hundreds of years, we wouldn't need your efforts. There have been and will always be movements like yours. Nonetheless, when you confuse the people, they'll revert back to the traditional ones they've stuck with," said the woman in the scarlet dress.

The man in the glasses added to their argument: "Your experience is with the youth, a fluid group of voters who are always rebelling. They'll soon grow up and assimilate into parties they once admonished their parents for. Like Elizabeth said, we just have to wait you out."

Markos froze at the advantage they lauded over Alana and Ephraim. There were rebuttal points, however, like the discussion, instead of it being a reasonable argument of how to help people, the aggressors used this time to discredit and weaken the team's resolve. Neither of them broke, nor did their emotions expose them.

Ephraim was defensive throughout the talks, leaving Alana on an island of her own to attack. Markos knew Ephraim hated threats. There was nothing Ephraim despised more than an empty threat. It showed a lack of respect for an opponent, an underestimation belittling the other side. If he was to threaten, he would do so if he could only deliver.

Ephraim looked towards the four, holding his anger at bay.

"Are you all aware of the story of Job in the Bible?" asked Ephraim, going off script.

Alana's legs stiffened and went dead as he chose to go on his own. Markos fought a ravishing desire to smile. *He's using Dad.* He let a hint of one creep out.

"Yes, I believe we're all aware," said the man in the glasses, the designated mediator. He looked to the others and saw approval in the nods.

They seem to move on one accord. The hate they show must be just for the cameras.

"So, as you all know, Job was of the most faithful followers of God. He loved Him, very much so. God seemed prideful of His servant and his belief in Him. In comes, however, the devil and for a looser term, teases God, and says that Job wouldn't be as faithful if he actually had been through some things," began Ephraim.

Markos was surprised at how informal Ephraim was. He was storytelling, wrapping them around his fingers, like their father once did with them. This one of Job, was one of the only religious stories their father loved, an important story he made them understand.

"God, as confident as He is, tells the devil that he can test His servant and that He is confident in his ability to not curse His name. As the story goes, the devil puts Job through it all, taking away his riches, killing off his bloodline, scarring his skin. Still, Job refuses to blaspheme Him," continues Ephraim, diving into the story, tapping the table as he spoke.

He continued, detailing the story for them, loosely exaggerating what he once learned.

"The worst part is that, over and over, Job begs as he looks to the sky to plead his side if he wronged God. He truly is clueless, as all of us are at the supernatural games being played. He pleads and pleads. His friends continue to tell him, he's wrong and that he obviously wronged God. They tell him of how crappy of an individual he is and that he really isn't what he believes he is. Throughout it all, he still refuses to curse God, but begins to ask for an audience with him. In the end, the devil loses, and God makes him whole. Who wins, however?" asked Ephraim.

Troubled looks came from the other side. All said they knew the story but were afraid to tell him they had not opened a Bible in some time. Only Campbell's face did not change at the turning points.

"Job," replied Joseph.

"Interestingly enough, Job was restored the best way God believed he deserved. I don't believe he was the winner of it all for he still suffered immensely and buried his bloodline. He was made whole with another family, but still. He gained an audience with God and spoke with Him. That proved *we* don't know anything about spirituality, but there is more to the story. Any more takers?"

Elizabeth and the man with the spectacles were immensely confused at his question. Campbell smiled as he pondered the question, respecting the origins and reason for the tale.

"Humanity," softly answered Campbell.

"Bingo," replied Ephraim, pointing at the senator. Ephraim's elbows then rested on the table.

"God, in light of a supernatural threat to his connection to us, trusted in a human to continue to have faith. With all the negative commentary on our desires and such, God trusted Job, his servant, a human. He persevered. There are many interpretations of this story, blaming God for allowing such a loyal servant to go through it, having bad friends who don't know you, and a bunch of stuff about how we are throwaway objects to God. But God believed in the perseverance and faith in Job, in us, humans. This is what I was taught. I will always persevere, we will as a team. My connection to the people I have talked to over the years has been out of genuine concern. I barely obtain a sustainable income doing this, living with my mother, as does the rest of the team. I will not succumb to the pressure and fight; this would go against the wishes of the people we have helped when our coffers were empty. I'll be here for them. *It is written for me to do so.* I will be here whether you wait or not, this meeting will be the last opportunity to create something that works for both of us, for we will announce what our next steps will be in the coming days in Oakland. Time ticks as you strategize," indicated Ephraim.

The four remained silent as Ephraim tapped Alana's shoulder.

"There's nothing more to say. We'll be in this hotel. You have our room number and my number. We are open to any form of deal where we can work with the both of you, and we *also* are open to working with one of you. We can extend our stay another day, but in about forty-eight hours, we will be leaving. We had initiatives, but you all came with your own agendas it seems," said Ephraim.

Alana and Ephraim both stood up, shook the hands of the four, and without a moment's hesitation, walked out of the room with Markos trailing them. The hours they spent with the politicians were useless. True deals and desires would only be shared once the representatives realized they were a formidable threat and not a social media phenomenon. Ephraim struck fear in them while also gaining their respect, especially Campbell's. He was the one with the highest position of the four. Ephraim knew they would now go to their superiors and offer what they could.

"You used Dad?" whispered Markos as they filed into the elevator in the lobby.

They stayed silent until the doors closed. The smiles of the two behind Markos showed itself in the elevator's glass walls.

"They pissed me off," replied Ephraim.

"Campbell will be calling. He'll want to meet with you Ephraim. You need to be ready. I don't think they'll offer anything though. Edwards may want to meet with me, out of respect, but to be honest, I don't think Washington is giving any leeway. We'll have to do it," added Alana.

"Wait, if it's necessary we will. They have a few days."

They waited and waited by the phone, refusing to leave the room throughout their stay at the hotel. Only Markos would take walks around, noticing the staffers and the representatives choosing to stay and delegate with Washington from the hotel.

"None of them called?" asked Markos, returning from his walk, hours after the meeting.

He dissected through the mess created by Alana and Ephraim. He saw the two of them hunched over the phone. They sat on the beds, both their heads near the lamp. While the sky darkened, the rain stalled, leaving sounds of car horns and pedestrians to be heard.

"No, we've discussed some things though."

"What does that mean?" asked Markos.

"We'll regroup with the twins. We didn't promise anything to them, nor did we threaten them with anything we can't take back. Losing the twins now would benefit their agenda and make us look more unorganized," suggested Alana.

Markos greatly approved of their recuperation efforts. The twins were vital to providing actionable programs. They made Ephraim a man of action.

Buzzing came from behind the pitch-black television. Ephraim dashed to his phone at the second vibration on the television stand. As he talked on the phone, Alana and Markos attempted to be very still to hear the muffled voice of the man on the other end. The man did most of the talking while Ephraim nodded and smiled.

"It was Campbell, he's downstairs. He wants to meet at the food court. He secured a table after they close in about ten minutes."

"Be careful, all the staffers and representatives are still here. It might give off the wrong message if you're seen. You never know," warned Markos.

Ephraim nodded and grabbed his black jacket. He quickly removed his tie and opened a few buttons. Markos inferred from the changes Ephraim made, it was an informal meeting. *Perhaps some drinks, maybe. Be careful Ephraim.*

"Don't worry, we're just talking. You both rest. We're just talking over dinner."

Alana and Markos wished him well as he strode out the door. They refused to talk of the monumental meeting. They all remained humble, even as they strong-armed the fundamental pillars of American politics. Alana, as she dropped her back to the mattress, deeply exhaled and smiled as she rubbed her hands smoothly on her face. Markos laughed at her lifted stress.

"You did great, Alana."

"We did great, we did something people will know about. We became lawyers and activists for stuff like this. We're really here after all these years, after all we've been through. We just can't mess it all up*,"* announced Alana.

Markos thought of the sacrifice Alana made, going to a good law school and dedicating her time to Ephraim, choosing family over a fortune she should be making. The frustration in her voice descended into true pleasure, recognizing the success of the decision. Doubts had begun creeping in, worrying her of next steps with the family, but she let the fears fade for a moment.

They waited, in peace, before the reality fused in with the thoughts of success.

"You know, like I do, the twins are leaving," stated Markos.

He ruined her joyful parade. She knew the truth, too. The effort itself may create an atmosphere for them to return, but all thought of breaking away needed to be forgotten for a reunion to occur.

"Oh well, we all will end up leaving. Depending on what happens after these meetings, we'll know where Ephraim's loyalties lie."

Markos slid his back against the headboard, rising from his lying position. *Keep your faith.*

"Would you leave him?" asked Alana.

No hesitation was needed to answer her question: "You know more than anyone else that I can't leave him. The only way for that to happen would be if he didn't want me."

"Good answer, but time will tell," said Alana. She turned over to her side and dozed off into a needed slumber. She left Markos with dark thoughts of what would become of him if the day came for him to leave. Fate spoke for him, there was no continuing of a lineage. He was alone, clinging onto the forced relationship accompanying blood relatives. The sweat-soaked shirt he wore in the warm conference room brushed against the cushions of his headboard as he dozed off. They both waited for Ephraim to make the decisions for the movement.

Following Markos's first stint in rehab for alcoholism, his deep slumbers became interrupted and flooded with dreams and reflexive movements. The punishing footsteps of the slightly overweight Ephraim would wake any light sleeper as he inched closer to the door. Markos noticed the time first, once his brother came in and patiently walked over to the desk. He pulled out a wooden chair and took a seat. Time passed, but the digit of the hour had not changed. They shared an inconspicuous look, refraining from speaking. Markos's shuffling movements on the bed, with the flicking light of the lamp as it turned on, awoke Alana. She turned to see Markos back in the same position she saw him in before she slept, while Ephraim sat in front of the television, between them, hunched over with his hands interlocked. He looked at his hands and rubbed them together before he spoke.

"So, umm, Campbell said he can't offer anything more than what we've already been given. He says the party can't be in charge of campaign promises. If that was the case, there are a lot of lobbyists in line waiting for their wishes to be granted. The dinner was a courtesy and he asked me questions about our start and our positions," started Ephraim.

"So, what, that's it for us?" asked Alana.

"He went on to tell me more about how he respects us and stuff like that. He did say one thing that caught my eye. Congress is afraid we'll break away, not just because of the support of the people, but because of the support we have in the House. He said if we were to break away, they fear some would defect. It's tense, that's why they set a meeting. They wanted to see if we were aware of our political support. Elizabeth reported that we're still misguided. He reported the opposite, though, but they went with her side, according to him."

Are you lying? She was the one most shocked by the story of Job. Did you come to a deal with Campbell?

"We can't do anything until we get back, we shouldn't. There's nothing from the other side?" inquired Alana.

"Joseph wasn't too happy to see us shake hands in the lobby. He instead turned around and went back to his 'war room'. He wasn't going to call, we insulted him," said Ephraim.

Markos watched as Ephraim's words rang through the air. The night was still, a consequence of the Sunday night's uneventful weather. The cars were all gone, not even people's voices could be heard. Ephraim's words frightened Markos.

"Use the truth to lie when necessary." That's what Dad taught us. You seem to be more like him nowadays, Ephraim.

"Let's sleep on it. We'll wait for morning. At least if no one calls, we can go home on time," suggested Ephraim.

At the order of his words, they all retreated to the beds, immediately sleeping in the formal wear they wore. As soon as the lamp was turned off, their eyes shut, welcoming the darkness. The storm awaiting them in the morning would require such rest.

Morning came with disruptions from a constant buzzing sound. The three ignored the clamoring of phones on the nightstand, but then one device's buzzing turned to three, even Markos's device going off. Markos was unmoved by the abnormal noise, dreaming again of his Elsa, her face shining in the sun as they made their way through the grassy, uneven field behind his mother's home. The gasps, the shock of Ephraim and Alana woke Markos up.

"Wake up, Markos," demanded Ephraim. The try at a pleasant tone made Markos uneasy.

"What is this Ephraim, is this you?" asked Alana. She looked deep into the headlines.

Ephraim stood up and began addressing the rumors, and soon, Alana followed as they calmed the baffled politicians who were calling after reading the headlines. Their phones rang and rang throughout the day.

Markos saw the emboldened words on the screen:

"Solomons, Leader of the large California-based social group, demands endorsed politicians be given top appointments in Congress. Bipartisan effort in dismissing his influence."

Ephraim remained cool, perplexed at yet another show of force. However, he was prepared with an ace in the hole. Alana vehemently yelled and answered the calls from universities and the student media correspondents who typically were given the scoop.

The next headline was the blow, striking unexpectedly. They were too focused to see how the game was played.

"BREAKING NEWS: Congress prepares for Solomons to break with politicians to create party of his own, an independent party, following denial of request for the appointments of endorsed candidates."

Ephraim's smile angered Alana. She initially thought of the smile as one shared after a successful ploy. Far from it, the smile was for the brilliant strategy of his opponents, whomever they were. They smeared the team, Ephraim, and his work. Instead of working with him, they too were disgusted by his threat. He was sure they were to be left alone and wondered if Campbell reneged on certain promises, promises Markos and the rest would always remain unaware of.

"Credit them for being as ruthless as they said they were. They make us look like we are trying to overpower them and then, they take away our honor. Whatever we do, we look like we're scrambling. They're forcing us to move fast. You see this!" shouted Ephraim in frustration.

Death to it all, thought Markos. He froze at the thought of being handicapped by people with no integrity, especially after being portrayed as having none.

"What now?" asked Alana, ignoring the calls on her phone.

"The choice is clear. We beat them by doing what they expect."

Running could be heard outside. The trekking footsteps progressively slowed as the sound approached the door. The three could feel the heavy panting of the individual on the other side of the door. They could feel the thought process of the individual, overthinking the next steps.

The rhythmic: one, four, two universal knocks scared the occupants of the room. Markos was the first to rise, knowing he was the one who needed to open the door.

He walked to the door, pumping his open palm in the air towards the two to tell them to back up. He rolled up the sleeves of his wrinkled white shirt, simultaneously removing his black tie and placing it near the television. Fiddling of some paper objects could be heard on the other side of the door. He looked through the keyhole, and due to his slow approach, footsteps of the knocker could be heard steadily pacing away from the door.

Markos methodically opened the door, maneuvering his body to sit parallel to the handle. His left pectoral was pressed against the door. He wanted to be able to use it to strike an intruder and protect himself if need be. His strong arm would be free to attack as well. He planted his feet as if such methods were necessary. Yet, no one faced him as he opened the door. All he found was an arrow, folded out of a piece of printer paper.

The arrow pointed to him.

His instincts told him to immediately pick the paper up from the floor. He knelt down towards the maroon carpet. The golden floral design in the carpet nearly hid the arrow in plain sight, but he grabbed the paper and unfolded the arrow.

Inside, he found a sketch of a donkey, drawn in blue ink pen. Three words were left smudged by the ink stains below the drawing.

"It was us."

He laid the paper down on the television stand, in the view of the two who stood disappointed by the revelations. They knew it to be Joseph's doing, out of pride and they deduced the party gave the final order. Ephraim took voters away from them, their liberal base.

Markos peeped his head out again to see the messenger of the note. In the distance, before they could turn the corner, he saw her. A staffer, the woman, the black woman he saw quickly stroll past him the day before. Her clothes were the giveaway. He could tell they were up all night. She was still in the same outfit he saw her in before the meeting. She kept walking down the hollow hallway, extremely long in length, exposing herself before she could reach the elevator. He yelled to her in order to get her attention, but she focused on her escape to the elevator and ignored his calls. As she edged closer to her turn, she betrayed her instincts and turned her face to Markos. He saw the petrified look on the woman's blank face. She turned out of a desperate desire to see him for what he became, to see him in the full form she once believed he could aspire to be. Despite the insults thrown at him years before, she turned for a moment. Angela looked up to obtain another look of him, before stepping into the path leading to the elevator, fading into the hallway on her way to aid one of Washington's political machines.

Markos, awed by her courage and mystified by the coincidental encounter, closed the door and retreated to the bed, ignorant to the importance of the ramifications of the last few minutes. He sat, hunched over the side of his bed near the lamp, stuck. He thought of Ephraim's words.

It is written.

twelve:
Vice City

"2. Liberate ourselves from the constraints placed on us from the belief that every decision made is final. Our systems are not final, and they still could be improved. A system is not ideal if it isn't fully fair."

"3. Put time into providing educational opportunities for those who sit unaware of the topics that affect us in everyday news cycles. Realign morals and tenets that were disconnected by unreformed education."

- Entente Party's List of Goals, inherited from the social movement of founder, Ephraim Solomons.

The smiles of the children reflected the vibrance of the shining summer afternoon. Lake Merritt was filled with hundreds of people who came to see the Solomons'. The whole family came to the event in a much-needed show of solidarity after the bombshell headlines. Participants of the day's festivities were in store for a powerful speech from Ephraim.

Tents were put up in the early morning. They mirrored the setup of the carnival the day Markos accepted his brother's offer. The Pacific breeze weakened the sun's punishing heat, offsetting the near-record highs for the season. Smokers and barbecues served as a gift and a curse, putting out a mouthwatering aroma while also raising the temperatures as smoke filled the covered tents. The leaves on the trees swayed in the whistling wind, providing the people with nature's sound before the speakers congested the air with the unique rhythms and rhymes of the Bay Area tunes. The freshly cut grass was originally wet from the sprinklers, but quickly dried as the sun rose to its highest point.

The family arrived early, helping those who needed the extra hands. Ephraim and Markos, along with Alana, had been working overtime since they returned from their trip. They did not take the necessary time to process the twins going back on their word. The twin's refusal to accompany them to Oakland served as the final break from the team after the news broke. Explanations were needless. The phone call was shortened by a lack of remorse from both sides.

The cheerful laughs, quirky jokes, and yells of the people were beginning to fill the sound waves around the lake. The event was sponsored by community members, the politically active offspring of former activists and retired politicians still involved in the Bay Area. They asked if Ephraim could be their keynote, as well as a member of their panel of speakers. Ephraim gracefully accepted the invitation at a discounted rate, aligning the event with the meetings he took with Congressional members in the East coast.

People flooded into the event after the first hour. Blankets and towels rested throughout the available grassy areas where families sat. Most spent the initial hour playing carnival games, cornhole and such, also buying from the businesses set up near the stage.

The sponsors rented a small black stage, wide enough to hold six black, metal foldable chairs and a microphone stand placed four paces in front of the chairs at center stage. The disc jockey remained hidden behind the chairs, where his system connected to two five-foot speakers, each on a different side of the stage. They were connected to stands, extending their height. His bass booster sat squarely in front of the stage, horizontally rested a few feet behind yellow caution tape. The tape cordoned off the stage and speaker system, circling a few feet behind the disc jockey. The setup was elegant. Onlookers viewed the speakers against the backdrop of the lake, while those on the stage were afforded a good view of everyone in front of them.

The small businesses, food service and all, flourished on this day where people gave time and effort to network with those making their own way in Northern California. It was the third year of the festival, *The Odyssey*. In terms of safety, the festival was always a concern of the city. Police were in attendance, as well as an army of privately paid security attendants. Still, small bookstore owners, artistry shops, family-owned bakeries, all who made up the small communities in the north, were together selling their products in a moment of Black solidarity.

A third of the way into the event, the cultural performances took the stage. Poets, Hip-Hop artists, and cultural performers representing the African Diaspora took to the stage. The passion of the performers was well received, even putting a smile on Rachel's face as she watched her country be well represented by a group of young women. The family were seated near the stage. They looked on, all of them, Alondra and Olivia, baby Darius and the matriarch of the Solomons family, Rachel. Markos and Alana chose to remain there with them. Ephraim asked for privacy before he spoke.

Markos felt the presence of something familiar in the moment. He feared nothing and felt no ill will lied with any in the crowd. He believed even those who appeared the toughest that day, came to enjoy the company of people.

Shortly after the dancing of the different cultures, a runway was set up in order to advertise the different clothing lines available for people to shop from. The essence and saturation of the colors in the dynamic streetwear were on full display, wowing the people with their ingenuity and the availability of unique designs. A brief intermission was then given to people with encouragement to replenish their plates and continue purchasing clothes. Ephraim's time approached following the intermission, beginning with the informal question and answer portion.

This is something you would've liked, thought Markos, watching his brother be introduced.

Ephraim was a victim of the excitement of the crowd, who roared at the entrance of the man they thirsted to question. The team avoided the cameras following the days in D.C., only releasing a statement Alana crafted, denying the allegations about the requested appointments. She, however, did not acknowledge the breaking away from the traditional parties. The previous days were filled with contentious debates and decisions about the next steps.

At Alana's request, Ephraim agreed to keep Peter away for a few weeks. She berated Ephraim for the departure of the twins and only requested processing time for the team. She thought this could give Ephraim some semblance of forgiveness before his speech. The day was for the family and as such, she argued only the family should be present. He complied, at ease with his decisions, appeasing Peter by divulging the details of the speech.

"Hello, everybody, you already know me. I will be your host. Today's questions were already typed up since y'all entered a bunch of them. We appreciate your participation, but we ask you to stay quiet, so we can hear them. Applause is okay, though," announced the host.

Ephraim looked at the famed comedian, laughing at himself for taking a discounted rate.

The panel answered all the questions thrown their way, mostly giving political answers to the well-crafted questions. Markos saw Ephraim already commanding the crowd before his speech.

"Mr. Solomons, your question. It's a little personal, but I read what's on the paper. It says, why hasn't your movement focused more on Black folks, going back to your ten-point plan? It doesn't speak of Black people, nor does it look as if you make an effort when such crises arise in the community?"

Ephraim's trademark smile crept out. The golden, coffee-stained teeth shined as the host walked over to the sixth chair on the end of the line to hand him the microphone. Unlike all who answered, he sat and waited before tackling the question.

"First off, I'm a Black man, whether or not others say I am. Growing up with an African mother slightly changes some of my mannerisms compared to other brothers. I'm a Black man *who so happens* to be fighting for the well-being of others. My preferences are without race, without gender, without class. Of all who would benefit most from the list, it'd be *us*. Getting caught up in what someone believes is useless.

"Speaking of certain crises, I refuse to criticize anybody, but I grew up in a time Black brothers and sisters were getting gunned down by police officers and abused at an alarming rate. The Hate Crime Bill and the joint civilian and police boards have curbed that, but before, your favorite celebrities were posting about it for ten minutes, unaware of what they were posting, but talking as though they did. The names of dead children were squandered and blasphemed at the hands of our own community, and we let others do it without understanding the profound effect our issues have on the homeostasis of America. When crises arise, is it not best I keep my head down and keep working instead of posturing?"

Throughout his address, his hands remained motionless, one holding the microphone to his lips. His monotone and soothing raspy voice carried the message to the back of the crowd, being met with thinking faces and calm, yet appreciative applause.

Ephraim's years in service immensely affected the youth. He started the rapid downfall of social media activism, antagonizing students in the crowd for the offensive methods on popular platforms, showing others they cared, when they did not teach themselves to emotionally invest in a topic. Students respected him more for calling them out for who they were. He attacked the privileged few who rebelled publicly but feared confronting their parents' views. Solomons outlined to them, if they could not confront their parents, they were opening a path for them to follow and repeat once their age of rebellion died down. He used his words to turn them to action, a practice the twins used on him.

"Back to you Mr. Solomons, you seem to be popular these days."

The joke pulled out a few laughs as people focused on the man they came to see.

"The question asks if you can infer from your experiences working with all types of people, what opinion do people in power have of Black folks?"

He took his time to answer this question, taking another small pause before speaking.

"That's a...um loaded question. From what I've seen, everything we do seems to be derogatory. For example, before, if you were Black and you walked into a job interview with tattoos, you weren't going to get the job," began Ephraim.

"Today, too!" yelled a woman from the crowd, getting laughs out of those on stage.

"Today, too, apparently. I have a few friends of mine, white friends, buddies from college who work in the private sector. They used to tell me of side conversations at interviews in which they discussed their tattoos. I was shocked and didn't really know how to react. It's the same with music. We listen to the same music, especially today, but when it's our car and it's loud, it's a problem. When we're loud in a restaurant, we're disruptive, when it's another family, it's festive. There are limitations to our existence because this isn't *our* land," answered Ephraim.

"Hmm," replied the crowd, applauding his thoughtful responses.

"What I've realized is we're on a short leash when it comes to what we are allowed to do. I feel like, especially when I'm in a room with certain power players, certainly always white, I'm putting on for the whole race. I felt like this in high school in those 'gifted' classes, I left like that in college, and I feel like that now. You see any other race, disruptive or misbehaved or whatever, you're not blaming the whole race. It's what they tell you, a bad apple. Sadly, we aren't afforded that, and I know you all know what I'm talking about when you go to work, or you are at school. You represent all of us the moment you step outside the house and walk into those cubicles and classrooms!" exclaimed Ephraim.

He put emotion in his voice, pointing his hands out at the crowd.

The strength of the applause was only contested by the ovation he received after his speech. The sentiments resonated with them, especially those fighting to return to the gentrified Bay Area communities.

"Mr. Solomons, I'm gonna stay with you. Sorry y'all, we're going a little off book, this is the last question. What can we do then to better our situation?" asked the comedian, shifting his tone, sharing his own curiosity.

"I'll pull another story out of the bag to answer your question, let me know if I need to move on," requested Ephraim.

"No worries, you're speaking next anyways."

"Well, I'll be quick then."

"Imagine...waking up in a field, stunned at the sight of your consciousness. You barely feel the blood flowing in your veins and as you feel your body out, you can feel the dripping of warm blood from a gash above your eye. You barely get to your feet. You concur from the blood-stained rock next to you, you were knocked out.

"I want you all to see a field, such as the grass most of you are sitting on, and to your right, you got a group of folks throwing rocks at the people on the other side, who of course, are doing the same. All the while, you're stuck in the middle. You're stunned, absolutely surprised at the hatred shown from both sides. They all yell for your attention, vying for you to join them, become them. Short of their one-liners and soundbites, you can't differentiate them from each other. You've barely been awake five minutes, and you're asked to choose.

"Nature is taking over and as you stall, you must dodge the boulders being hailed from each side now. Dazed and distracted, you see a glimmer of people ahead. It's tough, real tough...but you see a group of people ahead of you, walking forward, each alone and unaware of the presence of anyone near them. They seem happy, but it is at the refusal to turn back or help that they find joy in their own path. You wish to find their solace, yet you fear that you won't make it. So, us being us, we as black folks choose a side. When I was growing up it was people on one side from the suburbs hurling insults on people from the streets. Then it became liberals and conservatives in the twenties, I don't think either of those have changed in the thirties and now into the forties. We open ourselves to exposure by still criticizing each other for our views, especially on religion and economics. Regardless, you see how divided we are.

"We always say Black is not a monolith, but it should be. Don't get me wrong, we don't all have to vote the same or be in the same party.

Unity is togetherness in the face of different philosophies. You can be this and I can be that, but we are one, and we must protect the one. Until those people on the two sides come to an agreement and the ones who've made it turn back to help, we're doomed. We need to vote to protect us, we need to move to protect us, and we need to value the breath every one of us takes. When we integrated way back when, that's what got lost in the shuffle."

He controlled the crowd at this point, and they served at his behest. He saw as they clapped their hands in unison, the sun lowering to the back of Ephraim as he spoke.

"I think it's best if you would rise, good sir, and begin your speech," joked the host.

As he rose, the applause continued, refusing to die.

You have the momentum, Ephraim, finish off the day. It'll be historic on your account.

Markos saw the giant smile, his glasses fogging from the embarrassment. Ephraim was never shy, however, time removed certain motivations, and the routine speaking seemed to dry out his passion to put his emotion in the words. The day differed. While he wiped his face with his brown plaid blazer, he pulled at his white shirt underneath to distance his drenched undergarments from his outer attire. This was the day he envisioned, his moment. The sound of the clicks of cameras could be heard before he spoke.

Ephraim placed the microphone on the dark-brown, wooden podium. The antique podium had a black cushion under the miniature microphone stand.

Ephraim rested his hands there for the duration of his speech:

Again, thanks for having me. This speech will be more of an address or a public service announcement where I'll update you all on the state of my affairs and what I hope to work on in the near future.

I feel as if I took your time during the Q&A session, so I'll keep this quick. I know they told me we have to cut the microphone by six, it's 5:45 right now.

I want to first thank you for coming here, showing the support our community is in much need of. We've come far as a unit in the last few years, and that's due to our resilience and the support we've fed off of. I want to thank the folks who put this together. The timing couldn't have been more crucial to what I hope to accomplish, but first flowers must be given.

Those of you who've followed my journey since I was in college, I want to thank you, for today will be a historic day for our supporters. All of our hard work has come down to this day. The touring, the community service events, educational programs and seminars, all were implemented to accomplish a goal of ours. We wanted to create something with a strong foothold in the political arena, to open politicians' ears to the requests of those of us who've been ignored.

While doing so, we've interacted with different generations of folks who have forgotten the liberating facts that have been denied or lost in the shuffle. I can't tell you how many times we've talked with those who believe certain dreams and goals are so far from their reach. I've had to fight tears at statements of kids from difficult backgrounds, losing their innocence at such a young age, believing their aspirations are beyond reach. Pessimism has been taught to so many. People genuinely believe that they wouldn't be given opportunities laid out for others. My whole message was vested in emotionally and educationally, evolving and liberating those who've remained locked away in oblivion. We've taught kids about brand management, the importance of putting down resources to buy land and supporting others, things they couldn't think of before. They laughed at how within reach these goals really are.

I thank the motivated student pool who has been so vital to what we've done. The students, always a reliable demographic when demanding action, have been there through the years for us. Originally, I didn't believe they'd stay with us after many of them graduated, but they've stayed committed. For any of you who support us in the crowd, we owe it to their courage and discipline to listen to my speeches and act on it. They've been given unprecedented access to my team, and they covered us and always shared the truth of what we were about, never hiding or poaching for headlines. I am forever in debt to the students I've interacted with, a group I will not forget as I move forward.

Lastly, to the smiles of the people that have kept me going, the jubilation and open arms that have kept my family and I humbled and grounded, I am yours, completely, head to toe. All the cities I've had the fortune of visiting have always respected what we've done. You've discussed what you treasure most in your lives and what changes you want to see. Our debates and our joyful encounters live here, in my heart, engrained by the grace you've welcomed me with. I had no right to ask anything of you and you've stuck with me, listening to our words and requests. I ask, stay with me as I begin to wander into the unknown waters.

Politics is a sick game and the headlines this week are evidence of the deceitful tactics it's played with. I would never ask for such a request they accuse me of or butt my head into business that has nothing to do with me. I did not ask for those appointments, and I hope you understand that. We had a meeting to address the lack of action taken on certain bills and policies that we had been promised would be heard from recently elected officials, but they believed that we were too ignorant to understand the game of politics. We were laughed out of that meeting and told to get behind a line of lobbyists who at least had an open checkbook. We refused to play that game.

We've done so much without needing an insane amount of money. With your help and the help of many others, as a group, the time spent working with your own two hands has gone a long way in legitimizing this movement. It's funny how you would always be there when we needed folks to come out and help, all throughout this state, and the other states as well. It is an alliance, and as informal as it is, we understand each other and the symbiotic relationship between our requests and the actions we take together. I've been looking hard for a word for it, the understanding we share with all our supporters. Days and days went by before I finally found a word for it, scouring the dictionary for a word or a title, finally finding it with, 'Entente'.

It means what I've said, an informal alliance or mutual understanding. It has some historical significance, a name of a deal between France and England in the beginning of the twentieth century, used in the same context there as well. It's important you all understand that word, for it will be the name of our new political party, The Entente Party.

I appreciate your applause, but there is much work to be done. To not make this just a pipe dream, we must show them we are not in disarray, that we are in solidarity against the failing two party system. Years and years, they have fought against each other, stalling in the name of the party, while we've waited for the right thing to be done in the center of it all. I was disrespected, thinking I'd be heard as a voice of the people, a constituent. Instead, they leaked information, trying to weaken us.

We were going to wait before coming out as a political party, but the time is now.

We all watched as the mass exodus of the unprivileged and working-class people left California, and we saw as the parties bickered and blamed each other. They watched as the cost of living increased without the standards or the wages. I'm like many of you, unable to afford a home, still living with my mother. From my family's home, that's where I'll be working on creating a better situation for us all, slowly disseminating information and growing the party. We've set the foundation with your help, but it's time to collect and put our chips in together.

While this sounds good, I'll explain what's next. We'll be working with up-and-coming politicians and activists to begin grooming people for office. Our team will be in contact with people who've allied with us to see if we can turn others who still remain loyal to the ancient behemoths currently in place. It'll take time before you begin seeing us in the ballots, for mountains of paperwork and years of work still lay in front of us. It's now 2041, but in a year or two, we hope to have candidates switch to our side, and hopefully, run a candidate from the ground up. California's laws require a number of petitioned signatures for this to continue, so we hope to see your digital signatures when the time comes.

In conclusion, it is written, as I say, for us to do this. Never would I have thought that we could've done something like this. You asked me a question about who I did this for. Who more than us would benefit? Kwame Ture once said that we are the only ethnic group in America that must shed our own blood for the reform we want to see. I have been trying my best to prove him wrong. I wanted to be an active citizen, a member of my community that upholds the dutiful practices and standards that others hold themselves to. This is a necessary maneuver, and we hope, we pray, to see you all in the frontlines and the fortified trenches with us when the time comes. Thank you all and may you make it home safe.

"Our fate was sealed with his words," said Markos.

"The picture you gave me in the room, they snapped so many of us after the speech. Even the one you saw of that girl in my last lecture, all the best photos of them came from that day. He was at peace for one day, before he took on the vices of political power."

Anna and Olivia tuned into his story late into the evening as they transported the bags from the living room and the garage to the front door. The four duffle bags and the three backpacks would hold the necessities for their eventful four days in Los Angeles.

The day was filled with the twists and turns of the Entente Party's origins. The women were awed by his storytelling. He let emotion and excitement creep out of his usual monotonous attitude whilst he told his stories. He watched and ate as they packed up. They took breaks to eat and momentous pauses to ask the questions as the recollections became more intriguing.

"The twins were long gone. Alana said she talked to Jonathan after he called to congratulate them on the well-received address. They returned home to Los Angeles, keeping their head down and finding work down there. They were discouraged by how it played out," said Markos.

"They weren't open to returning? Did anyone ask?" asked Anna.

"No one asked, and to be honest, even we weren't needed after that announcement. As Alana, Peter and I completed the paperwork here at home, Ephraim was out there recruiting. We never wasted a day, sinking our head into the papers and spending our free time watching our phones. We ordered extra work phones for the four of us. We answered questions and tried to switch people over to our party. We had the voters, that wouldn't change. Originally, we didn't have people bold enough to run, though."

Anna and Olivia entered the kitchen and grabbed what foods they could find. The stories would conclude today, but they all had to wake at an early hour to drive down and avoid the torturous traffic. Markos verbally committed to arriving at his brother's school by noon. The clock numbered nine, and Olivia demanded lights be out by ten to give each of them ample time to sleep.

"Why didn't he run?" asked Anna.

"Because...he was the mastermind behind the party. His fingerprints needed to be on everything related to the party," answered Olivia.

Markos pointed his finger at Olivia, approving of her deduction.

Anna hopped onto the black marble counters, sitting beside the steel sink to her right. She rested her head on the water-stained cabinet doors. The wooden doors served as a pillow for her dead weight. She remained confused considering the explanation.

"Well, he should've run. He could've done more himself than pawning others off," shared Anna. She would never give the two men an excuse to rationalize their shortcomings.

She's right. No one asked him out of fear. He was a control freak those last few years.

"It didn't matter. Ephraim, in the first year, got state legislatures from both parties in Oregon, Washington, and California to agree to join the party once we finalized the paperwork. After a year of filing, conducting meetings throughout the state, and paying the necessary filing fees, our paperwork was streamlined through. It helped having friends all throughout the West who removed impediments along the way. In those days, we were overworked, but any success was welcomed. I even remember Liv, bringing us tea and bread. She was able to see that we were extremely stressed. I went from security to paper shuffler."

Olivia blushed at his memory. He finally called her the name she wanted to be called.

"The first year was shocking. I had faith in Ephraim, but I shouldn't have underestimated him. Senator Campbell, right after he won his reelection, said he'd run as a member of the Entente Party in the next election. I don't know what backroom deal was done, but he started coming around more and the phone calls with him and Ephraim were always private. It was a bombshell announcement, and it had a domino effect. Five representative seats switched and another senator, a veteran like Campbell, switched as well. The effect trickled down from the federal government. State and local governments followed suit. We grew slowly, but as Alana and I became less important, our relationship as a unit declined."

Olivia sat on an elevated stool she grabbed from the garage. Her back was to the oven, placing herself near Anna and in front of Markos. He faced them, leaning against the dishwasher, on the other end of the sink. The small square space of a kitchen housed the three as they indulged themselves with the unhealthier choices available to them. The alcohol remained in the cabinet; a few drinks worth of bourbon remaining. Instead, salted potato chips and caffeinated chocolate snacks took their attention.

"It seems Grandpa took control of the whole thing. That had to mess with his already paranoid outlook, no?" inquired Anna.

She's still interested. She wants to know why we fell out, why she can't see Alana. I can't give all of it up to her, but little by little she'll understand.

"Yes, he knew of my reservations and Alana's. He remained closer to Peter. He had his own agenda for the boy that he kept us away from. Peter was much more enthusiastic about the change than we were. Donations also flooded into the party, small ones from normal people. The five, ten dollars we received from working families was nothing compared to the progressive corporations who invested deeply into Ephraim's future. They saw the effect of his words and as long as he followed his famed ten-point plan, they were with him. With money, he afforded new lawyers, an army of them to help him game plan a larger approach to his politics. Alana became an outcast, relegated to an advisor role, even losing out on her job as spokesperson. A white woman didn't fit the demographic, apparently, of the people he wanted to attract. He focused on minorities, veterans, and students. She was virtually out entirely."

Anna smacked her lips as Olivia clenched her teeth. She was unaware of the falling out. Olivia was focused on her freshman year of high school while the party came onto the scene. She was distracted by the flurry of comments from her classmates.

"New allies referred him to security consultants and more useful people than me. I wasn't worried, that role was in name only. I was there so we could watch out for each other, but it had been years since he had paid attention," said Markos.

He took a pause to retrieve his cup of water near him. He felt as if he was going to cough if he continued. He refilled his cup and quickly drank before he continued further.

"After the paperwork was sent in, the money was received, and the new personnel was added, he even rented an office space near the Capitol building here in Sacramento. It's a relic now. They moved the party's headquarters to San Francisco. I went with him every day, but he paid less attention to the smaller details of his life: Alondra, Darius, and

Liv. They were much more important than anything we were involved with. They all saw him less, and quickly, he forgot about his responsibilities even in the face of tragedy.

"Two years after the speech, we buried Mom. She lived to about seventy-four. I was destroyed, a wreck. Out of respect for her, I avoided the bottle, but Ephraim was different. He didn't say anything, even though she loved him the most. I was the one that consumed her with worry, but him, he was her treasured baby. They argued like peers because she respected him, his work ethic and the fact that he refused to blindly accept anything she told him. He instead used the sympathy he garnered from her death as points in his political games. I detested it, and so did he, for he resented himself and carried around a soured attitude after she died. Her funeral was full of people I had barely met, only recognizing the twins, Alana, and Senator Campbell. The semi-familiar faces of the local politicians and community activists were also in attendance, never having an actual interaction with her. I truly hated it, and so did Alana. She was as much a child to our mother as we were. Alondra was even jealous she couldn't share that relationship with Mom. It was the last straw for Alana.

"When you lose a loved one, especially your mother, you wish you never wasted a second not hearing her laugh, eating her food, telling her what you were actually thinking. We sometimes lie to our parents to protect them or because we're afraid of them, but when they die, you wish you talked more. I didn't cry, I think crying comes from unexpressed emotions, but I was depressed. I wish I told her everything I thought about, all the things in my head that kept me reserved and distanced. I just went silent after she died."

Markos let the memories flood into full fruition. He remembered every core detail of the walks in the park she tagged along on, her shock at Ephraim's rise, every moment her patience was tested by him and Ephraim. He recalled the trips to her family's home and how her words could have a slow slicing effect.

Each departure, in those times, shattered his delicate stability.

"I have to leave. I'm thankful for the progress, for what we've created but it's time. He desecrated that funeral. He ousted the twins and lifted his Peter. I can't, I've been using my new free time to plan a way to live a life after all this. I'm sorry, Markos, I plan on moving far away from here. I'm never coming back. There's nothing left from the innocent kid in the past," argued Alana.

Markos illustrated the silence of the winter the day he spoke with Alana in the park. He and Alana walked and walked, passing the black fence separating the school, then circling around to the homes separated by the brick fenced barriers. The bark and mud between the barriers and cement path stopped at the right side of the walkway throughout the park, encircling the large grass field with cement as the inner barrier and the fences as the outer one. Every detail of the park was branded in his head, a place where his life twisted and turned, for better or worse.

The silence brought sadness to his eyes as the pain of another woman he loved, left him. He wanted to break down, beg if he could. He wanted to share in her great escape. He wanted to leave, but he promised to stick by Ephraim. She helplessly watched, wishing he would express his somber attitude in words she could reply to. She did not know how to respond, being the strong woman she was.

"All the people that love you are here," voiced Markos.

"Not all, Markos. I've used my new free time this past year to make myself available to others, beyond those who share the name Solomons. I've been lucky to find a great love, a surprise to me this late in life. It's helped me come to the realization I should leave with my head held high before I'm forced out."

His heart felt a feeling of grace. He fought tears while he laughed out of joy for her.

"I'm happy for you, the famed Alana finding love. He's a lucky man," suggested Markos.

"*She's* lucky, but I'm lucky I found her," interjected Alana.

He comically examined her as his smile grew from end to end. He had not found joy from a conversation in years, but as they left the park to walk her home, he smiled in their last moments.

"I'm happy for you."

"I'm sorry I'm leaving, it's for my sanity. I don't recognize it, the humble beginnings and the noble pursuit we chose to follow. He's power hungry. *Be careful,"* warned Alana.

They approached the doorstep and he hugged her with all his might, imagining a world where he did not have to let go of one of the defining pieces of his life. She held him together. She was the first to step back and give a tearful goodbye as she retreated to her home. She was gone, never to be seen by a Solomons until Olivia's dilemma with Anna's birth.

"No one ever talked about her sexuality?" asked Anna.

"Because it didn't matter, Anna. She was who she was, and she loved who she loved. If we were judged by our desires, there would be nothing sacred to be kept private," replied Markos.

Olivia was not prepared for such an ending to the story of her savior. The pedestal her father sat on was being challenged as she learned of the evolution of Ephraim.

"She told Ephraim before me, and he refused to tell me. I didn't know until he asked me if she had said goodbye already. I was stunned he hadn't begged, gotten on his knees and asked her to stay. I was so angry, petrified by the way he had thrown away someone who sacrificed so much for him," pleaded Markos.

"There was a part of him who hated who he was becoming. He was snapping at people and losing his composure. He was also very successful, very fast, and he absolutely had to change his ways, but it was a lot.

"He broke the party into committees to delegate the work, three of them to be exact. The influx of support and endorsements afforded him new volunteers and workers. He had a committee on education, split into two: one for higher education and one for adolescent education. The second was a committee on large scale economic policies, focused on small businesses and inner-city infrastructure. The last committee was on group economics, focusing on growing the network of entrepreneurs and small business investors in low-income communities. He and Peter, together, plotted out a list of separate goals to work towards and they dove right in. I took a backseat and watched as paper shuffling and an overly excited workforce congested Ephraim's movement."

"Did you ever plead to him, or even try and work towards getting him back to the things that mattered?" asked Olivia.

The surprising intrusion stunned him. Both the women were tuned in but saddened by the lack of fortitude Ephraim had.

"Don't get me wrong, this stuff all mattered. Like a war photographer, one may seem emotionless as he fixes up a wounded homeless man for a photo, but even if he doesn't look like he's helping him, he is. He's telling his story to viewers and moving on to help the next one. The position required Ephraim to be emotionless, but love and hope was what he used to grow, not money. He was not like anyone before him, family was involved in this. It's tough. I believed after Alana left, he'd notice his mistakes. I couldn't say anything, I was in a difficult position. I would've been a hypocrite, after all I put this family through, if I pleaded on behalf of our name. Months prior, he had already recognized I was not with him completely and I hadn't tried to hide it. I thought he'd notice. I became less active and avoided going to events and to the office. I stayed home, away from it all. I even moved out, I think when you were fifteen or sixteen, a year before Alana left. I showed him in all the ways I could without saying the words outright."

"You could've done more," suggested Anna.

She lowered herself from the kitchen counter. She dropped her weight onto the sofa, signaling to the rest of the family to meet her in the lounge area. Markos walked over in frustration at the lack of details he could not share with her. He could not tell her about the philosophical considerations behind Ephraim's control over him. Markos owed him his life and all the fruits of his labor.

"I see we're near the end of your relationship, what pushed it over the line?" asked Anna.

She's irritated, is it with me? I have to be careful; it gets worse. They need to remember him the way they did. He did it all for us. Repulsion has more energy than attraction.

"I'm gonna wait for your mother to come from the kitchen," whispered Markos.

He laid his glasses down as the moisture crept through his pores. Olivia was caught up in the thoughts of her father. She remembered her mute uncle's departure, but never noticed the decreased time spent with Ephraim. Her perception of his deterioration was moot, she never saw him anyhow. She met them at the sofas, considerably distracted with her own recollections of her absentee father.

"I don't like this. I don't like this at all," declared Markos.

He fixed his eyes on the road, serving as the driver for his brother and Peter. Ephraim's feet rested between the feet divider below the middle seat in the back. The blackened interior of the tinted sports utility vehicle was a gift of the private donors who wanted their playmaker to ride in style, protected from exterior threats.

Peter muted his thoughts, watching his mentor and his boss solve their familial dispute.

"Markos, it's a protest we're hosting. That kid did not have to die, you remember the things we grew up watching. We gotta get out there to remind these officers that that time is dead and gone," stated Ephraim.

Markos smacked his dry lips together. Deep in his thoughts, he ran through the security nightmare of such an event in his head. There were liabilities and risks associated with such an unnecessary photo opportunity.

"It's justified, beyond measure, but your presence is not," said Markos decidedly.

"He's here to show that his grounded roots are still intact. Since Alana's departure six months ago, some of our supporters are saying he went fully political," added Peter.

Markos scowled at Peter's arrogance. Being Ephraim's new protector afforded him the privilege of butting into the decision making of matters not pertaining to him.

"Nothing new there, everyone sees it," uttered Markos, hiding his comments under his breath and the radio.

"Regardless of how you feel, we need to be here. No one asked you to be here, I'll have security there anyway," said Ephraim.

"Ephraim, it's not about that. This is a delicate topic, and the police believe they are in the right in this situation. They already don't like you because you advocated for more civilians to be on the review boards. You're tackling more issues than you can handle," warned Markos.

"Issues are arising everywhere I turn!" snapped Ephraim.

He relaxed himself by leaning on the calmness of his deep breaths. Markos avoided his careless attacks.

My time is coming, thought Markos.

The protest culminated in more than thirty thousand people gathered in the downtown plaza. The outdoor park consisted of statues of activists from the twentieth century, the outlines of Martin Luther King Jr. and Cesar Chavez. The remnants of their legacy were in full demand in a day where people would be chanting and demanding justice for a young man, a Black man, killed in a police shootout. The details of the young man's death were fuzzy, for he remained over forty yards away from the initial shooting. As the suspects fled, mistaken identity cost him his life as he reached for identification. The officers were exonerated, circumventing the civilian and police review board by bamboozling the man's estranged father into signing a settlement awarded to the family. The settlement freed them from judgment, angering the community.

"I am as angry as you are!!" yelled Ephraim into the megaphone.

He shared the stage with local celebrities and athletes. Sacramento's full Civilian Force was in attendance, detailing the updates on the case.

They explained to the exasperated citizens how much the Entente Party will be involved in making sure this is handled better going forward. They, Peter and Ephraim, took their time to share how the mayor they will be running in the next year's election will be looking to punish the police force.

"Today, as we march, be as peaceful as possible. We don't want this to escalate into a situation we don't want. No one needs to get hurt," commented Ephraim, prepared to march.

He deferred to those who would be running the chants to orchestrate the voices of the crowd.

"We're going to be in front. The police set up barricades at our last destination, the State Capitol. They have roadblocks set up along the way, but we'll be fine. People will just be blowing off some steam," recounted Markos in his mind. The day's events went nothing like Ephraim said it would.

The crowd was more riled up than anyone expected. The group consisted of more college and high school students, along with a great number of young adults filing in by the second. They planned for no more than twelve thousand, overwhelmingly unprepared for those in attendance. They were astounded by the force of their yells reverberating through the alleyways and shallow streets of Downtown Sacramento. They walked through the different parks and skyscrapers, interacting with diverse groups of restaurant owners and homeless people. Their cries for justice garnered support through honking of cars, also receiving hate in the form of aberrant yells and empty threats. A few threats from passenger seat activists carried into the streets. Some protestors threatened to pull people out of their vehicles. Car windows were smashed by disruptors as the efforts of true protestors to bring about calm were ignored. Within minutes, arguments broke out between protestors who tried to maintain the balance of their message, and people who saw enemies in those who spoke out against them. It escalated into conflicts between peacekeepers and disruptors, breaking the solidarity they had walked with for an hour. However, these were small skirmishes, quickly subsiding after verbal exchanges.

"Ephraim, it's starting to get ugly. Sooner or later, police will be getting involved. We need to get you out of here at least. We can wait it out in the office if you'd like," pleaded Markos.

Ephraim kept his head on a swivel, watching as people in front of him shared some of the things transpiring in the middle. Markos shook his head as his brother ignored him and watched.

Boom! Boom!

The disarray from the shuffling feet of protestors boxed in people who chose to remain on the trek to the State Capitol. A third of the group deserted at the introduction of violence. Soon, protestors stood encircled by police and other antagonists behind them, shouting insults from the sidewalks. They could not move from the street. They were two hundred yards from the door of the Capitol Building, stuck on the street, blocking traffic. The officers employed tear gas, forcefully waking Ephraim to the dire situation he led people into.

"Markos! Markos!!" yelled Ephraim.

Markos, prepared for such an occasion, covered his brother's eyes and nose with a white cloth as he tightly clutched his blue shirt. He dragged him through the chaos, trapped in the screams of the terrified teenagers and unprepared collegiates. Those wise enough to stay in the back, slithered out of the group and retreated to their automobiles, wheezing and fighting to catch their breath. Markos sat trapped between the continued hurling of gas from the officers and the cornered herd blindly running around. The long, straight road leading the protestors to the Capitol Building sat between industrious skyscrapers, where most business affairs of the state were conducted. People were prepared for a protest and boarded up windows and locked all doors. The extra security in those buildings on that day stopped people from wiggling their way in to avoid police. Markos had no choice but to try and move forward.

The horseshoe formation of the police faced the protestors as they advanced forward. The only way out was from the back, but thousands blocked their exit. Markos could not clearly see anything in front of him, but he pushed through the white gas, being met with a strike from an officer's riot shield.

"Back up!! Back up!!" ordered the officer.

We're at the front of the formation!

Markos tried again to push through, but he was met with two blows from the shield, dropping both he and Ephraim to the ground. They were separated from Peter, leaving them alone to find a way.

"You get closer, I'll arrest both of you. Back up!!"

"Let them through! You know who that is, leave him!!" screamed an antagonist, laughing with his friends as they watched the mayhem with other onlookers and tourists behind the police blockade.

We need to go, this is not an ideal place to be, he is in danger.

Markos retreated and rose, violently clutching and dragging Ephraim. No resistance existed in his brother's movements. He surrendered control to Markos, fully aware of the errors of his decisions. Markos kicked and pushed Ephraim's supporters, working towards the back of the blockade. Many were still fleeing from the back, the only place with clean air and visibility. The news cameras were arriving to cover the raving madness of the protest, willfully prepared to spew their propaganda and cast blame on those they neither encountered nor spoke to.

A scuffle emerged from the rear of the group as a misfire from the police's formation caused more gas to be dispersed.

One of the young students grabbed the small metal tank of gas and heaved it back towards the police. The police broke formation. Moving in a frenzy to arrest the young man, they miscalculated the loyalty of the protestors who now found a common enemy.

Markos watched it all transpire, only worrying of the then and now, while his brother sank in his thoughts of the repercussions. He was nearly in the back, brushing against the backs of active protestors, spitting and salivating from his nose and mouth. He ripped his shirt to cover his nose and mouth, but his eyes, blood red, felt as if pieces of hot coals were inserted in the crevices each time he closed them. Barely able to see, he abandoned his idea to retreat from the back, taking advantage of the police force's broken formation. He was able to pull his brother to safety, still clutching onto him while keeping his other arm free to push others out of his way. They were able to make their way onto the sidewalks to their left, in front of a skyscraper. The tall, blue-black glass reflected the mayhem of the saddened city.

"Hey, you're not getting away that easily!"

Markos's blurred vision limited his ability to react. He could hear the increased pace of three spectators coming their way. He opened his eyes to liquid haze, blurred blobs yelling at them both.

"Ephraim, cover your face! Don't let people see you, we're six blocks away from the office, just work with me as I move," ordered Markos.

Ephraim did not say a single word, but his body obeyed.

"Hey, where are you guys going?!" screamed one of the three men, sarcastically.

Markos did not want to run until he felt they were clear of police. Markos made sure to cover Ephraim's face in order to avoid cameras and unwanted attention. They were being followed, and as his vision slightly cleared up, he could see the three males following them. He saw two middle aged white gentlemen, burly and out of shape, walking confidently towards them. They were enjoying the terror they imposed, while their Latin friend remained intrigued, yet silent, as he followed.

They were now four blocks away, jaywalking and increasing their pace each time they passed people up. The gentlemen behind them were beginning to jog, their impatience growing.

We're not going to make it.

They walked one more block before they heard the voices of their unwanted company on the street. The office was near the freeway and away from the businesses open on that Saturday. They were very close to their destination, but the men no longer needed to yell to get their attention, they were a half a minute away from being able to strike. Their unknown intentions frightened Markos, spurring him into decisive action as he planned countermeasures.

"Ephraim...Ephraim! Listen to me, I want you, when I tap you, to make a left into this alleyway. We're about fifteen paces from it, I want you to walk by yourself into the alleyway. Wipe your eyes, you won't have full visibility, but it'll be enough. Don't worry about anything. They'll creep up on you, but I'll be there, *I'll be there,*" stressed Markos.

As soon as they turned into the alleyway, the two brothers disconnected. Ephraim walked alone as Markos ran ahead, away from their view. He hid himself as Ephraim walked deeper into the silent alleyway. No homeless people nor bystanders were nearby. The alleyway opened to the entrance of a parking garage thirty yards away. Ephraim made it a few feet in before the three circled him. He wiped his eyes, turning around to see their faces as best he could.

"How may I help you folks?" calmly asked Ephraim.

Two remained in front of him, covering the street, while one stood behind him, his back to the parking garage. The one behind him did not hesitate to speak first.

"You messed things up, sir. As a guy that lives here, I'm pissed."

Ephraim was fearful of the man's sarcasm.

"I did not hope to see these types of things today, nor did I order anyone to do anything. I spoke and I marched alongside the people as a peaceful protestor. Your complaints should be voiced to the city," patiently replied Ephraim.

He wiped his face as sweat mixed with discharge from his nose.

"Well, I want to talk to you, big man. It's only you here, did your friend leave you?" asked one of the men blocking the street.

"No, he wouldn't leave. That's his brother I think," pointed out the man behind Ephraim.

"Can't trust your blood sometimes, eh? Don't worry, you're among friends," said one of the men by the street, striking Ephraim in his abdomen.

The soft cushion of his underbelly took the full force of the impact. Ephraim hunched over and spit out the discharge and snot in his mouth, gasping for his breath. The man behind him violently pushed Ephraim with his full force, forcing Ephraim to fall on his stomach. Unable to catch his breath and still inebriated from the tear gas, he let his body sink into the ground. He slowly curled into the fetal position in anticipation of a beating. The boldness of the men struck fear in him.

They would not get off any more blows before Markos snuck in from behind. He had sat in the middle of the alleyway and with his ripped shirt, he decided to remain seated and posture as a homeless man in a tiny crevice in the wall. The immense homeless population in Downtown Sacramento allowed him to be ignored by the attackers who he believed may have been affected by the gas. He sat on a bed previously slept in by a homeless man, stacked with cardboard and a blackened fabric blanket. He took time to grab what he could from the bed, an empty beer bottle and the blanket itself. He slowly walked up behind them, timing his step with the man's push, worming through on a vengeful quest.

He got close enough and smashed the beer bottle in the back of the head of the man who pushed Ephraim forward. The blow was so profound he cut his own hand on impact, completely knocking the man out cold. Markos wasted no time in taking the blanket he folded up horizontally to act as a rope, to choke the other man who punched his brother. With blood from his hand smothering the antagonist's face, Markos tightened and tightened his grip to not only snatch the air from the attacker's mouth, but to steal whatever life remained.

Markos cried at the detestable violence and emotion he utilized to hurt the man. He believed the man was like Peter once was, placed in a position where he was not privy to moral responsibility. The antagonist crossed the line, so as the flashbacks of all the heartbreaks of Markos's life zipped through, he strengthened his grip and backed into the wall of the alley as he obtained more leverage. He pulled harder, hearing the disorderly rhythm of the man choking. As he passed out, Markos was snapped out of his trance.

"Markos!! Markos! Let him go!!" screamed Ephraim.

He rose and saw the bloodied man to his left, unconscious and barely breathing, lying next to the first attacker. The third man, still quiet, lost all interest in remaining, but his legs stood frozen by shock at how the tables turned.

"Don't leave," said Ephraim to the man, slowly rising to his feet.

Markos submitted to his brother's control over the situation and saw as he silenced the ringing of his watch. He did not care to see who Ephraim was speaking with but he knew of the turmoil awaiting them. When the rage had consumed his body, as he attacked those who were hurting his brother, he remembered Malek's face when he returned from the police station, battered and beaten.

Malek endured the rest of his time in Morocco with delayed replies and cantankerous attitudes. As Markos accumulated the necessary materials to defend his brother, he feared the same fate for Ephraim. Now, it was his sentence he feared.

Peter was the first to show up and take the assailants to the hospital. Calls were made to party leadership. They and the donors who invested millions of their own money, were beginning to feel nervous from the situation. They put Peter in charge of the dilemma, employing him as a fixer, casting Ephraim aside. Police were not notified, and money was offered to the three. One of them, the man who took the bottle to his dome, was awarded most of the money since he lost large amounts of blood. He would be slow to recover, taking years to heal from the brain damage. All three signed a non-disclosure agreement, the whole situation, from settlements to pay-offs, orchestrated by Peter. He focused on the antagonists, invested in the task capable of putting him in good graces with the few who controlled the movements of Ephraim's party. He avoided Markos and Ephraim, leaving them to be treated before he would speak to them. He needed to secure their silence as well.

Ephraim was treated for dehydration and minor cuts he obtained when falling onto the ground. Markos received treatment on his hands from the broken beer bottle and the overt burns and marks from his handling of the blanket. After his treatment, he immediately snuck out to see his brother. He found Ephraim and Peter in serious discussion. A minor dispute, one no different from their strategy meetings, was visibly occurring in the room as he watched from outside the door. Markos feared his punishment, but he did not expect to be ousted.

"Markos, it goes without saying, you went overboard today," began Ephraim.

"You would've killed the man and put all this, all that *I've* done, in jeopardy. Look at me, look at me," demanded Ephraim.

Markos stuck his eyes on Peter outside. Peter did not want to look in on the brothers, he knew he was betraying the one who invested in and protected him the most.

"He's amassing more control. They gave him authority to fix this," whispered Ephraim.

"So what?"

"That's bad. If he gets the tap on the shoulder, I'm out as leader and he's in. Money is involved now, Markos, they own us at the end of the day."

It hurt him to say that. He knew and he did nothing.

"What do they want?"

"You're out Markos. You need to sign an NDA and you're out. If you choose to stay, they'll charge you now with assault and attempted murder for the other guy."

Markos sighed, he did not want to speak, but he felt an urge to defend himself. He did not know why, he was given the out he had desired for so long.

"Why am I the scapegoat for this?" inquired Markos, putting his attention to Ephraim's eyes.

"You're guilty Markos, you're guilty."

He's lying. He wouldn't cast me aside after I helped him.

"What'd they really say, Ephraim? What threat or offer did they give you?"

Ephraim looked away for a second, avoiding the perceptive glare. He turned back after a few moments to answer him.

"It's either you or me, and I have to weigh the benefits. You'll be locked out of all facilities and are banned from participating in any of the party's events. You also can't be seen in public with me, out of fear the encounter was recorded or in case the victims renege on the agreement. You have to sign that NDA," ordered Ephraim, changing his welcoming tone.

"I'll go away Ephraim, if that's what you want, I'll go away. I'm not signing my life away, though. I'm not signing," said Markos.

Annoyed by the lack of remorse and thankfulness of Ephraim, he stood up to leave.

"You're putting all the work I've done at risk of being taken from me!!"

The yells were heard through the hospital. Peter was ashamed of the necessity of these actions. Markos ignored his brother and continued his walk to the door.

"Markos, I'll have to tell the family what happened, what actually happened. I'll keep them from you if I have to. I'll tell them to stay away, always and forever. They'll learn of today. They'll know of the darkness I just saw in you. If that isn't enough, I'll have to tell Alondra and the kids about *Elsa.*"

Markos's arm shook when he reached for the door. He let his hand sit there after the cruelty of Ephraim's words. He was baffled at what he was to do as his savior and confidant sat behind him, threatening to blot him out of the family's memory, from the lineage. He sank, confounded at the lack of words as his lips slowly moved to speak.

"Why, why are we even signing anything? We're the party, you're the party?!" said Markos.

"Your interests haven't been aligned with our moves, and we have to make sure, Markos. We must be sure. These people aren't idiots Markos, their investment is in me, I'm their future. They know where your loyalties lie, they knew what Alana was thinking of all of this. *These people know everything,*" whispered Ephraim.

Ephraim spoke to him, fully transformed into the inner being he fought against and despised. His face was unchanged, stoic and everlasting. He was what the political machine required.

"Is this you? Is this him or you?" asked Markos, cracking his voice, beginning to break down in front of his brother. He did not care what he looked like.

He was hurt. He was broken.

Ephraim ignored his question. To his deathbed, Markos did not know which of the two removed him. He knew for Ephraim to fully immerse into the game of politics, voices like his and Alana's needed to go. But he was family, he believed he was untouchable.

"Markos, I'm sorry, truly I am. To complete my goal this is necessary, sign the paper. I can help so many others, so many people who need me, need us," added Ephraim.

Markos grabbed the yellow envelope sitting on the table of the recently renovated room in the hospital, the V.I.P room.

"Inside, it says if you break the agreement, your assets are inherited by the party. Prison time is also applicable. The statute of limitations will be set aside for this, and you'll be charged with a Hate Crime. You will be liable for a civil case from the three as well. You are to avoid contact with them, and again, we can't be seen together for a while. You'll...find something else."

"Ephraim, there's nothing that can be said between us after this moment. What you've done today will cement your legacy with that of Dad. There's nothing for us. I finally understand what Jonathan was feeling that day, giving you what you wanted before he left. I see the betrayal, and all the belittling. You've become something Ephraim. I will have to live with being the timid one, the shy, defected one. I wasn't strong enough to let you know, but this is it."

"Don't patronize me! I saved you and I was there for you. You think I wanted someone who'd always sit unhappy and depressed that his father left him. You think I liked sitting here and watching you drink over a woman who had a reputation of getting around. Read the paper, there's something else," attacked Ephraim.

Markos scanned through the paper, wiping his nose. He found the hidden portion.

"What is this?"

"You allowed this. I can't control him anymore. He has the authorization! If you let anyone know where he came from, the noose or anything from that day, I'll lose my position in the party and you will go to jail for this. The day of reckoning occurs the day you lose control."

Markos read through the paper in silence. He wanted the moment to bring pain to his brother, he wanted the picture of him signing the paper to be engraved in his mind when he thought of their end. In that moment, Ephraim eagerly watched him like a madman, emotionless.

"Ephraim, you are the one who lost control, you let this fester. The twins told you what would come, you basically ousted Alana for loving and protecting you. I'm going to sign this, but I'll be praying. I'll pray it all crumbles," said Markos as he signed, hysterical at the deception.

"I hope it all falls. Goodbye, Ephraim," said Markos, walking out of the room, escaping into the night as alone as he started.

He avoided all the cameras outside of the large hospital, even avoiding the patient Peter, who had waited years to be free of the secrets Ephraim held over him. He let Ephraim remain in control of the party, but alone. Peter loved them all, but he himself transformed into a politician.

Ephraim casted all his friends aside, losing the contagious smiles and camaraderie attached to the twins and Alana. He was never able to trust anyone in his party. He was never able to confide in anyone like he did Markos. Markos would never pick up his calls, refusing to hear his or Alondra's pleas to return. Ephraim was now the one walking in the park alone, burdened with dangerously high levels of stress. It took a toll on his life at home, worsening from the bickering of Alondra, who blamed her husband for his treatment of others. He would tell her of all the secrets he kept from her. He confessed it all: Elsa's ordeal, Markos's drinking, and all of his own actions as well. The stress overwhelmed him, his health waning from that and a worsening diet. In the night, years after his mother's death, his body crumbled piece by piece. He succumbed to a stroke in his sleep at the age of forty-three, a martyr to so many. He was a complicated figure to the loved ones who watched his rise. The ones closest to him kept their opinions to themselves when they thought of the forgotten deterioration.

The family did their best to keep the facts under wraps, but the living who kept the secrets hidden, paid a steep price.

Markos left out many things. He chose to tell them of the arguments in the car and how he threatened to leave the party while on the way to the protest. He shared how after the protest, he blamed Ephraim for the eighteen hospitalizations and the three hundred arrests. Markos, believing he was choosing the coward's way out, lied to them to preserve aspects of the family's relationship to a dead man. He did not wish to taint their knowledge of Ephraim. There were sacrifices Ephraim made that he could not explain to them in the time he had. He ambiguously detailed the origins of the agreement to protect them from the consequences.

He avoided talking of the dark aspects of the protest, the fighting and personal encounters with police. He wanted the story to be believable without ruining his brother's image or discussing Elsa. He expressed some of the hurtful words his brother said to him in the hospital. The women scoffed and gasped, livid at the inconsideration. He took the lion's share of the blame, however, explaining his regret ignoring his brother's phone calls or his absence following his departure. He refused attempts at anything real with Ephraim's children, always remaining in his room, choosing to never be alone with them when they lived together. He was on the road with Ephraim, so he, like his brother, was already absent. He feared they would be like him. He withdrew himself from them so they would not adopt a distant, fearful lifestyle. It was easy to keep that up when he finally left for good.

"Alondra was significant in keeping you all together, and sometimes, she updated me for a few years after he died. She stopped putting in effort because I refused to reply," said Markos.

Olivia cried at the innocence of her mother. She shed tears over the pride of men and the obstacles created by the brothers.

"You all could've done more. We were family, you all could've done better for each other," said Anna.

"In the present time, you think your actions are justified. You don't realize you're still a slave to time. You need to answer to the future for your decisions.

"Betrayal is difficult, because to his deathbed, he believed he was in the right. He believed all of his betrayals were necessary actions, and that we were the ones betraying his ability to adapt. I don't know what to tell you, I sincerely do apologize for the way it went down. Maybe he was always right, maybe he was prepared to face the difficult circumstances with the party. He could be right, he probably was. There was no place for us to be there together though, no place for me," concluded Markos.

"There was a place for you here. There was a home for you here. I was here, Mom was here, and Grandma was here. You should've done more; you all should've been better. Both of you were family before any political party was in the picture. His story ends unfinished because he betrayed family, just as you did," said Anna.

thirteen:
A Lonely Avenue

"4. Remove the obstacles to full integration. Today's conflicts arise from people unprepared for the consequences of demanded integration, racially and economically. Prepare others by notifying people of the status of your neighbors, regardless of their own beliefs."

"5. Sow the seeds necessary for such a momentum driven movement to be given away to those appearing after us. If we follow our words and act for the betterment of our children, all actions will work to create a better place. We must be quick to resolve and slow to conflict."

- Entente Party's List of Goals, inherited from the social movement of founder, Ephraim Solomons.

"Do you believe he's been telling the truth?" asked Anna.

Olivia shrugged as she looked in her rearview mirror. Markos prepared for his speech, resting in a state of deep sleep. The moment the car turned on, he used the space he was awarded to find the optimal sleeping position. He sat behind Olivia, resting his head on the window as the smooth electric car glided over the road. He was out and would spend the ride dreaming of the recent memories he brought to life with his words.

"Why would he lie?" asked Olivia in reply.

Anna's eyes sank as she applied pressure to her temple with her palms. She seemed uneasy by the thought of his deception.

"I don't know, I'm just wondering if he's taking our feelings into consideration. We may have overplayed our emotions yesterday. He hasn't let me get away with anything, but last night he didn't put up a fight when I told him to do better. *I know he's dying,* but – I don't know – I'm curious. I want to know more," said Anna.

Olivia believed her words to be meaningless suggestions. She lived through the arduous nightmare of hearing how twisted her absentee caretaker was. Running on fumes, she ignored her bodily signals as she drove. Her body repelled sleep the night before, instead battling with the silk sheets in the face of the intimidating darkness of the large, empty room.

"I don't know what to tell you, I've been thinking of Dad. I try to remember the good things. I was up all-night thinking of him. Honestly, I don't care to wonder if it's the truth. I believe it is, there's no harm in asking if it isn't though. He's not a stranger to you, he'll tell you if he's lying, he just won't tell you why he's lying. That's more important than the lies," stated Olivia.

Anna turned her head and looked at Markos. Her glazed eyes were reddened. She scratched at them in order to clear up the glossy tears forming from the cold air conditioning. She could see he was deeply entranced by the vivid pictures in his head. His mind boggled through past acts of betrayal, still honing on the chopped image of Elsa in the park. She tried to analyze him out of necessity but failed. A deep urge to go to him befell her. She felt an enormous feeling of empathy for him, watching him constantly shift in his sleep. She was disheartened by the lonely path he walked dealing with the events of his life.

"He lived alone, Mom. He lived alone for years, it's been twenty-two years since Grandpa passed. I've learned a lot about them both and I hope to never feel that. Grandpa was unfair to leave him to be alone after that heartache. I still believe they were both being immature, but Mom, I hope to never be in that pain. He looks constantly in pain," observed Anna.

"Pain goes away. It should've healed, and it was healing when he was with Grandpa, you can ask him. You can never recover from what he's faced, but scars are capable of slowly fading from the original gash. Family was supposed to stick by him. He carries some of the blame as well, he should've stuck by them. He chose to remain an outsider, choosing to be distant around those who loved him. Dad chose to look beyond that and involve him in what he was doing. They are both guilty, but more importantly, the family is guilty of rationalizing and allowing this," declared Olivia.

Anna took a moment, to breath, to think.

"We mattered to them. We still matter to him. It's in those lies he told in the beginning and the way he looks at us. He's grateful, but I feel like we were always in their thoughts. I didn't meet Grandpa, but I feel like he loved you. I mean look at the logo of his party, an olive branch on both sides of equal scales. It's the olive branch he put in there. I'm sure he thought of you at all times, but sometimes people who try to pass on a legacy to their children believe it's more important than the time they spend with them. There was no one to correct them, but they shouldn't have needed correction, as wise as they were. Maybe that's why they always remained alone, even at home. They were ashamed," continued Anna.

Olivia felt a mix of emotions at her daughter's analysis of the men's dichotomy. She spoke so softly, so nonchalant. She appreciated how Anna spoke out of a need to lighten the weight the words had on her mind, but the power of her sentiments needed time to be thought through. Olivia pondered if her daughter was talking about her. She was frequently working, trying to provide the best for her daughter. She worried she may have been excessive, even when she believed her daughter would benefit. Nonetheless, Olivia was comforted by assurances her own father loved her. She was speechless thinking of him, playing off her dumbfounded ignorance by checking her watch for the estimated time of arrival. She was told her parents named her for that, a baby of peace and unity. The logo consisted of a black ovular shape encircled by two white circular lines, serving as a frame for a scale equal in balance. An olive branch rested on both sides of the scales, signaling to members, regardless of the issue, equal ground would always be sought after. She remembered being told of the logo as a teenager, using the advantage against her brother, berating him about how she was more important. She smiled thinking of her significance to her father.

"We're gonna stop for food soon, I have to charge the car for a little while. The diner we always stop at is coming up. We're gonna have to wake him up in a little bit."

"Give him a little longer, it's going to be a long day for him. This is his last chance to get his message across," said Anna.

"It doesn't matter to him. He's been invested in his stories with us. He told us the story he wanted about the family. He's at peace," stated Olivia.

Far from the peace, Markos loitered in his dreams, confused and distracted by the state of his consciousness. His dreams were never really dreams, but instead torturous nightmares masquerading their way into his subconscious. He was locked to those memories refusing to leave him. That morning, he was haunted by his failure to find resolve between himself and Ephraim. He loved him and was still thankful, but he did not want to dream of him, he wanted Elsa. He wanted to see her in the park, before it went bad. He desired to see her. He was not angry at Anna when she politely shook him back to life, the existence he was stuck in. Past days were spent wondering where he was truly free, at the hands of his dreams or in the constraints of his lies and decisions.

"We're gonna go into the diner, Mom plugged up the car. After we eat, we have about three hours before we get there. Mom said it's best we change here after we eat because we'll barely make it on time. Come on."

Markos took some time to shake off his daze and stretch his bones. He rubbed his eyes and retrieved his glasses from the backpack under his feet. Looking back into the trunk, he eyed his black-on-black suit, zipped up in clear covers. His attire was the same Ephraim wore when he took on the politicians. His appreciation of Ephraim could never truly fade.

He refrained from using words when they ate. Like Olivia, his body refused sleep. Only when he snuck downstairs to drink a shot of bourbon, did his eyes shut, devoid of the desolate dreams. He was awakened by Anna in the morning. She only briefly delayed his sleep. He quickly carried himself to the car to quickly continue. He did not expect the dreams to return.

Markos chose to eat and avoid the conversations. He watched the two interact as he sipped his coffee. He ordered cinnamon French toast and poached eggs, choosing to box the meal after a few bites. Anna and Olivia knew to leave him be in the state he was in. They hoped he would snap out of it before the speech. Anna's words the night before affected him more than he liked. Her words mirrored those said by his father on his last visit, the memory of which was enough to ruin his appetite. The small diner, seating no more than five people in the early morning, brought him right back to that day his father visited him, upending his world with opinions on his life.

Fallen autumn leaves rustled through the front porch while the wind pulled them into the grass near the sides of the house. The warmth from the cup of black tea in Markos's hands was enough to defrost the chill that covered his whole body. The tea made the morning bearable. His gray sweat suit provided loose comfort in the presence of the fluid sounds of nature. The intruder was the outlier, trumping his picturesque peace.

"Can I get a cup of tea, too?" asked the intruder.

Markos looked at him before resting his cup on the cylinder-shaped coffee table to his left. He ignored the stranger's request and turned his head. His eyes glared at the untamed surroundings. He looked at the trees and closed his eyes, listening to the chirping of the birds and the repetitive sounds of crickets. Everything but his father obtained his attention. He was mad he did not have the restraint needed to stay inside to ignore his father's visit.

"It's okay, I had some breakfast before I came," uttered the man, laughing under his breath.

Markos opened his eyes as his father, again, interrupted the purity of nature's sounds.

"You are going to have to talk to me. We all live with regrets, especially me. If I leave here, without you talking to me, you'll have a life left with more regret," said Daveed Solomons.

"Regret was in my life far before you showed up on my doorstep. I can take more, but somehow, I believe I'll tack on extra if I continue talking with you."

He got up to enter his home, again, leaving his father alone with the birds. He paused as he put his hands on the golden knob of his carob brown door. He paused before he could push himself to turn the knob, contemplating the mystifying motivation for his father to appear in this moment of all days. Markos turned to find him looking at his shoes, dirtied from the walking done on the long path. Markos felt compassion in his father's brief moment of defeat.

"Do you want sugar in your tea?" asked Markos.

His father's head intensely shot up and froze, his eyes resting on his eldest. Daveed was entranced by his son's words. His mouth, slightly opened, could not push the words out as he shook his head.

Markos went in the house, pausing once on the other side, his shoulder leaning on the door. *Why today? Why any day?* His head rested slightly above the peephole. Markos faced the door for a brief second while he straightened his twisting feelings. He walked over to the kitchen and poured the warm water in the kettle into a black mug. The mascot of his father's school was plastered on each side. Markos smelled the ginger in the tea as he walked towards his father, a consequence of the heated ginger roots in the kettle. He brought out a black tea bag in his other hand for Daveed.

"Here," said Markos.

He first recognized his father's age in the feeble strength he used to accept the mug. He was slow to rest it on the table to his right. Most of his initial strength was used for the long walk down the road. He was nearing eighty, outlasting his youngest son and ex-wife.

"Thank you, I appreciate it," said Daveed in a deep, raspy voice.

There was a lack of corrected air flow in his words. Markos wondered if it was age or sickness. His time had come, outlasting the average lifespan in the fifties by ten years.

"Why'd you come here, today?" asked Markos.

Daveed guided his hand along the outside of the mug, dunking the tea bag inside repeatedly until the water blackened. He let it remain inside as he sipped. He provided himself the time to gather the words he needed. He had his reasons for coming, but the chill worsened his self-confidence after he caught a glimpse of his son. He resembled him most out of all the children he bore, sharing his large flat nose and the squinty eyes, both surrounded by the blackening bags of wear and stress. Markos was the recipient of Daveed's nappy hair and thick workman's hands. The likeness worsened the displeasure of their father-son relationship.

"I want to see you, I'm not sick or anything, I'm just at the end of my life and there are things left unsaid," said Daveed.

His tone was one of an elder statesman. He spoke as he once did, a father to his boys, authoritatively slow and patient.

"Say what you must to get it off your chest. I have nothing to say to you, nothing good or bad. Years went by as I sat contemplating what I could've done or said to make you stay with us. I don't know if life would've turned out better if you stayed. I'm not at peace, but I am not at war with your decisions."

"I didn't come to apologize. I can't, it'd be a lie. I ended up happier in a home where I was looked up to and not challenged. You boys, along with your mother, were much smarter than I ever was. I'd like to take some credit, and I will, but you both exceeded all of my expectations before you did the great things you both did. I want to tell you why I left, but I also *need* to hear your words and hear you, my wife demands it. She believes I can't be a man of God by avoiding you. I avoided Ephraim and Rahel before they died. I need to talk with you, for what she calls *eternal solidarity*," said Daveed.

Markos chuckled at the shield of pride he still blocked his emotions with.

"You found God now?"

"After I left you all, my wife thought that I should ask for forgiveness for leaving my first family. She said it was the right thing to do, a necessary thing if I wanted to marry her. She made me convert to Catholicism. I read the Bible again, forcibly so, but I found more accepting words and reason than I originally remembered," continued Daveed.

"She told you to find Jesus, convert, in order to marry her? Wow! I wish I had that same fortitude. So, instead of discussing your adultery and asking you to apologize to Mom, she wanted you to convert to marry her? You're perfect for each other, both of you work to serve yourselves," said Markos with an insulting chuckle.

Daveed rested his face into his tea. He watched his son relieve himself of his laughs. He was disappointed by the lack of respect his son held for him and his wife.

"Please, respect my wife, I don't care what you think of me. The woman has been through enough. Her whole family disowned her after she married a Black man. They believed she downgraded and diluted her bloodline after her first husband left her. We lost a child to a miscarriage, she's a righteous woman and far better than I deserve."

Markos surprised himself with the lack of empathy he had for his father. He wished he had some to spare, but he could not conjure up the necessary feelings of sorrow.

"You didn't leave Mom with sunshine, both of you can rot. They called Mom a bickering whore, a homewrecker, casting her out of all the things she loved to do. She couldn't come to our school without whispers of how the PTA president ran off with her husband and how unbearable she must've been to live with after losing such a 'nice man'. All of our friends and family looked at us with disgust and questioned how she made you leave. I have no sympathy for you or your wife."

Daveed tightened his grip on the mug. He kept his composure while his body stiffened.

"You're in pain, I get it. Life wasn't easy for you, I'm aware of all the things you've had to deal with. Life has always been unfair to you, and I take the blame for making you this recluse. I didn't allow you to start off thinking for yourself, only correcting my errors with Ephraim. I made you this way by controlling your confidence and restricting you in the way I raised you. I limited your words and let Ephraim roam free. I sincerely apologize, for I take that upon myself. I hear you've been slow to live life, and I hope to free you as I try to free myself," said Daveed.

Markos refused to let his body slip at his father's words. He was in control of his emotions. Markos moved his head around as he looked for the words.

Time went by before he found the right response to his father.

"Wha...what do you mean, you heard? How?" asked Markos.

Daveed smiled before answering: "Your mother, her pure soul never stopped sending me messages. We stayed in contact, never speaking, but emailing and texting. She waited a few years, but the photos and updates began coming in after your graduation. Um...wait," said Daveed as he smiled while digging into his chest.

He brought out his mahogany leather wallet from the right chest pocket in his peacoat. Markos caught a glimpse of his father's two stepchildren and his natural born daughter from a family photo on display. He tried to get a better look before his father dug into his wallet. From the back, Daveed pulled out the creased graduation photo, overwhelming Markos by the confirmation of his father's interest in the family.

He detested the absent effort and the photo of he and Angela.

"She would update me on everything, from you graduating college to Ephraim's ascension into politics. I saw the photos of him and Alondra at their wedding and I saw your photos when you were awarded your masters. She sent me a photo of you in your Air Force attire. Not what I would've imagined, but still, I was proud. I loved the photos of your trips to Ethiopia," said Daveed, pulling out all the photos he spoke of.

The small photos were now in Markos's possession, melting his hands as he clutched and viewed them. He was slow to examine each photo, each striking his heart with more pain as he could only think of his father's physical absence.

"If you cared, if you enjoyed these photos, why didn't you make the effort to at least try and meet? You couldn't have been afraid? You deserved all that you would've got from me and Ephraim. Why didn't you try?" begged Markos.

"I couldn't! I rushed it all, having kids and marrying a woman beyond my maturity. She was far more than I ever deserved, and I was blessed with kids I was unprepared for. You all challenged me, you saw the immaturity and the lack of resolve! You saw it, but Ephraim explored it with disobedience and when I finally lost the respect of Rahel, I veered away," concluded Daveed.

He implored mercy from his son with the passion he spoke with.

"You didn't raise your own kids!" argued Markos.

"Don't be a hypocrite!!" fired back Daveed reflexively.

Markos paused. His mouth slightly opened, then shut as his thoughts and movements were dulled. He sat motionless in his seat. His fingertips were numbed by the worsening wind as it progressed in speed throughout the conversation. Slowly, he regained function over his body.

"Who told...what do you know?" asked Markos.

"Let's leave it alone, I'm sorry I brought it up."

"No, no, no, no, no! What do you know?! Don't tell me it was Mom?" wondered Markos.

His face soured in horror.

"She told me everything. She told me, what do you expect? It's my first grandchild. I didn't judge," replied Daveed.

"I don't care for that, who have you told?" inquired Markos.

He tightened his posture and leaned in towards his father. Fear struck him.

"No one. Your mother told me it's just her and Ephraim that knows. I'm just aware of a tragedy, not the details, and the girl. The details, your mother kept to herself. I don't know why you did it, but I know Ephraim lied for you, lied to Alondra, and kept her."

Markos sat back in his chair and interlocked his fingers behind his head. He felt bare, naked at the thought of his secret floating in the air. He did not trust Daveed, he himself pried information out of his father using anger. Millions of scenarios played through his head where the man would ultimately reveal certain secrets. However, he turned again, and saw in his father's eyes, remorse. Daveed was still his father.

"Ephraim, Ephraim...he saved me. I was in no shape, he told Alondra that Elsa had passed away in Morocco. They were getting more serious, so he gave her a few details. We kept what happened out there between me, Mom, and him. The child couldn't have been raised by me after what happened. He saw how broken I was and how I was already resorting to my demons, the liquor and all. He took her in, he made it work with Alondra and he kept her."

"We're not so different," softly added Daveed.

"Don't do that, we are not the same. You folded; you had the opportunity to stay with me. I saw as surgeons ripped out a child from the love of my life, violently taking her away from me. She was the only one who forced out some semblance of personality from me. I was obligated to decide between her and a child I did not want, putting her in a coma where she was at more risk for loss of life while they ripped into her stomach. *We are not the same!"*

"Oh stop, you had the opportunity to get the child back with her, I know a little of what happened after. You know why you are the same as me, you saw the child and saw in a time of choosing, you believed they needed more. You knew your presence, while mine being extroverted and childish and yours, small and reserved, was a distraction to the child's growth. You saw her laugh and smile with a man who was better suited to be her father, *a better man.* I would only stunt what you could accomplish. I was scared that I would prove detrimental to my own kids," claimed Daveed.

"You know, whatever my decisions for *Selam* were, I thought of you and rationalized it through the lens that you looked at it through. I made a mistake not looking at it through my own eyes. There were times I sat fearful when you and Mom would argue, wondering if one day you would snap like those men on the news and really hurt her. I was scared, I knew you were like those prideful men, that you could hurt us at times with your words and with your fists. Still, I... I wanted you home, I wanted you around. I have tried to forget, but if I ever tell that girl who her father is, she'll see it through my eyes when you left us, the moral way, the right way. You should've stayed, you could've fixed me, and I could have had a shot to fix you. My greatest regret was not raising that child, at least trying. For that, I owe her silence, letting her enjoy the memory of the man who raised her," affirmed Markos, with the power of conviction.

He spoke with determination, no shyness or fear. He avoided eye contact, watching the birds fight the swift air. He was alone again.

At his words, Daveed shut down, reminiscing on the broken promises he made to his children and ex-wife. His hands shook at his son's words.

"I'm sorry, truly I am. I lived a happier life, but I couldn't sleep for years. Joy flowed through my body watching you boys doing great things. To this day, I'll stand by my decision, not taking credit for your achievements, but taking credit for not ruining you both. You remained true, as true as you could under the circumstances, and you each gave me grandchildren. As you confront death, I can only tell you it's better to answer the questions that remain in your head. Confront the girl. Call Alondra, give yourself the opportunity," begged Daveed.

"Not in this life, I swore to Ephraim if he took her in. I swore to my deathbed."

"Promises to the dead, die there. Promises with man are a slap in the face to God. He dictates what we live by, not people. Take pride you have a living daughter, an offspring of you, your ownership of time. I took full pride in my boys, always pointing to the screen wherever I saw you two plastered over it. I voted with pride as you took the country by storm."

"You see, that's where we are different. I was comforted when Ephraim would tell me a man like you, who turns to himself in every scenario, looking for credit, could never really change. You'd always revert to who you are and remain as selfish as the man who made all those inconsiderate decisions. He never had faith in you to keep your word. You didn't understand the weight of your words and the respect one should have for family. With us, you saw ownership."

Daveed, again, tightened his grip on his mug, holding an empty cup of tea. Markos would harken back to that last statement, never knowing how wrong he could be.

"You are the same as I am, truly. A time will come when you are extremely near to death, your body will tell you. You will revert back to the gory details of this desecrated conversation we are having on this very cold day. You will be a victim of sadness, at the wastefulness of this last opportunity to respectfully discuss some things with me. I wanted to be here for hours and discuss all your worldly exploits, why you chose to do the things you did. I wanted to tell you I saw you at your mother's funeral as I lingered in the back. We are the same, again, because I saw as you lingered in the back for your brother's funeral, uninvited, still showing respect. Don't come to my funeral, we've already discussed everything we've needed to. I came with regret, and I leave with sorrow that we couldn't find some common ground," said Daveed.

Daveed looked into the trees, eyeing the impending death he felt in his creaking bones. He mirrored his son's approach to eye contact. He was fearful of breaking down in his son's presence if he caught his eyes. He was dispirited by the lack of hope in Markos. He blamed himself, thinking of how bitter he raised him to be and how things worsened after his departure.

"You've come here divulging secrets you should've taken to the grave. There's nothing for you here, and you've been dead to me for years. Today is just a nuisance for me, another field trip to death's door, where I can only stay for a while before I am kicked out, as every day has become. Good luck, and if it is God you believe in, I will pray for you, truly I will. I pray that He doesn't judge you the way you deserve to be," said Markos.

He quickly cut his words to walk inside his sanctuary of a home.

Minutes passed before he would hear his father depart from his porch towards the long road. He watched from his bedroom window as his father walked away, for the last time, hearing from Alondra he passed two years later. Time went on, but Markos would continue to dwell on the point his father made. They were cut from similar cloth. Fear of this fact pushed him to email his sister-in-law months after the visit. He outlined to Alondra the truth of Elsa's accident, detailing how things changed for him once she was put in the coma and lost her legs from the collision. Fully aware of the situation from Ephraim's deathbed confessions, her reply, one of surprise, demanded now more than ever, he stay away. The child was no longer a baby, she had become pregnant. A revelation like this, she emphatically stated, would drive the child to depths the family feared would wreck her potential. Markos agreed with Alondra, a better time should be chosen.

Alondra, apologetic for how she treated him, met with him in secret, in his home. She brought with her a baby while the mother recovered at home. He had not seen the baby, other than a photo from her christening. He held his angelic grandchild, holding his direct kin for the first time, but the delightful visit came attached with a devastating request.

The smile on his face as he held the baby brought tears to Alondra's eyes. Markos had held his smile open from the moment the baby appeared at his doorstep. He was shocked by the visit, only expecting Alondra. She brought the baby to ease the pain of her request for him to stay away, for the duration of his life. She shared with him how the baby came to his daughter, a baby out of reckless wedlock. Following their departure, out of furious anguish, he beat his hands on the table as he sat helpless to their struggle. All he could do was beg Alana to help him and Elsa in doing something they could not, protect their child.

When his child was first seen, the family anticipated a flurry of questions from people around them. They decided to tell people the child was hidden, a child sprung on Ephraim from a previous relationship he had with a woman years before. Being a Black man, an extremely private man, people, as well as the local media exposed to Ephraim in the beginning of his rise, fell for the devious lies. Alana's trickery as a lawyer, as a member of the family, worked in hiding the truth of the child, making sure the paper trail made sense. Even she remained in the dark, however, about Elsa, the deciding truth mobilizing her into action for *Selam* when the time came.

Ephraim had told Alondra the woman had run away, and that she was the only mother the child would ever know if she married him. In a shocking moment of love for Ephraim and the family, Alondra accepted the arduous task, placing her own pursuits on a backburner to fulfill their goals of creating a family and taking on the world together. A lawyer herself, she became the guardian of the name Ephraim's mother once was, even as she sat with the credentials to live life on her own terms.

She accepted the needed assistance from Alana when the time came. She reiterated to Markos the instability in their lives as he held the baby for the duration of her visit, but, to him, they left as quickly as they appeared. He reluctantly agreed, understanding the difficult motives behind her justified requests. Out of love, he asked for a photo with the baby, always keeping it with him. He sent a copy of it to his beloved, sharing the message with her via postal, hoping to give her the jubilation he received from the baby's birth. Discouraged by the sure fact he would not receive a reply, Markos sat alone on his bed, for days on end waiting for another opportunity to arise, waiting an eternity for a time he knew was not coming.

The aftermath spiraled him deep into his own thoughts. He wondered if the family was truly cursed, for he knew he was. Markos, in the following days, could not sleep and when he did, was plagued by violent shaking and profuse sweating, keeping him from desired comfort. It was not long before he put devastating strain on his liver, relapsing for the final time, sealing his fate.

SURVIVAL

fourteen:
State of His Union

"6. Acknowledge our sins, and the sins of our mothers and fathers. The sins of the father and mother aren't ours, but the payment of their penance is. We must recognize and pay it while we deal with our own if they've ignored it. Lingering mistakes leave us open to risk."

"7. Everything is political, it bleeds into our lifestyle. We allow it to stain everything in our lives. The way the game is played must change, we must stop backstabbing and deception from being normalized by the way 'the game is played.' Our renewed forbearance will bring about discussion and end misused alliances."

- Entente Party's List of Goals, inherited from the social movement of founder, Ephraim Solomons.

"Come on!"

"I'm coming, we have to wait for your Mom. They told me we have to walk in together for you two to be escorted to Darius and his daughter. They told me he's already here," said Markos.

They barely arrived on time. The heat in Southern California was brutal on the summer day. The sun shone on the chic urban campus, uninterrupted by any clouds. They waited outside the parking lot of the university's indoor pavilion. Markos patiently glossed over the notifications in his watch while Olivia circled the lot. He was going to wait as long as it took.

The large line out the door was slowly moving into the stadium. The commotion could be heard from outside, yards away from the lot. The shuffling feet on the cement floors and the rambunctious cloud of voices fueled Markos's anxiety as he looked towards the large venue. There was a door for performers and speakers to enter, but he was forced to wait for his driver to reappear before he could enter the building.

"Let's sit on that bench while we wait, I'm too tired to stand in this heat," stated Anna.

Her white dress, kissed by the sun's rays, separated her from the students in streetwear. She sat on a blue bench near a mounted pole light ridden by cobwebs, near the first row of parking spots. Markos walked over in his black-on-black suit, burning up from the heat. He too, was tired of the weather, drowning in his own fluids. He sank in submission onto the bench.

"What are you going to say?" asked Anna.

"I have no idea," uttered Markos.

"What?" laughed Anna.

"I have words on paper, but I don't like them. I wanted to speak about other things."

"What does that mean?"

"I wished this to be a victory lap. I wanted to congratulate him. I honestly don't know if I should bring up more than that, it's not worth it," said Markos.

"Tell the truth, tell them he wasn't perfect, tell them what happened," suggested Anna.

Markos sat in the car reflecting on how daring he thought he was when crafting the speech. He puffed his chest for days in advance at how boldly he was going to approach his testimonials in front of his largest audience to date. Running through all his past shortcomings in his head: his father's visit, Ephraim's betrayal, and the requests put forth by Elsa and Alondra, he was fearful he would follow the route he took in each of those moments. In moments of crises, he relied on the coward's way out, and with the speech, things would be no different.

The school's security, in their baby blue collared shirts, escorted his rushed family through the gray, cemented tunnel underneath the stadium. They took the two women to their seats, escorting Markos as far behind the large stage as they could. The venue was used for the school's graduations and award shows, able to seat tens of thousands. He was still, remaining in deep thought under the cover of the curtains.

He looked into the audience while attempting to summon the courage he desired to cleave the sins off his chest. His eyes were distracted by the video cameras and the media outlets the school allowed in to watch his speech. What caught his eye were the men in dark black suits guarding the back door. Their eyes were focused on the treasured guest seated in the front row. He sat distanced away from the school's leadership and eager students, placed next to another security detail on each side. The Speaker of the House faced forward, awaiting the man he traveled across the country to see, serving as a gatekeeper of his party's secrets.

Markos's armor of confidence shattered at the sight of the Entente's protector. He looked to the crowd and saw as the rows became consumed with people. The arena was the shape of a large wave, seats placed higher and higher up towards the exits. The floor seats used were foldable, cushioned chairs. They provided a chosen few with favored arrangements over the students in attendance. All the venue's seats were filled.

He shook his head in self-disappointment at the thought of lying to the crowd. He saw the young girl in the front waving for his attention. Anna looked at him and smiled at the effect the name Solomons still had.

I'm sorry, it's always been the easy route. I'm sorry.

A roaring applause was given to Markos as his name was pronounced by the speakers connected to the stadium's roof. The lights near the speakers were focused on the stage. The lime green exit signs, the vending machines, and the private vendors near the exits were the only other forms of artificial light in the large spectacle. He cleared his throat and met their ovation with a smile of his own.

He went through the pleasantries and the resonating thanks he always gave to those who hosted him. Markos expressed private family beliefs in the initial moments, providing a glimpse of his family's thoughts on his brother's ascension. He gave small tidbits of information he never revealed to entice the crowd in the beginning. Outlining the exact moment his brother asked him to be a part of his movement, Markos engaged with the crowd's reactions at the sincerity his brother had in the face of his unexpected heartbreak. From their awe and empathetic reactions, he knew he carried sway over their emotions. He continued into his normal spiel of lecturing on his brother. He explained why his brother avoided giving his movement a name in the beginning, fearing how names could be used to label him and their supporters a certain way.

"He didn't want your parents to be labeled as something they weren't. We were nameless volunteers hoping to provide a meaningful service. We'd be here one day, then we'd be somewhere else in less than twenty-four hours. A shapeless body can shift into what it needs to be," added Markos.

The crowd yearned for more miniature details, thinking they or their parents made significant differences to the formation of the Ententes. Markos was glad to see the crowd soak up the useless information, but when he looked down in a brief moment of rest between his words, he could see his family's smiles and the frowning Anna.

She knew his tactics of deception, and none were more content than the Speaker. He watched with joy as the crowd interacted with the safe and calculated address.

She doesn't know what they could do, and neither do I.

Markos carried on for nearly two more hours before he took a victory lap for his brother.

"There's not much I can say to you all that you don't already know. He was strong, my brother, in how he maintained a foothold on politics. He wasn't perfect though and there were things he didn't expect to happen. He fought against the two-party system and noted its partisan failures. He berated politicians for protecting the pride of their party before they protected the pride of the people. He created his own party, and he didn't expect the upward trajectory and support of you all as the opposing parties conjoined as one. I believe you kids made a meme saying the elephant swallowed up the donkey whole. He didn't foresee his own party taking part in similar politics, the way the game is played to continue his legacy, I guess," observed Markos.

"He would have been honored by what was done in his name after his death. I cry at the news cycles that run around with his name every year on his birthday. I wished the outlets and politicians would have afforded him the same respect when he was living. I wished he would've seen the legislation pass that set limits on tuition costs at public universities. He would've been proud of the mandate some states added to have schools add food and housing in those caps, limiting capitalism in education. He would've been truly, truly proud. He would've been proud of the adoption of state-controlled health through public universities, giving health care for the veterans who can't afford it. The opportunities this afforded inner city neighborhoods and recent graduates would have brought tears to his eyes. When we were growing up, stuff like this was dreamt about and discussed as impossible. The Ententes, as much as I try to stay out of their way, do their best to continue his legacy. I'm proud of who he was, and the people you all have become in his name. Follow the list and keep the objectives pure. While a political party exists, remain the shapeless people able to mobilize at a moment's notice, for all future generations' hope," concluded Markos.

The stadium roared in applause, with rampant yells and whistling. Everyone was on their feet and deeply moved by the words of a practitioner of fiction. He wanted to see the people stay pure, but he hoped it would all sour and go up in smoke. The party cost him his family's peace and they broke the family's solidarity in the face of outside adversity. For Ephraim, he was proud of the great opportunities arising from the party's work, but he dismissed politicians' adept eye for submissive, partisan politics. He cursed them to his dying breath. They forced him to succumb to the necessary evil. The family's homeostasis was the price paid for this.

To them, a necessary sacrifice, thought Markos as he removed his smile, descending from the stage. The stairs on the side brought him down to the university-designated, important guests. He waited for the people to file in and ask for pictures, wishing it was instead his brother they were forever capturing.

Another hour was taken for the photos and to answer the questions of onlookers and news correspondents. One-word answers and small soundbites were all they could pry from him. He made his way back to the family, posing with them for photos for their own keep. The media took advantage of the sympathy a display of the family would obtain and quickly snapped their shots before packing up and leaving. Markos and the family waited them all out, waiting for him to receive his due payment for his services. He sat in the front row and looked to the black stage where he sold his soul for the last time. Anna and the family were predisposed with the university's officials who discussed future options with Markos. They held their stoic smiles as they planned years in advance for him to teach there, not understanding the lasting effort he put forth in his speech. There was no more in the tank for Markos. Darius, involved in the talks himself, assured the universities with arrogant promises to discuss all future opportunities as a family. Anna, separating from the conversations, walked over to the man, deep into his thoughts.

They did not share words as she met the cushioned baby blue seats with a shriek. The needed comfort of rest surprised her after she descended into the chair. Following her unintentional response, they sat in silence, as they looked at the darkening stage. The lights slowly dimmed, shutting off, as the view of seats behind them faded and turned into the black hole the audience felt like to Markos. Their steadied breath served as their conversation. In brief moments of talking with the media, she was able to see the demand others' requests can bring, as well as its toll. The veiled dialogue was needless, she loved him, and he had done what he could.

"Years ago, there was this Dr. Shepherd who was tasked by the government to do some research. He was a doctor like your mother, like a behavior type thing or a therapist."

She turned her attention towards Markos before he continued.

"The divorce rate, and the amount of people with kids out of wedlock had grown to an obscene amount. The government wanted to step in and figure out what was happening. Realistically, the study was conducted because white people were not having kids anymore."

She quietly chuckled at his deduction.

"Anyways, this young man, about forty-two years old, spent six and a half years talking to therapists, religious experts, professors, poets, musicians, and even some famed filmmakers. He interviewed people on the street, and had millions participate in his surveys. A lot of attention was put into his research. Each year, they televised his reports of progress to the legislatures who asked for the research. He was quite popular, a handsome fellow too," added Markos.

"He finally concluded that we can't fathom love without understanding mortality. Those who've gone through life and death tribulations with loved ones seemed to fare better in terms of the duration of their union. Those who've struggled with their significant other before marriage made it far because they knew the feeling they felt when they relied on one another in times of distress. Many of the elders who kept long marriages weren't perfect and were reported to be victims of things like adultery and typical boredom. But they survived hell with their spouse. Dr. Shepherd saw people who were getting married in his time were fighting biological clocks, seeing marriage as an issue of status instead of love. People settled in love and status, like they did with other goals. I give you all this to discuss the dilemma he posed," said Markos.

He paused before posing what they called, *Shepherd's Dilemma*.

"He posed this question in his last address to Congress, I think in 2053. I had nothing else to do but watch this young man, who visibly deteriorated from the research, discuss love. He asked if we were given immortality if we could love, love our partners, love our family, love anyone.

"He answered, 'How could we, we would not be afraid of death, we'd believe ourselves to be gods.' He shared how most people don't even visit their parents often until they are near death. Some older couples had told Dr. Shepherd that they feared leaving their spouse because they were afraid of what their short lives would look like alone, even as they lived unhappy. Some said he didn't know what he was talking about, being a single man himself.

"He always reiterated how we can't have love without the fear of death. With technology expanding, we fear death less and less as we become closer to gods, sacrificing love. The young man was so consumed by the stories he was told about love, he killed himself three years later.

"I say this to you to explain, me. I was shy, I am shy, and I will die a reserved man. I lived day by day, and if given immortality, I would live, day by day. While it may seem I was a fearful man, I loved harder than most. I gave my heart to love my father, I treasured my mother, and I would sacrifice my flesh for Ephraim. My love goes beyond words for Elsa. I am like this, because I lost each of them, unfairly. I became disconnected with some of them because of my fear of losing that love. Don't judge me from today, this is a result of decades of romanticizing things I did not understand and diving in without preparation. Maybe that's love? I do not know if I did it right, or if I was just unlucky. I don't want you thinking of today when I leave…"

I spoke to her about what I could, Ephraim.

They were both speechless to his defining displays of weakness. None wanted to intrude on the lasting effects of his devotion. They waited and waited, thinking on his life's experiences.

A child approaching, with a gleaming smile, was barely visible to him in the shaded dullness of the silent stadium. The lights near the exits were now the only source of light, being raised to a higher level than during the speech. She stood in front of him with her mouth opened wide, glaringly showing her toothless smile.

"Hi, you must be Uncle Markos. My name is Sophie, it is nice to meet you," yelled the exuberant girl.

Her neatly braided pigtails weakened any feelings of disappointment in Markos. Her introduction lifted his regretful infatuation with the words he shared with the crowd. He put out his calyces' ridden hands, and met her soft, innocent grip.

"It is an honor to meet you, princess. You know you are a princess, right?" asked Markos, sneaking a smile to Anna before again setting his sights on the girl.

"That's what they tell me," cleverly replied the child.

"She's a smart one, this one. Don't let her fool you, she's smarter than other six-year-old kids," added Anna, following the two into laughter.

In light of their new present joy, their serene affection was interrupted by a man's tap of Markos's shoulder. Markos slowly turned. His bronze teeth were widely visible as he remained comically indulged.

"Sir, there's someone who would like to speak to you," sternly said the large man.

Markos seized his laughing, the girls slowly following.

"It's him, right?" asked Markos.

The serviceman nodded. Markos made out which patron requested his attendance from the security's posture and inexpensive formalwear.

"If he wants to speak with me, I'll be down here with my family, please tell him that. If not, give him my good graces and wish him safe travels," answered Markos, returning to his family.

He carried on with Sophie and Anna, telling them tricks and stories the public could never hear about him and Ephraim. He shared his limited recollections of their parents, highlighting Darius's troublemaking capabilities and Olivia's outgoing personality as a kid. Sophie sat on his lap, comfortable in his security and entertained by the experiences molding him into the exact man he came to be in the precise moment. Accepting death and the maddening circumstances of his life, heartfelt admiration was what he held for the future of his family. Olivia was trapped in conversation, envious of the laughs she overheard and saw through the corner of her eye. As much as she wanted to be with them, she did not wish to alter the purity of their moment.

The task was taken up by another. A group of four, dressed in the same suits and carrying cordless earpieces in their ears, covered the doors and exits as a man descended down the stairs to take part of an exchange he required. Hearing the man approaching, Markos pleaded to Anna to take Sophie back to her father.

"We'll leave after this," assured Markos.

Anna complied while the man she deemed detestable walked towards her family. She took Sophie to her mother and Darius, but her eyes tracked his movements until he reached Markos.

The man, the Speaker of the House, sat a row behind Markos. They were two men in the middle of a sea of chairs. He tapped Markos gently on the shoulders. Markos replied by slowly grabbing the man's hand to shake the open palm resting on his shoulder.

Markos turned ninety degrees to the right and lifted his right leg onto the two chairs to his right. His body and head followed, not fully committing to face the man outright. His right arm rested on the top of the chairs his leg rested on. His eyes were still on his family. Anna and Olivia knew who he was speaking to. They split their attention with those they conversed with.

"Markos, long time," said the Speaker.

"Yes, it has been, Speaker," replied Markos.

"Please, you've never been one to be formal. Let's not start now."

"I'm sorry, I'm so used to seeing you in the headlines. It's been so long since I've seen you as a friend," continued Markos.

The Speaker snickered at the wise comments. Personally, he would say he missed them.

"I just wanted to speak with you and say what was needed. Too many years have passed without me apologizing for what was done to you. We've let you stand alone, and I know now what it feels to be alone. I'm here to say, I hope the payments you've received from these events have been sufficient," wondered the Speaker.

"Of course, I'm glad I was given your approval to talk about my brother at these types of things," Markos sarcastically retorted.

Markos himself did not know why he gave him a tough time.

"The situation isn't ideal, but we both know certain things don't have to be said."

Markos sighed, retreating from the attack. He let moments of aching silence pass.

"I'm sorry, I read in the headlines that you lost your daughter. No one deserves such a tragedy," said Markos.

The Speaker again snickered and slowly moved his head towards the view of the ceiling. His glares moved around the room, thinking of the daughter he buried merely weeks ago. Markos caught him off guard with a slight show of compassion, choosing peace.

"Family is the most important thing, I'm glad to see you try again," clamored the Speaker.

"Not much of a go, I'll be dead in less than a week."

The Speaker tried acting surprised. He was aware. They were in possession of a full workup of his medical records. He voiced to his team he wanted to be in the know regarding Markos. To most, it was methodical, to him, it was out of familial desire. He remained still.

"You know, you wouldn't come if you didn't. Say what's eating you," ordered Markos.

"I'm sorry," the Speaker replied quickly.

"I rose, gaining more power. I sacrificed all of the codes and promises you taught me to have, all to compromise myself for the top spot. With power, you become bitter as your mind fights with your body's desire for it. You worsen when you sit with popularity and fame. I detested what I became after my daughter's death. It was all for nothing. It was eye-opening when I lost her, sacrificing the time I had put in to be a worse off man than you found me at first to be. I loved the attention and hated myself for the corrupting principles I lived by to keep it."

Markos fully committed to looking Peter in the eye.

"Peter, you were my brother's pet project. He groomed you to be the defining member of his party. You are what he wanted you to evolve into. I blame his circumstances for his decisions, so I don't care to blame you for anything. Never did I hate you or him. I was just disappointed in the lack of empathy and loyalty. You, both of you, casted all of us aside, and left us out to dry," said Markos.

They paused. Peter felt comfort, while a thought came to Markos.

"My mother and I used to talk about faith in times of stress. I'd debate with her about a statement we all read in the Bible, that the meek will inherit the earth. Back then, I only had a surface level understanding of the material I read. We watched the news nightly and you better than anyone knows how the media works.

"I'd ask her, though, when would the meek inherit the earth? I was losing faith, day by day, with each sad story. She'd answer as calmly as she did when she'd be scanning through her students' papers. She'd say, 'they already have'."

Peter fixed his posture. He looked deep into the dying eyes of his mentor. Peter kept his comb over haircut over the years, allowing gray to subtly integrate. Another victim of rigorous discipline, his body was as immaculately shaped as time would allow. A rigid gut grew in place of a once slender core due to the drinks and depression of loss. His unshaven face was a clear indication of his trials. This was his first public appearance since her death.

"I would annoy her to try and make her explain. One day, she woke up real early, and as religious as Mom was, this question festered in my head. She made tea in the mornings, but this time, she had forgotten to turn off the tea kettle when she went to the restroom and came into the kitchen with steam shooting out of it so fast. The flames nearly burnt the bottom of the overused kettle. I caught her off guard after she sat down with her tea, and asked, when?"

Again, he paused, losing the air in his lungs. *They're near.*

"She looked over and said, 'from the beginning'. She quoted all the excerpts I overlooked, saying how the Earth was left for us and stuff like that. She was surprised to find me puzzled by what she meant. Mom explained it beautifully."

He felt himself recount the words in her voice so elegantly.

"The meek had always been those afraid to leave their willful power to a deity, or in the hands of others. They were those who were afraid to be judged, so they judged. They were the ones who were afraid to be hurt, so they would hurt. Those, to her, who saw earthly gain of power as something to fight over, those were the ones who inherited the Earth. They are the meek, ones who can't handle something beyond them, spiritual or natural. The meek were the few who'd enjoy unruly success and dictatorial empires because they believed and saw what was only in front of them, unaware of what awaited. They have always inherited the Earth and will continue to," finished Markos.

Peter's eyes glazed with the tears forming at the bottom cusp of his eyelids. He clasped his hands together, feeling the cushion of his mentor's wisdom again.

Markos served as a humble reminder of his origins and of his humanity. Prison cells and years of impatient probation officers were what awaited his life if Markos did not remind his brother of his responsibility to people.

"If I'm lucky, I'll soon tell her of her father's good heart."

They both rose from their seats to complete the awaited embrace. Photos were taken out of necessity for the party's image but were strongly discouraged as both of their puffed faces felt the weight of the other's remorse. They walked each other out, his family already waiting outside for the discussion to conclude. Anna and Olivia were hesitant to fully embrace the character they knew about. His rise in American politics was respected, for he was groomed and led the mass exodus of politicians joining the Entente Party after Ephraim's death. Within a little under twenty years, he was able to patiently grow the party into the leading voice of America's legislative branch. He was far from done, hoping to guide his fruitful ambition to the executive branch one day soon.

"It was nice seeing you, Peter. I wish you good fortune in the future," added Markos.

"Thank you, in this life and the next, my friend," said Peter as he waved from the car, one last time before his detail escorted him into his vehicle.

The family continued to wave, awed by the informality of the Speaker towards Markos.

"You're friends?" asked Anna.

"I'm trying to go to heaven," teased Markos, still waving.

The family moved to the edge of the parking lot. They waited for the three vehicles protecting and holding the Speaker to leave before they walked over to their cars.

"So, little Sophie, where should we go eat?" asked Markos.

"You guys want to swing by the house, first? Her mother wants to cook dinner," interrupted Darius.

"She doesn't have to cook. It's on me, you all didn't have to come here," said Markos.

"Well, she'll be mad if we don't eat with her, she's been waiting."

"Sophie, what's your mother cooking for us tonight?" asked Markos again.

"Steak!!" yelled Sophie.

"Her Mom has some steaks ready to be grilled for us."

"Tell her not to cook it yet. When we used to get together, from college or whenever we separated, Ephraim and I would cook with Mom. Let's try it out," suggested the eager Markos.

One last good thing, Ephraim.

The breeze from the air conditioning in the home forced Anna and Markos to grab their sweaters. They were well received by Darius's ex-wife to the surprise of Olivia and Anna. She was always drained by her husband's lack of emotional effort in Sophie's life. She gracefully accepted Markos's dinner proposition.

He saw that it was an empty home. He was told before he walked in of the unique arrangement Darius had with his ex-wife.

They were divorced, signed and done. They both wanted what was best for their daughter. They lived together and hid their outside relationships from the child. They co-parented, but Darius was never home. His time with Sophie accumulated to one month per year.

His former partner loved the genuine care Markos, and the women, took in talking with Sophie, interacting with her as they cooked dinner. The jobs were delegated as such: Anna to the salad, Olivia to the honey-glazed diced potatoes, Markos and Sophie to the rice and beans, while Darius and his ex-wife handled the steaks and steamed vegetables. Darius grilled the steaks, alone, in the backyard, while the group entertained his ex-wife with their jokes and clever debates about food. Markos noted how she hid a saddened feeling of emptiness, a side effect of the loneliness she suffered from. Her laughs would end with a trailing silence, signifying a deep fear of their inevitable departure.

Markos made an extraordinary effort to intermingle and socialize in one of his last remaining nights. He plucked out joyful laughs and ignorant jokes from all in the room, making a lasting impression on his family. Every action he took was reverberated with love and distracted him from what was to come.

Never, throughout the night, did he look to feel the creases of the papers sitting in his breast pockets. He ate and drank till he had his fill. They cooked enough food to feed them thrice over. He would harken to the discussions of the past during the dinner, seeing his mother at the table in Olivia's eyes, and seeing Ephraim's loud voice at dinner carry through the photocopy of a son he had in Darius.

Markos stood up from the large Greco-styled table and leaned over to the ear of his guide.

"Madam, would you lead me to the restroom? I could get lost in a large home like this," requested Markos.

"Yes, I can," pridefully answered Sophie.

She led him down a corridor left of him. They walked towards the restroom as he jokingly stumbled towards her. She bumped him to display her dominating resolve, laughing as she displayed abnormal strength. They continued the banter until he wrapped his hand around her shoulder, carefully placing it so he would not get his sauce-stained hands on her clothes.

"You remind me of a young girl I was raised with. You have her spunk," said Markos.

The abnormal laughing and joking took a considerable toll on the man walking to the restroom. His energy reserves were depleted from the day of addressing the masses of his brother's exploits. He was brought back to Earth in that moment, remembering he was a dying man. As the adrenaline slowly faded, his mind started to feel hazy. Pain grew from the point his pectorals met his stomach.

Still, Sophie kept her smile as they got closer to the restroom. He reached for the door's metal handle. His hand tightened and tightened, naturally gripping the door as his stomach turned. His body's crumbling was impulsive, striking the girl with fear. Her screams sunk deep into his ears. His warm cheeks were suddenly brought to the cold, tiled floors. The family rushed as his body seized to the natural inclination to crumble and tighten together.

Finally, his eyes shut, his body violently weakened from the episode. His arms had not moved. His rough hands clutched his left breast throughout the episode, protecting the letters.

fifteen:
The Creeping Demon

"8. Provide opportunities for people kept away in mental and physical prisons that serve as a barrier to their redemption. Show those with resources, the pains of them locked away, and open the path for mutual understanding."

"9. Make peace with our mortality. We must understand we are all a blip on the scale of limitless time. The words we leave on social platforms will remain to represent our names. As a group, we must sacrifice as each generation fights its own fight for the betterment of the next."

- Entente Party's List of Goals, inherited from the social movement of founder, Ephraim Solomons.

He found himself lost in the mirage of the misty morning scene. The air was glazed with a thick, grayish fog limiting his vision of the elements in front of him. From what he made out, he saw the people he loved most, interacting with one another in the park. Elsa, muted of sound, motioned forward with him through the park. Her mouth moved words into the air, but the emerging sound of oceanic waves was all that could be heard. Everyone's movements in the vision were slow. Crisis was near, averting the soft pleasure he once felt thinking of the moment.

Markos, in a time of dire calamity, returned to the day his heart shattered. The day was brought into his mind for it was one where his full family was in his purview. His head steadily bent forward as he examined himself in the weary recollection. He had his clear white shirt tucked into his straight navy-blue jeans, complemented by his spotty black dress shoes. The outfit had not changed, only the perception and speed of the events. Down to the sweat stains on his shirt and smudges on his shoes, the details of the people in attendance and their outfits remained the same.

He feared danger nearby, obstructing his memories.

His movements were a slave to the sluggish time lapse of the trapped, convoluted memory. Markos did his best to keep his head on a swivel. He shifted left and right as he looked for the cause of the distorted moment. His legs were caught in the simulation and moved as the dream did. Mimicking the effects of sleep paralysis, his head became still when he saw the controller.

A black figure, shapeless and formless, stood a distance away from him. He stood at the opening of the park, parallel to his location near the school.

The figure was comfortably waiting for him to circle, refusing to relinquish a strategic location in the dream. The figure shared the form of a human's anatomy and outline. It waited and waited, unmoving in its patient pursuit to return Markos to his Master.

A tapping noise, relentless in its rhythmic signaling, jolted Markos out of the mental strain of the demon's attraction. He fought the memory's control over him. His time in deep sleep was ending.

Tap, tap, tap.

Repeatedly, his mind listened to the tapping break the scheming figure's control of the once devastating events of the day. He shifted into a medium state of consciousness, stuck in limbo as the memory gradually faded to black. His bouts with the creeping demon in times of near death were occurring more often as he tiptoed on the line of cognitive awareness.

Tap, tap, tap.

He tried to move his body in the limbo, but he was caught in a chilling stillness as the sound grew stronger. His eyes were the first to escape. At his own shivering pace, he regained control and limbered his stiff muscles and joints to follow. He cracked his neck to loosen up before he investigated the source of the tapping noises.

He lifted his hand and understood from the tubes and cotton ball attached to his hand where he lied. The local university's V.I.P-designated room was much larger there in Los Angeles, than in his hometown. The room was covered in the school's colors, blue and yellow. The school's shade of blue was the same in the tint of the walls and the outline of the shades covering the window. The school's name and mascot sat on the face of every document and poster detailing the needless everyday health tips the masses ignored. A tablet sat on the sliding table near his bed, along with two of his letters, both unsealed as he last left them.

An unshakeable fear seeped into his bones.

Who read the letters? He wondered who would break his trust.

As his eyes continued to scan the room, he saw a dark raven creeping between the view of the shades. The raven's path hid the bird from his direct view, forcing him to imagine the creeping bird's full outline behind the drapes. The repetitive taps of its beak on the window brought him back, but now, pestered him with its presence.

He lied in the room for quite some time to gather scattered thoughts of the events leading up to the hospital stay. He remembered the dinner and his request for the restroom, but his memory ended there. Markos was worried of what he might have done or said in his deep state of disorientation. Lazily shifting his point of view, he glued his eyes to the opened letters beside him. He wished not to answer for them when he lived, hoping death would bring them closure.

The monitors were periodically beating and pumping the necessary fluids and nutrients into his malnourished body. He was alone in the room and let the rhythmic sound of the beating and cranking of the devices hold audible control. The raven left him to lie alone in the scratchy sky-blue blanket. He painfully maneuvered his body, slowly pulling the table towards him and sliding the top of the table to sit directly above his stomach. He examined his letters and the smudges of someone's oily fingerprints on the tablet next to them. He unlocked the tablet, triggering a messaging system to the nurses, alerting them of his awakening.

The first to walk into his room was a small nurse, short in height, stubby from the aged stress she allowed to loom over her. She did not say a word to him, hovering over his blankets and the meals left on the counter for him if he was to wake. Markos wondered if she was aware of his coming death. She carried the divine silence of those who knew another was going to the afterlife soon. Her sneering attitude towards Markos's unconscious state riled her up. She was in charge of his food and drink, as well as waste disposal. He had not awakened in some time, worsening the stress she had for her patient. She dropped the food near his tablet with the necessary utensils, then left the room.

I hope death is more welcoming than her.

The family rushed into the room with the doctors once the message was relayed by the voiceless nurse. Markos was deep into his meal, plunging his knife and fork into his mashed potatoes and dry pieces of saltless tri-tip. He kept a smoldering attitude towards the doctors as they spoke of his near death in front of all his family, including the uninformed Sophie. Markos took his time as he masticated the dried meat and wallowed down the rest of the food. They read off the excess conditions and abnormal readings in his nutrient levels. As he finished up his burnt dessert, crispy honey cornbread, the last statement by the two doctors stuck with him.

"It's about comfort now."

By the time they left the room, his hot pink hospital tray was cleaned off.

"Welcome to another V.I.P room."

"Ar…are you okay?" asked Sophie.

She was met with a controlling tap from her father. He was leaning over the counters near the windows, seated next to Sophie who sat upright on a yellow loveseat.

"Don't worry, I won't be here in a few days. Time runs out for us all," replied Markos.

"Let the adults speak," ordered Darius.

The father and daughter positioned themselves to sit more comfortably. She watched the elders speak on the inconsequential next steps they deemed important. Darius leaned in close, still next to her on the loveseat, actively attempting to engage in conversation.

"First...did anyone read these letters?" asked Markos.

No one spoke to reply to the man. He could not go further without being absolutely sure.

"No one read them. When they stripped you out of the clothes, I took them from your pockets and left them for you. No one read them," assured Anna.

She was on the stool beside the bed while her mother sat on another loveseat by the sliding doors. Olivia turned the windows to "Obscure" before she continued the difficult conversation.

"We...we need to discuss arrangements," Olivia said, shakingly.

She's been crying.

"Go ahead," said Markos. He was unphased by the conditions.

"There is a possibility you won't, you won't make the drive back to Sacramento. Do you have a problem if we buried you here? They've put us in contact with some people who could help with the transitioning to get this done," requested Olivia.

"Maybe, I should take Sophie outside?" suggested Darius.

"No, let her stay. She knows what's going on, she's smart. She'll mature faster when she sees death," continued Markos.

"You can bury me here. This is the city my parents fell in love in, the city my father is buried. I'll forward you the name of the site he is buried at, near the family he lived his life with. I've been alone too long in Sacramento, he can't be left alone either," said Markos.

He toggled with his tablet as he spoke, protecting himself from their tears. He fought the urge to look at them, knowing he would follow their show of emotion.

"Okay, we need to again ask if your estate and affairs have been settled for?" asked Olivia.

Anna scoffed at the questions being asked. Time was ticking. She burned with desire to ask her questions before the time came for him. She turned away from the eyes of the others.

"They've been taken care of. My full bank account and investments, numbering a little under a million, will be given to the kids, Anna and Sophie, as detailed by my will's statement declaring any kids who carry the name keep the money. There will be a financial advisor who will go over the details of my account, they have your number. The contents of the house and the house itself are given to you, Olivia. Darius, I apologize, I haven't seen you in a very long time, I did not know where to include you," calmly answered Markos.

Darius was stunned, along with the other women, at how his resources were amassed. Markos did not spend much of his own money in his lifetime, holding onto all the money he received from the Air Force, the teaching program, and all speaking engagements following his brother's death. He made sure to keep it all away while buying a home in cash to shield himself from outsiders. Inheriting most of his money after his grandfather's death, he made sure to keep the money working by tying it up in investments, a lasting gift to those he would leave.

"No apology needed. I am glad you thought of Sophie. That's fine for me," asserted Darius.

Anna's tears now flowed down her face uncontrollably while not making a single sound. He did not hint of any wealth, nor did he seem deeply interested in the well-being of the family following his departure. She looked away to give herself ample time to recuperate. They quickly thanked him before moving on.

"Do you have a request for the house?" inquired Olivia.

"Do as you please, sell it, strip it, I don't care. No good memories lie there. You can make it a vacation home or Darius can keep it if he wishes to stay near the family," said Markos.

Darius shared a look of disappointment with his sister, hiding confessions with their impolite gazes towards one another. Anna looked away in disgust. Markos saw something was off.

"For the funeral, anyone you wish to ask for?" asked Olivia.

"Just you all, Alana and Peter," replied Markos.

"No one else?" impulsively asked Olivia.

He shook his head with a growing smile on his face. He laughed at the ask, knowing she did not plan to verbalize the rude question.

"Okay, it all seems to be solved, I'll ask if anything else arises."

They sat in deathly silence. They looked at Markos who remained focused on the tablet in front of him. Nothing was said. They pointed their inquisitive looks towards him as they watched him visibly wither away. Anna's desire to ask questions was itching at the tip of her dry tongue.

"Um, we're going to get some food. Sophie hasn't eaten since last night, we'll be back," said Darius, exiting with his daughter.

Sophie shared a toothless smile and a wave to Markos as she left the room. He shared a forced smile, and with his hand, weakly waved back.

"I'll follow, I have to share these details with some of the folks carrying out this process."

"*Liv*, I emailed you the name of the site," said Markos. The words sunk on his lips.

He took a deep breath while watching them file out.

She nodded, pausing at the door, then leaving Markos to attend to Anna's questions.

Her head whizzed over to Markos after she watched the family leave. Tears still spilled down the side of her cheeks. She wiped them away, then clasped her hands together under her chin. The wheels under her chair motioned towards the hospital bed after she pushed the ground with her feet. Her elbows rested near his legs on the bed, giving her prime view of the dying man.

"Um, thank you, for the money," squeezed out Anna.

"Hopefully, it'll make up for me and Ephraim," replied Markos, leaving the tablet alone.

"You aren't as sad or shameful as you think. Darius, who you just offered a whole house to, he's a man who should feel shame."

"What do you mean?" asked Markos, pushing his body to sit up.

Anna's fists clenched tighter, fighting her pulsating annoyance.

"He told Mom, last night, in the hospital, his wife gave him an ultimatum before we arrived in LA. She told him she would be leaving the city for a job, and that she had done enough in taking care of Sophie, and that it was his turn to raise their daughter. Mom had let it slip that I may be moving for work, and he begged her to take Sophie. This man has the nerve of a…"

"Anna, he wants what's best for his daughter, and so does his wife. He isn't what's best for Sophie. He looks at you and knows that his answer is Liv," said Markos.

"He had no shame in asking, no right to do it right now at least," politely exclaimed Anna.

He basked in a soothing silence. He waited for her nerves to calm. No time was available to argue in useless anger.

"You can't be mad, if you left, Sophie would be great to have at the house with Liv. You never know, you may get a few offers in Sacramento, you can take my house or Liv can take it. You have endless possibilities," added Markos.

He clutched his stainless-steel cross before he continued further. The long-lasting pendant accompanied him through all his shortcomings. Its journey was nearing a purposeful end.

"The most misguided statement made that people are always told is that they should be fruitful and multiply. People will then believe, as they always have, that they have a right to have children, when it is in all seriousness the most endearing privilege one can have. Before they even have a partner, people are already dreaming of how they're children will do everything they never were capable of doing. They dream of the athletes, the scientists and doctors they will bear. When it's time for the child to be actually raised, they throw in the towel, and things like divorce and midlife crises come into play," stated Markos.

"That's a cynical way to look at it," jokingly added Anna, both struggling to laugh.

"It's the truth, you see it in Darius, your father. He thought he would be bearing a Solomons, but he couldn't raise a child with that pressure.

You have those who accidentally stumble upon children and do their best, and most of the time, they create or continue a cycle of hurt. It took almost fifty years to forgive my father, and after I did, I relapsed. Some people aren't worthy of having kids and the family they imagine because they want those things for the wrong reason."

"Hmm," thought Anna.

"Darius, as far as I'm concerned, falls into the masses who had a daughter out of joyful love with his wife and then couldn't figure out their relationship when it came time to do the grunt work. I don't blame him or her, but the innocent will get stuck in the middle. I think Liv should take Sophie; the money is there for her."

"You never thought of having kids?" asked Anna.

His heart felt like it hesitated in its rhythmic beating. He lifted himself in the bed before replying. Markos smiled to give off the guise of comfort, clenching his teeth before answering.

The truth. He cleared his throat.

"Years ago, right before I went to rehab, I was in Sacramento as I told you. I had an opportunity to reclaim an opportunity for a family. I told you, love was first a trivial thing to me, and with all the stuff that surrounded Elsa, there was no love left after her accident. I couldn't love anything beyond her. Even with her though, I never wanted kids and we agreed. I was scared I would fail like my father and do damage to a child. She was scared she would become distant like her mother. We were too in love to involve other people.

"I had great people around me, but come or go, with them, I never really cared. I understood mortality, but with her, being in love, it made me unreasonable. Even when she was here..." said Markos, pausing to clear his throat as his emotions took control.

She shared a supportive smile before he continued.

"Even when she was here, I was beyond terrified what would happen if we settled down. I only loved her, and I didn't fully understand my feelings toward her. It was divine, a creative anomaly. I was never sure if I could replicate it if we had a child. These opinions about children had been in my head after my father left. Neither of us said we wanted kids, but we knew time could change things if need be. I was never worthy of that privilege though," vocalized Markos.

His eyes refused to focus on any object. They looked at the room all over as Anna listened.

The heavy, tired footsteps of Olivia were nearing the door. Once she reappeared into the room, she withdrew to her loveseat. Her head lifted towards the sky in frustration, keeping her words to herself. She moved her gaze to him, guiding her attention now to Markos.

"I had a few questions, since this may be the last time to speak with you," said Anna.

"Anna, leave him alone and let him rest."

"Don't worry, time for rest is coming," said Markos, calming Olivia's tension with his hand. He put it over her hand as she walked over to check his vitals, intaking her stress as his own.

"Thank you. I just want to know if you lied in your stories," wondered Anna.

"Absolutely, I had to protect certain secrets of your fathers and also Alana's," declared Markos, without hesitation.

"I told you," whispered Anna to her mother. Markos playfully sneered at her remark. As mature as Anna was for her age, hints of her childlike awareness eased Markos. She needed joy.

"Seeing that the eternal rest is near, could you divulge some of *your* secrets? If you could just put it out there for the family, that'd be appreciated."

Her comedic tone eased the seriousness. He loved it.

Olivia brought her head down towards him to see if he would share some of his secrets.

"I won't give them to you outright. I'll truthfully answer the questions you have."

"Great, I don't have a lot, just a handful. Did you ever sleep with Alana? There are rumors."

"Anna?!" said Olivia in desperation.

Markos wanted to laugh at the simplistic questions. He could not expend the energy required to do so. She distracted him from the future and the discussion he needed to have about his letters.

"No, I didn't. There were times we came close out of being tired and in the mood."

Olivia's head turned away to smile as quickly as Anna's smile took over her face. They both glowed at the small details of such a larger picture.

"I'm enjoying the honesty. I heard Grandpa was a womanizer before Grandma, is that true?"

Markos nodded to keep the lie the family created alive, with a mix of truth embedded: "He was always good with people, I've never seen anything like it," added Markos.

Olivia smiled at the questions, she herself had some of her own: "What is the truth behind you and Dad's issues, in the end I mean?" asked Olivia.

Markos soured at the serious turn of the inquisition. He waited before giving them the truth.

"During the large Sacramento protest, we had to leave quickly because of the resistance we faced. We got run down by some people. I put a few of them in the hospital, one of them even had some long-term damage. They casted me out and made me sign an NDA that Peter also used to get out of the leverage we had on him from the noose stuff. It was unexpected, but because we were all family, I thought I'd be safe. Ephraim said some things that shouldn't have been said to make me sign," revealed Markos.

In peace, Markos thought. He silently gasped at the boulder removed from him.

"Thank you," said Olivia, concluding her curiosity. She did not see the need for more.

Anna's was not yet quenched. Her eyes widened at the possibilities of what was hidden.

"Why'd you protect him?" asked Anna.

"We're blood, I forgave him, there's no need to drag his name further in front of the family."

"Were all your lies in this form, a form of protection?" asked Anna. She knew he would not lie about this.

"Yes, there's things that should remain shelved. It's forgiven."

Olivia's question was a point of no return. Anna desired more unknown facts, but they were unimportant and remained unasked. Gossip tales and talking points were needless to the three of them. Their only serious, recent daily human interactions consisted of the people in that room.

"I forwarded your request for the plot," interjected Olivia.

Markos grinned at her compliance: "Thank you, my father's family moved away after his death. They didn't part on the best of terms, but it'd be nice to be there with him."

"Were you close in the end?" asked Olivia.

"No, he came to me once, years after Ephraim and my mother died. After that, I never spoke to him again," said Markos.

The significance of the conversation concluded after she confirmed the burial site with him. He shared with her the contact information of Peter. They were able to hear from him quickly. He awkwardly assured Markos of his attendance at the funeral while at the hospital. Markos left contacting Alana to Olivia, forwarding the relevant information he had of the lost compatriot. He was confident she would appear at the funeral, out of the love shared.

Markos put his hands over the table and interlocked his stubby fingers above the two numbered letters. He twiddled his thumbs around, stopping only to tap them together in an anxious frenzy. He calmed his breathing whilst continuing his tapping. His toes curled, nervous to bring up what he thought of every breathing second he was awarded in the last month. He took a few deep breaths while Olivia and Anna tinkered their gazes towards him again, wondering if he was going to pass out. His calmed breathing brought him back.

"Um, I've, I've been carrying these letters in my pocket for some time. I want to leave these to you, Anna. I know it's corny, but it's something. You'll understand me a little better. I have a few requests before I give you these letters," said Markos.

Olivia leaned over to get a better view of the letters he asked about when he first woke. Anna's watery eyes mirrored Markos's.

"I want you to promise me, you won't open these letters until I pass. Take your time, especially with the first letter, but you should not read them until you put me in the ground. It's something I want to leave you both with, to make up for the time I've been gone. This will be my apology for the time lost, along with whatever material things I can pass on. It'll answer some of your questions," said Markos, controlling the tears that wanted to flow down his eyes. He needed strength to make the requests, and he gave all he had of it.

The letters he protected and clutched onto were now being passed to Anna, his legacy. She would keep his promise, but the letters themselves, were a piece of his heart being torn and shared. He visibly shook as he handed her the fiery torch of his soul. Her emotions ravaged her expressions, puffing and watering her face as the mascara she had on smeared. She handed the deed to his soul over to her mother who kept it safe in her purse while they awaited his death.

"My term is over, and I apologize for the family and what we've done to you, and to you. You both deserved better and we let pride get in the way. We should've fixed the issues for all our sakes. We built a house of lies to help others, forgetting about family. Forgive my sins and the sins of your father and mother. Do better with Sophie, she deserves better, as you both did.

"I once loved staying home in the dark and I cursed any form of sunshine. I cursed those who enjoyed the shine and the happiness that came with it. I stayed ignorant on purpose, and even in the midst of hot days, there was no light that ever came through my blinds. I cursed what I did not know. But with you both in my life, I watched as the sun rose in the park, finally feeling the joy that comes with it. Don't trust anyone without regrets, even small decisions come with regret. I regret I didn't step outside sooner and learn more about what I did not know.

"Life is boring, very monotonous and routine. It comes down to five days, maybe ten, where important decisions are to be made and you are given opportunities to make up for your failures. You will have those days soon, and I hope you both make better decisions than Ephraim and I. Enjoy those days you have the power to shift the trajectory of your life. I sank in every one of those days and chose the easy way out," concluded Markos.

All three burned with torches of slow realization. None of them combusted into all out emotional outcries, but there were deep scars forming in their piercing tears. The women let them flow down throughout the night, while Markos waited to be alone. There was a sense of truth in his end, with his last words. In the hours remaining, he gave them honesty.

"I'll note all of this down as great life advice to be followed. However, let's pass the time in a better way. I snuck a little something in when I got up this morning, before you woke up."

She walked over to the counter, pulling out from under it, a two hundred milliliter bottle of his favorite bourbon. The small bottle was connected to three plastic cups hanging upside down on the cap. Her mother grimaced at the sight of pure strength in the tiny bottle.

He apologized once more for his lack of courage to return to the family. He shared, while they drank, how he gave them years and years of stories in a matter of days and hours. He apologized for his weakness, unable to give them the time needed to share Ephraim's mannerisms, and the small facts of the family that made them the stars the people loved. They would never know the miniature moments of joy in their group discussions, their playful arguments, what many considered life's boring days. How could he find the time to share the discussion Ephraim had with Markos after meeting his love in Ethiopia? Where were the recycled sands of time needed to share the joy found in the card games during their road trips? He loved their last moments, but in the back of his mind, there was too much dying with him.

Regardless, his thoughts did not stop them from sharing deep laughs and diving more into the stories of each of their lives, all through the afternoon. The three carried on their discussions once Darius and Sophie returned as well. When they finally departed, with Anna choosing to stay with Markos, he fell into a slumber, letting fallen tears blanket him after she fell asleep.

Hours after his eyes shut, he saw his creeping demon once again, closer than he had ever seen before. By the time he was given the leeway to react, his hand had touched the demon's, turning both of their attire white. The face of the demon cleared, exposing his father's youthful face, along with the jubilation in his stained golden teeth. His smile comforted Markos away from the dire panic he felt from the initial touch. Together they turned their bodies and began their walk home, leaving Anna behind as he enjoyed his eternal, dreamless night.

sixteen:
Truth in Finality

"10. Carry a good spirit with all foundational work. We must work towards The Peace, upholding every opportunity we can for the future. We are surrounded by those who've learned to fight for us, but let us be the ones to also teach the future to keep the peace for us all."

- Entente Party's List of Goals, inherited from the social movement of founder, Ephraim Solomons.

Olivia's effort in coordinating the intimate last ceremony celebrating the shelled life of Markos was one he would smile down upon. An Ethiopian priest, a friend of Darius's, was called in to do the last rites in the hospital. As promised, he conducted the ceremony in Markos's native tongue, fulfilling a promise Olivia made with Markos.

The priest spoke as if there were hundreds in attendance, thunderously excavating the words from deep within to carry Markos's departed soul to its rightful place. He spoke to the saddened six who knew him as best they could.

To Sophie, her first experience with death was one filled with her own concerned questions of his final resting place. She enjoyed his brief humor, loving his investment in her in the brief time shared. Like a grandfather first seeing his own, he flourished in emotional displays of affection. He did what he could to be what Ephraim would have been better at. He felt free in the last dinner he shared with what was left of the family. He curiously pried the info he required to ease his mind before he would pass. Sophie's guiltless mannerisms gave him a full view of the family's bright future. Markos left them in peace, worry free of the family's status.

The two in attendance who knew him the longest were the ones who held the deepest misconceptions of who he was. Peter saw him in a mentor role. He was heavily invested into his own growth to see his mentor's secrets and struggles. In the end, he saw a man full of grace and compassion, forgetful of the guilt consumed in the past. Peter saw what Markos allowed him to ingest of his character, never its true form. The playful banter and the meaningful lessons were only a requirement to fulfill for Peter to gain the prerequisites needed for his role.

Alana's relationship with Markos was divided in hypocritical stages of friendship and times of sincere moments. She was aware of his innocent intentions and the thought process he retreated to. Alana was also aware of the fathomless skeletons in his closet, but she left him to transform, alone, in a time of needed comfort. For decades, she was nowhere to be found. He carried the unbearable weight of failure and regret in his mind, alone, when she held the key to possibly reintegrate him into the world. There was a chance he could have rekindled a relationship with Alondra and been involved with Anna and Olivia. She knew, she was aware of his itching desire to return after losing any opportunity at happiness with Elsa. Alana decided to live her own life, doing what mattered most to her. For that, with his admirable love for her, he refused to blame her intentions. She was never able to see what he turned into. Nevertheless, the presence of Alana and Peter would bring pleasure to his heart, but their tears would mean nothing to him.

There were no tears shed by Anna and Olivia, nor did Darius share any. They watched the ceremony and the tears of others being discarded for Markos. He pleaded to them to not shed any, because for Markos, tears were a sign of a lack of effort and unresolved love. They said what needed to be said in the time afforded.

"You've put in the efforts for this family, save your tears for the living...you gave me a purpose in these last few weeks of my life and I'm going to rest with ease. People mourn, but to me, tears are sometimes either an act or a display of a lack of effort when a loved one dies. It isn't a weakness, but sometimes unnecessary since they show the guilt of some. Don't cry for me, you did more than could've been asked," begged Markos, hours before he departed.

Anna watched them all speak for Markos, sharing words one by one, of the man they all never understood. She attempted to avoid any form of judgment on those who came, but she had words for each of them. She put aside her choice analysis, desiring a peaceful send off for Markos. A dichotomy of awe and anger flowed through her empty mind.

The group circled the open grave, all victims of soaring heat and the windless air of the dry afternoon. Alana and Anna faced one another across Markos's grave, Alana's eyes following Anna and her mother to Anna's left. Peter stood right of Alana. He was traumatized by the similarities shared between the ceremony and his daughter's send off.

Facing the sun, Darius, his daughter, and the priest stood over the grave. Markos's lying body and tombstone encapsulated the full circle. Anna noticed, as the words began first with Peter, Alana's glares focused on her and Olivia. Alana's slow tears trickled down faster the longer she stared at them. She sniffled before she spoke, clearing herself of the urge to cry.

"I left him years ago, it has been so long. We loved one another but time worked against us. One thing he once said to me was that he found one preconception of his to be wrong. Love was not developed. He said the realization of true love happens at an instant. You see everything with the first gaze, even tragedy. He was never poetic, never one who divulged information about emotions and what not. He...he only shared it...when he lost Elsa, his wife."

Anna's eyes imagined all the hidden, unadulterated truths lying in the grave in front of her. Darius and Sophie were unchanged by the word, *wife*. Olivia tightened, bringing her hands over to her daughter's. They gripped each other with surprised concern, a matched emotion, masking their disappointment.

Alana's gaze tightened on the two women in front of her before she spoke. She knew she rocked their existence with a single word. They stood composed, awaiting the next words.

"He went on about love, arguing with himself one day on the road. He believed people have real love for you if they can love you for what you are, not for what they hope for you to be. People have the capability to look at their partner and imagine a bright future. He said it's selfish to seek a future with what people believe to be an unfinished product, when in reality, it is a future for themselves."

She let her tears fall, their path interrupting her. She paused before forcing his words out.

"He said to me, true concern and heartfelt connection comes when you admit to yourself who your partner is at the moment, and you accept it. Love is when you look at yours, happy, and you realize it is as good as it gets. That's when you accept, *you're in paradise.*

"He lived believing the flaws he saw in himself were the worst kind. He never believed he could be loved by others. He looked for an angle in all his friendships and relationships, a reason they could've been forced, by blood or popularity. He was untrustworthy with emotions, but he shared that with me, the power of love."

She put a rose, as Peter did, down in his grave once she concluded her words. Darius and Sophie declined to speak, instead putting their roses down. Anna was overwhelmed by their decision to decline to speak. She looked up to Alana's eyes focused on her, again, serving to heighten her nerves before she spoke. She feared breaking down in front of people she did not completely trust. Participation in this, for her, was far from optional.

She then wiped her face with her sweat drenched hands, clearing her mind before she spoke.

"Um, I'm not prepared to speak like I thought I was. I honestly have known him for only a month, but I've listened to all his stories in that time. As boring and as reclusive as he thought he was, his life was as eventful as anyone's life could be," uttered Anna.

"With his stories, you can tell who he was closest to. I was always surprised by how certain things in his life played out, the speed of the way the events occurred. I asked him about it the night he passed.

"He started by saying how life was like a day at the beach. I asked him more about that, but he said I'd understand later. He sure was a man with parables. But he also talked to me about how we know who we'll trust long term in a matter of minutes. He talked about how he knew about Elsa, regardless of how long he was out there. The speed of time moves differently when you are invested, he would say. He reiterated that people's schedules or timelines for how your life should play out should never be placed upon you by someone else, especially by your family."

Her mother handed her a tissue, eyeing the tears consolidating under her eyes.

"He, uh...he, mhmm. He told me, after I said we'd only had a month together, that he's never been so comfortable with anyone in his life. He felt like he had lived with Mom and I for a lifetime. He went on to say that the sands of time were thicker in his time at home. He told me, don't worry about what seconds have passed, what did time feel like when we were together, how did it lapse?"

She smiled, knowing the answer to his question.

"He was a man with words he believed no one wanted to hear. I wanted to hear it all, always. He said...time makes family, not blood," concluded Anna, placing a rose in the grave.

Olivia hugged her daughter. She kissed her on the cheek when Anna took two steps back to return to her original position. Following her daughter's return, she dropped her rose into the wide opening. She looked at the picture of young Markos placed next to the open grave; a picture taken when he was a young teacher with his students in Morocco. A year into his teaching, the photo showed a man in a time of optimal happiness. She looked at the picture again, smiling.

"There will always be love with you here, next to your father. There will always be love for you among the living as you now have among the dead."

She retreated and watched as the priest concluded the rest of the ceremony. The soaring heat thrashed the holistic sentiments of the funeral. Towards the end, Sophie's youth showed in her complaints of the heat. Darius used her as an excuse to escape. The priest noticed, rushing the rest of his ceremony, beginning to feel the drowning rush of his own thickened perspiration and dampened fatigue.

"Thank you," said Darius, returning from his car to get the priest.

The priest nodded as they continued a conversation to the parking lot. Darius and Sophie were the first to say their goodbyes to Markos, then to the family. They hugged Anna and Olivia, shaking the hands of the prolific characters in attendance as well. They returned to the car, taking the priest back to the church.

"Well, we should get something to eat, then hit the road. I want to make it back to Sacramento, at least before it gets dark."

Anna nodded in agreement. She was fascinated by a conversation occurring between two attendees, Alana and Peter. From what she heard, she did not expect such a closed and lifeless conversation to happen. She watched the cordial acting play out, Peter shaking her wrinkled hand. Her blonde hair was slightly grayed out. The slight wrinkles and the gray did not take away from the subtle beauty Markos underscored. Peter, with a busy schedule and a deep hatred for inconvenient funerals, ran out, waving to the family as he departed with his security detail. Alana, however, walked over to the mother and daughter before she left.

"Those were nice words," said Alana, putting her hand out.

This was the first time Anna saw her round, green eyes in person. They still could mesmerize anyone in front of her after all these years. She spoke with confidence, with knowledge of information that the two women did not have.

"Thank you, you too," hesitantly replied Anna, shaking her hand. She was the same height as Anna, but she held a noticeable power over her she could not completely understand.

"Nice to see you again, it's been a long time, Olivia. Your daughter looks a lot like you...a lot like her grandmother. The resemblance is uncanny," uttered Alana, trailing off towards the end of her statement.

Anna whizzed a quick look to her mother at the peculiar words.

"Nice to see you, thank you for coming. We hope to see you soon."

"There's pain back home. Anything he shared couldn't have done what happened justice. I do apologize for my distant behavior. I can forward you my contact info. I'm in San Diego with my own law practice. If there's anything you ever need, I'll be there."

The women smiled. She was once a celebrity to young women around the nation, a powerful figure who demanded respect. They took her card, assuring her of a call to come once they got situated. She asked what their plans were, as they floated the idea of staying in Sacramento or moving to Los Angeles. The women left all their options open for the future, watching Alana relish in their interactions with her. Anna's contempt towards Alana was weakened after hearing her speak. Similarly, Alana's eyes sparkled at the spoken words of the women. Small talk carried on for a few minutes before they returned to their cars. The goodbyes were short, expressed with endearing looks rather than empty promises of tomorrow. Both parties avoided any vows of future meetings, instead thankful for the funeral's chance in bringing them together. Alana, before she walked away, again reiterated her prior statement.

"You have no idea...you both truly look like your grandmother. I'm sorry, you both are beautiful beyond what any of us could have imagined," said Alana, tearfully walking into her car.

They laughed off the slow words of Alana, waving to her as she left. They entered their car and waited a moment. The car started, but they looked upon his grave from their windows. They had not slept since he passed, adding days to their trip they did not plan for while they took care of arrangements. The anguish in their eyes would sit unchanged for years.

"Alright, we should leave," said Olivia, pulling off and away.

"*Goodbye, Markos,*" whispered Anna.

The drive was filled with spontaneous silence. No one in the car cared to speak up about what transpired. In his last days, time passed too quickly for Anna to remember everything about him as she wished for all the memories to flood in. The car's speed subtly slowed the flow of their thoughts. The silent six-hour drive gave them time to think about every detail they overlooked the last few days: Sophie's dilemma, Markos's last words, Alana's revelations. They put the man who reignited their life into the ground, and to them, life would return to be as slow as it was, as problematic as it was. Hours in, the truth of his finality set in.

"Mom, where are the letters?" asked Anna.

She needed any form of distraction to take her away from the thoughts of normality.

Life is full of eventful days. Five to ten days will be offered for big decisions that can shift life away from normalcy, but normalcy is inevitable. Find people you love, make normalcy interesting.

She remembered Markos's words. She saw him speaking as her eyes closed, hearing the soft words float in the hospital room.

"It's in my purse, right behind my seat," said Olivia, her right hand leaving the wheel to point to the bag.

Anna turned her body to retrieve her golden purse. She immediately found the two letters, one in an envelope, the other sealed by its own flaps. They were in the large front fold in the outer portion of the purse. It was unzipped. She returned the purse, weakly clutching the letters.

"Why do you want to read it now?" asked Olivia.

"I'm not trying to think about tomorrow," replied Anna.

She saw the numbered letters. She placed the second one on her lap, unfolding the papers within the first envelope. She found the letter sent to him to be addressed to the school. The papers popped out at her from the address chosen, surprising her before she read.

"Read them out loud, I'm driving," ordered Olivia.

Anna glanced over to her mother, smiling: "I'm going to read it before I read it to you."

Anna, motionless, was rocked and swayed by the words of the paper. Methodically, the cursive words popped out towards her, patting her puffed, sensitive cheeks with each sentence. Deep in her inner sanctum, tears were produced for the promises and pain within the paper. The droplets fell on the paper, smearing the blue ink.

She flipped the sheet, anxiously pushing through the words on both sides of the paper.

Quickly, she sped through page two, then onward to the last one.

Anna slowed her breathing, afraid of what more she was to uncover in the next letter. Her breaths were warm as they left her mouth, escaping the grasp of her lungs as her body demanded more oxygen. She rested the three pages under her legs. Not a single fiber in her arsenal twitched as the car moved past traffic. The end of the rustling of papers came as a notice to Olivia. Smiling, she looked over to her shell-shocked offspring, playfully wondering.

"A…Anna, what's in the letters? What did he leave you?"

Anna could not hear her mother's intrusion. She could not hear the rugged eighteen wheelers to their right, clogging the road with their permissive lane changing. The sounds of an emboldened group of dogs striding through the field of immobile cows to her right were mute to the frozen woman. In a moment, the lapse of her time froze, as she grasped the meaning of the first letter. The written scripture was ingrained in her now. She attempted to make sense of the tumultuous life of the man she buried. A sense of admiration, with a mixture of sadness and despair, engulfed her whilst she wondered how to tell her mother. She was concerned how the letters would interrupt her driving, capable of conflicting their safe commute with impulsiveness. All concerns were considered in how she would recollect the words and share them with her mother. Her concerns nearly distracted her from the presence of the second letter.

Little by little, Anna's possessed fingers lifted the flaps of the paper. Fear shook her heavy fingers as she overcame the dry mustard stains on the golden sheet. A few sentences were plastered on the paper, leaving her without a shred of doubt. The small photo left her with the evidence she needed. All she desired was confirmation from her mother. She put the papers and envelopes down, resting her elbow at the meeting point of her glass window and door handle. Her hands were clenched into a strong fist, tightening her grip as she held the picture.

She gave herself time to cry, laugh, all the emotions needed to express the joy and hurt in the letters. Olivia looked over, believing her daughter was overcome with the grief of his death.

"It's okay, Anna, this is a tough time. We'll get through it."

Anna sat steadied by her incomplete words. *The importance of information,* she thought.

"It's not for him, it's for all of us."

Olivia inquired about the letters, but Anna wished to stop before a conversation took place. Anna shook her head while looking out the window. The water stains, the declining sunshine, nothing took away from her thoughts of the quiet evening. The news within the letters bounced around her mind, gnawing at her as she attempted to deduce how Markos felt in every second of his isolation, every moment he had with the two of them. She tried to feel what he felt. She aimed to put herself in his timid lifestyle. She tried to find a meaning, a reason to complete life the way he did. As they pulled into the driveway of their home, she thought of what emotions ran through Markos, waiting to die in their company, in the home he was raised in.

"You want to let me know what's in the letters?" asked Olivia, grabbing her purse from the backseat, resting it on her lap. Hours had passed since Anna chose to sit muted of sound.

Anna's dried lips were unprepared for audible words. They were under the covering of the home in the driveway, in front of the garage door. She hovered her hand over the light near the rearview mirror. The shining white light lit up the front seats in the darkness of the evening. She grabbed the papers in her lap, still clutching to the photo in her right hand.

"Is this me in the photo?" asked Anna.

Her mother was disturbed, nodding in approval. Anna paused before she began reading.

"This letter is to be sent to you upon my death."

"Dear Markos," began Anna.

Olivia froze. Fear struck when her daughter looked up for her reaction.

"Where to begin, love. I wrote down my ideas for what I would say to you, how I'd say it, but I told myself I shouldn't be worried if I'm not alive to answer the letter. We have a lot of things to discuss. If you wish to discard this letter, I simply say three things: thank you, sorry, and we did not deserve what we wanted nor did we deserve what we were given. I wanted to write this in English, I don't want any confusion of my sentiments. I want to leave this for you before our words and promises submit to death."

"I love you, and I have always loved you. It has been an eternity since we have seen each other, but I have never had another lover. Never did I look into the eyes of another, nor has another enjoyed what we shared. It's tough to love when the only time it was real, it was met with devastation. I know I played my role in it, as did you unknowingly, but we did what we did."

"There are days when I think of the beach, and how you shared how you felt about me. I reminisced, every night I slept after your nightmares subsided, how you peeled away all the hurt and how you reached out to love. There were times when I would wake up and after decades, would try to pick the phone up and call you. I obviously couldn't, as you could never do. I think of how it escalated so quickly, but the warmth and joy felt like an eternity. We were destined to love as hard as we could, but we tempted the world with how much we truly cared for one another. We tempted God with how much power we gave each other to dictate our lives. We did not care what we were to others, we neglected other people's meanings of what life should be, what our relationship should be. I thought of all the judgment we faced, the stereotypes cast on you, on me, and how we lived. This letter begins as a thank you for what you allowed me to feel. I grabbed time as you said, and I was able to feel its power over life."

Anna was visibly trembling before her mother took over. It was unnecessary for Olivia to read the letter aloud, but a feeling came upon her to do so, a reflex of some sort.

"I think of the day we were interrupted. The day that car crushed me, I was awake enough to feel the force of the vehicle's impact. I do not pity the position you were put in, from the memories of those around me, I hear it was not a pretty sight of you. I could not stop it, but I wish I could have been there for you. I could not have handled it like you did, I would not be here if it was you on the other end. With the child, and the decisions necessary, I do not know what worse event could have transpired if it was me on the other side. You sat as they removed my crushed legs, put me to sleep, and dug out a child. I love you, but our relationship was never on the receiving end of good luck."

Olivia glanced, again, over at her daughter.

"The tough times had already occurred in building our partnership, and to be hit with a dreadful thing like this, our emotional capabilities were pushed too far. We were pushed after my mistake. If only you felt the pains that day on the beach and the days that followed. I was sorry, and I know you said you forgave me, but I don't think you ever did. The pains in my stomach were too much. I did not think to tell you I stopped my contraceptives, my pills, by order of my doctors when they gave me medicine for my stomach pains. I believe it was a consequence of the overconsumption and distraction of love. We were too scared the mass was going to be cancerous, we were scared we'd be interrupted. We were crazy to live how we did. I love you for the effort you put in after. You tried to show me you saw the best in the situation, but you were scared and hurt by my mistake. We weren't prepared, but you distracted me with your phone calls when you returned home to tell the family. Even after the accident, I don't ever blame you for thinking you gave up on me by leaving. I sensed that's what you felt every time we spoke after the accident. After I woke up, my parents told me of the arrangement and the calls you made during my rehabilitation. Your interest in me helped

recuperate from the tragedy. This is the last thank you I can share with you before I must move on to what has been burning inside for so long."

"I apologize for what happened, following the accident. I was slow to meet you in the US. I was afraid and wondered if you could still love me. It was not all about love, it was more about the fact that I worried if you could love me after I realized that I was going to be the one to break the promise. There was no way we were going to build a family. The eternal relationship was easy when things were good, but when this child came as an accident, we both knew we could not handle it. The crash destroyed any chance at trying. The day we came to the park, months after the crash, we saw her smiling with Alondra and Ephraim in the park. I remember how much you were sweating, feeling the pressure of our family in one place for the first time, awake at least. From my face, you knew it was wrong. We could see her, happy and giggling as she ran across that field. I had not been accustomed to the cane, with my prosthetics, barely able to hold myself up in front of our daughter. I whispered the name we wanted to call her in the mirror at the hotel, again and again, hours before my parents took me to the park. Selam, Selam, Selam. I knew she wouldn't reply to it, but the thought of my Selam running to me made me happy. I'm glad Ephraim respected our decision to give her a name with the same meaning, peace, even if it was not in your language. She was meant to be the offspring of two destructive parents. Her name was appropriate, le rameau d'olivier, formed between us."

Olivia wanted to pause, but she thirsted for more.

"I cried immediately, and you followed after we came to the same realization. The way you hugged me after that, I have never felt that much love from you, a spiritual form of it. The unreasonable affection we had for each other all shifted to her in that moment, knowing we could not take her away from a superhero, to be raised by no names. I turned away, shaking Ephraim's hand and letting him know as you sat down, defeated in your thoughts. I believed he expected that to happen, but that, I'll never know. I left you a kiss. Somehow, I knew it'd be the last time we

were to see each other. We did not have the courage to raise her, and it is how you said, we must make sacrifices for children, everything is for them. The greatest success we could have had in raising her was giving her to Ephraim at that moment. We were selfish with the extra life we brought into this place; we did not deserve a child."

"Markos, it is tough for me to even write her name, but we did not deserve her. We were polar opposite creatures who had fun loving one another. We meant too much to each other to afford to love anyone else, we were reckless. Jesus, Markos, you forgot a suit for our own wedding. I remember how we had to navigate through your mother's old neighborhood to find one. I cannot blame you. We rushed that wedding because I forgot to tell you about pills."

"I write this, because my time here is near an end. My heart could not take the aches and pains of being alone. I buried my father and mother, and they left me money for a nurse to take care of me, even though I'm beyond repair. There were complications with my mobility as I aged, but life has been full of loneliness. I want to tell you how much you meant to me, and how you should enjoy what is left of your life. I doubt you will listen, but live, laugh, and integrate in the girl's life. I have no regrets, except one, not shaking the hand of the child I held for so long. She was there to walk me down the aisle, she survived a crash with me, and yet, I never introduced myself to her. I was told you went to rehab, and you avoided her, how much I despised hearing such news. We didn't deserve her, but she is being raised by good people, we could at least try to be there. Be there for her now, as I go, for the both of us. I will prepare a feast for when we all meet again, pestering her of our annoying love, telling her how we once met at a silly dinner."

Olivia's eyelids were shaking as she attempted to hold back the floodgates of tears.

"Sincerely, The Wife of Markos, Mother of Olivia."

She put the letter away as if nothing happened. Anna watched as her mother became possessed with the same uncertainty she was seized by.

Anna put her hand to Olivia's shoulder. Olivia crumbled at the touch, slowly leaning her head to her daughter's hand.

"There's another one, Mom."

Olivia slowly nodded in the clutch of her daughter's hand.

"*Dear, You Two*," declared Anna, chuckling as she put a sound to the words.

"*Circumstances affected what you both were able to learn about me, but love for you never left me or Elsa. There is truth in death, because the complications of life become untangled when the disruptors pass. I experienced the death of my emotions at a time where life came from me. I looked at her through the glass, worried for her and only her at that moment. I did not think of the child crying beside her, to even look or hold her in her initial moments of living, a shameful fact that brought me to the bottle in the end. I could never be a father after that. These things are what they are, truth. Truths revealed in these letters are the only way the dead speak. After we failed to reclaim our daughter, I resented the position we were in, I resented life, I began resenting her. I was afraid, I never thought I could have been a father or a grandfather, I believed myself to be too altered by time. Parents grow with their children, but neither Elsa nor I wanted to grow, our love was symbiotically connected to our immaturity. I was not worthy as Ephraim was of that mantle. I rest, however, knowing that as I lived, my hand dug in the sand, on the beach of life. With my love, we both dug in. When my time comes to depart, as hers did, we're comfortable knowing we leave with sand in our hands, our daughter and granddaughter, our own piece of posterity.*"

Olivia sobbed as Anna concluded his letter. She wet her daughter's hand. She was momentarily disabled at the thought of how close she was to her father, how close she was to holding him without ignorance, wishing she could be like a child who first puts their hand to their father's palm. She thought of her mother's wishes and regrets, how she will never be there to remedy her pains. Saddened by the lack of answers, time would pass before she was to look for them through Alana.

"Do you want to see the photo?" asked Anna.

Olivia rose her head as Anna handed her the creased pocket photo. She saw her daughter, as a young newborn, a recognizable bronze face, in the clutches of a man momentarily filled with unattainable happiness. In one of Markos's last remaining happy moments, he was captured on camera as a proud grandfather to a child he was bound by promises to remain distanced from. The smile, the tingle in his blood, never was to be replicated. The photo captured the initial moment he held his direct lineage in his arms, unafraid of what was in front of him. On his deathbed, as the priest read his rites, he remembered holding her. In the photo, each time he laid his eyes on it, he felt Elsa nearby, and the strength Olivia had to withstand the crash and survive in her mother's stomach. He posed for the photo believing it to be a far-off dream, a moment awaiting him only in heaven, yet captured on Earth. The room the photo was taken in was the victim to many of his drunken nights. It was a consequence of the memory of Anna fading each night he tried to remember her small hands, the soft feet, the innocence of her movements and cries.

He left this time knowing they would know the truth, requiring him to only wait. Never again, would he have to do so alone.

Writing One's Posterity

I began writing to be free from the psychological cage I put myself in. College put a lot of things in perspective for me, what I wanted to do, who I wanted to be, etc. I was no different than anyone else. There was nothing, no major to encompass what I wanted to do.

I went through catalogues of different schools during the end of my second year, and still, I was lost as to what I wanted to do. I searched, but I ignored what I should have known. My therapy had always come from stories: novels, movies, poetry. I knew so much about films and books, but never did I think it was something for me. I grew up imagining myself as a superhero, some cool teenage spy, a civil rights leader. I created different scenarios for myself whenever I could not pay attention in class, wanting to be these characters that I created a story for. I was too invested in what others wanted for me to see that I wanted to tell stories. My friends know, I'm always telling a story. I often meet new people when recounting wild stories. This was a way to break social barriers.

This story was inspired by the quest I wanted to take for the duration of my life. I wanted to be like Markos, eternally searching for something. He doesn't know what it is, and neither do I. Writing this book, you hope for success, but its purity is in the story and in the wish you have for others to sense my aspirations.

It's important to look at how along his quest, I thought of what this world may throw at a young black male: love, divisive politics, health issues. These are terrifying to an individual who's afraid of control. That's what we all fear in a way, taking control of our lives and failing. We may fail on our own accord or fail because of the things we cannot control like Markos. However, love can be restored despite these obstacles. Anna and Ephraim were the indicators of that. We can easily forget that power love has. No matter how they ended up, they grew through love. Complications arose as one chose love of wisdom, while the other chose love of man. Still, both of their efforts showed there is no greater way to unify than through that which can bend space and time, love.

Writing *One's Posterity* was for the audience to realize we ignore so much due to the things we focus on daily. We ignore the hidden cycle causing us to fail at relationships and friendships while we choose to attack things we can never change. We need to first answer for the sins we have neglected within our families and our communities. We can change so much with simple conversations with those we share a car, a classroom, or even a dormitory with. We choose platforms where we speak to millions at a time, when the true work is diving into the issues with heartfelt honesty, with tears, showing our humanity to one person at a time. This writing process taught me a lot, and I wish to discuss more with all of you if possible. That is my obligation as your storyteller.

About The Author

Daniel Mistir is a college student in his last year at the University of California-Davis. He is from Sacramento, California. This is his first novel, with another novel, *Pride of a Nameless Nation,* to be released in early 2024. He is in his last year in college, concluding his Bachelor of Science in Biomedical Engineering, with a minor in African and African American Studies.

He is a self-published novelist hoping to find success not just in novels, but in the filmmaking business as well. He is a screenwriter and wishes to follow in the footsteps of many novelists who were trailblazers in both avenues. His staple of blending subtle romantic tones with minimalism was inspired by the work of independent novelists and filmmakers, a group of people who shift the minds of an audience intimately, one by one. His wishes to continue with the same purpose through films, poetry, and novels, as a true storyteller.

Made in the USA
Middletown, DE
11 May 2022

65651760R00241